. . . .

Midnight LEMONADE

ANN GOETHE

DELACORTE PRESS

Published by
DELACORTE PRESS
Bantam Doubleday Dell Publishing Group, Inc.
666 Fifth Avenue
New York, New York 10103

LIBRARY OF CONGRESS CATALOGING IN PUBLICATION DATA

Goethe, Ann.
Midnight lemonade / Ann Goethe.
p.   cm.
ISBN 0-385-30807-8
I. Title.
PS3557.O3225M5   1993
813'.54—dc20   92-1649
                                                        CIP

Interior design by Christine Swirnoff

Manufactured in the United States of America
Published simultaneously in Canada

April 1993

10 9 8 7 6 5 4 3 2 1

BVG

For
Conrad and Candy

and
A.J.C., S.J.

With profound appreciation to

Sandra Dijkstra for her tenacity and guidance;
Chris Thompson and John Van Ness for their faith and
support; my wonderful editors Jackie Farber, Mary North,
Diane Goff; the Reynolds Homestead; the Virginia Commission
for the Arts; FEORC; Kathy Saideman; K.B. Schwarzenbach;
the Kemah Walkers; and, of course, Molli Wagner

Midnight
LEMONADE

It is an old sin, several years old. I am racing through the Alabama darkness. It is three o'clock in the morning. The backseat is down in the station wagon, and my three children are asleep. They are so little and needy that they sleep in one small tight bundle. Through the rearview mirror the back of the station wagon looks empty. This has been a hard year for their childhood and sometimes it seems the only time they are truly young is in sleep. So, I hoard my children's sleep, count the hours as if sleep is gold coins, precious treasure.

I am driving very fast. The Southern countryside is deserted. My father is waiting for me in a Louisiana hospital. He stopped talking out loud; he speaks only in whispers. Maybe he is in on some cosmic secret and now I might be included. This morning he whispered for me. And my sister called and told me to hurry. I have pulled my children from their North Carolina schoolrooms and now am breaking the Alabama speed limit, trying to reach Louisiana by broad daylight.

1

A n n   G o e t h e

Suddenly, from nowhere, a dog appears and freezes in my head-lights. He should run fast across the road or, since there is no other traffic, should wait until I pass him by. He does the very worst thing, this goddamned German shepherd. He holds in the middle of that blank black highway, pauses as though I have just called his name. He looks to me for salvation. I'm going too fast. If I hit the brakes, I'll wake my children, spin the station wagon out of control. The four of us will sail high over midnight's deserted cotton fields. I'm thinking inanely, "Gwine to Alabama with a banjo on my knee" as I hit the dog. His yellow eyes glare betrayal at me as he passes the windshield on his way to somersault across the roof of the station wagon. A grisly game of fetch, which I imagine leaves him openmouthed with amazement behind me on the road. Where I do not find him because I do not stop. I leave him to die, like my father dies. Alone in the land of cotton. Old times there are not forgotten. If I had gone back for that dog, to pull him from further harm's way, to lullaby him to his final rest, to get help if there could be help for him. If I had done that, my father would have lived. I know this is true because I have set spells, made vows, and kept bargains for the lives of my children. And they live.

CHAPTER I

"*A*NY GIRL WHO KISSES BOYS IS GIV-
ing her husband a sucked-out orange when she marries." Sister
Helena is framed by French doors. In the garden behind her
camellias are blooming; beyond them, the row of oaks laced with
Spanish moss leads to the convent's main building. Sister Helena
has changed my life. She made Shakespeare more real to me than
the Cleaver family, I know Dante the way my peers in the outside
world know Frankie Avalon. Sister Helena calls me her "little
Emily Dickinson." I will languish in a garden writing beautiful
poems that no one will read until after I die. I will die juicy.

I turn to see how my two best friends are taking Sister's
metaphor. Susan rolls her eyes. I am not surprised. She is a Yankee and the only Protestant in our class. Also, we know her IQ
sails somewhere above 180. We have recently discovered IQs, and
they are very big. High IQs question things. Marie is blushing
and shoving viciously at her cuticle. I would guess some boy,

back from around her family's plantation, has tasted of her citrus lips. The Act of Contrition says "I firmly resolve, with the help of thy Grace, to sin no more and to avoid the near occasions of sin." I won't be so blatant as to share this insight with Marie. Her conscience is her own. Besides, I work very hard at balancing letting the Holy Spirit into my heart and acting out being a beatnik intellectual. Susan's influence, of course. We have smuggled Ferlinghetti's poetry into our room and are amazed at his references to the great secrets of womanhood. The beat poets provide us with our few clues to said mysteries. As far as near occasions of sin, unless hiding candy and dirty poetry in your room counts, we're in the clear. Our boarding school is set so far back into pastoral splendor that, if a car horn would sound, the entire population of Holy Name Academy would turn snow-headed in a second.

A white ceiling fan spins indolently in the high white ceiling of our 120-year-old classroom. The French doors are open to the early spring scent of sweet olive and confederate jasmine. Heady perfume, seeping around Sister Helena's next pronouncement. "Men are made to take, women are made to give." This is a beautiful concept. I press my thighs together and plan a marriage of noble silent sacrifice. Rhett Butler slowly unbuttons my soft linen blouse. I am his wife, he may take what he wishes from me. His cruel, but tender, shadow falls across the curve of my yielding breast.

Beyond the garden we can faintly hear the gardener's mower. I look around at twenty sets of feet, placed ankle to ankle, on the polished wide board floor. Only trashy girls cross their legs. Demerits are given here for crossed legs. All of us in the junior class are ladies, and we are all virgins. I am the president of our class, I have never been Queen of the May. My secret is: Who'd want to be President when she could be queen?

Jackie is queen. It is late March. Kennedy was inaugurated a year ago and it is the heyday for Catholicism in America. Question: What's the new phone number at the White House? Answer: et cum spirit two, two oh. Last January we wept watching the school's tiny black and white television as Robert Frost, blinded by white light on white paper, stumbled through the poem he'd written for the new President. Verse to usher in a thousand days of Camelot. I cried because it was beautiful and fraught with mortality, a new age of poetry pronounced by that old old man, his words lost and found again.

Susan, Marie, and I are sitting on the cushioned floor under a long row of pines. The trees form a cathedral ceiling thirty yards overhead. The trees are so old and dense that the late afternoon sunlight filters down in pale yellow streaks, making this place as hushed and almost as dark as the chapel it leads to.

Marie earnestly leans forward, her delicate high-boned face and sleek black hair haloed in dim light. "Arthur's realm reeled back into the beast, but Guinevere was lucky, she got to go into a convent. She could atone for her sin. What about poor Lancelot? It was too late for him to be a priest." Marie's French accent, Acadian French, makes everything she says sound musical and, to me, slightly out of context.

"Guinevere was crazy, is what." Susan is much taller than Marie and I. She has never cut her thick blond hair and wears it in a bun which is so heavy it tilts her head slightly back and lends our friend a consistent look of haughtiness. She looks like a Viking princess. When Susan washes her hair it takes so long to dry in the Louisiana humidity that it always smells slightly mildewy. "I mean, what do you Catholics have confession for anyway? This whole sin thing is nuts. You go to hell for murdering a hundred people and for eating a ham sandwich on Friday and for French kissing."

"You just don't understand, Susan." I brush a pine needle from my gray pleated uniform skirt. Marie and I have made a pact to pray for Susan's conversion, and we have promised ourselves to be patient.

"Well, explain it, Katherine."

My coup de grace. "Listen, if it's good enough for a great

thinker like St. Augustine, smart as he was, I think we ought to be able to accept what the Church says about mortal sin on faith."

Marie is always a few beats behind Susan's and my debates, and now proudly quotes our school chaplain. "Father Shea says that French kissing is bad because 'what goes on upstairs invites bad business downstairs.' "

"Whatever that means," says Susan despairingly.

"It means, well, he means you shouldn't take boys upstairs if that's where the bedrooms are. Which they are. Usually." Marie tries to keep her voice full of conviction.

Sister Rita stands on the front gallery ringing the handbell that calls us into study hall. In study hall we will sit in our assigned seats, bathed in the gold of late afternoon and lulled by the clacking of Sister Helena's rosary as she glides among the long aisles. This time of the year, being indoors feels like a slap in the face of God. My friends and I reluctantly leave the haven of the pine trees and walk along the brick path that leads past the front gallery.

As usual, I pretend not to see Sister Rita. I have held a silent grudge against her ever since the December afternoon I discovered the little round nun spraying Lysol disinfectant over the student lounge right after our Christmas party for the children from the Colored Orphans Home. Maybe, if there can be bad pennies, there can also be bad nuns.

. . . . .

In the evenings, after the nine o'clock lights-out bell, Sister Helena sits behind a small desk at one end of the long marble hall of our dormitory. The hall is very dark except for the glow of Sister's reading lamp. If a girl is drowning in a spiritual crisis, or has recently lost a parent, she may tiptoe down the hall and sit at Sister Helena's feet. If her loss is particularly painful, she may rest her head on Sister's lap and weep. I have actually prayed for a spiritual crisis and confess to wishing for a near death experience for one of my parents. I have even considered faking a spiritual crisis. Sadly, the parable of "The Little Boy Who Cried Wolf" is too much with me. I want to go to Sister Helena and tell her how very much I am disturbed by desires, which must mean that I am meant to be a great poet. I would tell her how I lie awake at night tortured by mute verse. How some unnamed longing makes me so restless that the very touch of sheets against my body stirs me to aching wakefulness. The world seems too immense, yet I would open my arms and legs to it, hug the earth tightly within my very limbs, and move with the world to the rhythm of the tides. I think Sister Helena might offer me some assurance, but impending great poethood is not reason enough to follow the shining path up the marble hallway. Our school is small and our collective home and spiritual lives are fairly settled, so it is seldom that anyone shares Sister's light at the end of the hall.

"Oh, that is so embarrassing!" Marie covers her head with a pillow.

"So liberating, you mean. I call it the sweet squeak of freedom." Susan strides purposefully to the other end of our room and knocks lightly on the wall.

The knock will echo down all twelve rooms on our side of the hall. A nightgowned figure will dash across at the row's end and the knock will carry up through all the rooms on the opposite side of the hall. Sister Helena has but one vice; she loves to indulge in a romp in the bathtub. Her bare bottom squeaking up and down the tub assures us that she is fully nude and the upper school can hit the closets to read, quietly gossip, or cram in additional studying. So many layers and confining contraptions are built into the nuns' habits that it would take Sister a full ten minutes to re-dress herself. Marie just hates to think of Sister Helena having a "be-hind," so our room next door to the nun's is torture for her. The closets have twenty-watt light bulbs; Susan settles in to peer at Heller's *Catch-22* and I am squinting through a second reading of *Doctor Zhivago*. During my first reading, one of the nuns asked to borrow it from me, browsed through the book herself, and then had it banned from the school library. I have begun my second read to discover why the book was banned and to mark the "good" parts for the next readers. Marie, inexplicably, settles in with a Kafka essay.

. . . . .

"Katherine, you say you won't lie, yet you write papers for other people and let them turn them in under their own names." Susan and I are sitting on the front gallery, chancing a barrage of demerits by propping our feet on the wrought-iron railing of the old porch.

"That's different, it's not a lie, it's an act of charity."

"Why?"

"Why"—I rock back and forth in the cane-bottomed rocker —"because Fay and Ellen and Mary Beth hate to write and really don't do very well. And—and it's easy for me. It's fun."

"It's a lie," insists Susan.

I stop rocking to make my point. "It helps people. That's good."

Susan gets out of her chair and leans against the railing to face me. "That's situational ethics and if you believe what you say you believe, writing papers for other people is wrong. It's—it's like girls who think it is all right to do it, just as long as they keep their eyes closed."

"What a disgusting comparison!" I rock out of my chair, hook my arm through Susan's, and tug her back toward our dormitory.

. . . . .

My hometown of Bellebend is almost a three-hour drive from Holy Name. Susan's father's parents live in Lafayette, twenty minutes away from the school, so we spend most of our weekends at her grandmother's house. The large, rambling Victorian house delights me for the same reasons that it drives my more aware friend insane.

"Grandmother," Susan moans as we are awakened on another Saturday morning by two maids walking into Susan's turreted bedroom, carrying two large, loaded mahogany bedstand trays. They fasten the trays to our beds, lift the silver covers, shake out our napkins, and, almost silently, back out of the room as we thank them profusely. I love this. It feels like being in a Katharine Hepburn movie. There are little crystal bowls of marmalades, delicate china egg cups, hot biscuits and sweet breads, fresh-squeezed orange juice, a small silver plate of breakfast meats.

"Don't touch anything, Katherine. We're carrying this stuff downstairs. I have told Grandmother and told her that we can get our own breakfast. Lily and Chris have better things to do than wait on two perfectly capable—"

I have already buttered a croissant. "We thanked them, Susan. We sit in the kitchen and talk to them all the time. I even gave Chris a copy of *Black Like Me*. It's better for them to wait on people like us than on bigots, or let's face it, your grandmother. Besides, why do you want to hurt your grandmother's feelings?"

Susan's grandmother fascinates me. She is not a nice person, in fact she is an awful person. Though she is always nice to me. She is very fat and very short and spends all day in a plush red velvet chair in her front parlor. She wears her dyed black hair in stylized curls mounted on top of her head like Little Miss Sunbeam, the curls bound by a velvet bow the same color as her dressing gown on any given day. She sits with a silver-headed cane propped between her knees and uses the cane to hit out at any of the servants who come within her reach. Other immobile old people watch television or play cards; Susan's grandmother jabs at passing blacks or pounds her cane on the floor calling for service of any invention. She is always in a terrible mood.

Susan's grandfather, on the other hand, is the most courtly

9

gracious man I've ever known, next to my father. Everyone at Holy Name Academy agrees that, if Clark Gable had lived, and had been an ounce more handsome, in his old age he'd look just like Susan's grandfather. Mr. Blake has a thick mane of pure white hair, a flowing white mustache, and bright blue eyes, which always seem to convey patient amusement. He stands almost six and a half feet tall. Whenever he arrives at the school in his ancient, silver Cadillac, about half of the student population leans out of the windows swooning. Mr. Blake is as gentle as my father, only more dramatic. Marie and I think that we might truly be in love with Susan's grandfather. Susan and I are convinced that her grandmother purchased Mr. Blake with her fabled wealth. Whatever their bargain, he certainly keeps his part. You'll never see a more attentive husband.

On Sundays, the servants' day off, Susan's grandmother always insists on sending the two of us out to Sunday dinner with a hundred-dollar bill. It is impossible to spend a hundred dollars on a meal for two people in Lafayette, Louisiana, in 1962. Susan tries to tell this to her grandmother and she tries to return the change. Her grandmother won't hear her and won't take back any money. The waiters at Jacques love to see us coming. We get fancy cocktails—only in south Louisiana can young teenagers, without question, be served whiskey sours—and appetizers, soup, salad, at least one entrée each, dessert, and usually a round of liqueurs to top off the meal. We leave a copious tip. After four years of Sundays, Susan will save enough from the dinner change to buy herself a new car when she gets to Radcliffe.

When we leave the restaurant, Susan drops me off at her grandmother's. Though we are usually three sheets to the wind after all the excess, Susan, impossibly, drives over to the university to spend the last few hours, before we have to leave for Holy Name, in the library. I usually pull all the shades and pass out for a deep dreamless sleep on the pale apricot satin coverlet of my bed in Susan's secluded, round-walled tower room.

One Sunday afternoon something causes me to wake early.

Struggling awake from a tipsy midday nap feels much like trying to swim to the bottom of a pool of thick opaque water. "Shhh. No, go back to sleep." Susan's grandfather whispers in the muted light of the dusky many-windowed room. He is sitting in a chair he has pulled to the side of my bed. His legs are crossed and his arms rest, relaxed, on the tapestry arms of the chair. I start to sit up and he slowly shakes his head, looking disappointed in me. I don't want to displease this kind, gentle man. I check and see that my skirt is modestly covering my knees, then lie back on the pillow and close my eyes. Perhaps he has been doing this for as long as I've been taking afternoon naps at Susan's.

Every Sunday after this one, he comes to watch me. It is always the same. He sits the same way, leaned back and graceful, in the large tapestry chair. He never touches me, we never speak. I begin to dress more carefully, to prepare for my sleep, which is seldom completely feigned. Lying there, with my eyes closed, I feel the way I feel when reading passages in certain banned books, excited, warm, tight in my lower stomach. Though I have been waiting for him, I almost never hear him enter the bedroom. I think I can only hear my own breathing, then realize two people are breathing in the stuffy golden dusk. Our breaths join, perhaps the way runners resting side by side join their breathing, until I really fall asleep. By the time Susan comes crashing into her room, the chair is back in its place by the curving front window. Mr. Blake and I never speak of our afternoons. He never changes his courteous, amused, treatment of me in the full daylight. I never tell anyone.

. . . . .

May arrives, as does the annual contest for who will get to crown the Blessed Virgin Mary. The person who writes the best poem about Holy Mary, Mother of God, is chosen to be Queen of the May and gets to crown the pale pink statue that stands in the south garden grotto. Every girl in the school must submit a poem. This is the only writing competition in the school I have never won. And this spring is no exception. There is only one year left for me now. Only one more chance to be Queen of the May.

Our junior year ends traditionally with most of us weeping good-bye and making promises to write to one another all summer as our fathers patiently load a school year's worth of luggage into the family cars. I will spend this summer working in Michigan. Nice Southern girls don't have jobs but my Northern mother thinks I should work. The only solution is to go North. My mother's brother-in-law inherited several businesses in Michigan. I will be working behind the ice cream counter of my Yankee uncle's drugstore.

. . . . .

It is the summer of the Twist. My aunt, her husband, and their friends are as wild as teenagers. Most of them don't have children and they don't behave like any adults I know at home. They have supper with friends just about every night and after dinner play records and dance. But they don't know how to do the Twist and I do. It is my entry into what seems a sophisticated late night life of lipstick stains on cigarettes and tangy summer drinks made with lots of lime and lots of gin. My uncle is always adding extra gin to my drinks, and he even slow-dances with me at their parties, so that I am never left out. I can hardly believe these people in their twenties actually let a sixteen-year-old girl stay up late with them. I teach them the Twist, and we twist and twist the night away. All of them, even my aunt and uncle, insist I call them by their first names, Linda and Luke.

My parents would die. In Louisiana, even if you're sixty years old, you always say Miss, Missus, and Mister to people older than you.

Often we spend the evening at the home of my aunt and uncle's best friends, the Wests. They are my favorite of all the wild adults I've met. Veronica talks to me like I'm the same age she is and tells me all about how she met Jim and how much in love with him she is. His family had a lot of money and her family was poor, but proud. When she and Jim started dating in high school Jim's parents tried to break them up. But Jim stood by Veronica. Even after she got pregnant. When he said he would marry her, no matter what, Jim's parents cut him off. They haven't spoken since, though his parents went ahead and let Veronica and Jim take over their vacation house on Jordan Lake. It's the reason the Wests settled in this small town. Veronica lost that baby in her fourth month of pregnancy, and, even now, when she talks about it, she gets tears in her eyes.

I love Veronica and wish I were tall, busty, and red-headed the way she is. I also love Jim, though he doesn't talk to me much. I can tell he likes me, because he catches my eye almost every time he starts in on a story or a joke. Jim is an insurance agent and seems like a proud, uncomplaining, fallen aristocrat to me. He has wavy auburn hair and soft brown eyes, like Veronica's. They could almost be brother and sister. He is definitely the most handsome man I have ever seen.

He calls me his "swimming buddy" because he and I are the only ones in their crowd who can swim all the way across the lake and back. Before we do this, Jim always drives around to the other side of the lake and leaves two cigarettes and a kitchen match on the opposite shore. Usually in the late afternoon we take our swim and each smoke a cigarette before swimming back to the group in the Wests' yard. We joke about being in training. Their house is where we have most of our parties. The Wests have a little three-year-old boy, so that's the reason most of our late nights are at their lakeside house. None of the other couples have children yet and it saves the Wests from having to hire baby-sitters.

Sometimes I feel sorry for little Jimmy when he shuffles sleepily into any of our really loud parties. Sometimes it gets on my nerves when I'm having a really good time, but I always walk him back upstairs. I have made up an imaginary friend for him, an elf named Ivan. "So, Ivan is out on the water, see? And he's trying to trick a sparrow into taking a thread of yarn into his beak and—"

"Where did he get it?"

I pull the covers under his pale, serious little chin. "Get what?"

"The yarn, Kat. Where did he get the yarn?"

"When your mother wasn't looking, Ivan very carefully unraveled the sleeve on one of her sweaters she hardly ever wears." I tell him Ivan lives in the roots of a tree down by the lake and has a little canoe and one day Jimmy and I will learn a magic spell that will turn Jimmy into an elf and me into a fairy and we'll go riding all around the lake with Ivan in his teeny-tiny canoe.

One evening my aunt and uncle and the Wests go nightclubbing. All the grown-ups are sorry to leave me. Sadly, Michigan is not like Louisiana, there is no way that I can be sneaked into a nightclub with my new crowd, since I'm sixteen and actually look twelve. I sleep over at the Wests' because I'm the baby-sitter for the evening. Sometime in the night I hear Jim and Veronica return, laughing and stumbling up the old wooden stairway that leads to the hallway of bedrooms. I turn over and fall back to sleep.

It is later, maybe much later, when I feel someone grabbing at my foot beneath the covers. "Psst." I wake up and see Jim sitting on the foot of my bed. "Get up, let's go swimming."

"Swimming? Jim, what time is it? Where's Veronica?"

My swimsuit is on the windowsill where I left it drying after our afternoon swim. Jim grabs it and tosses it on my bed. "Veronica's asleep. I'll meet you on the dock in two minutes." He closes the door quietly behind himself, and I slip out of my baby doll pajamas and groggily pull on my still-damp bathing suit.

It is a beautiful, almost full moon, night. The lake shimmers like an antique glass bowl ebony-colored and set on the dark table of night. The rippled bowl reflects back a swath of silver moonlight poured among the shadows of ancient trees. I dread the icy water. "Are you afraid?" Jim had been sitting so quietly on the dock's edge I hadn't even seen him.

"Of course not. It's just, well, I guess it'll be pretty cold."

" 'Prutty coll,' " Jim repeats after me, sounding like a Yankee's imitation of a Southerner. Which sounds nothing like a Southerner. "I could listen to you talk, Katherine, till the sun came up."

I lean over and lower my foot to test the water. "How come, with the water so black, it seems like there are creatures under the surface?"

He steps up and balances on one of the pilings. "So, you are afraid."

"I most certainly am not." To make my point, I dive headfirst into the satiny, icy depths of the lake. I hear him splash in behind me. It is cold, but it is wonderful, silent; even our bodies gliding through the water are silent, not kicking or splashing, just barely moving our arms, floating, sliding through the water the way I imagine seals move.

We swim and swim, weaving back and forth like shadow dancers in a mute minuet. Jim glides under the dock and I follow him. It is getting very cold and I hope we go back inside soon. I begin to fantasize about the quilt folded at the foot of my bed. Jim's voice sounds hollow and gurgled, slapping against the wet pilings. "I was so afraid you wouldn't want to come out here."

It had never seemed an option to me. I mean, tell me to baby-sit and I will, tell me to go swimming and I will. I wasn't raised to question authority.

"Are you cold, Katherine?"

"N-no," I chatter back.

"Here." He kicks off from his piling and glides over to mine. "Here, I'll warm you." He takes my hand off the board I'm holding and pulls me, facing outward, into his chest. Which is amazingly warm, but my bare back against his hairy wet chest feels very strange to me. "Better?" I nod, though my teeth are still chattering. "Good." His hand holding me is flat against my stomach, and I notice I really like the way that feels.

We aren't saying anything and I grope for a topic of mutual interest. "Jim, did you see *Creature from the Black Lagoon?*"

"Nope." He pulls me in closer, if that is possible. And then— and then he kisses me on the back of my neck and begins to speak quietly into my ear. "I love you, Katherine. You know that, don't you?" He kisses me again. I am staring straight out at the lake, worrying about my pounding heart and what I am supposed to do next. "You are so full of life, tiny, pretty Katherine. I love you."

Suddenly I realize I love him too. When I realize this, I think of Tristan and Iseult and feel tragic and happy at the same time. I twist around to face him as he holds me up in the water. "I love you too." I put my fingers softly on the hollow of his temples, press my palms against his cheekbones, and kiss him on the lips. Jim and I kiss and kiss, wet, cool, adult kisses. Kisses tasting of clear lake water and gin. The entire time we are kissing, he holds me up in the water. I think of how I will describe this to Susan and Marie. "He is tireless and strong. We stay kissing under the dock until we see the first signs of dawn lighting the water."

When I get back to bed I am shivering, shivering because I am colder than anyone should ever be in late July and because I know my life has changed forever.

· · · · ·

On most afternoons the pharmacist goes off to my uncle's country club to have a midafternoon drink with the golfers. On the days I work, I am left to hold down the fort alone. One day a heavy-set, very hairy man walks in. He is wearing the kind of undershirt Stanley Kowalski wore in *A Streetcar Named Desire*. It is half tucked into faded madras Bermuda shorts. "Do you have any Trojans?"

Instantly I think of Helen of Troy. "I beg your pardon?"

The man grips the countertop in impatience. I'm sure that if he leans any closer I will smell garlic on his breath. "Trojans, you know, condoms."

I am failing some test here. My uncle will be really mad. "I'm sorry but I don't—"

The man steps back in disbelief. "Condoms, rubbers, rubbers!"

"Galoshes?" I ask. "Boots?"

"This is a drugstore, surely you have rubbers?" I have backed against the display shelf behind the cash register, shaking my head. The man turns and slams his way out of the drugstore. When Jim walks in, a few minutes later, I am still crying.

"Sweetheart, little sweetheart, what's the matter?" We are very careful in front of other people, but, since the store is deserted, he takes the chance of leaning on the counter and stroking my teary cheek.

I tell Jim about my encounter with the rude man, and he begins to chuckle. "Why are you laughing? I'm not supposed to know everything in the whole store. This is just a summer job, which I would like to quit so I don't ever again have to talk to a rude, horrible, smelly Yankee walking around in public in his underwear!"

As I speak, Jim almost twinkles with delight. "You are so incredibly innocent. I love that in you. It makes me want to protect you."

For the second time in five minutes, I am left without a clue. Protect what? He pulls a handkerchief, lovingly washed and ironed by Veronica, from his pocket and dabs at my face. "Well, what is a Trojan? I mean, I know that gorilla wasn't referring to any ancient Greek lore." I walk around the counter and sit on one of the round red leather stools lining the front of the ice cream section.

"Honey, you truly haven't heard of condoms?" I shake my head. "Do you know what birth control is?"

"Yes, it's a sin."

Jim laughs and gives my hand an affectionate kiss. I wish we could go to the back of the store and really neck.

. . . . .

The summer is whirling by, landmarked by kissing places and kissing times. We have already made a plan where Jim will find a way to sneak a plane ticket through the mail to me at school. I will get my friends to make up a story to cover for me when I meet him in Detroit on Thanksgiving. I'll tell my parents I'm visiting Susan's mother in Princeton. Jim and I are seldom alone, but at the wild dinner parties we slip off our shoes and touch feet and bare legs under the tables. We stay longer and longer at our cigarette times on the opposite side of the lake. We take Jimmy to the park and make up games to play with him that let Jim and me hold hands. I try to pay even more attention to Veronica.

Some days I think she knows about Jim and me, some days I am positive she doesn't. I often feel her watching me. But this could just be because she likes me so much. I mean, Jim loves me, but not like he loves Veronica. When I think about it, I think that Veronica is his life. I'm just a summer love. She's like a beautiful mansion and I'm a little treehouse, set up for a season. On my days off I help her with her housework, a first in my entire life.

"Veronica, what is the trick to getting this little leftover line of dirt into the dustpan? I've worked it over two whole rooms already. I think it's getting bigger."

Veronica laughs and later, at the parties, tells about all the messes I made helping her. The rest of the wild grown-ups laugh too. I am the star of the summer. Even my aunt's husband seems fascinated with my Southern ways. Jim sits back smiling. Jimmy hardly lets me out of his sight.

We have extended Ivan's genealogy and travels, and Jimmy talks of our make-believe elf with endearing conviction. We are both terribly worried about Ivan's winter wardrobe. A worry compounded by Jimmy having no recall of the past winter and my never having seen snow. "Kat, 'pose all that snow gets in Ivan's tree? What will he do?" We are hanging out by Ivan's tree, hoping for a glimpse of the elusive fellow.

"That's the good part, he can cover himself with snow. Snow is very soft. It's the ice we need to worry about." I have worked hard to win Jimmy's heart and it is completely mine. I think this makes it fine for me to go sneaking around with his dad.

. . . . .

The day before I am to leave for Louisiana, Jim and I rent horses and go riding deep into the Michigan woods. Veronica packs our lunch and cheerfully waves us off. I am equal parts terror and anticipation over the prospect of spending four hours alone with this handsome older man. It is almost too much to believe. Most of my childhood fantasies revolved around horses. Now to have a horse and romance, all on the same day. This will be the first time Jim and I have ever actually been alone, not within at least a good stone's throw of other people.

We ride side by side. I memorize the slashes of light crisscrossing the dirt trail, the strange Northern birds, the feel of the cool woods, the rhythm of the horse beneath me, the way Jim looks in his tight faded jeans and scuffed cowboy boots. I try to hold every detail to tell Marie and Susan our first night in the closet back at Holy Name.

The horses' hooves are quiet on the dusty trail. Jim takes my hand. "I have it all planned, Katherine. In five years, in five years you'll be through with college. Then we can get married."

I rein in my horse and stare at Jim in disbelief. "You're already married."

Jim's mare dances a little as he neck-reins her to pull closer to me. "Katherine, I love you."

"But what about Veronica? Don't you love her too? You'al are in love. She told me. You fought for her against your parents. She's your wife."

He reaches over the small distance between us and takes my hand. "That was then, Katherine. Things change."

"Not love, love is forever." His horse is trying to pull away. I take back my hand to keep my balance.

"I know I'll love you forever, Katherine."

"Isn't that what you thought about Veronica? God, Jim, in five years Jimmy will be eight years old!"

"But he loves you so much. You know that. When he's scared at night he calls for his 'Kat.' It will be O.K. because Jimmy loves you." I say nothing and Jim reaches over for my horse's bridle. "What did you think was going to happen?" I keep my horse away.

"Let's race, let's gallop the horses while it's still so cool!" I kick hard and the horse bolts. I give him his head, push my cheek tight on his neck, and feel the wind against us, the power of the horse between my legs, his mane tangled in my fists. Jim is galloping beside me, I don't look at him. I'm confused and angry because of what he said about Veronica. We had never talked about the rules and, suddenly, I find out we're even playing different games. I think about my father and mother, what it would be like if one of them was disloyal to the other. I think how I am the only star in my father's blue heaven, how proud he is of me, and now somebody else's father wants to get married to me. My father would be so ashamed of me, too ashamed to even believe it.

Jim pulls ahead and blocks the path and I have to rein in my horse. We hold on the edge of the trail and let the horses lower their heads to graze in the roadside grasses. "What did you think was going to happen, Katherine?"

I run the flat of my hand over the horse's damp neck, the sound of the two horses breathing makes the forest seem noisy. "I—I don't know." And I really don't know. "I guess, I guess I thought it would stay the same. Everyone loving one another. And sometimes you and I would get to be alone."

Jim swings his leg over and drops down to the ground. "Well, we're alone now."

We lead our horses through the woods to a small clearing rimmed by a fast-running creek. There are no such streams in Louisiana, the land of sluggish muddy waters. I kneel, mesmerized by crystal water rushing over smooth pastel stones. Jim has tied our horses and joins me. "I have always longed to picnic by a babbling brook," I say, hoping that we are changing the subject. Jim laughs. This is the summer I discover I'm funny.

"I have always longed to kiss you by a babbling brook," he says. I brace my arms behind myself and raise my face to be kissed, the way I present it to the sun when I'm sunbathing. We kiss and kiss, long breathy kisses that, if I don't get to confession, will send my soul straight to hell. I don't care, I love this kissing. It isn't anything like the years of groping car and front porch kisses back home.

I feel as liquid as the stream behind us when Jim gently lowers my head to the grass. He lays his fully clothed weight over me and I think this feels too good to be true and murmur a protest when he rolls off me again. He is still kissing me as he unsnaps and unzips my riding pants. I pull my face away and push at his hands.

"Don't worry, Katherine, it's not what you think, don't worry. I can wait." He is breathing heavily, and so am I. He presses the flat of his hand on my stomach, the way he did when we were under the dock. I keep my hand on his wrist as he gently presses my stomach and continues kissing me. I start to feel wonderful and careless and let go my hold on his wrist. Then my heart drops as he slips his hand inside my underwear. This is sick. Before I can push him away, his fingers are probing between my legs, and my body begins to move and shiver on its own. Small sounds come from me, like a puppy crying, and I think I faint.

Faint and wake up in seconds with my body shaking as though I am cold, even though the sun is searing my exposed stomach. My hair has fallen into the creek, I can feel the ends of it being softly pulled by the water. Jim is kneeling beside me, not looking worried at all. He is smiling. "You can do that to yourself. Do you understand what I'm saying? When you miss me and you are alone—"

I want him to stop talking, so I kiss him. I sit up, take his face in my hands, and kiss him. I don't want to hear anything else he has to say. Then I stand and walk into the shadows of the trees so I can zip my pants in privacy.

On the ride home I hardly speak, I am so shaken. On the same day, I discover the man I love is a pervert who likes to sneak his fingers inside people's underpants. Then I also discover that I am probably an epileptic.

The next day the Wests gather at my aunt's house to tell me good-bye. My uncle is driving me to the train station. "Kat, can I come with you to the Dossianna?"

"No, Jimmy, I'm sorry. I have to go see my own mama and daddy and my sister; then I have to go back to school. Here, here is something I made for you." I kneel and give him a drawing of an elf's cap and a short poem I'd written about Ivan. "Jimmy, when you miss me, or you're afraid you're gonna forget about Ivan, ask somebody to read this to you. O.K.?"

Jimmy is crying and Jim is crying too. I hope it looks like Jim is crying because Jimmy is so sad. I'm sad too, and when I hug Veronica, I want to whisper a warning in her ear. I want to tell her to look out, that Jim isn't the nice person she thinks. Instead I just hug her and I hug Jim, and pretend telling him good-bye is just like saying it to the others. I hug my aunt and get in the car and leave that little Northern town forever.

. . . . .

"We galloped our horses together. The sun came through the trees in long golden slashes, the horses' hooves were muffled on the velvet path. Then we found a place by this incredibly beautiful stream. Jim helped me down from the horse. A breeze was ruffling this lock of hair on his forehead. I could hear the water rushing over rocks as he gently kissed me."

"And then the horse crapped all over your foot."

"Susan! You're ruining it." Marie has been hypnotized by my story.

When I had stepped out of the car at Holy Name I could hardly wait to rush into the dormitory to look for my friends. We all promised to write, and I hadn't heard from anyone all summer. Susan worked as a research assistant for a friend of her mother's at Princeton University. Marie was in Europe with her parents. That night, in the closet, we all agreed my summer was, by far, the most romantic. I leave out the parts of the story that don't fit.

.   .   .   .   .

In October, when a box of candy arrives for me at the school, I lift up the row of chocolates and, along with an airplane ticket to Detroit, find a letter from Jim. It seems that Veronica has "accidentally" become pregnant. Jim writes that Veronica has been careless. I don't understand how a little baby coming into the world can be an accident. I remember Jim's face, the way it looked when his fingers were prodding inside me. I carefully reseal the box and send it back to Jim's office in Michigan.

When I'm home for Thanksgiving, Jim phones me. Hearing his voice makes me shivery and afraid. I hate thinking about the way he was breathing when he was touching me. I think about him as if he were an old man, an old man rubbing himself against me. I remember his fingers again and how they made me feel as though I had nothing to do with my own feelings. Maybe Veronica felt that way too and now a baby is growing inside her. I tell

23

Jim that I'm sorry, but hearing his voice makes me sick to my stomach. I hang up while he's still talking. He sends one more letter to me. I can't believe a grown man would beg someone my age the way he begs in that letter. During the summer he was in charge, like Rhett always was with Scarlett. Now he's acting like that sissy who married Scarlett in the beginning of *Gone with the Wind.* I don't answer the letter.

In June my aunt will write and tell me that the Wests have had a baby, a little girl, and they named her Katherine. I will carry a picture of Jimmy in my wallet until I have children of my own.

. . . . .

"You girls are living in a time of change. Our President has said racial injustice will no longer be tolerated."

Ellen raises her hand. "Sister, the colored people don't want equality. They want us to take care of them."

"Do you know that for a fact?" Susan has spoken without raising her hand and Sister Helena doesn't do a thing. "And do you really think cleaning our bathrooms for two dollars a day is anybody's idea of being taken care of?"

Though I did not know it then, there would never be another time in my life where the line between right and wrong would be so clearly drawn. It was the same line that divided black and white. The issue in the Deep South of the early sixties was segregation. Goodness and evil came in two colors.

On one of my weekends home I am sitting on the hood of our car waiting for my sister to come out of a friend's house. A heavy-set black woman walks by, dressed for church and leading her little boy by the hand. The little boy is about Jimmy's size. I say hello as they pass me, the child smiles shyly and his mother returns my greeting. They are almost a block away when a bright red car full of boys drives by. The windows of the car are open and I can hear their radio. "Paper Roses" is playing, and I can hear their catcalls. "A jigaboo. I see a jigaboo!"

"Two jigaboos, a mammy and a picaninny."

"The picaninny's only two points."

"Seven points for Ralph!"

They pull the car near the curb where the black mother and her son are walking. "Git ready, aim . . ."

They have set the windshield washer nozzles sideways and, as they pull beside the woman, someone presses the washer button. It sprays the woman. She doesn't move. The four white boys are laughing and honking the car's horn. The little black child is crying and pulling on his mother's arm while she stands immobile as the spray drenches her face, her church dress. I do not pick up a rock and fling it at those stupid redneck boys. I don't run to intercede, I don't yell at them. I do not even go to help the woman after the boys drive off. My mother, my strong mother would have helped them. I am too ashamed. Ashamed of my color and ashamed of my passivity.

When my sister, Eve, comes outside and I tell her what happened, she is outraged and activated. Eve knows the boys and immediately begins to gleefully plot high school revenge. One of her plans involves eggs and the shiny finish on the red car. I have no such outlet. I promise myself that, if my failure in courage and charity can be forgiven, I will never step back again.

. . . . .

We are sitting in senior year theology, taught by Father Shea, a large kindly Irish priest. He and the gardener are the only men we see at the school. I have always hung on the priest's every word, every pronouncement. There is a long-standing Holy Name rumor that Father Shea lived a wild and passionate youth in the uptown section of New Orleans. A tragic love affair sent him to the Jesuit seminary more than twenty years ago. We speculate endlessly and are especially conscious of not crossing our legs or

appearing in any way trashy during theology class. It is an honor
to be taught by this wise and involved theologian. Today Father
Shea is talking about the personal conscience; his massive cas-
socked body leans, amazingly gracefully, on the edge of a dark
oak teacher's desk. I raise my hand.

"I don't understand, Father. You are saying that my conscience, how I examine any particular moral issue, is the final
dictate?" He nods. "Higher than the Commandments, more final?" Again he nods. "Well, how come we're just hearing this? I
always thought the Ten Commandments and the Commandments of the Church were the last word."

Father Shea steps away from the desk to stand more eye to
eye with me. "The laws of God and the Church inform the conscience of the individual."

"But," I say, "but when push comes to shove, the individual,
I, makes the final choice on a moral issue?"

The priest smiles at me. "That's exactly what I'm saying."

I am confused and look back to see if Susan plans to enter
this discussion. She signals that it is all mine. "But why are we
just hearing about this?"

Apparently none of my classmates see a conflict. "Because
you are in the final year at a superb Catholic preparatory school.
You have studied the greatest thinkers of all time, you have had
classes in ethics and theology, and you have been prepared to
think on your own." He crosses his arms and leans back on the
desk.

"I know my Catholic friends back home aren't hearing about
this. And I would bet they aren't teaching it in the mission
schools in South America."

"Exactly," says Father Shea. "Those people haven't had your
education."

"So, if you'll forgive me, Father, it sounds like what you're
saying is that rich Catholics get a break."

Father Shea encourages debate in class and throws his head
back to laugh at my challenge. "It has nothing to do with money,

Katherine. And we're not talking about 'breaks,' we're discussing moral choices."

I am having very upsetting thoughts. "Is this why . . . Father, is this why a lotta rich Catholics only have one or two children and most poor Catholics have herds of children? Is it because poor people aren't allowed the inside information on the Church's laws on birth control?"

Father Shea is getting a little bothered that I am missing the point. "Katherine, it has nothing to do with economics. I've just explained, you need a background, an education, you need, so to speak, the tools for choice before you can ever choose properly."

I know he will fix this, he has to help me understand. "Oh, so only smart Catholics are allowed to use birth control?" The bell rings, it is time to change classes.

"Katherine, that is an oversimplification. You are deliberately misunderstanding." He leans down for his papers and book, turns and walks out of the classroom.

We have to file out of the room in order. I am sure Father Shea will be waiting for me in the hall so he can explain. But he is gone. He has taken the money and run. So to speak.

That night I walk down the shining path to Sister Helena's desk. At last I am having a spiritual crisis. The dim pool of orange light frames her like a halo, her small desk could be a shrine. "Sister?"

She looks up, her thin stern face framed by the starched cowl. This woman knows everything. I have done the right thing coming to her. I am one of her favorites and she gives me a rare smile. She will save my faith. "Can I talk to you, Sister?"

"You mean 'may I.'" She smiles again, amused by my poor handling of Emily Dickinson's language.

"Yes, Sister, I mean may I." I can't help myself, I think of all the summer twilights I spent as a child playing 'Mother, May I.' "That's what I meant, may I please speak with you?"

She indicates the place beside her on the marble floor where I may sit. I sit, tucking my legs neatly under my powder blue robe.

She leans over to brush a tendril of my unruly hair away from my eyes, and I almost start to cry.

"Sister, today in theology, Father Shea talked with us about the personal conscience." She nods, encouraging me to go on, and I recount the morning's dialogue. As I speak, she serenely fingers the black wooden rosary beads that hang from the side of her habit.

When I finish, she is very quiet, I look at the shadow we make on the back wall. She drops her beads, folds her hands, and says, "You do know that Father Shea is a brilliant and very respected priest?" I nod my head in agreement. "And that we are fortunate that he gives us his time?"

"I know, Sister, I just—"

"Does it occur to you that there are complexities, layers of interpretation, that Father knows might be difficult, if not impossible, for a schoolgirl to understand?" She smiles, teasing and intimate. "Especially a schoolgirl in danger of failing chemistry."

I don't want to change the subject. I suspect Sister does not quite understand that I'm in a crisis, not a sparring match with Father Shea. "Sister, the poor look to the Church for guidance and—and for the truth."

She rests her hand on my head. "And, Katherine, the Church takes care of the poor. You know that. Jesus loved the poor. You know of the work of St. Francis and you know of our missions all over the world."

"It's not the same, Sister. It's not all right, it seems to me, it's not all right to lie to people just because you're feeding them."

She moves her hand. "Lying? Don't you think you're speaking a little strongly, Katherine? Don't you think the Church, with her long history, is best suited for guiding those who can't guide themselves? For deciding what is the truth?"

This is not going the way I'd hoped. I reach over and hold one of her beads between my forefinger and thumb, feel the hard and simple wood between my fingers. "Sister, when we talked about segregation, you said the whites had no right to decide that we know what is best for colored people." I don't look up at her. "Isn't this the same thing?"

She opens her mouth as though to speak, then she takes a deep breath and softly taps her lips with her three middle fingers. In the silence I think that I am sixteen years old, and questioning the Church is very different for me than it would be for someone who has burned her bridges, vowed eternal obedience to an invisible bridegroom.

"No, it's not the same thing at all." She opens her book. "Go and pray about it, Katherine."

My roommates are waiting up for me. "Well?" whispers Susan.

Marie crosses over to sit on my bed. "Did you cry, did you rest your head on her lap?"

I am actually very shaken, feeling I've gotten more than I ever bargained for. "It's like in Trixie Beldon when her little brother skins his knee and comes to find out what he hurt himself on wasn't a piece of glass, but a diamond. All of a sudden something very normal becomes very big."

"I like Nancy Drew, I never did read Trixie Beldon." Marie flips down on the pillow of my bed.

"I'll bet she stood up one hundred percent for Father Shea. Because he's a priest and because he's a man," Susan says in a low voice.

"She told me to pray," I whisper back to her.

"Is that with an 'e'?" asks my Yankee friend.

. . . . .

Our last year at Holy Name is hurtling by. After the Christmas holidays a series of weekend house parties begins. It happens that I never return to Susan's grandparents and I will only see her grandfather again at graduation, where he will be as courtly and amused as always.

The twenty members of our class draw even closer. One classmate's parents invite us all to their New Orleans home. They have an enormous dinner for us on Friday night and have managed to secure dates for everyone for the entire weekend. The next morning we all have breakfast at Brennan's, a time-honored New Orleans tradition. We have many drinks and disrupt the white linen dignity of the old French Quarter restaurant.

Most of us have grown up in a south Louisiana Catholic culture where drinking is a natural part of daily life. Sex is taboo, but the sensuality of good food and drink is encouraged and exalted. In the South of the early sixties we have been raised to be "ladies." Ladies don't curse, don't wear trashy clothes, or "make out." Ladies hold their liquor and keep their knees together.

This weekend in New Orleans we are celebrating one of our last times all together; we are convent girls set loose in the City of Sin. Saturday afternoon is spent sipping alcoholic fruit drinks around the pool at our hosts' country club. That night the twenty of us and our dates go to Pat O'Brien's in the French Quarter and sing at the sing-along, then take over the fountain in the old courtyard. All the modest girls of Holy Name, with our years of indoctrination in the graces of femininity, have a drunken water fight in the patio of Pat O'Brien's. Sunday, at morning mass, all twenty of us droop in the pews like those corpses people sit up in chairs at certain ethnic wakes. On the bus ride back to school, we sleep, two to a seat, cuddled up together. Many of us dread our approaching graduation as though it is an execution date.

. . . . .

May comes around, my last chance to win the poetry contest, to crown the Virgin, to be Queen of the May. Fay Lemmon wins the contest. With a poem written by me. I'd written a group of poems and distributed them among my nonwriting classmates. I saved what I considered the best poem for myself.

The school is assembled on the lawn in front of the statue of

Mary. "Bring flowers of the fairest, bring flowers of the rarest," we sing. "From garden and woodland and hillside and dale . . ." Fay walks between us, carrying the crown made of flowers. She is crying, in shame. She meets my eyes as she passes me and I am crying in frustration.

As we walk back to the main building after the ceremony, Susan hooks her arm in mine. "In Eastern religions, this experience is known as karmic justice, Katherine. All action matters. I don't think Buddhists recognize degrees, like venial and mortal."

. . . . .

It is the night before graduation. Marie, Susan, and I have sneaked out of the dorm. We are sitting in the late May moonlight, on a marble bench by the school's formal pond. "As long as I live, the sound of water frogs at night will remind me of Holy Name," I say. "I remember the first week here when I was so unhappy, so homesick, the sound of these old frogs kept me awake. Now, when I'm away from the school, I can hardly get to sleep, for missing their night croaking."

"I can't imagine any frogs singing in Boston." Susan had nearly perfect scores on her college boards and was able to choose the college she would attend on full scholarship. She has chosen Radcliffe. She will enter the northeast academic establishment during the tumultuous sixties and none of us will ever see her again. A story will circulate that she is editing a Communist newspaper and another that she is living out of wedlock with a Chinese man, a Harvard professor. Later, there will be vague rumors of SDS and expatriation. In my life, I'll never meet a more naturally brilliant person than Susan of the tilted chin and musty golden hair. Marie and I will manage to keep her a presence in our lives, a voice of reason.

"I dread tomorrow," adds Marie needlessly. "We'll never again have this much peace, and I'll never have anyone I love as much as I love you'al. I know St. Joan's won't be the same."

31

Marie is going to a Catholic women's college in New Orleans. In her senior year she will have to have a minor operation. For several years afterward the surgeon who performed the operation will keep Marie as his mistress in a small house in the Garden District. She will be estranged from her wealthy French family and a long time coming into her own. Marie and I will continue to see one another. We will always be able to talk, but will never be able to help one another.

. . . . .

"Katherine, this isn't like you. Everyone is waiting."

"No, I won't do it. I won't leave!" I am sobbing and Sister Helena is, quite literally, pulling me while I hang desperately to my white iron convent bed.

"Katherine, you've written a beautiful speech. The class is waiting, your family is waiting. Everyone is here."

"I'm afraid to leave, Sister, nothing will ever be the same." I let go of the bed. "I'm afraid."

Sister Helena puts her arm around me and we walk toward the chapel where I will dedicate our class to God and to the future. Holy Name has done so much for me; the school has been an island, a haven, from the storms of adolescence. My rough edges have been smoothed, my friends and I have been given the rare gift of a place for contemplation. But we have not been prepared, in any way, for the world beyond these gardens.

We are twenty girls, dressed in white. We walk slowly up the alley of pines leading to the chapel. We are singing a song in French; the song says God loves the world and will always watch over us. Our voices weave through the branches of the ancient trees and take to the air and are lost long before they reach the sky.

CHAPTER II

I *AM SANDRA DEE PLAYING TAMMY TO* the professor, I knock on Eric's door, on Dr. Frederick Pierson's office door. "Come in." He pulls off his wire-rimmed glasses to look at me. "Speak now or forever hold your peace."

I have just turned nineteen and am a college dropout. My unruly ash blond hair is supposed to be in a page boy, but one side always curls up and wispy curls frizz around my face. I am thin and bony and not very tall. My gray eyes are my best feature.

Years later, when I look back at photographs taken in the early years with Eric, I will see that I was very pretty. If anyone ever told me that then, I was unable to hear it. On this day I especially don't feel pretty. I am intimidated by this college professor; his thick mass of chestnut hair shows faint gray streaks at the temples, and he has an amused expression on his handsome Waspy face.

I take a deep breath and stumble over my recitation. "I don't believe in grades. I love poetry very much, and—and I believe that it is more important to live as a poet than to be a poet and I'd like permission to sit in on your class. I'm not a student, I mean I haven't enrolled or paid any tuition or anything."

. . . . .

In a desire to escape the bigotry of my beloved South, I had fled north to school. At my Chicago women's college I met real bigots, people who didn't even want to eat food prepared by Negroes and people who said it made them sick "to think of niggers holding white babies." If my sister or I had ever said that "N" word, we would have gotten our mouths washed out with soap.

It would take several bars of soap to clean up the way a lot of these girls talk, racial slurs being just one portion of their dirty talk. When I first arrive, the Yankee girls in my dorm are nice, and seem interested in me. I make friends easily and begin to seek the close friendships I shared with Susan and Marie, friends for sorting out the major issues of our day. But it's like these girls are always looking over my shoulder, checking to see if someone more interesting may be on her way to join the group. Conversation might be called "the lost art of Illinois."

For fun, my classmates use fake driver's licenses and go in dateless groups to bars to drink beer. Beer! I'd never even seen a female order a beer. It seems, too, the more illegal it is to drink, the less you can hold your liquor. I get embarrassed for these sloppy drinkers. I hate beer and can't believe girls go to bars without escorts. In the smoky beer places boys hang around our tables and my new Yankee friends talk in front of the boys the same way they talk back in our dorms. Cursing and everything. In Louisiana it is an unspoken code that conversation with boys is light and flirtatious. The best example being Scarlett O'Hara's behavior at the Twelve Oaks barbecue. Real talk is what goes on with your girlfriends, after the boys are gone.

. . . . .

"Photosynthesis." The biology teacher scribbles numbers and letters over the blackboard. "Photosynthesis, the process in green plants which converts incident light to chemical energy and, at the same time, synthesizes organic compounds from inorganic compounds—for instance, carbohydrates from carbon dioxide and water—with the simultaneous release of oxygen."

I look around, my classmates are copying the numbers and letters from the board. None of them are scratching their heads in confusion or moaning and drooling in despair. I want to stand on my desk and scream out "What in the world are you saying? Speak English, sir! Can you translate, I mean, how would William Carlos Williams say this? You are discussing plants, right? What happened to sunshine, sunshine, rain, and soil?"

In my classes I either know too much, or, in most cases, too little; it feels suffocating. Holy Name had smiled upon my ignorance of multiplication and the periodic table. My informational voids had all been part of my feminine artistic nature. Those holes in my secondary education would have been very helpful in the math and science classes that are requirements for college freshmen. The discussions, debates, and investigation I expected from college degenerate into cramming for grades. Everybody here seems to be competing, there is little sharing of notes or after-class challenges. I miss the small and supportive atmosphere of Holy Name Academy. I've always been a big fish in a series of small ponds. Now I am without gills, and gasping for air in a vast body of water.

"You knew about this 'photosynthesis' already, didn't you, Susan?" My worldly friend has called me from Radcliffe and I am trying to squeeze instant tutoring out of an expensive phone call.

"Light hits the plant, a chemical reaction turns it green. Surely not all of your new friends are as unenlightened as you are, Katherine." Susan sounds more amused than concerned.

Surely there are some enlightened people around, but, six weeks into the school year, I am too cold to look for them. Any extraneous movement seems too difficult and hibernation becomes an attractive alternative. Even before November, the Lake Michigan wind lays ice crystals in my bone marrow. I long for the sight of green, and I hate the campus pressure to date.

. . . . .

The couple in front has disappeared below the seatback, I hear a few grunts and the rustle of clothing. The car windows have an inch of icy frost on them and the air is thick with smoke. I am chain-smoking, keeping a cigarette constantly in the center of my mouth, so I don't have to kiss the skinny boy with the flattop who has all but hopped onto my lap. With his right hand he is trying to hold on to my right hand, but he keeps letting go so he can dry his palm on the knee of his corduroy pants. His left arm is flung, at an unnatural angle, over my shoulder. I'll bet he has a monster neck ache by the time this night is over.

I have abandoned my courteous attempts at conversation, so we are pretending we can see the lake through the impenetrable windows. As I put out my tenth cigarette, simultaneously reaching for my eleventh, this youthful Ichabod Crane slams his mouth onto mine. He pushes hard with his mouth, at the same time angling to swing one of his legs over my pressed-together knees. I compare this to Jim's smooth easy way of kissing and I want to laugh. But I can't, my head is shoved into a painful position and the boy's sweaty hand is groping around, lost, under my sweater.

I try to pull his hand away, while he pants, "Come on, come on, Katherine. Just let me touch it."

A lost voice from childhood, *"Touch it, little girl, touch it . . ."* frightens me enough to make me abruptly push my damp, hopeful, winded date halfway across the seat.

I just stop dating, ignore all offers. I am tired of sweaty-palmed Yankee boys trying to grab my small breasts. I also hate the tricks my body occasionally plays on me, how I sometimes become flushed and breathless when someone, whose conversation bores me and whose looks repel me, slips his tongue between my lips.

· · · · ·

"The President's been shot!" I think the voice yelling down the dormitory corridor is about to tell an Abraham Lincoln joke. I put my head outside the door to hear the punch line.

The school gathers in the chapel; for twenty-five minutes we pray that the President will live. I promise God that I will become a nun if God will let the young President live. After the second announcement, after they tell us that he is dead, most of the girls stay in the chapel to pray for Kennedy's immortal soul. I wander out of the chapel, not nearly so concerned with his immortal soul as I'd been with his mortality.

The next few days I watch my classmates watch all the heart-breaking gory details over and over. I sit alone in the student lounge, with my back to the TV screen, and shred napkins. I cover the sticky Formica tabletop with parade confetti I've made from paper napkins. I drive my thumbnail into my palm and try to draw blood. I tear up stacks of napkins and try to make sense of the faces of my classmates. I want to be deaf and blind and home. I want time to stop and go back, I want there to be no Dallas. Televisions are on everywhere and the front pages of all the papers seem like those sensationalist detective magazine covers. Even the picture of little John-John saluting his father's funeral procession is too awful for me to look at. When I glance at that picture on the front page of the *Chicago Sun* I feel like I've been slapped by the newspaper, slapped the way you hit a dog you're trying to housebreak. Who would put that little boy's picture out there for strangers to pause over? That little boy who is going to grow up without a daddy. It also seems no one can get enough of the sight of Jackie's bloodstained pink suit. Jackie, the queen, scrambling on the back of the limousine, losing her husband, but not her hat.

The people poring over pictures, watching the television reruns, are like vampires to me. All I see is our great hope for change, dying. White and black people side by side, poetry in the White House, young Americans fanning out over the globe to help those less fortunate—all that hope, gone. In class, without my stack of paper napkins for diversion, I listen to self-important professors pontificate about the fall of Camelot. There is no one to talk to about the world ending. Barbra Streisand sings a song about how lucky people are who need people and the Beatles sing about wanting to hold someone's hand. And I quit school.

I break my parents' hearts. After three months of college, I just walk away. College seems irrelevant and empty. I am also failing most of my courses and, given the choice, would always prefer to reject before being rejected. I'd expected to quiet my Southern conscience by making real friends of Negroes. Even though there are a few dark-skinned classmates scattered throughout our dorms, they are as self-protective as their Southern sisters. The difference is the enemy here is not tradition, it is the human heart. My Southern liberalism, engendered by my parents, is as out of place in Chicago as my convent feminine charms or my ability to down whiskey sours in a place where only beer is available.

In my isolation on the barren shores of Lake Michigan, there was too much to learn about myself and I wasn't ready. If I couldn't be the belle of the ball, I wouldn't dance. I decided higher learning was not for me.

. . . . .

Two nights after our first meeting in his Laffitte College office, Dr. Pierson invites me to be his guest for dinner down in the French Quarter. We go to Arnaud's, a very old restaurant, a place of dark wood and aloof waiters. The menu is in French, which Dr. Pierson speaks. He insists I call him by his first name and my handsome date shows me how to order wine, he explains years and vineyards. When the waiter presents the cork, Eric exhibits it so I can see that the wine has remained properly sealed, the cork is not stained. It is my first taste of red wine. We share a bottle and, after a brief awkwardness, where Eric graciously puts me at ease, begin to tell one another our deepest secrets. We laugh to discover we love the same poets.

"Because I could not stop for Death . . ." I say in a low clear voice. "He kindly stopped for me," Eric finishes. "The Carriage held but just Ourselves—and Immortality." He clicks his wine-glass to mine.

I begin any line of poetry and he can finish it. We are amazed at what we have in common. He has one brother, I have one sister. We've both gone to boarding school, mine for girls in the South, his for boys in the northeast. His grandfather was mayor of their hometown, my grandfather mayor of ours. I don't think we notice what we are eating.

As we sip after-dinner brandy, he reaches across the table and takes my hand. For the first time all night, we are silent. It feels to me as if even my heart stops beating. In the quiet we look long and deeply at one another. His light brown eyes are kind and wise and I gaze as steadily as he does. This distinguished professor is actually holding my hand. The candle on our dinner table flickers and burns out. We have sat here for hours. When we walked into Arnaud's, I was so shy I could hardly order my dinner. Now Eric, not Dr. Pierson, now Eric is the person I know best in the world. Our waiter is glaring at us. Eric laughs and leaves a large tip.

We step outside into a misty French Quarter rain. "I can never get over your Southern rains, the warmth."

"When I was at school in Chicago, the first time I tried to walk in the rain, I nearly took pneumonia."

He laughs. "It seems to me you're so tiny you'd have to run around very fast to even get wet." He takes my hand. The cathedral clock tolls midnight as we turn the corner toward the old market.

Suddenly, we have stepped into the Twilight Zone, one more magic happenstance in this night of magic. As far as we can see through the fog, 1920s automobiles are parked bumper to bumper. The buildings, of course, are far older than that. There is no evidence, anywhere, of our decade. A few people rush past us in the light rain. The women have on flapper dresses, some of the men wear spats and fedoras. I even search for a tiny woman I heard about in childhood who dressed in pale green satin in the Roaring Twenties. We have stepped across more than forty years of time.

Eric takes both my hands, and we face one another in wonderment, then he draws me to him, and we kiss. We step back and look at one another in the soft strange New Orleans rain, as if it is our first glimpse of a long mystery. Later we will learn a movie about Prohibition was being filmed in the Quarter. Later is soon enough to know facts. This night is all fantastic mystery.

The next afternoon I am sitting on Marie's roommate's bed. WNOE is playing "The Sweet Elusive Butterfly of Love" on the pink plastic radio turned down low on the dressing table. Marie has cut class to hear about my date with the Laffitte professor. Through the open window, we can hear the clanging of the streetcar as it wobbles down St. Charles Avenue.

"Eric takes my hand, and we run laughing through the rain like children. We spin around and kiss under streetlamps. When the rain becomes heavy, we take shelter under the eaves of St. Louis Cathedral and kiss and murmur endearments."

"Right in front of the church? Suppose a priest, or something, had come out of the church? What would you have done?"

I stand up. "Are you kidding? This was about two o'clock in the morning." I settle on the open windowsill.

"Go on," Marie urges.

"Eric ran his hands up and down my body; he lifted my damp skirt and grabbed me, two-fisted, and pulled me close into him. I wasn't afraid, this new way of being held was part of discovery and magic and rain. We pressed our hips together in the rhythm of water falling from the eaves of that pristine, ancient church."

"This is so romantic. It practically gives me fever." Marie is literally bouncing on her bed. "Then what, Katherine? What happens next?"

"It was Thursday, we both had work the next morning. He drove me home and we kissed good night for a very long time." I turn my back to Marie and shout out the window, "I am hopelessly in love!"

. . . . .

Degreeless though I am, I have a teaching job. In Louisiana, during the civil rights upheaval, an eighteen-year-old college dropout can actually get a job teaching high school. This particular school is set up to exploit kids who have criminal records or who have been kicked out of regular schools. Unless they attend some kind of school, it is juvenile prison or reform school for them. The man who runs the school is getting rich on the desperation of children. Someone in their miserable white trash lives finds enough money to buy off the authorities by penning these kids up all day with a group of unqualified teachers. I take the job with the intention of turning their lives around by sharing the beauty of our native tongue with them. I know that once they understand Emily, Byron, and e.e. cummings, they'll change their wicked ways.

Their hearts go out to me, but the kids patiently explain that nothing I know will ever be of any help to them. They aren't going to go to college or read books, ever. Their lives will be their parents' lives. As young as they are, they've already accepted the patterns and paths of their futures. I quickly discover all that the director expects of me is that I keep the untamed youth in the classroom. I make my peace by introducing the kids to some of the beat poets, who briefly hold their attention by reference to sex and the scatological.

. . . . .

On our second date Eric takes me to a cocktail party given by one of his colleagues. My roommate lends me clothes and fixes my hair into the semblance of a French twist, but I still look like an adolescent playing ladies. Eric's colleagues do not seem surprised to have him walk in with a date younger than most of their students. Eric keeps his arm around my waist as we walk through the room for introductions. "Doing O.K.?" He smiles down at me.

"Look, these people teach English, right? About the only thing I do know how to talk about is books." It turns out, no one in Eric's crowd reads the books I read. There is something very hot, called *The New Criticism*, and this is the rage.

By habit that reaches probably as far back as the first time my younger sister tried to speak and I wrestled the attention back to myself, I gradually take over the floor. I begin to amuse an ever-growing group with stories of my teaching job.

"They're only in ninth grade, but all my little girls dress like streetwalkers. One day Wanda comes in dressed halfway decently, so I say, 'What a pretty dress, Wanda.' And Wanda says, 'What size dress you wear, Miz Roberts? I'll lift one for you, too.'"

"The only time I have anything resembling order is on rainy days, 'cause I let them keep their motorcycles in the classroom." My audience laughs and Eric winks at me. "If anyone causes any trouble, out all the bikes go into the rain. Which is hard on me too, because I don't have a car and my ride to and from school is on the back of Violent Vernan's motorcycle." More laughter. "Which is never boring because neither Vernan nor his motorcycle has a license, so we dodge the cops coming and going." Even more laughter.

I feel a little twinge. These kids really like me a lot and think I stick up for them. Which I do. Usually. Tonight they are, as the Beatles' current song goes, my "Ticket to Ride."

As I look around the room of mostly middle-aged academicians, I fail to catch the irony in my pride at being included. One of the reasons I thought I left college was to avoid these people. Yet, here I am tonight feeling honored to be among the pontificators. Time is going by, and I'm still thrilled to get to stay up late with the grown-ups.

. . . . .

After my Chicago fiasco, I had kicked around the house smoking cigarettes for about three months. My sister, Eve, my loyal sidekick, pulled a chair up beside me at the kitchen table one afternoon and lit into me. "You know, big sista, you have always been the star around here, the Great White Hope. We don't have any money, but the family scrapes together enough to send you off to a boarding school for rich girls. You do well there. You don't do great, but you do all right. I'm back here making straight A's and wearing your faded hand-me-downs. Mama and Daddy and you and I, we all think this is O.K. because you're a star."

I remember Eve was straddling the chair backward and talking to me over her crossed arms. I couldn't believe this conversation, because my younger sister had always been my greatest fan. "It looks like we might be right because, lo and behold, despite mediocre grades, your uniqueness is recognized, and you are awarded a scholarship to another fancy girls school, a college this time, in the faraway North, the promised land. It turns out this means nothing to you. You toss it away, without looking back, without talking to any of us, who had all our bets on you. Without talking to any of us, you throw it all away."

Eve got up, pushed her chair back to the table, and turned to me again. "Now I'm a junior and I'm looking at catalogues for colleges, trying to decide where I want to go and it turns out I don't get a choice. I go to good ole LSU with all the good ole rah rahs and sorority girls, or I go nowhere. The family coffers are empty. We truly placed all our bets on you."

She turned and walked out of the kitchen. The next day I took a Greyhound bus to New Orleans, determined to make my fortune, determined to win back my family's trust. My first day of job-hunting, I landed the teaching job.

. . . . .

After the party Eric takes me to his apartment. Which makes me very nervous. Unlike the thrown-together and extremely filthy apartment I share with a friend of Marie's, another dropout, Eric's place is decorated with antiques and is impeccably clean. He walks me through the four large high-ceilinged rooms and nothing is out of place. Eric watches me, and I can tell he is eager to put me at ease. "Why don't you go in the next room, and I'll get us something to drink. Anytime you're ready to go home, Elfin One, just say so." He kisses me, sweetly, like a brother, on the top of my head.

I sit on his deep green velveteen love seat with my ankles together and my hands folded in my lap. Eric walks into the living room carrying two glasses of brandy. "Now I really do believe you are a convent girl." I must look embarrassed, or uncomfortable, because he puts his glass down and strokes my cheek. "You are the most refreshing little thing it has ever been my privilege to touch."

He kisses me lightly again, then walks over and opens a large oak cabinet. "Why don't you select a record? I have a new Debussy you might really enjoy."

Eric goes back into the kitchen and leaves me behind to figure out what a Debussy is. A quick perusal shows me that he has no Bob Dylan, no Beatles, not even an Elvis. When Eric returns carrying a tray of cheese and crackers, I'm back in the convent position, and there is no music playing. "Didn't you like my collection?"

"That was the problem, I liked it too much. I'm a real bad decision maker." I remember myself, and cross my legs, and lean back casually on the arm of the love seat. "Men are better at things like that."

Eric puts on a record which may, or may not, be Debussy. It certainly has no words.

He lights a small, dim lamp and places it on the table beside the love seat; he takes off his glasses and places them beside the lamp. Then he walks over and turns out the bright overhead light. He kneels at my feet, which is embarrassing and encouraging at the same time. "I know it's only been two nights, and I know I'm a bit of a philanderer, but, Katherine, I think I might be falling in love with you." Eric folds his hands on my knees and looks up at me, and I fight the impulse to pinch myself. This can't be happening. He pushes the hem of my skirt up and kisses my stockinged knees. I stroke the back of his head, my fingers play with his thick hair.

"Me too," I say. "I mean . . ."

He takes my hands, and I kneel on the floor in front of him. We are kissing. This isn't like kissing an eager clumsy boy. Eric isn't rushed, or pushy, he knows what he is doing, I don't have to be in charge. I am with a man, an unmarried man; a man with streaks of silver in his hair.

Eric runs his thumb back and forth across the scoop neck of my dress. His fingers slip down to brush lightly over the top of my breasts, he moves his hands back up to my neck, down my shoulders, my ribs; he lingers, encircling my waist with his large hands, kneading; his hands slip down to my hips. All the time we have been kissing and his hands have been moving over me, my hands have been holding on to his shoulders. This feels to me almost the way it does when I'm crouched in the water on skis, waiting to be pulled up by a motorboat.

Suddenly, Eric sits back. "Katherine, you're wearing a girdle."

I'm embarrassed, but this is no boy, this is a man. I have to explain myself. "Yes, of course I am. I have on stockings. What's wrong—"

He is kissing me and laughing. "Your little chastity belt." He takes my hands again and sits me on the love seat. Then Eric kneels in front of me, runs his hands under my skirt, and reaches to undo the garters of my tight little girdle. When he looks up at me, tears are running down my cheeks. "What's wrong, little one?"

I am trying not to cry. I have a job and an apartment. This man is a college professor. "I'm afraid," I blurt out.

"A-afraid you're . . . ? Oh, Elf Child, my precious, precious Elf Child." He pulls me down into his lap and rocks me while I sob.

"I'm afraid it will hurt. I'm afraid I'm gonna hate doing it, and I'm afraid I might go to hell and I'm afraid you're gonna get mad at me." By this time I'm sobbing in hiccups and wiping my eyes and nose on the hem of my skirt.

He pulls my skirt hem from my fingers and kisses my tears and my neck. I burrow my face into his shoulder, and run my hands down his chest. Soon we are lying on the floor kissing and touching desperately.

Eric loves my virginity and his love of it makes it seem the greatest possible gift I could give to him. I can't believe his tenderness. I want to give him everything, anything. Whatever a man might want from a woman is what I want to give this tender, tender man whose tongue is tasting the nape of my neck. Four nights ago I didn't know he was in this world. Now the thought of leaving him cracks my heart in two.

My clothes and my little girdle stay on, but they are damp, wrinkled, and rumpled. Eric doesn't take me back to my unkempt garden apartment until almost daylight.

The next night we make love. We go all the way. It doesn't hurt like I thought it would, and being with Eric is nothing like my furtive suffocating experiences with college boys. Despite the

Blessed Mother's example, despite a vague and disturbing child-hood memory, I love this lovemaking.

The next day I break it to Marie that I'm not a virgin. Two months later Eric and I are married. Seven months later Made-line is born.

. . . . .

When we decide to get married, five weeks after we have met, I proudly take Eric home to Bellebend to meet my family. I return to Bellebend vindicated for my discarded education. My fiancé is a college professor. My mother is pleased, because, among her fears for us, is the fear that Eve and I will marry Southerners. That we'll settle down to dull lives in Bellebend, or some other dull, slow Southern town. Eric charms my no-nonsense mother, they engage in casual intellectual banter, and I am proud to see my smart mother hold her own. It occurs to me that my hus-band-to-be is chronologically the same number of years younger than my mother as I am from him. I think how nice it is that he can close the gap, in a manner of speaking. My father is beside himself. "Dr. Peterson, it's a pleasure, a real pleasure."

"Please, sir, call me Eric."

"Daddy, it's Pierson, not Peterson." My father is so proud and so relieved, his little girl is no longer going to wander, uncared for, in the careless world.

Eve joins us briefly in the living room for a drink and then excuses herself. I follow her.

"Now what's wrong, baby sista?" I slip off my high heels and snuggle up beside Eve on our old bed.

"Nothing, Katherine. You look very happy and he's certainly a charmer. I liked that special little squeeze he gave my hand. Real brotherly."

I sit back to look at her. "I'm missing something. What are you trying to say, Eve?"

"Oh, nothing, Katherine. It's just, it's just that I thought you

47

were going to make something of yourself. I always thought that."

"Eve." I take my sister's face in my hand. "Eve, I'm marrying a professor, a college professor. O.K., I messed up getting an education, but now I'm marrying one. Don't you get it?"

She takes my hands from her face and holds them. "No, I think you don't get it; he may have it, but you're not gonna get it. Not with him."

I shake my hands loose and stand up. "Eve, I'm not leaving you. I'm still gonna be your sister. Things will be almost the same. And look how pretty you are. People stop in the middle of the street to stare at you. When you're ready to get married, you can pick anybody you want."

"Why does it have to be about looks? Katherine, you're smart. You're real smart. How come you think your brains are just one more cute little charm for your charm bracelet?"

"I don't understand why you're begrudging me this happiness."

"Shit, Katherine, I'm still in high school. How come I feel like the big sister?"

. . . . .

Though the notice is very short, there are several parties for us. Eric's colleagues host a supper for us uptown at Commander's Palace restaurant, with wry good grace. One party held by a friend's pool in Bellebend has me holding court in the dressing room.

"This being in love, really in love, is a zillion times more than we ever thought it would be. Sometimes I look at Eric and I remember that this man, this perfect man, has kissed me, and I have to touch my lips. It's like pinching myself again and again. Can this be real? He makes me laugh, he makes me cry, he makes me forget my very name."

Marie is starry-eyed. "Katherine, I always knew something like this would happen to you."

My friends, who are all college students, are thrilled for me, speechless around my professor fiancé. The same night we decided to get married I scribbled a letter off to Susan at Radcliffe and keep expecting a phone call or a telegram from her. I can imagine Susan and Eric meeting, their glib and bright conversations.

The kids at my school put on an enormous wedding shower. They must have stolen over a thousand dollars' worth of loot. Though it is evident they stole only one big roll of wrapping paper, since the more than twenty gifts are wrapped in the same paper. Eric is too busy to attend the shower. I am sorry he has to miss it, because my children really give a wild and wonderful party. They put together a rock 'n' roll band and sing a song written especially for Eric and me. We have Cheez Whiz on Ritz crackers and cases of Coca-Colas, probably lifted from the nearest National Food Store. My favorite of all the tacky hopeful gifts is a giant book that rotates on a pedestal. Across the front, in gold leaf, is written "The Good Book," and when the Good Book is opened, it contains a complete bar set, shaker, full booze bottles, jiggers, glasses, the works. For months after we are married, every time there is a knock at the door of Eric's apartment, my new husband and I laugh and pretend it is the police coming to repossess our wedding gifts.

. . . . .

On my last visit to Bellebend before the wedding, my mother comes into my old room where I am reading. "Is there anything you need to talk about, Katherine? Anything you'd like to ask me?" She looks amused and serious, at the same time.

"You mean, like the 'facts of life'?" We both laugh.

A moth is caught in the shade of my reading lamp. The taps

of its escape attempts make a soft rhythm behind my mother's voice.

"There's so much you haven't seen or done, Katherine. Eric seems like a wonderful man and I assume he's crazy about you. It's just that you're so young. I hope this all isn't too rushed. I'd hate to see you settle now, then regret untraveled roads later." She sits on the side of my bed. "You've had such a brief time between your daddy and me and the nuns. And now a husband . . ."

"I'm just a few months younger than you were when you married Daddy." The little thuds of the moth make me turn to watch its shadow through the shade.

"I know. I guess that's why I'm bringing it up. I—"

"And you and Daddy are so romantic." I put my book aside and sit straight up. "I mean, look how much Daddy loves you. After all these years."

I'm almost awed to be having this heart-to-heart talk, such an uncommon thing with my mother. I can't wait to tell Eve. "Eric reminds me a little bit of Daddy. I think marrying an older person can make up for being young when you get married. Eric is so smart. Did I tell you he speaks practically perfect French?"

"Well . . ." My mother has gotten up and cupped her hands inside the lampshade, capturing the moth. She walks to the raised window and unlocks the screen with the knuckles of her cupped hands, pushes the screen out, and releases the moth into the night. "Well, Katherine. Just think about it. Right up to the altar, you can always change your mind." She pulls the screen back in and snaps the lock. "Remember that."

She walks out of the room and our heart-to-heart has ended. I'm just not sure what it was about.

. . . . .

Our wedding is in April. I wear a pale green silk suit and Eve is my maid of honor. The reception is in a small old-fashioned uptown hotel in New Orleans. It is a much nicer event than my parents can afford. I hardly notice my family, though. I only have eyes for my handsome groom. He looks at me as though he loves me. I know I don't deserve such love, but I am determined to become worthy of it. We stare at one another across the room of our wedding reception.

The only shadow of this day is the fact that I haven't heard a word from Susan. I thought surely she'd try to make the wedding. Also, I try to entertain and divert my aloof in-laws. Eric's lawyer father and petite silver-haired mother seem to deliberately set themselves apart from the raucous south Louisiana gathering. Even his brother and sister-in-law seem to be standing back.

Only after we leave the reception do I remember I haven't kissed my father. I haven't even said good-bye to him. I only vaguely recall hugging my mother and my very quiet sister. On our wedding night Eric and I have dinner with his family. I neglected my own father on my wedding day, and have to sit quietly on my wedding night listening to Eric's father talk about people I don't know.

We don't go on a honeymoon, it is too near the end of Laffitte's semester, Eric has too many papers to grade. I certainly don't need a honeymoon. Going to bed and getting up with this man is a miracle, a gift, a holiday. Whenever Eric wants me, I am ready for him. Sometimes I wish he were in the mood more often. Sex, to me, is like a wonderful delicious feast where you can have as much food as you want, yet never get full. Being married, and having sex, is the same as actually owning the restaurant where an unending feast is held.

· · · · ·

Susan finally calls me from Boston. I don't ask why she missed the wedding, instead I go on and on about my new life. "He's just brilliant, Susan. You two will really get along. I can't wait for you to see our apartment. To think that I will get to do this for the rest of my life! It is the most immense and glorious thing I know."

"But what else, Katherine, what else are you going to do with your immense life?"

"I swear, Susan, you sound like my sister. Just you wait until you find love."

. . . . .

Eric and I fix supper together every night and socialize with his colleagues on weekends. We take long bike rides through the Garden District and grade papers sitting side-by-side in his study. I try to keep up with Marie, but neither of us seems to fit in the world of the other.

During the summer session we go to Eric's family's beach house in Delaware. It is here I discover Eric's family isn't anything like mine. In Delaware we dress for dinner and have many cocktails before sitting down to dinner. Eric, his brother, sister-in-law, and his parents all drink martinis. I drink weak vodka tonics that grow tepid as I hold them during the much too long cocktail time. They discuss politics, over my head, so to speak. In Louisiana I am always outspoken and precocious. In Delaware I seem to be seen and not heard. I'm a listener sitting in Danish modern furniture on a screened porch facing away from the sea.

I hear Eric's father say, "If poor people want to get ahead, they should go to college."

All the poor people I know struggle just to keep their kids in high school. I wonder if Northern poor people go around turning down options that don't seem to be available to Southern poor people. Another time I hear him say, "Think of the poor stockholders!" Think of the stockholders. Here I am, practically a grown woman, and I have spent my entire life without ever giving "the poor stockholders" a thought.

I am homesick and want to go back to Louisiana and am too ashamed to say so. After Eric falls asleep, I cry. I listen to the

Atlantic pounding the shore near our window. I think about my own family and the sounds of riverboat whistles out on the Mississippi, and I cry. I hate that I didn't kiss my father on my wedding day. I want another chance.

Eric's family seems embarrassed by my pregnancy. When we planned our wedding, I sincerely did not know I was pregnant. Years later, when I ask Eric why he married me, why he seemed in such a fevered rush, he will confess that he was fairly certain I was pregnant. I was taught reproduction by nuns and only discovered my pregnancy days before we left for Delaware. I was under the impression that there was only a second, or two, in each menstrual cycle when the woman's egg was in position to be whammed by the man's sperm. You'd think I could have noticed the world's population and figured that, unless there was a great deal of round the clock copulating, the law of averages was against basic Holy Name Academy biology.

I am so thin that my growing stomach becomes immediately evident. When the family entertains, my new sister-in-law lends me flowing Hawaiian dresses to wear. The Piersons are uncomfortable, but it seems to me they are also relieved. As if, here at last is an explanation for Eric's taking an ignorant Southern child, twelve years his junior, for a bride. This is not to say they aren't kind, only that they aren't very interested.

. . . . .

When we return to New Orleans, I have nothing to do. Eric is up for tenure and is busy with committee work. At home he is distracted and doesn't seem to want to talk. He closets himself in his small study with a drink and only emerges for dinner. At the end of my school session, when I told the director of my pregnancy, he had said it would be best if I didn't return in the fall. The work with those untamed teenagers was too dangerous for a pregnant woman. I never tell my class good-bye, and I never go back to visit them. Instead I go to sleep.

. . . . .

"*Cat Ballou* is really supposed to be a funny movie, Katherine."
Marie's voice on the phone seems very far away, though her dorm
is a ten-minute streetcar ride from Eric's apartment. "You don't
have a job, I don't have classes this afternoon. Come on."

"Another time, Marie. I'm just exhausted. I have to nap in
the afternoons. I just have to."

. . . . .

Sleep is a warm ocean, I am seaweed. I only want to sway underwater. I don't want to think or talk or breathe air. I want to be
left alone to be moved by tides and currents beyond myself. I
sink into warm salty sleep, a shadow beneath the surface of day,
and the surface closes over me.

I can't wake up for anything. Or the only thing I wake for is
love. I pull myself from bed to make breakfast for Eric. I shower
with him, we kiss and play in the shower. Then, as he gets
dressed for work, I stumble back to bed. I set an alarm to ring at
four in the afternoon so I can walk to the National to buy groceries for dinner. I am learning to cook, and have dinner waiting
when Eric returns home at six. I am asleep again by nine.

When Eric asked me to marry him, I said I'd never be interested in cooking or keeping house. He laughed and lifted me up
in the air. "I'd never want you to be a housewife, Elfin Child."
When I lost my job, it didn't make sense not to be something.

One night we attend a play at an all-black university. The
play is very contemporary. It is by a black writer who hates white
people. Eric and I are the only white people in the audience. I fall
asleep. I would fall asleep in a swimming pool, I surely fall asleep
in this warm, crowded room. While I am sleeping, one of the
actresses leaves the stage, walks through the audience, leans over,
and shakes me by the shoulders. "Wake up, white bitch!" she

says. I stay awake for the rest of the night. Eric and I stop going anyplace in the evenings.

One morning, when we go to shower together, we see that my stomach looks as though a lion has ripped at it. The taut shiny skin of my pregnant belly has stretched as far as possible, then has ripped open in great streaks. I am horrified. When I look at Eric, I see that he is horrified too. The next morning I don't go into the shower with him. He doesn't ask me to, either. After my cute distended belly turns grotesque, we don't make love anymore. I miss lovemaking very much and don't know if this is normal. I don't know if it is normal to stop having sex when you're pregnant. I also don't know anyone to ask.

We live near a home for unwed mothers. Sometimes I watch those poor girls, those girls without gold bands on their fingers. Sometimes I daydream about asking one of them over to Eric's apartment for a visit. It still feels like Eric's apartment, not our apartment. Maybe I'd make lemonade.

One day, during my walk to the grocery store, a woman hisses at me, "You can't be more than fourteen. Children, opening their legs for anyone. How disgusting."

I want to tell her that she is wrong, that I'm almost twenty. Instead, I keep walking, but now my fingers are laced together over my swollen belly. I don't know if babies can hear the outside world. I don't know anything about babies. I'd like to cover this baby's ears.

Late one morning I'm awakened by a long, hard pain in my lower belly. When I go into the bathroom, my underwear is streaked with blood. All this time I thought the baby would come when I was ready. So I haven't been getting ready. I want my husband to myself a little longer. I want to be the only child. I want to stay up with the grown-ups just a little longer. I haven't read any books about pregnancy or childbirth. I always think about other things when my sweet, elderly obstetrician talks to me on my visits to his office. I am humiliated when he looks between my legs. When he asks if I have any questions, I always smile and shake my head. Eric and I haven't bought a diaper, we don't have a baby bed. Nothing is ready. But suddenly I know I am about to have a baby. I don't want to phone Eric. I hate calling his office. It always sounds as though I am bothering the department secretary and I want her to like me. The hospital is only seven blocks away. So I walk.

In the labor room everything happens at once, and none of it is anything I expect. They take all my clothes away and give me an enema. I have to walk down the hall wearing a gown without a back, walk down the hall afraid I'll go to the bathroom in the hall. In the bathroom I'm afraid the baby will fall out into the toilet bowl. Back in the labor room, an efficient, unsmiling nurse shaves me between my legs and I'm propped on a bed in such a way that anyone passing can look between my legs. The ceilings and walls have been painted the only shade of green I hate. I lie there looking at the ugly green and wishing my stomach didn't hurt, wishing I could put my legs down.

Someone has called Eric and I hear him in the next room. The nurse with me leaves to tend my husband. It seems that on the way to the hospital Eric was so rushed, so excited, he slipped and fell. Now the staff is swabbing and bandaging his brush burns. Finally, someone comes back in the labor room and pulls the sheet back down over my feet so Eric can come into the room.

He strokes my face, smiling very hard. "Oh, Elf Child, if you could see your face. Your eyes are as big as saucers."

I take his hand, close my eyes, and take a deep breath. "Eric, they—they shaved all my hair. You know, down"—I gesture—"down there."

"Hmm, sounds very sexy."

"Eric!"

The doctor arrives, and Eric can't stay with me anymore. "When the pains come a little more frequently, we will give you something called the Twilight Drug. It will enable you to sleep between contractions."

I don't even know what a contraction is. "Dr. Ballus, I haven't had anything to eat. The nurse says I can't eat, but I was—"

"What would you like to eat, Katherine?" He is smiling so helpfully.

"Well, anything that might be around."

"The hospital has wonderful facilities, name something you'd really like, love."

"Anything, really?" He nods. "Well, then I'd like a hot fudge sundae."

"With whipped cream?" he asks.

"And, I mean if they have all the stuff, whipped cream and roasted pecans." Dr. Ballus asks the nurse if she has heard my order. She nods but doesn't leave the room.

Time passes, the room gets dark. Someone gives me a shot. My stomach still hurts, it hurts more than I can bear. I wake up as the nurse twists a flat metal needle into my arm. The needle is connected by a tube to a bottle full of liquid. I ask about the hot fudge sundae, but everyone seems busy. I think I hear screaming in another room. Maybe the screams are in this room. Maybe I'm screaming. I wake up from a dream where Eric is chasing me, trying to rip my belly open with a knife. The dream seems funny because my belly is already ripped. I am moving, floating down a hallway.

In a cold white room Dr. Ballus leans too close to my face. Now I am dreaming Eric and I are having sex. Everyone in the cold white room is watching, cheering, as I arch my hips into Eric. Eric enters me again and again. People shout each time, "Push!"

Dr. Ballus is wearing a shower cap, and he is bossing me around. His shiny, round pink face isn't kind anymore, it's mean. "One more time," he says, sternly. "One more time, Katherine!"

"One more time means one more time. Don't say it any-more!" I am tired of people bossing me around. Everything hurts too much and I am tired. The nurse who never smiles lowers a cereal bowl over my face.

"A beautiful little girl." Eric is leaning into my face, like Dr. Ballus. "We have a daughter, Katherine!" I need to get back to sleep. First it was too quiet, now it's too noisy. "She's so tiny, Katherine."

"Where is the hot fudge sundae, Eric? Everyone promises . . . I'm so hungry."

When I wake up again, it is morning. My father is sitting by my bed. This is a hospital, how strange for my father to be here. He looks so worried. Everything will be all right now, because my father is here. He won't like it when I tell him how much those people hurt me. He'll be on my side.

"Katherine, honey, I rushed here. Your mama said I had to wait, that we'd wait until the weekend. You know how practical your mother is, saying you'd be tired and we couldn't hold the baby until you were home. I couldn't wait. Your mama will have a fit, but I just couldn't wait to lay eyes on that little girl. She's beautiful, Katherine."

Now I remember my father hasn't looked me in the face for months. I'm so glad he's looking at me. My entire pregnancy my father has talked to me while focusing on a place about two feet away from me. My swollen belly embarrassed him. And it embarrassed me when I was around him. Now he's looking at me again. His eyes are watery.

"Who, Daddy? Who looks like me?"

"Your daughter. My granddaughter." He seems confused.

I sit up. "I've been asleep, Daddy. I've been asleep for a long time. I—I . . . now I remember. The baby, the baby came!"

"You haven't seen your daughter, sweetheart?" I shake my head. Everything is happening at once, but it's happening in slow motion.

"I'll be damned!" My father is walking out of the room before I know it.

He returns followed by a nurse who is carrying a bundle. My father walks to the bed, and then moves back like a gentleman opening a door for a lady. He stands away and the nurse steps to the bed and leans over to place the bundle in my arms. A perfectly round head is in the bundle, hooded in a thin white blanket. A bundle, so light, moving slightly, settling in my crossed arms. My daughter, not the red anonymous newborn infant I expected. This is my daughter.

Though I didn't know I had been waiting for this life all my life, I would know this bundle anywhere. She settles into my arms and becomes my arms. I am holding a perfect baby, tiny and perfect, a valentine dreamed by the angels. Eyes that are not supposed to see yet look at me, and don't let go. My daughter's small body turns toward my body, twists in her newborn dream, and five miniature perfect fingers reach up to tap at my chest. Fingers, the size of hummingbird feathers, softly tapping on my heart. A little visitor, come to stay. My arms fold her to me as she keeps her steady knocking. I let her in.

CHAPTER III

"*MOON TARS, DADDY.*" *I AM A LIT-* tle girl, scrubbed and shiny from my bath, dressed in a cotton nightgown. I reach for my father, stretching my arms high overhead. My mother is in the rocking chair giving Eve a bottle. It is a ritual with my father and me that, every evening before bedtime, we go out to look at the sky, at the moon and stars.

He lifts me onto his shoulders, and we step out into the night. We cross the River Road and climb through the damp grass and wildflowers to the top of the levee. Night is a velvet cloak rich with diamonds my father has flung over the darkness for me. Crickets in the grass and frogs from the river ponds fill the night with music, and my father is the conductor of this orchestra. The Mississippi glimmers through the trees, my father has parted the curtain of trees so I can see the river. The night is scented by that wide swath of muddy water, and by honeysuckle and confederate jasmine. Beyond the great curve, a riverboat sends a plaintive faraway whistle. All of this is magic, a storybook my father has written just for me.

On my wedding day, as he prepares to give me away, my father will stand, nervously clearing his throat, in the entrance of the church. He will begin to speak, trying to remind me of that little girl who asked for the moon and stars. Leaving one man for another, I will be too impatient to hear out his tender prepared speech for me.

My mother says, when I was born, my father thought babies were like puppies. When he saw me with my eyes open, only moments after birth, he was convinced I was a genius. My mother says he never changed his mind. I think that I am the only star in his blue heaven. That no matter how high I jump, he will always catch me. I think that all my stories will have happy endings because my father is a magician who will wave his wand for me and make it so. As a "Grand Knight" in a secret Catholic society, he has an ornamental sword. When he tells me he has slain the devil with his sword, I believe him. I am happy for the world that the devil is now dead, proud that my daddy saved the world from hell. When he says the South won the Civil War, I believe him.

Eve is two years old, and my mother is still wearing maternity dresses, drawn in by a belt, because they have no money to buy new clothes. Yet, without even consulting her, he buys my mother a beautiful diamond ring. Another time, when they are still very poor, he buys a big tricycle for me that costs more than one week of his teaching salary. I am small for my age and, by the time I can reach the pedals of that expensive toy, I am a first-grader and wouldn't be caught dead riding a tricycle. He is foolish with money, my mother says, because he was born with a silver spoon in his mouth.

"Tell us about the lovely Madeline." Eve and I have heard the story of our father's brief and tragic first marriage a hundred times, but it is still our favorite bedtime story.

He leans with his back against the open window by our bed.

His dark hair is streaked with silver and one wave of hair has fallen over his forehead. He is framed by the broad branches of the magnolia, it is summer twilight, and the shiny leaves are holding the very last light of day.

"I was a handsome young man of twenty, a student at Loyola University in the Crescent City, the City of Dreams—"

"The City that Care Forgot, the City of New Orleans," Eve and I chime in.

Our father loves New Orleans. He laughs at our recitation, then takes on a faraway look, the way he does when he's getting down to brass tacks in telling a story. "I was a guest at a debutante ball, and I was standing alone, sipping a glass of illegal champagne. Champagne smuggled in from France, because in the late twenties our country was dry, dry as northern Louisiana, dry as a Baptist wedding. Then I saw her, the most beautiful, liveliest, golden-haired girl I'd ever laid my eyes upon. Until I laid eyes on your mama, of course. She was surrounded by a group of friends and seemed to be regaling them all. I put down my glass—"

"And she was dressed in a pale green satin gown," Eve adds.

"Yes, she wore a pale green satin dress. I put down my glass and crossed the room in great, urgent strides. And, apologizing for interrupting, I ask the beautiful young girl to dance."

This is always my favorite part. It reminds me of when Rhett asked Scarlett to dance at the wartime benefit ball in Atlanta. "To my amazement, she accepts," my father continues. "I discover this night is her birthday, her name is Madeline, and she has just turned eighteen. We danced until the musicians stop playing, even then we continued dancing. Her brother had to come and take her hand from mine. That was the first night of the carnival season."

Eve kneels upright in our bed, "Twelfth Night!"

He gently takes my sister's shoulder and lays her down again, pulling the sheet over both of us. "Yes, Twelfth Night." He smiles. "And we are married the second Saturday after Easter."

Our father sits down on the bed to tell us the sad part. Eve and I hold hands under the covers.

"For our honeymoon Madeline wanted to go to Charleston, South Carolina, but I insisted we go to St. Louis. She said she had never seen the ocean and longed to walk along the Battery and watch the ships come in. I had my heart set on a wedding night aboard a riverboat. I thought of standing on deck with her each evening at sunset. It would never have occurred to my gracious fiancée to argue. She was very disappointed, but, of course, agreed to the St. Louis plan. She even mustered a show of enthusiasm by reading several books on St. Louis."

Eve and I know that if it were our mother, instead of the lovely Madeline, if our mother had wanted to go to Charleston, that would have been the end of any talk of St. Louis. That's for sure.

"Our boat ride was everything I could have hoped, springtime along the Mississippi." At this part of the story, he always speaks more slowly.

"Every evening we stood on the deck and watched the sun set. To this day I can see her delight in that ethereal display. After our leisurely cruise up the Mississippi, the boat trip ended in St. Louis, where we had the bridal suite at the King Louis Hotel. I had cabled ahead and the room was filled with flowers."

He pauses for a moment. Eve and I push in closer to one another.

"The great canopied bed had a cover of red velvet and antique lace, our balconies looked over the river. On our second night in St. Louis, Madeline fell very ill. The hotel doctor was drunk, and, by the time we could fetch decent help, Madeline was delirious. She had meningitis. In her fever dreams she hummed the song that was playing when we met."

" 'The Viennese Waltz,' " I murmur.

My father leans over to stroke the hair away from my forehead, his voice is very soft in the dark room. "She hummed that waltz and talked and laughed, saying, 'See, Jason, I knew you would like Charleston best. Look, look at the light on the ocean.' Madeline hummed that song and talked of Charleston all night long. She died shortly after sunrise."

Our father stops speaking, stands and gazes out the window, though it is a moonless night and there is nothing to see.

"Green is my favorite color. Do you know that, Daddy?"

"Yes, I do, Katherine. And one day I'm going to take you to Charleston. I promise." He hasn't turned back to me. He continues looking out into the darkness.

Though she surely knows the story as well as we do, sometimes our mother stands in the doorway to listen. It is as though she is looking down some passageway to find her husband young and full of spirit. The three of us like to watch him wander down that passageway, maybe because he always comes back to us.

. . . . .

My father's mother died when he was seven years old and, from what the old-timers say, my father was a wild young trouble-maker after his mother's death. We heard that once he shot out all the streetlamps in Bellebend with his BB gun, and another time dropped a stink bomb from the balcony of the Grand Theater. He was the terror of the town. That all changed when he was ten and his wealthy father married a very stern German woman. She made sure the large household was clean and well organized, but seemed to have felt no affection for my father. His days became regimented and he was miserable and twice tried to run away and join the priesthood. Each time my grandfather had him brought home to Bellebend again. His stepmother took what seems to have been a mischievous fun-loving boy and molded him into a quiet, uncomplaining scholar. His adolescence must have been very solitary. My father went off to the university at sixteen and was just finishing his degree in education when he met Madeline.

Sometimes I imagine that I was alive, and lived next door to my father when he was a boy. I imagine I could have kept him from being lonely. We would have had adventures and secrets. I would rescue him from his mean stepmother and would help him laugh at his troubles. We'd do everything together. At night, after the mean stepmother was asleep, I'd throw stones at his window, like Huck Finn did to Tom Sawyer. And off we'd go. Just my daddy and me.

After the death of his beloved Madeline, my father seemed determined to put love and the Mississippi far behind. He took a teaching job in a school for American Indian boys run by the Benedictine priests in Oklahoma. It was right after oil had been discovered in Oklahoma and before the government had figured a way to steal this land from the Indians too. So most of the time my father was teaching there, many of the boys had rich chief fathers. The chiefs would come to talk to the teachers about their sons and my father said they'd light up their cigars with five-dollar bills. My father got a kick out of that. He told us the Indians were wise, they knew that money was nothing and land was everything. And whenever he'd start to remember about everything being taken away from the Indians again, my father would get mad. He taught us about some of the treaties made with the Indians and broken. They didn't even believe that anyone could own land anyway. He taught us about Chief Joseph, who said, "From where the sun now stands, we will fight no more forever."

My sister and I loved hearing that quote. My father would tell it with such a solemn face. "From where the sun now stands, we will fight no more forever."

"What does it mean?" I'd ask.

His own father had died shortly after our father left Louisiana and my father turned all of his inheritance over to the Benedictines. He had been teaching and living at that school for fifteen years when one day a beautiful young reporter from the local paper walked in to interview him. Our mother was twenty years old, a slender, gray-eyed blonde, and, the way our father always tells it, he looked up and said, "I'm a goner!"

Our father seems to have a thing for whirlwind courtships. Within a half a year Jason and Emily were married. This didn't sit too well back in my mother's native Michigan. My mother's family very much objected to their oldest daughter marrying a man sixteen years her senior. And the Benedictine priests seem to have forgotten our father wasn't a priest. Emily and Jason caused a small scandal. He wrote off to his hometown and the school authorities offered my father a teaching job. He'd left Bellebend as a wealthy, eligible young man. He returned almost twenty years later, poor and with a Yankee bride.

Our father can make the most ordinary thing sound like the world's greatest adventure and he can tell the biggest fibs with his eyes wide open and completely sincere. Whenever we want the hard cold facts on anything, Eve and I march up to our mother and ask.

There is no mistaking our mother for anything but a Northerner, even her skin feels cool. Yet, she was always a rebel too. She refused to go to the college her parents chose for her, so she didn't go to college at all. She talked herself into a newspaper job before she even finished high school. Then, after high school, she got hired as a reporter on a weekly paper way off in Oklahoma. She never accepted a penny from her parents after that. Sometimes, when Eve and I spy on our mother while she is talking with her friends, we hear her talk about her teenage years. It sounds like she was pretty carefree back then, and normal. It's hard for us to imagine. Our mother keeps her feet firmly on the ground. And she does her best to keep Daddy's feet there too. That's a harder job. Our father says that she was "scarred by the Depression." He tells us that her own mother never kissed our mother, ever. Even though she is a Yankee, our mother hates to be cold. On the very hottest days, her skin still feels cool. With the slightest chill in the air, she bundles up like Bellebend was the North Pole.

. . . . .

Growing up in this little Mississippi River town, my sister and I have always felt special, chosen. Bellebend is a place of miracles. When the Yankees were going downriver during The War, they fired on the town, and their cannon ball sailed through the tower of the old convent and was stopped by the Blessed Mother's finger. Anyone not believing that can go to St. Vincent's this very day and see the statue with a stub on her right hand. Next to the deformed Blessed Mother there is the finger in a box full of cotton balls and, next to the finger box, the cannon ball. St. Francis also appeared to a man down the River Road and saved his son from death. Every year on the Sunday after Easter there is a procession from that man's house to the Sacred Heart Church in Bellebend. Most of the people walk barefooted.

There are bigger places than our town. We know about Paris and Istanbul and Detroit. But Bellebend is the home of The *First* National Bank and, though hardly anyone from the town attends, it is also the home of The *First* Baptist Church. When we visit our mother's boring Yankee relatives, none of their friends have ever heard of Bellebend. We can hardly believe it. We don't understand why Bellebend isn't marked in great red letters on the map of Louisiana, if not on the map of the entire United States.

. . . . .

Once, when I am about seven and we are visiting in Michigan, I go alone to play in the park near our grandmother's house. Eve is helping my grandmother bake bread. I hate squashing dough between my fingers, so I've gone by myself to the park. I swing for a while and try to swing hard enough to wrap the swing around the top frame, the way I've seen older kids do when no one is in the swing. A man has been walking across the park and stops to watch me. I hope that, if the trick works, he'll still be watching. In case Eve doesn't believe me. After a while swinging gets boring, the swing will go just so high and no higher, so I head for the jungle gym.

To my surprise the man doesn't stop watching me. He even walks over and sits on the bottom rung of the jungle gym when I climb to the top. He is wearing a dark green work shirt and work pants. He must be pretty bored to have nothing to do but watch a seven-year-old climb around.

"That sure looks fun," he says.

"It is pretty fun." I try to impress him by standing on the second from the top rung with my arms outstretched.

"I wish I could climb up there." He is rubbing the palms of his hands up and down the top of his pants leg.

"I bet you could, if you tried." I say this even though I can tell he's too old to climb up on a jungle gym.

"You want to come down here and show me?" I don't want to hurt his feelings, so I climb on down.

"See, it's easy." I put my foot on the bottom rung and reach for the bar above it. The man doesn't move, he just looks at me, the tip of his tongue shows between his lips a little bit. Like he's getting ready to lick his lips, but doesn't.

"Here, you can do it," I say encouragingly.

"Maybe if you would hug me first, little girl. Maybe then I could do it."

It is a strange thing for him to say. I don't want to hug this man, but I can't hurt his feelings, or run away, which is what I really feel like doing. So I just stand there. Then the old man stands up and pulls me close to him. His belt buckle cuts into my chin and I can't breathe. I feel frozen. He is rubbing his front against me the way a dog will rub its back against a tree to scratch itself, and breathing like he's out of breath. He holds me that way for a long, long time, his big hands tight against my back.

"Touch it, touch it, little girl," he says to me in between his hard breathing.

I can't move, and if I could, I don't know what I'm supposed to touch.

He's rubbing against me harder and almost crying. "Please, little girl, touch it!" He grabs my hand and I pull away.

Somehow I am able to pull away and I say, "My daddy, my daddy is calling me. I have to go home now."

And I back away from the old man and turn around and run to my grandmother's house. Even though my daddy wasn't calling me. My daddy didn't even know I was in the park.

. . . . .

By the time I am nine years old, I have read just about every piece of fiction and poetry in both the Catholic and public school libraries and every book about horses. I love horses beyond all belief. Bellebend is too small to have its own town library. By the time I am ten, I will have read *Gone with the Wind* twice. Reading and daydreaming about my reading are about the only things I do. I read in arithmetic and history and geography class. I am in big trouble with my fifth-grade teacher, Sister Justine. I have skipped third grade and now I'm about to fail fifth.

"Jason, this has gone too far. I felt it was a mistake to have her skip a grade." My mother runs her tapered long fingers through her pale hair, then reaches for her cigarettes. My parents are sitting in the kitchen having an argument about me. The two of them face one another across the thick oak table that takes up the center of the black and white tiled floor. The big Kelvinator hums in the background. I am kneeling just outside the kitchen doorway, listening.

"Emily, I tell you, the child is still bored. She needs to be challenged."

I happen to know this is not true. I have absolutely no idea of what is going on in arithmetic class. And we've started writing in cursive, and I can't shape my letters at all. I'm the dumbest kid in the class. I read all the time because I like to read.

They don't get really worried until I don't hear them when they call me to dinner. When my parents finally get my attention and get me to the table, they don't really have me. If I'm reading a book set in pioneer days, while the rest of my family eats pork chops, I gnaw at bear meat beside the fire. One night I look through the smoke of the campfire on the lone prairie and see both my parents staring at me.

The next day I am in a psychiatrist's office in Baton Rouge. He is working in the new field of hypnotic therapy. "Katherine? Katherine." He leans over and takes my book away from me. "Katherine, what is the worst taste in the world?"

"Lima beans," I say, reaching to take my book back.

He hypnotizes me and tells me that if I read anything but schoolwork for the next month, my mouth will be filled with the taste of lima beans. It works. But by the time I am cured of compulsive reading, I have missed the multiplication tables and beginning division. I never catch up.

. . . . .

"Daddy says that Louisiana is God's paradise," I say to Eve.

"Mama says everybody is married to their own cousins, so they're all retarded," she responds. "Well, not everybody in the whole state, just in Sacred Heart Parish," she adds as an after-thought.

The lines are clearly drawn; I'm Daddy's girl, and Eve belongs to Mama. I'm glad to be my father's favorite, though having my mother around always makes me feel safe. Daddy is a dreamer and Mama is smart, real smart. She keeps Daddy from doing really foolish things with our family's small bit of income. Eve and I are pretty sure we'd be in a poorhouse, like in the Charles Dickens books we devour, if Mama didn't put her foot down. Just as our parents are very different, Eve and I can hardly be taken for sisters. She has our father's shiny, very dark hair, which she wears in a blunt, sleek Buster Brown. She has large, brown, mischievous eyes and, though she is two years younger than I, she is almost as tall. I am small-boned and have fair hair and skin, my mother's coloring. My hair is always a tangled mass of knotted curls. My mother chops at it about once a month.

"And what about that man with the bug in his ear?" We are sitting on the roof of the shed in our backyard. This is a secret place tucked behind a chinaberry tree. We play house here and jungle and Holy Mass.

"What man?" I ask, though I really know.

"The man Dr. Nolan told Mama about who got a bug in his ear and his wife tried to help him get it out by spraying a garden hose up through his right ear, thinking she could blow the bug out of his left one."

"Well, what's wrong with that?" I ask, trying to get on Eve's nerves.

Eve starts to climb down the chinaberry tree. "The brain, that's what."

I pound my chest like Tarzan. "The Mississippi is the greatest river in the world!"

I spend long hours wandering alone near the ponds behind the levee and along the riverbank. Always our father talks about our ship coming in, what a great day that will be. How he's going to get silk pajamas for us, a different color for every day. When I was little, I wandered the riverside looking for a silken-sailed ship. I wanted to be the first to see it. I wanted to run over the levee with the good news that our ship had come in. Our ship was docking in Bellebend and now my parents didn't need to fight about money anymore. The poorhouse wagon would never come to fetch us. My mother could stop worrying and settle back and enjoy her silk pajamas.

During the summer low tides there is a little island, made by the roots of an ancient oak tree, that I can reach by jumping from the riverbank. I spend a hundred afternoons reading there, with my back leaned against that great tree. Sometimes massive ocean vessels pass on their way upriver. Sometimes, if he sees me, the person in the pilothouse may blow the ship's whistle and some-times crewmen come on deck and wave. I like to pretend that one day Roy Rogers will be coming upriver touring the South on a great boat. Just as they are passing, one of his children, maybe the little retarded one, will fall overboard and I'll dive into the river and save the child. Roy Rogers will say to me, "Katherine, how can I ever thank you for saving my little retarded child's life?" I'll say, "Oh, it was nothing, Roy. But, if you really need to thank me, you can give me Trigger. Don't worry, I know how to take care of a horse."

．　．　．　．　．

"Mama, do you love us?" Eve and I climb beside our mother as she is reading on the sofa.

"I'm trying to read."

"But do you?" Eve insists. "Do you love us?"

"Can't you two find something to do?"

"Karen's mother says she loves her all the time. She tells Karen every single day," I say. "Karen can't recall a day of her life without hearing her mother tell Karen she loves her." As I try to rest my head convincingly on my mother's shoulder, she slams her book shut and walks out of the room. This makes Eve and me giggle, kicking our legs up in the air. We never doubt our mother's love, but to her, it is something you do. You don't display it or talk about it. When we grow up and fall in love, we will no more discuss love with our mother than we would talk to a nun about going to the bathroom.

．　．　．　．　．

"Helen, how come you have children and you don't have a hus-band?"

Helen works for us every day but Sunday. She is a tall, big-breasted woman with strong, prominent cheekbones, deep chocolate skin, and a broad nose; she always wears a bright-colored kerchief tied tightly around her hair. Today she has the ironing board pulled right in front of the window fan, and her voice is a little wiggly when she answers me. "Lawd, don't I have enough problems with all those churrens? I sho don't need no husband to compound it all."

My mother likes to tell the story about when Helen first came to work for us. My flat-chested mother wears falsies. "So, I'm sitting in the living room," she says, "hosting a coffee for the ladies of the school board, Bellebend's answer to the Daughters of the Confederacy. In comes Helen, carrying these two dripping masses of foam rubber. If that's not enough, she pipes in, 'Miz Roberts, you want I should hang these li'l titties out there on the line?' It surely shook those blue hairs. I've had a special place in my heart for Helen ever since." Eve and I love hearing our mother tell this story.

Our world is one of "white" and "colored" water fountains and rest rooms and schools. A small colored boy is in front of me in line at the Dairy Queen. Jess LeBlanc, who is the manager, looks over the little boy's head, just looks at me and asks what I want. If another white person comes up, he'll do the same, again and again. That little boy will just have to stand there waiting. Jess doesn't question that, and I don't, and the little colored boy doesn't. My Yankee mother makes a few noises now and then.

"Jason, for the life of me, I don't know how you can get your blood pressure all up talking about land being taken from the Indians and fail to work any fury over the Negroes being taken from their land. We are surrounded by a people whose ancestors were brought here by force. Abduction is surely as bad, or worse, than theft."

But, besides our mother's lectures, for a long time our family generally doesn't do much of anything about race issues. Except Mama won't let Helen sit in the backseat when she drives Helen home. Daddy does, though.

One winter, when I am about eleven, things start to change. A colored man, from up North, comes to town. Like a lamb going to slaughter, he makes the mistake of attending Sunday mass at Sacred Heart, the white church. It's an early mass, and the church isn't very crowded, so nothing much happens until the man goes to receive communion at the communion rail and the priest passes him by. Just like Jess LeBlanc did to that little colored boy waiting for ice cream. The man, who must have been brave, or like my friends said, "stupid," just stayed at the railing until the priest had given everyone up there communion and had walked back to continue mass at the altar. He stayed there a little longer. Mass went on and the congregation had to look at that lone person, still waiting for communion. Finally that colored man pushed back from the communion railing, genuflected, and made the sign of the cross. He turned around and walked straight out of the high-ceilinged, marble-pillared white people's church.

When my mother hears about this, she has a fit. "That does it, Jason. We are changing churches, we are going to St. Anthony's." My parents are sitting in the cleaned, late night kitchen, their favorite place to argue. Eve and I are kneeling on the dining room floor, our favorite place to listen.

"Emily, honey, we can't go to the colored church, I'll lose my job."

"You will not, Jason, and you know it. This town still venerates your father's memory, like he was God the Father. Which makes you Jesus Christ in their eyes."

"Hush, Emily, that's a terrible way to talk." Our father hates any kind of sacrilege.

"Here you are protecting the name of God and not doing a thing in the world about 'God's house' turning away the 'least of our brethren.' It is goddamned hypocrisy. And you know it!"

My father does know it. He just hates to make waves. We always tell him not to worry about making waves, we'll make them for him. Really, Eve and my mother make waves, I just follow behind because I don't want to look chicken. So we change churches and there are four white faces in a sea of color every Sunday at the St. Anthony's ten o'clock mass.

· · · · ·

"Mama, how come Helen has children and she's not married? I thought only married people have children." Eve has gone to the National Food Store with Daddy and I sit carefully down on the bed where my mother is folding clothes.

"Well, Katherine, it's—it's complicated. I'll tell you some other time." She stands up as though she is going to walk out of the room. As though Helen can finish folding the clothes, even though Helen is outside hanging today's wash on the line.

I'd only asked my question for something to say, something to say in this rare time of having my mother to myself. Now it seems like I've stumbled onto an important subject. My mother looks uncomfortable.

"Why not now? Tell me now, please. Tell me how you can have a baby and not be married."

"It's a . . ." She unfolds the pair of Eve's shorts she'd just folded. "It is something a man and woman do together and after they do, do this thing . . . well, nine months later a baby comes."

"What is it they do, that both of them do? What is it like?"

"It's called 'intercourse.' " My mother abruptly scoops up a stack of clothes and heads out. I block the doorway.

"Mama, why do they intercourse if they know a baby comes and they aren't even married?"

My mother looks impatient, eager to put away the folded clothes. "Because—because they're curious."

"But Helen has more than one baby. How come she keeps being curious?" My mother is walking rapidly down the hall.

"It doesn't make any sense!" I call after her.

A n n   G o e t h e

. . . . .

One afternoon in late spring I have been picking blackberries behind the levee and am just heading home through the tall grasses of the levee when I hear an ominous buzzing. Suddenly, something stings me on my rear end, then on my arm and my cheek. I throw my bucket of berries and begin to run. I am running through a cloud of bees and they are stinging me everywhere. They are stinging my legs and my ankles beneath my jeans, they fly down my blouse and are stinging me again and again on my small new breasts, my back, my ribs. They cling to my neck and tangle in my hair. I am running and running, trying to shake bees out of my hair, trying to scream louder than the buzzing in my ears, louder than the pain. I can't outrun the bees. Cars park along the River Road to watch me screaming, batting at a cloud of bees and shaking my head until the sky is green and the ground is blue, and I am rolling down the levee, rolling and crying, slapping at my chest. I am breathing bees.

I wake up in my bed, lying on my stomach, wearing only my underpants. The sheets feel icy on my skin. In the next room I hear voices speaking quietly. ". . . even slightly allergic, she'd be dead. She's a lucky little girl. Add a little warm water to this, it'll soothe her. If the fever doesn't go down, call me."

My father sits beside my bed and places a bowl on the bedside table. I hear a cloth sloshing in the water. When he wrings it out, it sounds like the bowl is laughing. He carefully pulls the sheet away from me. It takes all afternoon for the sheet to move. My room grows dark. I fall asleep and wake up again as the sheet slowly billows away in a cloud. The water laughs in the bowl again. Then a warm wet cloth sucks tiny fire arrows from my skin. My father whispers, "There now, there." The bed is a boat with silken sails my father and I ride rocking in water that whispers "there, there." The fire arrows fill my father's hand, and he is saving my life, crushing the arrows in his wet fist, putting them to his mouth and swallowing them.

"It hurts, Daddy. It hurts so much."

"There now, there," he whispers.

"My front, Daddy, my front." He needs to take the arrows from my small new breasts, they hurt so much. I try to turn, and, as I turn, the sky turns green. "Here, Daddy, here." I touch my chest.

He pulls the sheet up. "I'll get your mother."

"No, you, Daddy, just you." I push the sheet away and pull at his hand, try to bring his hand to pull the fire arrows from my chest. "Please, Daddy, just you."

I hear the bedroom door close, and I am all alone until a great horse made of black flames leaps into the room and I mount him. I open my burning legs and close them around the sides of the horse. The inside of my belly is on fire. "Just you, Daddy." I turn on the horse's back and look for my father. I want him to ride the wild stallion with me, but he has gone. He has left me here, straddling black fire that leaps for the sky. I am riding a black and flaming horse, moving with the horse as it climbs through the empty hot air toward the sky. The swirling velvet sky that sparkles with diamonds my father has flung away.

. . . . .

That summer life begins to change. I look around and find a world beyond books and river and family. The gateway to this new world is the Wednesday night dance. These summer dances are held in Bellebend's American Legion Hall, and all the teenagers of the parish attend. Romances begin and are severed there, boys fight out back, and girls weep over broken hearts in the graffitied bathroom. "Shit on Nancy Greff" the walls say. "Fran Dupre swims naked with boys." "Serafine loves Andrew."

It is a time-honored rite that seventh-grade girls enter the Wednesday night dances to be picked off by the ninth-grade boys. Our petticoats, layers of petticoats, have been starched. We wear little flat pumps with nylon footlets.

Our mothers have helped us get ready, as though this is the logical extension to our Saturday afternoon ballroom dancing classes. We sit on folding chairs lined along the walls in the big narrow room, pretending to be wrapped in our own charming and witty conversations, while the boys cruise us. I am never chosen, but I understand this. Girls always like me a lot, but the boys don't even notice me. I am flat-chested, and no right-thinking ninth-grade boy is going to ask a flat-chested girl to dance. Marilyn Monroe is an actress and a fantasy. Audrey Hepburn is only an actress. I'm just happy to be here, happy to watch the older kids dance and fight and pass around brown paper–wrapped bottles of sloe gin. The drama of it all astonishes me. And the music is great.

One night the band plays "Girl with the Red Dress On" for forty-five straight minutes. Nobody stops dancing. Even the unpaired people left lined up against the wall are so carried away we jump out on the dance floor too. "She can do the birdland all night long!" The wide world opens to me in the glimmer of sweating bodies, moving hips and feet, heads swinging and tossing sprays of wet heat. Everyone is an animal and that animal is one animal moaning and screaming with the wild, wild music. "Shake that thing . . ." the black singer on the low stage yells, and everyone does. We are jumping and gyrating until the air above our heads is wavy with moist light. All the dancers have dripping wet hair and bright red faces; the girls' petticoats are limp and damp and slap their legs, the boys' shirts are sheer with sweat. When the band finally stops, the whole crowd bursts through the front door, like a shout, out into the sultry Louisiana night.

My friends and I can't believe how wild it is, how hot.

"Look at me, I'm red as a tomato, I swear!"

"You're red? What about me!"

"Did you see Jimson Blanchard?"

"Which one is he?" Our cluster gets tighter.

"The junior, from Catholic High? The one that lives behind the parts shop."

"What about him?"

"He did the split, I swear!"

"You mean the real split, like a majorette or something?"

"Or like Little Richard."

"Who is he? Who is Little Richard? Does he go to Catholic High too?" I ask.

That night on the ride home, with Mrs. Uness driving us, I hang my head out the back window and let the lush, jasmine-scented, humid wind tangle my damp hair. The moon looks immense and close. No matter which way the car turns, dropping off members of my new gang, the moon follows me. I know I am chosen and that I will be wild. I will be wild and dance all my life. I won't sin, ever, but my passion will be eternal.

When school begins in the fall, because we are eighth-graders, we are finally in the high school building. Catholic High is divided by two long wings: one for boys, one for girls. The sidewalk for the girls' side runs in full view of the windows for the boys' side. Our classes change at different times. I am sure no gauntlet of American Indians standing with switches to whip the young pubescent braves was more difficult to run than that walkway. Unlike the native rites of passage, this is no one-time deal. It is every fifty minutes, six times a day, five days a week. The bell rings, the boys all turn to the windows, and we walk by, a meat market of virgins. I always feel like the back of my uniform is ripped open, I'm not wearing underwear, and I have concrete blocks on my feet instead of saddle shoes. Several minutes before each class change, the compacts all come out, and there is a rush of hair combing, lipstick application. I catch sight of one of my classmates unbuttoning the top button of her uniform blouse.

I don't own a compact, and my father is adamant that I not wear lipstick. My friends feel terribly sorry for me. They think it must be a nightmare to have a school principal for a father, even if it is the public school. They lend me their lipsticks and help me wipe off my mouth before I return home. I begin to pointedly ignore Eve. I can't believe what a "square" she has become. When she asks me to do anything with her, like climb up on the shed or walk by the river, I just roll my eyes. When I talk about him, I start to call my father "my old man." My friends tell me I am rebelling, like James Dean in *Rebel Without a Cause.* I start smoking cigarettes and learn to talk with the cigarette still stuck in my mouth.

It is Saturday night and Halloween. Catholic High is having the first dance of the school year. My friends and I have been getting ready all week. We decide costumes are childish so we've been lending clothes back and forth. Virginia insists I borrow her green sweater because it looks good with my eyes. Kathleen lends me an outgrown bra and suggests I put socks in the cups. We all agree that bobby socks are out of the question, people would notice. I arrive at the dance with one nylon sock in each bra cup.

We have come as a tight little gang, Suzanne's mother is supposed to drive us home at eleven. We are definitely going to stick together. This is our first high school dance. We sit all together in the folding chairs lined against the wall. We talk just to one another, we don't look at the boys across the dance floor. Crepe paper is strung from the ceiling of the gym in purple and gold, the school colors. There is a large jack-o'-lantern on the apron of the stage, and some uncarved pumpkins are piled in one corner. A few of the unpopular kids are drifting around looking jerky in their costumes. One of the younger lay teachers is in charge of selecting and putting on the records. He is pacing two fast songs for every slow one.

By the third slow song, all my friends are paired off on the dance floor. I am alone in the middle of a row of five empty chairs. The nearest other unpopular girl is Phylis Gimbroni, a girl I have never spoken to in my life. She may have a lot on her mind since she is staring blankly with her tongue half in and half out of her mouth. I am thinking of pushing down the row of empty chairs to make friends with her when I catch sight of Gabriel LeBlanc. He is probably the most handsome boy at Catholic High, and he is looking at me. His gang is pushing at him, and he heads toward me, then heads back. I am almost positive he is on his way to ask me to dance. At last the older boys are noticing me. As Gabriel crosses the floor toward me, I try to get Virginia's attention over her boyfriend's shoulder. I want her to see this.

Gabriel is standing in front of me, looking very shy, reluctant. I smile encouragingly. "Katherine, uh, we . . . anyway, my friends back there"—he twists to the gathered group of about six boys who are watching us—"my friends want me to ask you where you got your new titties."

I expect my nose to start bleeding, my face feels so instantly flushed. "They were on sale in the fruit section at the National, mixed in with the apples. Why, do you need a pair?" I stand up and walk out of the gym with Gabriel still looking surprised.

I use the nickel I was going to spend on a Coke to call my father. "Daddy?"

"Hey, baby, I thought you were at the dance."

"I am, but"—I am fighting tears—"it's not all that fun, and —and I think I'm getting a headache and I was wondering . . ."

"How 'bout I come pick you up, honey? Is the corner of Church Street a good place?"

"Uh-huh."

While I wait for my father, I keep my back pressed against the brick wall to shield my face in the shadows. A few people are still arriving at the dance and I feel that anyone seeing me would know the entire story of my humiliation. I hate boys. I hate boys so much. I'm going to save up my allowance and buy a motorcycle and run over Gabriel LeBlanc's face. I'm going to get my father's Knights of Columbus sword and run it through Gabriel's heart! I furtively reach under my sweater, remove the nylon socks, and slip them into my purse.

My father must have walked out of the house the minute he hung up the phone because I do not wait very long. When he reaches across the seat to open the car door for me, I think he is Moses parting the Red Sea for my escape.

Instead of turning the car to head back up the River Road, my father drives toward Bellebend High. "Honey, I hope you don't mind, I promised the teachers chaperoning the dance at my school that I'd stop by and check on things."

There is still a lump in my throat that makes it difficult to talk. "Naw, I'll just wait in the car."

"The heck you will! I'm not going to be responsible for leaving a pretty girl outside all alone. The word could get out and it might empty the place. I know you go to Catholic High, but you still wouldn't want to be responsible for the Bellebend High dance ending three hours early."

"Daddy!"

When we walk in the door of the gym, I am amazed to see that the public school has a live band. Right now they are playing one of my very favorite songs, "You Cheated." We walk up to the refreshment counter and my father orders a Coke for me and says he'll be right back. The icy drink stings the back of my throat and tears well in my eyes like relief. I am swallowing hard and looking toward the street through the open double doors of the gym when there is a tap on my shoulder.

"Katherine, can I get you to dance with me?" Frankie Lotile is smiling at me like he's really glad to see me. Frankie is a junior and I know him because his family raises horses. I have been horse crazy since I was five years old and I know everybody in the parish who has horses. Also, Frankie really likes my father. So I've seen him in my daddy's office a lot.

"Sure," I say, and carefully place my Coke in the corner of the refreshment stand.

Frankie and I dance through the end of "You Cheated" and have started to fast-dance to "Splish, Splash" when one of Bellebend High's best football players cuts in and, before I know it, I'm being twirled and practically flipped on the dance floor by another junior, this one a giant. I am suddenly having so much fun and try not to look in my father's direction because I don't want him to remember that it's time to go home. My father surprises me by not looking me up until the band takes its break. I have danced every dance since "You Cheated." If only my gang had been here to see this.

My father's hand in my overnight popularity doesn't occur to me until years later.

. . . . .

Finally the blood comes. I am the last of my friends to have her period. It is a Wednesday afternoon in the summer after eighth grade and I am at Virginia's house. All my friends have felt sorry for me, worried that I am so underdeveloped. When I discover the blood in my underwear, I am elated. Virginia is so happy for me that she gives me a big hug. I call my mother with the news and she comes to pick me up.

When we get home, my father is pacing in the living room, and I can tell my mother has told him why I am home early. He doesn't look in our direction as my mother walks me into the bathroom. She opens a cupboard, reaches up to the top shelf, then hands me a sanitary napkin and an elastic belt with strange hooks on either end. Then she backs out of the bathroom and closes the door.

I stoop, bleeding, in the middle of the bathroom floor, and try to figure out what I'm supposed to do. I could certainly turn the elastic into a fine slingshot, but I can't figure what it has to do with my period. I know what the napkin is for, but I haven't a clue about its relationship to the belt. When my mother returns to check on me, I am still crouched in the middle of the floor with the belt in one hand and the napkin in the other.

"For heaven's sakes, Katherine!" My mother had so hoped she would have intelligent children. She brusquely demonstrates the way the ragged ends of the napkin slip into the rounded hooks at either end of the belt. I put my hand on her shoulder while she holds the belt out so I can step into it. Then she turns and walks, wordlessly, out of the bathroom in her fast Yankee way. I stand there alone for a minute with my legs slightly spread. I wish there were a long mirror in the bathroom. I think maybe the Kotex is like a loincloth and that I might look like some kind of Indian princess.

That night I am standing in a circle of friends at the Wednesday night dance. Suzanne elbows me, and I look toward the front door of the American Legion Hall and see my father heading into the room. This is a nightmare of embarrassment. No one over twenty ever comes closer to the Wednesday night dances than the front curb of Mississippi Avenue.

I furtively swipe my lipstick off, twirl out of my group, and rush for the door. "Daddy, what are you doing here?" I am trying to walk him back outside as I talk. "Parents don't ever come inside."

"Get your purse, honey. It's time for you to come home."

I stop in horror. "Daddy, it's nine o'clock."

"Do you want me to get your purse?" He heads back toward the inside of the hall.

"No! I'll get it." I rush inside and grab my purse. All my friends are staring like suddenly we're in the middle of a Nancy Drew mystery. I shrug and run out to join my father before he walks back inside and ruins my life.

By the time we reach the car, I am almost screeching. "Why? Why, Daddy, why do I have to go home? Suzanne's mother is driving us at eleven. I always come home at eleven!" He gets in the car without answering me and I stand outside pounding my fist on the roof.

He reaches across and opens the passenger door. "You get in this car, young lady, or I will spank you right here on Mississippi Avenue."

Nothing more horrible has ever happened to me. I can hear the music of the band; out of the corner of my eye I see my gang of friends crowding the front door of the dance hall. Impossibly, my father starts the motor, and we are driving away. It is nine o'clock, and we are driving away from the Wednesday night dance. All year my friends and I have talked about last summer's dances and planned for this summer's. My father is pulling me away two hours early, and he has no explanation. Also, he won't look at me. He hasn't looked directly at me all day. I feel like I've become a stranger to him and this makes me furious. The closer we get to home, the more outraged I become. I will be an adult before I equate my period beginning with my father's sudden panic over my being out in the night, in the world of boys and bluesy music and booze.

"Why! Tell me why you are making me go home!" He just keeps driving. "You have to answer me!" But he doesn't.

Finally my rage is larger than my heart. "You're old enough to die, why don't you just die!" Still he says nothing. And I say nothing else. He pulls into the driveway, and we get out of the car. I rush to my room.

Two hours later, when my friends are probably just leaving the dance, I am still crying. Eve, pushed far on her side of the bed, falls asleep through my sobs. More hours pass and I have cried my way into a sore throat. He is old enough to die. My father is much older than anyone else's father, and he could die, and it will be my fault. If God will only let him live, I promise I'll become a nun. Or, if not a nun, I'll work among the poor and will never marry.

I tiptoe down the hall to my parents' room. I kneel outside the closed door and try to listen for my father's breathing. I hear nothing. He could be dead, of a broken heart. "Daddy," I say, hoarsely.

"Yes, sweetheart." My father, who is a family joke for his ability to fall immediately to sleep and to sleep through any noise, is, impossibly, awake at three o'clock in the morning.

"I don't really want you to die, Daddy. I want you to live forever."

"I know that, sweetheart."

85

"Daddy, I love you," I croak.

"And I love you, Katherine." I sneak back to bed and cry until dawn with the relief of the forgiven, the absolved.

. . . . .

That summer my father catches me wearing lipstick and punishes me. While I'm punished, I defy both my parents by shaving my legs. Eve is a nervous witness. The first swipe I take at my leg removes so much skin that blood shoots across the bathroom and Eve has to run for help.

One day, while my father and I argue, I try to make a point about the respect owed to teenagers. "You know what, Daddy? When I used to walk down the streets of Bellebend, people would say, 'There goes Jason Roberts's daughter.' Now when you walk down the street, people say, 'There goes Katherine Roberts's daddy.'"

"What!" my father roars. "What!"

They find a switchblade knife hidden in my top drawer. Virginia had asked me to keep it at my house until her boyfriend's birthday, but my parents don't care that the knife isn't mine. I'm not allowed to go to the Wednesday night dances anymore. I don't speak to anyone in my house for days. I steal cigarettes from my mother and sit on the roof smoking. I hide whenever anyone walks out in the yard. One night, when I think my parents are asleep, my friends come by with Virginia's boyfriend driving, to pick me up for the last hour of the dance. When I get home, all the lights in the house are on and my parents are furious. They take me back to the psychiatrist in Baton Rouge. He says I am rebelling and I should be placed in an alternate environment, like a boarding school.

. . . . .

As we drive off down the River Road, Eve chases the car. She woke me up this morning crying. Ever since it was decided I would go away, my little sister has shadowed me. I watch her through the back window until a curve turns her out of sight. I comfort myself with the thought that, after all these years Eve has been claiming I was on her side of the bed, now she can finally have the entire bed to herself.

My father and I are in the Landrys' car. Sue Landry is going to be an eighth-grader at Holy Name Academy. I will be a freshman. She is going away to school because her family is rich. I'm going away because I am just too wild, I am a handful. Her mother is sitting in the backseat with us, the two fathers are in the front. My mother is staying home with Eve. I could tell my mother was sad to see me go, but all she did was pack and repack my suitcase about a hundred times. I also know she was glad to stay home because she would have hated being in the car with Mrs. Landry. Every time Mrs. Landry says something I think it is the most boring thing I've ever heard. Then she says something even more boring. After a lifetime with her mother, boarding school is going to feel like a trip to Disneyland to poor Sue Landry.

We have been driving for almost three hours when we turn onto yet another back road and suddenly see the school. We drive through a row of live oaks and pass formal gardens, a massive row of pine trees leading to a small chapel, a huge columned main building with graceful galleries and wrought-iron railing. We turn through an arched gateway and stop in front of the dormitory of Holy Name Academy. Sue's mother begins to cry and hug her daughter. I get out of the car. Mr. Landry opens the trunk, and my father pulls out my two suitcases.

Holy Name nuns and students are at tables in the large marble foyer. I leave my father to fill out the forms and get directions. I am not interested in his stupid paperwork or in any of the girls my age who are welcoming new students. I wander into the student lounge and look at the photographs on the wall of prisoners of former years. My father comes to get me. It is time for us to go upstairs.

One of the older students leads us up the curved stairway and down the wide marble hall to what is to be my room, then tactfully withdraws. My father lifts the suitcases onto the bed. I turn to look out the window. The window overlooks a large artificial pond. I wonder if there are goldfish in it.

My father clears his throat, and I continue to look out the window. "I remember the day you were born."

I am still looking out the window and he begins again. "I remember the day you were born. It seems like only yesterday, and—and here you are . . ."

I don't turn around and my father stops talking. He clears his throat once more. I am pacing his punishment, his punishment for dumping me in this prison. After I feel he has suffered enough, I turn. He is gone.

I walk down the hall, then down the stairs; as I reach the front door of the dormitory, I see the Landrys' car driving away. I run out of the building and cut across the lawn, I slash my arms on the sharp leaves of camellia bushes and stumble over low hedges. I am chasing the car the same way Eve chased it this morning. Chasing the car and watching it disappear as I call for my father, for another chance to kiss him good-bye. Already I can't remember his face. All I can remember is that I've always been the star in his blue heaven. That he has always rescued me and praised me and asked nothing back from me. By the time I reach the alley of pine trees I am winded and sobbing so that I can't breathe. I stand on the carpet made of a century of pine needles and lean against a tree crying, "Daddy, Daddy . . ." My James Dean days are already behind me.

CHAPTER IV

WHEN SPRING COMES TO NEW ORLEANS, the fragrant lusty spring of the City of Dreams, I begin to roam the streets with Madeline in her baby carriage. I am searching for an unsoiled place of smooth grass. A place I can spread a blanket, stretch out, and watch clouds with my baby. The only place we can do this is Audubon Park, a three-mile walk from Eric's apartment. I long for green. I feel I'm robbing my daughter of her first spring because we have no patch of land that is ours. I can't imagine how it is possible to raise a child in the city. New Orleans becomes a ghetto. I beg Eric for weekends with my parents in Bellebend. I want to show Madeline the river. I want to take photographs of my soft round blue-eyed baby surrounded by the levee grasses.

"But why can't we go to Bellebend? Last weekend you said we could go this weekend. Now you say no. Why, Eric, why?" I am pacing the living room of our apartment, holding Madeline and patting her diapered bottom in time to my "whys." The three of us have just returned from a Saturday brunch where Eric and I consumed many Bloody Marys.

"What is it about you Southern girls that you always have to be racing back to your mamas and daddies? You're married now. This is your home."

I follow Eric into the kitchen where he picks up a sponge and begins scrubbing away at the stains in the sink. "Maybe if you'd figure that out you'd start taking care of this place."

"I thought—" I have to stop talking because Madeline has slipped her fingers into my mouth. I pretend to nibble on them, and this makes her laugh. "I thought you didn't want me to be a housewife." Her fingers are back in my mouth and I'm making faces and lipping her fingers to keep her quiet so Eric and I can finish this conversation. It seems, since Madeline was born, we never have time to finish any conversations.

"What were you thinking of doing instead of housework, Katherine? Maybe performing brain surgery or teaching my classes for me? Or—" He is still talking when I run out of the kitchen.

"That wasn't fair, I'm sorry." Eric sits on the side of the bed. I am kneeling on the bed, with my back to him. I hold Madeline against my chest and am rocking her and crying. Madeline thinks this is another game and is dabbing at my tears with her fingers and then tasting her fingertips. "Really, honey, I'm sorry."

Eric lifts my braid and begins to lick the back of my neck. I have never been able to resist this and Eric knows it. I want him. I don't turn around, but I stop crying and lower my head and begin to nudge my neck into him. Eric slips his hand over my shoulder and down my blouse. "Little Katherine, sweet little Katherine. Let me kiss it and make it better."

His hand kneads my breast and Madeline reaches for his hand. "No, Maddy girl," he says, "that's for Daddy. Here we go, upsy daisy." He lifts our daughter and deposits her in her crib. To my amazement, she doesn't cry, just stands balanced holding the crib railing.

I am on my back now, Eric is on his knees straddling me and slowly unbuttoning my blouse. I raise my hips to him and he pulls off my underwear. "Little cotton undies," he murmurs, tossing them across the room. He always says this. I think he gets a kick out of my convent girl underwear.

"Now, Eric, hurry. Now, now . . ." This is going too slowly, I am eager for sex. It seems we have it much too seldom. I want us to be naked, and start to unbutton my husband's shirt.

"Ma-ma, Ma-ma," Madeline says. She is leaning in her crib trying to see my face over her daddy's shoulder. It bothers me that Madeline sleeps in the same room we do. Dr. Spock says this is not a good idea. "Ma-ma-ma!"

I stop unbuttoning and roll away. "We can't, Eric."

"Oh yes we can." He scoops me up and carries me into the bathroom. Madeline begins to cry. The fuzzy bath mat is under my shoulder and my head is pushed into one of the lion paws of the tub when Eric mounts me.

"The baby, Eric, the baby, I just can't, I—" He puts his hand over my mouth.

"Let me finish!" And he does. Then he gets dressed and slams out of the apartment.

. . . . .

"Do you still write poetry, Katherine?" Marie and I are sitting on swings in a little neighborhood park near the apartment. We had to pick our way through the dog droppings. I left Madeline in her stroller and the stroller on the sidewalk to save the wheels.

"I haven't written any poetry since Holy Name."

"Well, what do you do? I mean, you don't go to movies and you don't go to classes. I try to imagine your life and I—"

"There's so much to do, you can't imagine. Like in the after-noon, Madeline wakes up from her nap and I put her in the stroller and we go to National Food and shop. I've been reading this German cookbook. Eric just loves German food. We went to Kolbs on one of our first dates."

I push back and start to swing. Marie pushes her swing too and we stay in rhythm. "Anyway, I've been reading this cookbook and . . . When I tell it, Marie, it sounds boring. But it really isn't. I guess loving Eric is what makes it all worth it. I mean, really loving my husband, having this perfect husband, and having this perfect baby." I point to the stroller where Madeline sits happily watching the traffic go by. "You wouldn't believe how good Madeline is. And sex. Of course sex is great. You just wait."

. . . . .

Eve didn't end up having to go to LSU after all. She got herself a scholarship to the University of Michigan at Ann Arbor. Her letters to me are from another world. In one letter she writes about going on an LSD trip. Another letter casually mentions that two boys live in the same apartment she and another girl are renting. All of this makes me feel like while I was in the lobby getting popcorn, the movie changed from *The Glass Bottom Boat* to *Hud*. I expect Doris Day, and get Patricia Neal. When Eve comes home at Christmas, Eric and I pick her up at the train station and she is wearing a shirt that says "Draft Beer, Not Boys."

"What is that supposed to mean, Eve? 'Draft beer, not boys'?" We are driving to Bellebend, I'm leaning over the front seat, Eve is in the back holding Madeline. They are so cute together.

"We're organizing against the draft. Ever since the Gulf of Tonkin Resolution there's been a real buildup of troops." Eve hands the baby back to me. "We want the U.S. to cool it."

"To 'cool it,' what does that mean? I keep saying that to you, 'what does this mean?' 'what does that mean?' " I'm bouncing Madeline on my lap to distract her from her aunt who seems to have lost all interest in my baby. "But really, Eve. I mean it's not like they're drafting college boys."

"Just you watch, Katherine. It won't be long and, besides, they shouldn't be drafting anyone."

"I tell you one thing," Eric adds, "it sure turns giving grades into another ball game. I had a kid come to me and beg me to raise his grade. He said that if he flunked my course, he'd be out of school and shipped off to Southeast Asia. All of a sudden a simple F in English can be a death notice."

"And it's not just the draft." Eve raises her voice to speak above Madeline's fussing. She seems a little irritated. "We're opposed to U.S. involvement in Vietnam. Period."

"We're just helping those people, Eve. They asked us to."

"Bullshit!"

"Eve is right, Katherine. Think what this country would be like if the British had come in and helped the South during the Civil War."

"Eric, you never told me that you thought the Vietnam thing was bad." I have given Madeline my finger to chew and this quiets her.

"Well, I do." He reaches over and ruffles the top of my head. "I'm very opposed to 'the Vietnam thing.' "

I turn to my sister again. "Eve, remember how Daddy always told us the South won the Civil War? And we absolutely believed him!"

. . . . .

After spending the holidays with Eve I realize I'm terribly out of touch. When I listened to my parents, my husband, and my sister talk around the table after dinner I felt like I had when I was a kid, sitting on the floor outside the kitchen listening to the grown-ups. While I was folding diapers and heating sauerkraut, the whole world changed.

I work an arrangement with Eric where he watches Madeline

in his office on Tuesday and Thursday afternoons for an hour. I run across to the Laffitte library and devour some of the *New Republic* magazines and whatever other liberal periodicals I can find. It's a good arrangement because it gives father and daughter private time together and it gives me a chance to move in the wide, wide world. Some days I don't even read, I just sit at a library table and watch the students. Other days I am engrossed by what I read and shaken to find the United States wearing the black hat instead of the white. I read a great deal about the Catholic hierarchy's absence from the civil rights movement and revisit my schoolday thoughts about the Church's hand in the poverty of Catholic countries. These revelations come gradually and seem to waver peripherally, just beyond the edges of my tenacious attempts at homemaking.

One afternoon I must have wheeled the stroller extra fast down St. Charles Avenue because Madeline and I arrive early at Eric's office. Eric's door is closed, so I knock and then push the door open. This is a mistake because I seem to have interrupted an important conference. A pretty young student, with her hair cut in a silky bob, slips off the edge of Eric's desk as I walk in.

"You're early, Katherine," Eric says inanely. "This is, a . . . Betsy, this is my wife, Katherine."

Betsy is definitely not interested in Eric's "wife, Katherine." She walks out of the office without a word.

"So, they're letting Yankees into Laffitte, I see. What a rude girl. New Jersey, maybe?"

"Speaking of rude, Katherine, I agreed to watch the baby for an hour. Not the entire afternoon. You're early, I hope you're not planning to run late again."

. . . . .

Eric is invited to interview for a job as assistant department head at a small university in the mountains of North Carolina. We leave Madeline in Bellebend and I go to Leeston with Eric. Our

94

host drives us along a curving mountain road from the airport to the small college town, fifty miles from any city. I fall in love with the rounded green mountains folding away from the road in deep swells. I fall in love with the countryside and I fall in love with the town. Though we are told the university is entering a growth phase, the small town has one store that still has a front porch. Old men, wearing overalls, sit on the porch watching the mixed population of students, professors, and mountain folks parade down the town's one main street. Other campuses are beginning to stage demonstrations against the war, take over administration buildings, and demand the legalization of marijuana. We are told that, on this campus, there is an ongoing debate about whether coeds might be allowed to wear slacks on campus next term.

Eric is offered the position and, on our second wedding anniversary, we celebrate by deciding to move to North Carolina. This last spring in New Orleans Eric and I, almost frantically, bicycle through the Garden District, crisscrossing the tree-canopied streets. We are trying to crowd in as many memories of the City of Dreams as possible. Every bike ride uncovers some dense graceful mansion we've never before noticed, huddled just beyond its flowery lawn, tall fringes of Spanish oak, or crepe myrtle, or magnolia trees. An old black man drives a horse-drawn cart filled with produce along the quiet shady streets. He sings, "Bananas, I have ripe ba-na-nas and apples." He is the last of his kind. Little Madeline careens on the seat behind her daddy, blissfully oblivious of just how much her short life is about to change. In less than a month we'll be leaving this shady, slow, European-like city for a little corner of Appalachia. We'll be entering a land of seasons. We'll be leaving her beloved granny and papa far behind.

Eric and I have a last romantic dinner at Arnaud's. We think we have the same waiter as on our first night together. "You only grow more beautiful, Katherine. You're a little mother and we could put you in a school uniform and you could walk the halls of your beloved Holy Name Academy with no problem." He reaches for my hand and kisses it. The candlelight flickers on his face. In the distance I can hear a horn playing "Just a Closer Walk with Thee."

"I didn't think it was possible to love you more than I did on our wedding day, but I do, Eric. I do."

. . . . .

A week before her graduation Marie and I go out together for a drink. She's had some kind of tumor removed from her ovaries and is still looking wan. "I don't know how you did it, exams and major surgery all in the same month."

There is now no trace of Marie's French accent. She has cut her amazing black hair and is wearing it in a pixie. "Jackson, that's my doctor—I still can't get used to calling a doctor by his first name—but he wants me to. Jackson says I'm very strong. Daddy told me just to let the semester go, that I could pick it up in summer school or something. But I tell you, Katherine, I am sick to death of school. I also don't want to go back to the country. I'm going to get an apartment and stay here in the city. Maybe get a little job, or something. I know Daddy will just have a fit."

I can't imagine Marie with a job. I doubt if she's ever even done her own laundry. Marie splashes the slush of her daiquiri around its oversized glass. "Jackson says he thinks I'd be real good with flowers. One of the girls I'm graduating with has an uncle who owns that big florist place on the avenue. Maybe I'll work there."

I'm tearing at the lime slice from my drink. "Or you could move to North Carolina with us."

"Yeah, Eric would really like that. He rolls his eyes when he finds me at your place even for five minutes after he gets home from work. He'd just love it if I moved with you."

"Eric likes you." I signal for the waiter to bring us two more drinks. "It's just that, with the baby and all, our time alone is precious. Maybe he's too protective."

"Katherine, I'm going to die of loneliness without you. We've been friends for a hundred years. First Susan disappears up North, and now you."

"Marie, North Carolina isn't 'up North.' It was one of the first states to secede, for God's sake."

The most difficult leave-taking, of course, is from Bellebend. My father and I go for a farewell walk along the levee. Where has time gone? Only yesterday he was carrying me up this very same hill, offering me the heavens. Suddenly it is twenty years later and my father is disturbed that I have recently "lost my faith." The last two visits home I refused to go to mass with him.

"You're the one who taught us that religion was about goodness. Show me something the Catholic Church has done that is good. Cardinal Spellman has been so vocal in favor of the war and the assumption is that the Pope will speak out against the Pill. All those poor little starving babies in South America and then the Pope will tell 'em they can't even use the Pill? Daddy, the Pill! There is nothing about the Pill in all that 'spilling your seed upon the earth' stuff in the Bible."

It is a hot day, and a muddy breeze reluctantly ruffles the high levee grasses as we walk. I turn back to look at our house, the curving driveway, the white front porch with its bright green floor. I see my mother rocking Madeline, singing to my daughter. Home.

"Honey, the Pope is behind the times. I'll grant you that. And the Church ought to do something about the war, like Eve says. But the Church has lasted for two thousand years and it's lasted because of the guidance from Rome."

"Come on, Daddy. That's like trying to get to town in a car without gas, or without wheels. We can sit in the car, bouncing on the seat all day, saying 'Last year it drove us to town.' The car doesn't work anymore. The Church doesn't either."

"Shh, shh, I hate to hear that kind of talk. Your wild-eyed

sister off at that crazy university is one thing, but you, Katherine? A Holy Name graduate?"

"It's your fault, Daddy. You raised us to question stuff."

He pulls a tall thick blade of grass and pensively chews its end. "It's your mama. I like things to just keep rolling along. It's your smart, beautiful, Yankee mama who got you girls all riled up. I'm still learning. Like you, I'm still learning."

. . . . .

Though I had hoped we would find our own idyllic country house in North Carolina, we move into a brand-new apartment complex instead. I am able to get over my disappointment, because the apartments are surrounded by meadows, and beyond the meadows there are mountains. Another bonus to apartment living, one I had never thought of, is we are living among young married people with children Madeline's age. Eric had been, by far, the youngest faculty member in his Laffitte department and he is twelve years older than I. After over two years of marriage, this time among the other graduate and faculty wives would be my first taste of two-way conversations about babies and recipes.

Eric has just left for his first day at the office when there is a knock on the apartment door. I open it to find a long-haired, slender blond woman, wearing very short shorts and a toddler affixed to her hip.

"You *are* a pretty young thing. You were the talk of the sandbox this morning." She uses her shirttail to wipe her baby's face as she speaks. "We always check out the new people." I must look a little stunned. "Sorry, no manners. My name is Rosa and this little gorgeous bundle is named Harmony. Jeff and I aren't even flower children. We just liked the name."

"Hi, I'm Katherine Pierson, would you like to come—"

The woman has been looking over my shoulder and steps into the apartment. "I heard you had a little girl too."

"Yeah, Madeline. She's in the playpen in the den. Would you like some—"

"Coffee? I'd love some." It occurs to me this is the first time I've ever offered anyone, besides Eric, a cup of coffee. Marie and I always drink Cokes, or brandy milk punches. I feel like I'm playing ladies.

"I'm going to drop Harmony in the playpen, O.K.?" She is around the corner of the den before I can answer. I go to turn on the coffeepot.

Harmony lets out a yelp as I join the gang in the den. Madeline has a handful of Harmony's sunny curls in her chubby fist. Rosa is standing back not looking very disturbed, so I pry my daughter's fingers open.

"You'll have to forgive her. She's never seen a peer before. She thinks Harmony is a grown-up someone left in the dryer too long. She's not really pulling your daughter's hair, she's trying to stretch her back to full size."

I lift Madeline out of the playpen. She starts to cry and reach sadistically for another chance at Harmony's curls. "Calm down, Madeline. You're short too."

"Let them battle it out. I don't think they can really do much harm, do you?" Rosa has her arms folded and is looking amused while Madeline makes another lunge at Harmony.

"It'll be another story when Madeline has your daughter's scalp swinging proudly from her diaper belt."

"You're funny, Katherine. I didn't know Southern women could be funny. This is getting better all the time."

"Well, you certainly didn't have to tell me you're not a Southerner. I guessed it," I shout over Madeline's noise as I head to check on the coffee.

"The manners thing. Right?" she shouts back as she follows me to the kitchen.

"I've seen more mannerly bulldozers," I add. And we both laugh.

My homesickness almost disappears. Two years after getting

married, I enter the life of young married people. Rosa and Jeff have Eric and me to their apartment for dinner, we invite them back. Unlike New Orleans, there isn't a good restaurant to be found, so the people of Leeston entertain in their own homes. Some days Rosa and I cook together.

"I thought, if you held your breath, the onions wouldn't make you cry."

"Naw, Katherine, just hold a piece of bread in your mouth. That does it."

I mumble, over the piece of bread, "When I married Eric I'd never boiled water. I didn't know if the little bubbles or the big bubbles counted."

"Only a Southern girl could stay so untouched by life on the planet. Did your 'mammy' boil all your water?"

"No, my mammy was the one holding my parasol to shield me from the sun. I don't want you coming over here again until you've read *Gone with the Wind.* I thought you had a college degree. What use is an education if you haven't even read *Gone with the Wind?*"

. . . . .

There is a beautiful river not far from the town. The first time I see it I want Eric to stop the car immediately. We park on the roadside by large gray boulders, and roll down our windows so we can hear the falls rushing over rocks. The water is the color of Coca-Cola bottle glass, clear and fast running, and the river is wide. I think of the wide sluggish Mississippi and how I would love to show this pristine river to my father. A car horn disturbs my reverie. Rosa and Jeff are following us and are impatient to start our picnic. We drive a little further and find a small deserted beach in the curve of the river. We carry blankets and picnic baskets to spread over the white sand. I take off Madeline's diaper and pull on her checked pink swimsuit. Eric starts to pour

Bloody Marys from a thermos he has brought. He turns to offer one to me, but I am already in the water.

Madeline is splashing in the shallows with Harmony; Rosa, Jeff, and Eric are sipping drinks and laying out our picnic. I can just hear all their voices; the baby chatter, the easy adult conversation sound like music over the water. I float on my back in the easy current, looking at the cloudless sky, and watching a pair of hawks swimming with air, dipping and soaring on unseen waves. Deep green mountains line and shape the riverbed. I think I've found a home for my heart.

. . . . .

Rosa introduces me to another faculty wife from the psychology department, an outspoken, foul-mouthed New Yorker whom I surprise myself by liking almost immediately. Even though Esther uses the worst language I've ever heard. "My suck ass husband is never home. He's not up for tenure for two more years, but the asshole is the first person in the building every morning and the last out at night."

"You sure it's tenure, and not the Little Woman keeping him away from home?" Rosa asks, smiling.

"I may be hard on his ego, but I also keep his dick hard. The man has good sex, and he knows it. Don't you worry about this Little Woman."

I glance nervously at Madeline, but she and Harmony are off in their own babyland fantasy. Esther is oblivious of her impression on me. She is short and stocky and wears her light brown hair in an incongruous permanent. She runs her nail-bitten fingertips through her Shirley Temple curls and reaches over to light yet another of her unfiltered cigarettes. Tall thin Rosa and stocky Esther have been fast friends since meeting two years ago at a faculty mixer, a gathering Esther irreverently refers to as a "Suck Hop."

"Look at those two." Rosa points to our daughters, who have flung themselves into a pile of leaves.

Esther has a son in kindergarten, so is easily bored with Rosa's and my earnest conversations about teething and potty training. "Tune in, girls, the times they are a-changing. Let's talk current events, or almost current. Can you believe Johnson's latest Supreme Court appointment?"

The three of us are stretched out in lawn chairs, enjoying the unseasonably warm weather. Esther has a house out in the country so Rosa, the babies, and I are spending the day in pastoral bliss. The colored leaves of autumn, the mountains on fire with gold, literally take my breath away.

"Are you talking about Thurgood Marshall?" asks Rosa. "Old Lyndon is really coming through. The Great Society is keeping some of its promises."

"I'll bet the good bigots of Bellebend are having fits. A black man on the Court!"

" 'Here come da judge, here come da judge,' " adds the disrespectful Esther, in a parody of Flip Wilson.

"We're going to see some changes," Rosa says, not taking her eyes off the little girls. "Some long-overdue changes."

"I bet they reach us in about a decade. You wouldn't believe my sister's letters. When I read what Eve says is going on at the University of Michigan it makes this place sound like one long, slow-moving Tupperware party."

"Well, shit! Let's start stirring stuff up here." Esther stubs her cigarette out.

"Good idea," says Rosa. "I wonder if they have toddler-sized gas masks?"

"You're about to turn the conversation back to kids, aren't you, Rosa? The revolution is starting to rage and you and Katherine succumb to maternal lobotomies."

A breeze tosses leaves from a giant maple and the little girls twirl and laugh, their heads flung back to watch the falling colors.

· · · · ·

It is a warm autumn night, the windows are open letting in a breeze sweet with the scent of ripe leaves. Eric has just turned off the light and I'm drifting into sleep when I feel his hands slowly rolling up my nightgown. I pretend to be asleep as Eric runs his hands over my breasts and begins to breathe into the nape of my neck. This is something Eric loves, when I hold very still as he makes love to me. I like it too and try to seem unexcited and asleep. He opens my legs, then leans back to pull open the drawer of the bedside table. I turn. "Honey, don't. Don't use anything."

He is tearing the wrapper as he speaks. "What do you mean? Fertile Myrtle, you should know. I don't use this and, boom, you're pregnant."

I kneel in the shadows and take his face in my hands. "I thought that was what you wanted. You said you wanted me to have lots of babies. That was the main reason I went off the Pill. Eve and me are two years apart and Madeline is already two years old." I wrap my legs around his hips. "It's getting late."

"Eve and I, Katherine." He drops the half-opened package on the floor and tenderly lifts the nightgown over my head.

· · · · ·

"We're losing this girl!" I wake up in a crowded delivery room to an atmosphere of panic. My baby. I've had another daughter and now she's dying? People are rushing around; just out of view, a red light near the ceiling is flashing. Somebody grabs my arm, twists the vein in my arm. A large bottle of red is gurgling overhead. They are giving me blood. A nurse smiles down at me.

"My baby?"

"Your little boy is just fine."

I've had a son. He's all right, my son. *Who* are they losing? The doctor and another doctor, or an intern, two men are peer-

103

ing between my legs. Someone shouts something about pulse rate. The doctor grabs a long banner of gauze, I see his fist rise up from inside my belly. I faint.

"We almost lost you, little lady. Placenta acreta, the placenta is supposed to peel out, like a tangerine, after the baby. Yours actually grew into the wall of the uterus. One in ten thousand cases that'll happen."

"I thought women stopped dying in childbirth a century ago. Are you sure you guys are doing your job?"

"Anyway, that's the reason for the hemorrhaging, you tore the uterus," the man says, without humor. "You're going to be in here for a while."

"My baby, my son. Dr. Williams, can I see my son?"

"That's the nurse's business. You just press that button for the nurse."

. . . . .

"I miss Madeline!" I'm crying and Eric is sitting on the edge of my hospital bed. "I hate this stupid place. Imagine not letting children in!"

Eric strokes the hair away from my face and leans down to kiss me. The nurses have told me that during my emergency, Eric was in an absolute panic.

The next night Eric comes to visit carrying a very large bag, topped with a bouquet of roses. When he walks in, he looks clandestinely around, then carefully places the bag on the floor. He takes the roses out and my daughter's head pops up. "Surpleyes!" she shouts. Her arms open, her fingers spread, her little round face crinkled with her smile. Her straight blond hair hasn't been brushed in days, but her daddy has dressed her in her very best pink dress. I could eat her alive.

. . . . .

" 'We're losing this girl!' one of them yells. And the first thing I think is that the baby is a girl. Then when I get the picture, you know, that it's me they're losing, I want to ask for the baby and then I want to tell the nurse to please make sure my son knows his mother held him before she died."

"You're really thinking that in the middle of all this chaos?" Rosa asks. It is my second day home and I'm regaling my friends with the tale of my brush with death.

"You bet I am. But then I think how embarrassed I'll be if I live. I'll probably be haunted for the rest of my life by my Claudette Colbert scene. Like something from *Imitation of Life*, for God's sake."

Esther throws back her head in one of her plaster-shattering blasts of laughter. " 'I want my quack-quack. I want my quack-quack!' " We'd seen the old 1934 film together, with the Cinema Club, and we all laugh.

"God dammit! I'm trying to get a little work done!" Eric lets out his own blast from the den. We hush, and Rosa raises her eyebrows.

"We were up all night," I say in apology. "Madeline is falling apart."

"Displacement anxieties," says Rosa wisely.

. . . . .

"Did I suck on your bosums too?" Madeline is watching me nurse Toby. "Sure did," I lie.

. . . . .

For the first time since I discovered it, I am not interested in sex. On the other hand, Eric is terribly interested. I haven't talked to him about it, I don't know how. Our lovemaking is silent and sometimes even painful. Tonight, as Eric rolls back to his side of the bed, I start to cry. I want him to take me in his arms and ask me what's wrong.

"Katherine, I've got to get some sleep. Ever since the baby, my lectures haven't been worth shit. I'm tired all the . . . Can you just, just—"

He stops himself and reaches over and lights a cigarette and sits in the darkness smoking. The bedroom smells like gin. I lie and watch the glow of Eric's cigarette coal until Toby starts to fuss for his feeding.

. . . . .

"Eric has been a dream, but even he reaches his wits' ends. Having two kids is very different from one. I can't believe it. Madeline is a changed child. I feel so sorry for her. The apartment is falling apart, I can't seem to get my head above water." My family is visiting for the holidays. Eve and I are out on the town for lunch while my parents watch the children. I am so excited to be in a restaurant, to be out without the kids that I can't even remember how to order. Eve has to take over.

"Katherine, you want me to cut your meat for you, or anything?"

"I'm not that bad, tell me I'm not that bad."

"You're fine, big sister, and your big tits look great."

"It's been a dream of mine, Eve," I say facetiously. "But there's stuff about large breasts we didn't know. Like, for instance, when you run, they jiggle. And you can't see your feet in the shower."

My flat-chested sister reaches across the table and returns the roll that I'd just knocked off the edge of my plate. "You are telling me this at the right time. I've been torn between graduate school and going to Switzerland for breast implants."

In truth, Eve has been accepted for graduate school at Berkeley and will head West in the spring. In truth, Eve wouldn't be caught dead wearing a bra, even if she needed one.

"Look, I may live in Appalachia, but I've read about you wild feminists. I've been hiding my nursing bras, for fear you'll put a match to them."

"I have vays of making you talk. Vere are da cursed bras?" Eve says, with a crummy German accent.

I want to ask her about Berkeley, but am afraid my questions will make her feel sorry for me. Her eyes glaze with boredom when I begin talking about my daily routine and, since Toby's birth, my feeble grasp of politics has become a joke. Our lives couldn't be more different. I can't even imagine hers and it's obvious she wouldn't want mine. Many years have passed since I was the brave big sister and Eve was the little sister sitting home waiting for me to bring her stories of the world.

When my family drives off the day after Christmas, I sink into a terrible depression. I'm horrible to be around and Eric stays at the office longer and longer every day. Sometimes he even goes back to the office on weekends. The mountain winter is endless. Rosa and Jeff have moved into a wonderful new house, but neither of our families has a second car, so I seldom see Rosa. Madeline misses Harmony and I'm too tired to attempt amusing my unhappy daughter. One day I hear Toby screaming and go in to find teeth marks on his infant nose. "How could you do that to your brother? How could you bite his little nose?"

Madeline is not contrite. "I didn't mean to. I weally wanted to bite off his yittle head!"

One night I dream I am on an airplane with my two children. There is an announcement that a terrorist is on board and that the plane is going to be blown up. Just at that moment, Madeline slips away and comes back leading a man by the hand. "Here is my new friend, Mommy," she says in the dream. I look up, and her friend is the terrorist. He leers at me, then he hits my daughter and her face begins to bleed. "My friend doesn't like me anymore," she sobs, her heart broken. Time has run out. Suddenly the plane is blowing up and I can save Toby or I can save Madeline. I want to comfort my heartbroken child, yet my baby is so tiny, so unprotected. I can't save them both. I can't decide which child to save. The plane explodes.

. . . . .

"Those are snow drops and those are crocus. They're the first, but just you wait, Katherine, in a month everything will be bursting into bloom."

It is a warm day in early March and Eric has dropped the children and me off to spend the day at Rosa's. She's walking us around her new yard. "Katherine, you are not tuning in. This is about the longest case of postpartum I've ever seen."

"I'm fine," I say, and shift Toby to my other shoulder. "Except that in the mornings when I wake up, instead of stretching, I hit my heart with my fist, pretending I have a knife in my fist."

"That sounds very healthy," says Rosa, rolling her eyes.

"I mean I had this perfect little girl who is now probably going to grow up to be an ax murderer because she's so pissed at not being an only child anymore. I'm so bitchy around my husband that he's taken to leaving for the office before it's full daylight. And I'm a failure in bed. When Eric touches my breasts, I want to bite his hands off."

"That is normal you know."

"Which of those things, the ax murderer? The lust for death?"

Rosa kneels to brush some soggy leaves away from a small waxy flower. "Well, all of it, really. But I was talking about sex. The old drive often goes way down when you're nursing. As for your daughter . . ." She points to Madeline, who is holding hands and telling secrets with Harmony.

"Why don't you start her in nursery school? She's a kid's kid. You probably bore her. Tell you what"—she leans back and wipes her hands on her jean knees—"we'll start Harmony too and work out some kind of carpool." She stands up, shoving her pale slender hands into her back pockets.

"Rosa, do you know all this stuff 'cause you finished college, or because your mother is more verbal than mine?" I hug my friend and smile for the first time today.

It turns out things do right themselves. Madeline loves nursery school, I love the time alone with Toby. And shortly after I wean my baby, my sex drive returns in full gear.

We've been invited to a party at the department head's house. We make a night of it and split a bottle of wine at dinner before the party. The party is dense with smoke and conversations that, as usual, exclude me. I drift through the talk of university politics and literary deconstructionism, not paying much attention. I do find myself in an argument with the English department's resident "Pound man."

"Of course I like his poetry, what I can understand of it. But his politics, his politics were awful," I say.

"He was misinterpreted."

"Oh, so he wasn't anti-Semitic? I honestly can't understand why T. S. Eliot stood by Pound."

"Well, you know the help Pound was to Eliot, how much of Eliot's poetry was actually rewritten . . ."

I stop listening. I think I see my handsome husband across the room talking much too intimately with a student-type. Eric sees me watching and pushes back from the wall, turns away from the girl, and starts toward me. He is stumbling slightly. I'm not in the mood to confront Eric, so I go upstairs to the host's bathroom.

It is a large, ornate affair, gold fixtures, fake green marble floor, a walk-in shower, and a large lit mirror over the green sink. I look at myself in the mirror. I surely don't look like the tiny thing Eric married, I'm still a little plump from having Toby. But I'm not a dog. I comb my shoulder-length hair with my fingers and open the door to step outside.

Eric is in the hall and grabs the door. "Ah, my bride, my bride," he says, hanging on the doorframe with one hand while the other starts to unbutton the front of my dress.

"Eric!" People are in the hall, on the stairs, people are every-where at this crowded party.

Holding my dress closed, Eric backs me into the bathroom. "I've been looking for you all night," he says. He staggers as he pulls the shower door open.

"It didn't look like you were looking for me, it looked—" Eric is nudging me into the shower stall. He closes the frosted glass door, and lifts my dress and kneels. I go to push him away, but when he touches me with his mouth, I forget. Soon I'm trying to unbutton his shirt. Someone comes into the bathroom. We didn't lock the door. I think Eric will stop, but he doesn't. And I don't. We make long, quiet, damp love in Dr. Hanson's shower stall, with people coming and going.

. . . . .

"You what?" Esther is laughing on the other end of the phone. "When Charlie has too much to drink, he immediately goes to sleep. And he snores. So just how frosted was the frosted glass?"

. . . . .

At the end of the summer the children and I fly home to visit my parents. "Look, Madeline. There's Lake Pontchartrain. See it?"

"I want the clouds back. Are we gonna get more?"

When I walk into the New Orleans airport, carrying Toby and leading Madeline, I can't believe my father isn't waiting for us. I have missed him so much. I've missed that proud incredulous way he has of looking at me, like he can't believe his little girl is so good at playing ladies. We start down the long hall toward the main terminal. Maybe he's had a wreck, maybe he got the days confused. The only person more excited than I about this trip was my father. Suddenly he pops from behind a doorway.

"Papa!" Madeline opens her arms to her grandfather, who has to put down the giant bag of toys he's holding to lift his granddaughter up. He was so busy buying too much loot for my children that he almost missed our arrival. I love watching his easy natural way with my daughter. I wait for him to look up and open his arms to me.

· · · · ·

The old house is the same. "And there, Madeline"— I point through the front window—"there's the levee where Papa used to walk me every night before bedtime."

"And where I'm going to walk you, Madeline," he says.

"And not Toby, wight, Papa?"

My father looks over at my sleeping son and winks at me. "Who is this 'Toby' guy? Some kind of mule, or an alligator?"

"Oh, Papa!"

My mother walks into the living room and I run to hug her. She backs up so she can take Toby from me. "I still can't wrestle a real kiss from you, huh?" I laugh.

If anyone else stepped away from my affection the way my mother does, it would hurt my feelings. With my mother, it's just her way. We've even talked about it and I know she doesn't like sex either. She says none of the women from her generation like sex. This seems hard to believe. Sex is my favorite thing about marriage.

· · · · ·

"What a pretty little house. Oh, Marie, don't you just love it? You couldn't have all these things with kids around, believe me."

The children are in Bellebend with my parents and I've come to New Orleans to spend the day with Marie. She turned away from me as I entered her house and now seems withdrawn. I find myself talking too much. I lift a tiny jade sculpture from the ebony coffee table. The piece surprises me, it is of an oriental woman, nude, with her hands opening her own privates. "You certainly couldn't have something like this around kids."

Marie's lover, the doctor she met in her senior year, has set her up in a small shotgun house that has been completely remodeled. The cypress floors are bare and highly polished. The furnishings are sparse and obviously expensive. A delicate-looking red brocaded sofa and two white leather chairs are arranged around the coffee table; a sideboard, filled with what looks to be antique china, dominates the rest of the long room. Very dark red drapes are pulled, blocking out the late morning light.

"You with a lover. Who would have thought it? Susan and I spent one entire phone call speculating. She was in Amsterdam, I bet it cost her a trillion dollars. I told her I'd get it from the horse's mouth. So, talk, tell me about this Jackson fellow. The good doctor." I'm early, as usual, and seem to have caught Marie unready.

"Did you know she was in jail?" Marie doesn't even sound like herself.

"Who?"

"Susan. Susan was in jail, before she moved to Europe. My mother told me. She heard it from someone in Lafayette. Something to do with that bank in California those Communists blew up. I mean, of course Susan didn't blow up the bank, but she was involved. She hid some of them, or something."

"My God, Susan in jail. Yet, when you think about it . . . any chance we can open the drapes? The light out there is wonderful. When you think about it—"

"I—Jackson—Jackson doesn't like the drapes open. It's bad for the art." My friend keeps her face turned from me and settles on the far end of the couch, her legs folded beneath her. "Do you think we'll ever see Susan again," she asks. "I mean, it's been six years."

I nod and drop into one of the chairs. "Of course we will. Remember how shocked we were when we heard she'd hitchhiked across the country? With a boy!" Marie smiles. "Now they all do it. Everybody's hitchhiking and living together. I just missed all that wild stuff. I mean, I wonder if I would have married Eric if . . . You know, it never occurred to me not to marry him, after we'd done it. And look at you! Susan and I were positive you'd be a virgin even *after* your wedding night. Sister Helena's veil is probably standing straight up."

"You want some coffee or a brandy milk punch, or something?" Marie is definitely not her usual babbling self.

"No, I'm already wired from three cups of my mother's stuff. You can't get that good dark roast in North Carolina. I thought we'd wait till we got to Commander's for a milk punch."

Marie turns to face me for the first time. "Katherine, would you mind very much if I bowed out? I don't feel much like, well I have a headache and—"

The right side of her face is a mottled bruise. "Christ, Marie!" Someone has slammed an open hand across my friend's cheek. "What happened? Did—"

She covers her cheekbone with her hand. "That's why I—" She starts again. "I fell down the back stairs last night. I was carrying the garbage outside and I fell. You remember my two left feet, right?"

"Talk to me. I've been your friend for over ten years, what is—"

Marie stands to move away from me. "I already told you I have a headache. It's not a good day for talking. Jackson might be coming by soon, and . . ." Her voice slips into the shadows of the darkened room.

On the drive to Bellebend from New Orleans I roll down the windows and turn the radio up as high as it will go. At first I speed down the Airline Highway, screaming threats and plotting revenge upon the "good doctor." Then I turn off the radio and drive slowly, smelling the dank roadside swamps, remembering other trips down this flat rundown highway. Remembering the Holy Name Academy bus ride after our wild senior weekend in New Orleans. That girlhood seems so far away, so lost. Nothing is turning out the way we thought or hoped. First Susan marches off into the unknown, now Marie seems to be disappearing into unspeakable horror. I feel angry, abandoned, and powerless.

. . . . .

The year Toby turns two we find a rambling old farmhouse, not too far from the university, and buy it with money given to us by Eric's parents. I am twenty-five years old and pregnant with our third child when we move into our dream house. The old brick farmhouse has bright green shutters, high ceilings, a stone fireplace, an out-of-date kitchen and dining room, four bedrooms, a study for Eric, and a view of the mountains. The house is on a sloping hill and our land is bordered by a shallow creek. There are fruit trees in the yard and lilacs and giant maples. The lawn is rich with grass. I will fill picture albums with photographs of children playing in the mountain grasses. I will mark the passage of time by the ages of my children.

"Eric, see how beautiful everything looks. It was worth all those years in an apartment." My hand rests on the slight swell of my stomach, I can feel the baby turning.

"It needs work, it needs so much work. The ceiling in the dining room is about to fall in."

"Did you remember that Rosa and Esther volunteered to organize a work crew next weekend? We'll have like a barn raising. I'll put on a big pot of chili and we'll stock up on beer. Esther says that's how they put in their sun room."

I walk to the window to watch Madeline struggling to pull Toby, in his red wagon, up the sloping lawn. "The kids can play outside without my having to worry about them."

"And the mommy and the daddy can play inside." Eric runs the chilled rim of his drink glass along my collarbone and leans to chew on my neck.

"Eric, there's gin in there! Honey, it's two in the afternoon." Eric puts his hand in the center of my chest and nudges me backward until my back is pressed too hard against the kitchen counter. I turn my head away from his afternoon breath smelling of gin, as he opens my blouse.

. . . . .

"I'm as likely to go to the moon, as to California. Susan, you don't have a clue what it means to take care of two children. I couldn't ask Eric to do that, even if you did pay my way. And even if I didn't look like a rutabaga. I'm eight months pregnant."

I'm having what will turn out to be my last phone conversation with Susan. She is in the States for a few days and has called to ask me to meet her. "I hate that you don't have time to come visit. It's so beautiful here. And our house, Susan, I wish you could see our house! Sometimes I can't sleep at night, I feel so lucky. It really is a dream life. My smart romantic husband looking after us, the happy children rolling in the green grass of our lawn on a hill looking over the mountains, forever."

CHAPTER V

I HAVE ALWAYS BEEN FOND OF THE BEginning of *Glass Menagerie*, where Tom says something about his father being "a phone lineman who fell in love with long distance." What is it that is supposed to be so romantic, even heroic, about wandering husbands/fathers? Ulysses is an epic hero who comes to mind. Gauguin and even Gandhi are among the men who left their families to find themselves, their causes. On the other hand, wandering wives/mothers have always been seen as villainous. It doesn't seem to be a feminine option.

"Why don't you, Katherine? Why don't you just pack up and leave? Make your little newspaper job a full-time one and just leave." Eric is still holding on to the paper he was grading when I so disrespectfully interrupted him. I am standing in the doorway of his study.

"Leave the children, with you, for good?" I decide to ignore his slam at my thirty-cents-an-inch, sixty-dollars-a-month job.

"Yeah."

We both know he is bluffing, still I have too many points to make. "Eric, you can't even leave your work for their birthdays, never mind their lives."

I enter the sanctum and settle my weary self on the edge of his desk. "You're deliberately twisting what I said. You know I'm not asking to abdicate. I just want a sympathetic ear. I—I just want a weekend off. I want to go out to Rosa's cabin and read an entire book, for Christ's sake. I haven't read a book straight through in eight years. Not since Madeline was born."

I stand and pull myself up to my full five feet to make my point. "Either it is very difficult to take care of three kids, in which case I need a break. Or it's a piece of cake, so what's the problem with you watching over them for two days?"

"Are you finished?" he says, lowering the red pencil over the still-clutched papers.

I turn to look out the window, but it has become dark outside, and all that I see is my reflection. Myself looking back at a woman of almost twenty-eight who looks ten years older; limp uncared-for hair, crow's feet beside my tired eyes.

"Please just hear me out, Eric. I am fighting to survive. I am terrified that I will end up a mindless old lady living to laugh at the jokes the stars tell on 'Hollywood Squares.' I just need a little space, a tiny bit. Some dignity. I used to have a mind. I almost remember that, I—"

"And who is going to grade these papers that are already several weeks late?" Eric interrupts me, then turns back to his work.

I stand there for a minute and look at him in the glow of his work lamp. Time has not been good to Eric either. His thick hair has lost its dark gloss, the chestnut color has turned salt and pepper, his brow folds into deep furrows. His eyes are watery and red-rimmed behind his glasses. This year he was passed over for department head. It was a sure thing and somebody else got it.

At night, when he makes love to me and touches me between

117

my legs, Eric holds his hand out afterward, away from himself. As though he's touched something dirty and doesn't want to spread the mess. Once, when we had a dog, she rolled in some horrible dead thing, then Toby played with her. I carried Toby to the bathtub by his suspenders. His small, round struggling body held away from me. I feel like that dog, that I've rolled in something unspeakable. I take long showers and wash inside myself, hard and earnestly, scrubbing between my legs. Eric and I seldom even have conversations, yet I am always hungry for him, always eager for sex. The showers get hotter and hotter, my skin becomes chapped and dry. Sometimes there are places where the skin has cracked open and bleeds.

Our old farmhouse seems haunted. The three years we've lived here feel like a long, slow slide through some sort of haze. A fog of boozy evenings and monotonous days, punctuated by Eric's petty infidelities. Madeline wanders the night in her out-grown nightgowns, talking of smoke and fire, of burning houses. When I carry her back to bed, she makes me promise our house will not burn down. I promise her, then return to my own bed, smelling the air for smoke. Toby sees witches in his dreams and screams out. When I rush into his room, he is cornered, out of bed, his five-year-old body pressed in the far-most corner of his room, his gray eyes wide with fright, his thick mop of hair damp and sweaty. I turn the lights on and take his hand. We walk together all around his room. I make up chants to send the witch away and tuck him back in his bed, turning the pillow to break the spell of the bad dreams. Three-year-old Beth, on the other hand, has begun to sleep longer every night and often asks to be put down early, before she has even had her supper. On windless nights the house seems shaken by storms that the bright dry autumn mornings turn to lies.

. . . . .

My husband is a Henry Higgins who falls in love with a long line of Elizas. The phone rings. When I answer it, the person on the other end hangs up. It rings again, Eric picks it up in his study. I hear his voice, steady and low. I stand in the hallway outside and press my whole body against the wall. I don't even know if I am trying to eavesdrop or trying to take in the tenderness, the intimacy, from the other side. Take it in, so I can have a share of it.

"Mommy, what are you doing?" Madeline stands beside me, her pale, freckled eight-year-old face contorted by concern. Her braids are coming loose, and I realize it has been a couple days since I brushed her straight blond hair. I wonder if "benign neglect" is an oxymoron.

"I'm trying to move the wall so I can sweep under it," I tell my daughter. "Remember that time you helped me move the couch? Well, I'm trying to move the wall now."

Once I read that the Chinese have a way of preparing turtle soup by filling a large pot with water and very peppery spices. They put the living turtle into the seasoned water, then they turn on the heat. As the water gets hot the turtle becomes thirsty and begins to sip the seasoned water. Of course the spices make her even more thirsty and the turtle desperately drinks more of the water, trying to rid herself of thirst, trying to escape the heat. This method seasons the turtle inside and out. My marriage has become unbearable. "If you can't stand the heat, get out of the kitchen." All the exits are blocked. I'm like that turtle, everywhere I turn I hit a wall, everything I drink makes me thirstier still. I reach for Eric in my desperation. And Eric is what ails me.

· · · · ·

I run my hand along Eric's side of the bed and feel the cool blank sheets. I turn on the light and look at the clock. It is two o'clock in the morning. I am horrified that he hasn't bothered to come home or even bothered to call with a made-up story. It feels as if the blood has left my body; my hands are shaking as I sit and reach for a book. I try to read until I hear the car drive up. I quickly turn the light off and pretend to sleep as Eric stumbles quietly to bed. I think he is deaf and stupid because he can't hear my heart beating. I suddenly want him so desperately, it takes all my will not to push my ass, spoon-fashion, against his belly.

. . . . .

"Look, Eric, I don't blame you." It is another two o'clock in another morning, and I have turned in our bed to watch Eric's cigarette glowing in the darkness. In the silence I think: no one sleeps in this house except Beth. Maybe she has taken all our sleep, the way old-timers say a cat will suck the breath from a baby's mouth. Tiny Beth has slipped through the house, sipping all our sleep away. My Beth has murdered sleep. My husband doesn't answer me. I try again. "I don't blame you. I just think we ought to talk."

"There's nothing to talk about." He jabs his cigarette out.

"Right." I turn my pillow over, wishing grown-up nightmares could go away with the flip of a pillow. I slam my fist into my useless pillow and move as far to my side of the bed as possible. Our twin clocks tick out time from either side of the vast bed.

"There's nothing to talk about because, because it's over." He lights another cigarette. "It's over, O.K.?"

"Over?" I crush the sides of the pillow into my jaw. "When?" He gets out of bed and stands at the window. The silhouetted November tree is almost bare of leaves, and Eric looks like a shadow trying to climb the empty tree. "When?" I ask again.

"This afternoon." His voice breaks. I realize Eric is crying.

"I'm sorry, Eric. I'm really sorry. It must have felt so good to be clever and right again."

He dashes across the room and kneels on his side of the bed, reaching over to slap me hard. "Katherine, I don't need your sarcasm!"

I touch my hand to my cheek and am almost relieved. It is as if I have been waiting for violence for weeks, the way you wait for a summer storm. He needed to do this, and I needed to feel something. "You know what John Knowles said about sarcasm, Eric?" I pull back the covers to let Eric know that his place is still in this bed. "He said, 'Sarcasm is the protest of the weak.' Even though I might be weak, I swear I wasn't being sarcastic. I meant it. It would be lovely to speak well again, to be admired."

Eric stretches out on his stomach. I place my hand on his shoulder and he turns to pull me into him. "For you, I did it for you and the children, Katherine. I gave her up for you." He is sobbing as he pushes my nightgown up and enters me. Maybe we will be all right. Maybe our bodies are night vessels that will save us all from drowning.

. . . . .

The late winter of 1974 is a severe one in the mountains, blizzards followed by long freezes. The schools are often closed and the children and I rattle aimlessly around the farmhouse that I can never get quite warm enough. It is too cold for even housework and we wander in the clutter of the high-ceilinged, dusty rooms, illuminated by stark outside light through frosted windows. The cold gray afternoons are endless. Rosa has returned to school and is working on a graduate degree. When she visits me she is full of talk of her classes, or of Watergate, the growing national scandal, and I have nothing to say. I search for something interesting to say and am humiliated by my mundane life. When Rosa voices her concerns about leaving Harmony with sitters so much, I am not sympathetic, only envious. We seem to have lost the pitch and catch of wordplay. I think I have dropped the ball. Rosa visits less often.

Esther is Rosa's opposite in that she seems totally unconcerned about her son; she has started a job selling real estate and avoids my house of children as if it is something contagious, like flu or the plague. My friendship with Esther seems reduced to dutiful phone calls.

If I had a car I could drive the children into town, we could go to the library. I'm too tired to even take on any free-lancing for the newspaper. The year Beth was one, I talked myself into very part-time work, something I could do at home. I think I had visions of following in my mother's early journalistic footsteps. So I'd gotten a little newspaper job for myself; in a show of independence, in the hope of having some money to call my own.

The people at the newspaper have stopped calling me and I never phone there. I stay in my nightgown all day long. Sometimes, when Toby and Madeline are out of school, I tuck all three of the children into bed with me through the long afternoons, and try to read. I am desperate to read, and think I can feel my brain growing soggy and stale, like graham crackers left too long out of the cookie can. I read my novels out loud to the children and disguise my voice so they will think I am reading storybooks. They pull the books from my hands and ask to play cards and simple board games. I hate games and stack the children up before the television, force them to watch soap operas and old reruns so I don't have to play Monopoly. Beth is too young to stay in front of the television, but seems content to return to her crib, napping and talking to herself. Her curly dark blond hair is always matted, from being pressed on her pillow. I know I should check on her, shouldn't let her stay alone so much. But it's too much effort. Everything is too much effort. If only I could read one book, cover to cover. Eric stays at the office longer, and I fall into the habit of feeding the kids canned soup early and parking them in front of the television. Then I wait for Eric so he and I can drink our supper.

Beth goes to bed with the winter sun; her brother and sister fall asleep on the den floor most nights before I remember them. On those nights, Eric and I stumble our way upstairs, each carrying a sleeping child. Sometimes Madeline and Toby tiptoe downstairs and beg for more supper. I let them nibble on the cheese and crackers and chips that Eric and I have to go along with our drinks. Then I walk them up to bed and read to them, skipping entire pages in my rush to go downstairs and drink more.

. . . . .

During the winter it is discovered that my mother is, as they say, "riddled with cancer." Her illness is an unreal event that takes place in a green land, a place where birds call out and flowers bloom. The children and I fly, away from the ice and snow, down to Louisiana.

They have moved her from the big four-poster bed to the room Eve and I shared as children. I sit beside my mother, as she lies in my childhood bed, and search for some real thing to say to her. Sometimes I clear my throat, as if I am getting ready to make a speech. Maybe my speech will be about what my mother has meant to me. The cool fire of her. How I have loved the light of that fire and pitied the coolness of it. How sometimes, when I hold my children, I hold them the way I would have liked my mother to hold me. The way I think she wished she could have held me and my sister. When Eve and I were little, the way Madeline and Toby and Beth are little now. I think I would like to tell my mother who I am this winter, about my life. About the mess I'm making. I'd like to ask her for help. Though I realize her time for helping is past. I'm beginning to find out what she has always known—that we survive our mothers.

Eve bustles in and out, checking on Mother, running the household, keeping the ship afloat. My mother and I have no tradition of verbal intimacy, and all the things I plan to say sound like bad movie scripts. So I sit silently by my mother's deathbed and contemplate the light on magnolia leaves outside her bedroom window.

I am relieved that my children are with me, but not my responsibility. Trips home have always been an opportunity for me to abdicate motherhood. This visit is a painful one, still I know my children have been saved by it. Released from their ice palace of neglect. My children are with their grandfather and I can sit at my mother's bedside and grieve for her. Cancer has stripped the flesh from her and my lovely spirited mother has become a thing of bones. I can remember my childhood with my mother so well. Now I try to remember what being with her has been like since I became a mother. I can't think of us as "fellow mothers." I am her child, she is my mother. She is "Granny" to my children, but my mother, and I am losing my mother.

One day, while I am sitting beside her, my mother turns to me and says, "These things happen sometimes." I don't know if this is meant as a lifeline or if it is a non sequitur. She closes her eyes again. Maybe she was talking in her sleep.

My father takes the children off on Louisiana adventures. He takes them to the state capitol building in Baton Rouge and shows them the bullet holes in the marble wall where Huey Long was shot. He buys them sailor hats and gives them rolls of quarters to spend at TG&Y. He cooks extravagant dinners for the children and, afterward, sits on the edge of the bed they share and makes up bedtime stories. When all three of the children are asleep, he comes into my mother's room and paces until she becomes irritated. Then we hear him pacing in the hall outside her room. He is in awe of her sickroom, just as he has always held her quick mind and tongue in awe. He seems courteous and fatherly before this evil suitor at his wife's door. He is so much older than she, and now she's beating him to that great finish line in the sky. It is a cruel joke, and my father will be angry at God for the brief remainder of his life.

I try to console my father, to distract, to engage him in conversation. He looks at me as though I am some alien. Even when he is off with his grandchildren, his heart and thoughts are with his disappearing wife. Seems I wasn't the star in his blue heaven, after all. Turns out it really always was my mother.

Eve has come home to live again; she's given up her job

teaching in Colorado to come back to nurse my mother. Later she'll get a job at LSU and will commute from Bellebend to Baton Rouge. She will stay on to ease my father's transition. My mother is in terrible pain. Eve takes an orange and a hypodermic and tries to show me how to give my mother injections. I can't even watch the needle enter the bright skin of the orange. The small sharp intrusion, searing its way into the tender pulp. I turn my head away. My younger sister knows how much it would help me to be able to ease my mother's pain. But I can't. Once again, Eve pulls into the lead.

"You drink too much, Katherine. We aren't a family of heavy drinkers. What's going on, big sister?"

The household is asleep. Eve and I have just watched the late news, Watergate, more on the Vietnam troops returning, impeachment talk. Now we're having a midnight visit.

"My mother is dying, our mother is dying. That's what's going on." I rattle the ice cubes in my bourbon and water and try not to resent my collected, capable sister's probing.

"I don't think so. Or I don't think that's all of it. The last couple times I've called North Carolina in the evenings, your speech was distinctly slurred. Now what's wrong really? Trouble in paradise?"

"Of course not, everything's fine, wonderful, Eric is—" Eve leans across the table and presses her fingers to my mouth.

"Something's wrong. I hardly know your kids, this time. Madeline has become an insomniac and cheerful Toby is one pissed-off kid. Beth sleeps all the time."

I surrender and take my sister's hand. "You know how it is with Daddy, how he just wants to hear the good things?" She nods, smiling. "He thinks I'm off in this beautiful old farmhouse in the splendid mountains with my adoring professor husband. He wants our stories to be happy. Me too, I'm his daughter. So I always make the story happy. All my stories are beautiful. I feel like it's the least I can do for Daddy. Now, on the other hand—"

I take a big last sip of bourbon. "Mama has always wanted the truth. I've never quite known how to talk to her, but if I could figure that out, I'd tell her the truth. I always understood Mother has been our safety, the voice of reason. But you see, she's dying now and it's too late for me to ask her to save us. I feel trapped, Eve. Like Rapunzel with a crew cut. Instead of the prince being the savior, he's the one who has locked me in the tower. He's locked me in the tower and gone off searching for other long-haired maidens. Too late, I discover I've been waiting for Mother to come to the rescue."

When it is time for the children and me to return to North Carolina I rush around my parents' house gathering last things to pack. I've left a hairbrush beside my mother's bed and run in to get it. As I turn to leave the room, leave my mother for good, I see that her eyes are open. I stop, poised to run again. "I love you, Mama."

It is difficult for her to talk, and when she does, her voice is so weary. "I know you do." She closes her eyes. I am absolved, since I have never doubted her love for me, only if she knew of mine for her. She dies two weeks later.

. . . . .

"I might have some respect for you, Eric, if it was the same student." We just aren't quite drunk enough, it is still dangerous to speak the truth. Eric has confessed a new adultery, a quickie while I was at the funeral. "And in my bed, you bastard!" I am stripping the sheets off the bed. "Help me, help tear these." I am using my teeth to start a rip.

"Aren't you overreacting? I mean, I told you. You wouldn't have found out on your own." All the lights are on in our bed-room. We had been getting ready for bed and our clothes are tossed over the room. He is wearing a pair of boxer shorts and is leaning, unsteadily, against the dresser with his arms folded.

"I can't get this son-of-a-bitching sheet ripped. Help me with this!" Eric hates when I raise my voice and he really hates when I use foul language.

He crosses the room and throws me down on the bare mattress. With one knee on my belly, he takes the shredded sheet away from me and slowly tears it, laying the strips across my spread-out arms. I don't move. I realize I am frightened. He is breathing heavily and I know he could just kill me. There is nothing but unmasked hate on his face. His knee in my stomach is painful, he could shatter my face with his fist, he could strangle me. Instead he runs one tatter back and forth over my breasts. Spittle has collected in a corner of his mouth. When he leans over me, I can smell the gin on his breath.

"I guess you don't want to hear about my dream." Madeline is standing in the doorway of our bedroom with her small fists braced on her hips. She looks disgusted. I can think of nothing to say. She turns and is gone.

Eric moves off the bed and I kick away the strings of ripped sheets, pull on a robe, and walk down the hall to my daughter's room. She is lying in bed with her face to the wall. I climb under the covers with her and fall asleep.

· · · · ·

I attempt an affair with one of Eric's junior colleagues. I seduce him with a feigned interest in Restoration drama. We scheme deviously for weeks, though I doubt either of our hearts is much involved. We finally find a night Eric is out of town and I can get a baby-sitter to stay late. We meet for drinks in the Caribbean Room. By the time we weave our way to a rented room at the Travel Lodge he is impotent from a near lethal overdose of Zombies.

In one of our rare visits, I have been telling Esther about my night of sin. "You should have known better when he ordered a Zombie. Any man who orders such a foolish-sounding drink, with a straight face, surely can't hold an erection."

"Esther, please remember my tenacious inexperience."

"Now those Volcanoes are something else," Esther adds. "Don't you think a man that can drink a Volcano from the Caribbean Room has a thing this big?" She parts her hands about a yard wide. "Eruption City!"

"Esther, you have a trashy one-track mind."

"Katherine, it is the obsession of the monogamous. Here it is, the seventies, there's a sexual revolution going on out there. All my talk, and Charlie is the only screw I've had for years. Some fucking revolution. A fuckless revolution in my case."

"Well, it turns out I am still monogamous. Eric is the only man I've had. Ever." I look heavenward. "You hear that, Sister Helena? It was only a 'near occasion' of sin!" I light a cigarette. "I mean the only earth that moved was his. It looked like he was on very unsteady ground when I left him retching in the Travel Lodge bathroom. The next morning I'm here in the kitchen distributing tiny oriental paper umbrellas among the children. Madeline and Toby fight over the only purple one."

"So much for Peyton Place, Katherine." Esther reaches over and fondly grabs a fistful of my hair. "Shit!"

Since becoming a real estate agent Esther has been wearing fake fingernails and she's torn one off in my unkempt hair.

"And so much for Restoration drama." I untangle the nail from my hair and hand it back to her. "God, I hate all that 'mistaken identity' business. It's in every play."

· · · · ·

Spring comes inevitably. Even to the damned it comes. The yard is filled with blooming lilacs. Before we moved to North Carolina, I'd thought lilacs were only some poetic metaphor invented by Whitman. As in blooming in dooryards, whatever dooryards were. The lavender clouds of lilacs, the cherry blossoms, forsythia, and dogwoods paint our yard like the water-colored beginning of a Disney fantasy. Only my family is out of place. There is a mockery of butterflies and brightly colored birds in the sweet-smelling air. Our young cat is pregnant. She doesn't understand the change in her body and tumbles clumsily when she tries to leap after butterflies. I'd meant to have her spayed, I just didn't know she could get pregnant so young. Beth dresses the cat in baby bonnets and wheels her around the porch in her doll carriage. When the swollen cat leaps heavily out of the buggy, I hear my own lisping baby call the cat a "tupid tunt."

. . . . .

It is our wedding anniversary, our ninth, and I have the bright idea of involving the children. Beth and Toby have helped string streamers over the dining room, and Madeline fills a large vase with flowers we have cut from the yard. I put my grandmother's lace tablecloth on the table and set five places. I have told Eric of the plan. He is still very late getting home. He has been unavoidably caught in a long-running tenure and promotion meeting. Eric insists on a before-dinner martini, then another. Though the kids are hungry and sullen, I am amazed to see them on good behavior. They don't see very much of their father and tend to treat him like powerful company.

Beth curls up under the table, and I have to wake her up when the candles are finally lit and we have gathered at the table. Eric starts to propose a toast, then sees that the children have already begun to eat. He drains his wineglass instead of offering a hollow speech about all our happy years. I pour more wine for him. With a little food eaten, dispositions at the table improve and the children are chattering among themselves. Eric tries to fill me in on the tenure situation.

"Mommy, Toby is chewing with his mouth open."

"Am not," Toby says, deliberately opening his full mouth in Madeline's direction.

"Am not," echoes Beth, proudly dribbling her milk down her

chin. These are not even interruptions to me and I don't see why Eric has abruptly stopped talking.

I prod Eric to keep the conversational ball rolling. "But how did Wilson vote when the—" Toby reaches for a roll and knocks Eric's wineglass over.

"You bastard, you little bastard!" Eric shoves Toby's chair away from the table and it skids against the wall carrying its small ashen-faced passenger. There is what seems like a full minute of silence before Beth begins to wail.

"I can't, I can't do this anymore." Eric stands, kicking his chair over. "I hate it, all, all . . ." He gestures around the table, then deliberately raises his voice to be louder than Beth. "I hate it!"

He rushes from the room; we hear him start the car, then the spray of gravel as he speeds out of the driveway.

He comes back, of course. He's not a monster. He comes back with ice cream for the children. But Beth is sound asleep, and the two older children are already in bed and say they aren't hungry. I eat Eric's ice cream. I eat the whole carton. Eric goes to bed, and I sit at the deserted table eating ice cream and watching the candles melt over my grandmother's lace tablecloth. The ice cream melts through the carton and spreads over the tablecloth too. I sit and lick the empty spoon until the metal taste burns my tongue.

"I don't love you anymore, Eric," I whisper into the darkened dining room. "I just don't love you anymore." I drop the spoon into the carton of lukewarm cream and begin to clear the table.

. . . . .

"I mean, I couldn't tell the melted ice cream from the melted candle wax. Maybe next dinner I'll use—"

"Are you going to do anything about it, Katherine?" Rosa's voice sounds so concerned. Concerned and professional. She'll soon be a licensed counselor.

I have finally broken my vow of silence and, without really thinking about it, in trying to make it a funny story, meandered into telling Rosa the gory details of the Pierson family's happy anniversary dinner. Only when it was half told did I see there was no humor to be pulled from it.

The phone is damp against my ear. I pull it slightly away when I talk to my friend. "What can I do? I guess I'll just keep on keeping on. There are worse ways of living."

"I'm not sure I agree. Look, I know I told you I was working on my thesis, but I can't believe you took that to mean you should stay clear until it was finished. I've got seven years to complete it. In fact—"

"Oh, I know that." I switch ears, hold the phone in my left hand. "I just don't have any energy, and the kids are out of sorts, and . . ."

Rosa picks up where I interrupted her. "In fact, Katherine. Why don't you and Eric go off somewhere? Just the two of you. Jeff and I can watch your kids. Maybe you can work things out, put a little romance back. You can use our cabin. Or go off to the beach."

I should have kept our little nightmare to myself. "That's so nice, Rosa. Maybe some other time, huh? I think Beth is calling me. I gotta go, O.K.?"

I push the button down without waiting to hear her say anything else. I push the button down, then leave the phone off the hook. The truth is, even if I could summon the spirit to go off with Eric, I'm pretty sure he'd turn the offer down.

. . . . .

It is the middle of summer, a summer of heat and rain. I have avoided everyone I know for months. I've returned to writing poetry and have written a poem that says the walls of our house are furred with mold and that slugs copulate in our garden. The poem seems cheerful compared to my life. It is very late at night, and I am very drunk. Eric is in Washington for a week of modern language meetings. I suspect he is not alone. But I am. The children are asleep, and I am alone. I try to make love to myself and am unsuccessful. Despite all the manuals I have read, it still seems such a hollow empty act. And I cannot sleep. I light the small lamp at my vanity table, open the drawer, and pull out a tube of bright red lipstick and a brush. Leaning close to the mirror, I carefully paint in the line of my lips with the brush, then I fill in with the tube, going round and round and round. I make my lips bigger, bigger than they are, swollen. I paint on swollen, shiny lips. I open my mouth and run the lipstick up and down my tongue. This feels good to me. I pick up the brush again and carefully, slowly, paint a very thin line around the rim of each areola. Then I take the tube and fill in with red, flicking my nipples over and over until the lipstick is thick and glistening on them. I have drawn a crooked red line down my belly and am standing and just reaching between my legs when I hear Toby calling from his room.

"The witch, Mommy, the witch! Help me!" Without thinking, I am too drunk to think, I run down the hall to his room. When I turn on the light, Toby begins to scream and scream.

. . . . .

I wake up slowly, and on my own. This may be the first morning of my motherhood that I wake up this way. No baby crying, no small voices arguing or calling me, no child's hands pulling away my covers. My head aches, my mouth is sticky and dry. I am confused by the red smears on the sheets. I lift the covers and look at my streaked breasts. Then I remember. I remember my son's nightmare, that I became my son's nightmare. It is a bright summer morning and I hear no sounds in my house. Suddenly, I feel as though a hawk has been loosed in my chest and is trying to beat its way out. My children, where are my children? Then, like the distant thunder of the cavalry's hooves, I hear the faint sound of the television.

After a quick, scalding shower that stains the white enamel with lipstick streaks, I get dressed and go downstairs. Madeline and Toby are sitting on the floor in front of "The Price Is Right." They don't look up from the television when I walk into the den. "Where's Beth?"

"She's down with the kittens." Madeline is concentrating on a description of the features on a Maytag dryer.

"Let's all go to the kitchen, and I'll fix pancakes."

Madeline still doesn't look up. "I already made breakfast, you don't have to worry."

I put my hand on Toby's head, his hands are squeezed into white-knuckled fists. His red tennis shoes are on the wrong feet. "Well then, help me make sandwiches. We're—we're going to go to the river and have a picnic." A woman on the screen is weeping, she is so happy to have guessed the right price of the dryer.

"We don't want to go to the river, we'll miss our shows."

I lean over and turn off the television. When I pick Toby up, his body is stiff and unyielding. I carry him downstairs and wordlessly bend his body to sit him on the counter beside me as I make the peanut butter sandwiches.

Eric has been promising for a month to take the station wagon to the shop and, at first, I can't get it started. The children are stacked in an angry little row in the backseat, and I can almost feel them cheering for the stalled motor. If we have to walk, we are going to the river. When the engine catches, I hear Madeline whisper "Shit." I race the motor to charge the battery, then back out of the driveway.

"Why tant we take da tittens to da river?"

"Beth, believe me, the kittens wouldn't enjoy it. Cats don't like water."

"Me neither," mutters Madeline. Toby still hasn't said a word.

I light up a cigarette and roll down my window. "Put on your seat belts, kids. Mommy is going to drive very fast."

The first sight of the river is like balm, like a cool bath to me. It opens in a wide blue swath at the base of a green high mountain. As the car rolls down the hill and curves to follow the course of the river, we can see the falls where a great crack crosses the riverbed and climbs up the mountains on both sides. The water is all lace and foam while it races and falls over the massive boulders. We drive past slowly; I hope that the sound of rushing water may soothe my children too. We don't stop here because this is where the college students gather, and today I don't need to see any of Eric's disciples. Besides, I need these children to myself.

I follow the asphalt road until we lose sight of the river. Soon afterward I turn onto a rutted dirt road, cross a set of railroad tracks, and park the car in the shade of a willow tree. Madeline and Toby walk ahead of me, down the bank to the river. I am left to struggle down the hill with our picnic basket and blanket. Beth trails behind me, dragging her beach towel through the railroad cinders and down the grassy bank; she finally abandons the towel in the white sand at the river's edge.

My children seem not to notice the blanket I've spread on the small beach and the picnic lunch I've set out for them. If I can get over a hangover, they can damned well get over me. The day is so beautiful, they will have to fall under its spell. The river is running as clear as spring water and the sky is empty of clouds. As far as the eye can see, there are only the marks of nature. No phone or electric lines, no boats in the water, not even a beer can in the shallows.

I walk over to where the three are digging a network of canals from a small puddle on the beach to the river. "Look, kids, no sign of people. We could be Indians, we could be the first people who ever lived here, we could—"

"Native Americans, Mom, not Indians." Madeline's voice is

world weary with all the knowledge she has garnered in three years at the university's progressive school.

Toby stands, kicks in his handiwork, and walks over to the blanket. He picks up a peanut butter sandwich, walks down to the river's edge, and flings it into the water. I think of how Mr. Rogers would say something really helpful, like "You're angry, aren't you, Toby?" Toby sure as hell is angry and this picnic is not exactly a picnic for any of us. I try again.

"Toby, remember last summer when we used to come here and I'd swim out in the water and you'd hold on to my back and swim too? Remember that?" He shakes his head, the sun catching the red highlights in his hair. "We did it a lot, ever since you were a little bit littler than Beth. I bet we can still swim together."

"You'd just drop me." He is gazing out to the river with his hands clasped behind his back, like a very small, very worried old man.

"No I wouldn't. Tell you what, if I drop you, if I lose you in the river, you can . . . I'll let the cat get up on the supper table while we're eating tonight."

"You would?" He turns to face me for the first time all day.

"Don't believe her, Toby!" The girls have been close enough to eavesdrop.

"Tuppose da tat dumps off da table?"

I lead my son out into the river and kneel in the pebbles and sharp stones of the water's edge. He tentatively takes my shoulders with his small hands, then slips onto my back as I crawl toward deeper water. I feel his full and desperate weight. When the water covers him, he pulls his arms tightly around my neck. I begin to swim, carefully opening the water with my arms extended in front of us. I do a modified breaststroke, taking my arms back far enough to run my fingers along his slippery calves, which are digging into my sides. I swim slowly and carefully, the same pattern over and over.

"Me! Me now," Beth calls urgently from the shore. Toby's

135

arms tighten into a vise, and I can't tell if he is trying to drown us, if he is really that fearful, or if he is hugging me with all his five-year-old strength because we have found one another again.

The sun is low as we pile our sandy blanket and towels back into the car. Everyone is going to be sunburned tomorrow. Still, I am Super Mom, "Put your seat belts on, you guys." The car starts immediately and we bounce up the rutty road. As we mount the railroad tracks, the car dies.

"This is like a song that was popular when I was a kid." I'm twisting around to talk to the children as I try the key in the ignition. "A girlfriend and a boyfriend, teenagers, are out for a ride when their car stalls on the railroad track and a train—"

Incredibly, I hear a train. A train is coming. On a late July afternoon a train is rushing toward us, down the railroad tracks that follow the river. My babies are belted into a car that is stalled on the railroad tracks, and a train is coming. The train sees us; the engineer is blowing the whistle. I am turning the key, again and again. How can I get them out of this car and, at the same time, turn the key? Turn the key!

"Mommy!"

I promise whatever, whomever, is listening that I will never drink again or desert these children or break any righteous law. I am making vows, here. Please don't let this be happening, please don't let my babies . . . We can see the man in the train's front window. The ignition catches, the station wagon fishtails off the track in a whir of flying cinders, and dies again. The train zooms by. It is so loud, so close, we cover our ears, and it shakes the car.

"Why are you crying, Mommy, why?" Toby is leaning over the seat, smoothing the hair away from my forehead.

"Fun! Dat was a fun wreck!" Beth is bouncing happily inside her seat belt.

In the rearview mirror, I see that Madeline is white beneath her sunburn. The ignition catches on the second try. On the way home I teach my children all the words to "Teen Angel."

That night I call Marie. She has recently left her sadistic lover

and, after a long silence, we've fallen back into the habit of calling one another.

"Jesus Christ, Katherine, I'd be in a mental ward. I'd look up
and see that ole train bearing down on me and I'd just plain
check out. You'd find me in a padded cell. With snow white hair
on my head and drool dripping down my chin."

"To tell you the truth, Marie, I feel like I have been in some
kind of mental ward; like I'm just getting out, just recovering
from shock treatment. Marie, I realized today, looking at my little
ones in the clarity of almost losing them, I realized I could be
Eric's wife or I could be a mother to my children. I can't do both.
And it's no contest."

. . . . .

"A tisket, a tasket. Shit! A tisket, a tasket, a green 'n' yellow
basket." It is two days after the narrow escape with the train, and
I am crying again. Singing a stupid song, crying and trying to
stuff kittens into a green and yellow picnic basket. Only these
kittens aren't going on a picnic, they're going to the gas chamber.
I have called ahead and the vet is waiting to put all these multicolored fuzzballs and their mother to death. It's just that the
kittens won't stay in the basket. They keep flipping the wooden
lid up. My arms are covered with scratches and the mother cat is
howling on the porch outside, howling and jumping up at the
kitchen window. I can't look at the kittens' little faces, or feel
their fur as soft. I am already surrounded by more innocence than
I can bear. Here I thought the basket would be a humane means
of transport, but I am bruising and mauling the crazed kittens as
I clack the basket lid down again and again.

The children are at Rosa's house for the afternoon. They are
playing with other children. If they actually remember how to do
that. If they could see me now, they would know just how un-
trustworthy their mother is. But we're jumping ship and must
travel light, as little baggage as possible.

137

Friends. Impossibly, I still have my friends. I haven't returned any of their calls for months, haven't accepted any invitations, anything that would get in the way of Eric's and my drinking nights. I wake from the great sleep, the lost weekend, blinking in the blinding light of second chances. I've been gone, maybe for more than a year, and now, I discover friends among the salvageable. People were out there all this time. Normal people, living their lives, going to their jobs, driving their kids to the swimming pool, hosting barbecues, doing whatever good people do in the summertime. The good old summertime. Women that I know have, in a matter of hours, begun to orchestrate my life change. My friends are going to come out here and help load mattresses and the kids' toys and my books and our clothes. They're going to move us into a little three-room house my real estate agent friend, Esther, has found in town for me, and that I have rented. These friends who don't even ask me where I've been for the last few seasons.

. . . . .

"Those days are over, Katherine. You need to help us, honey." Rosa, Esther, and Esther's friend, Dena, are looking at me with little-masked concern. I pull my head from the oven I've been cleaning and try to figure out what they are asking me to do.

"Eric can clean the oven now," says Dena. "You don't have to lift any heavy objects, but your crew here needs a few suggestions about what you want moved to town."

"There's a stain back there I just can't get out." I go to lean back into the oven when Rosa takes my elbow and Esther takes the scouring pad from my hand.

The three women gently, but forcibly, escort me through one last tour of the farmhouse. This final resting place for love's lost illusions. I point to Beth's walnut spindle youth bed, the double mattress of Madeline's bed, Toby's bed and dresser. Dena and Rosa lift the bright red toy box, and Jeff grabs Beth's bed.

Esther keeps her arm around my waist, and I lean on her shoulder in muddled confusion. "You know, you're a kid playing ladies, wobbling around in your mother's high heels, giving tea parties with tiny tea sets. And before you know it—even if you still think it's playacting—it isn't pretend anymore. It's for real."

"It is for real," Esther tells me, "and you're going to do real good, Katherine. Don't you worry."

. . . . .

"How will we get any money?" Madeline asks pragmatically. We are sitting in a pathetic circle on the floor of our new house. Our friends have just departed, after an afternoon of moving and cleaning. They've taken the feigned holiday spirit with them.

"I have a job. It really starts when you start school."

"If you have a job," says Toby, "who will take care of us?"

"Me, goofy, same as always. I'll take you three to your schools. A different school for every kid, thank you very much. Then I'll go to my job. When you get out of school, there I'll be in the old station wagon, waiting. Same time, same place. The only difference is that Beth will go to the full-day program. Instead of half, like you guys did when we lived in the big house."

"Like Ella?" asks Beth.

"Yeah, like Ella. Maybe her mom and I will even carpool now."

"What kind of job could you get?" Madeline wants to keep this discussion on track.

"You know how I've been writing sometimes for the paper?" Madeline nods. "Well, now I'm on the staff full-time. I'll have my own column about the university and I'll write editorials and articles."

"I heard you tell Daddy that the newspaper pays 'bird doo.' We're gonna be poor, aren't we?" Now it's my turn to nod. "Great, I'll go to school dressed like the Little Match Girl." Madeline flops, spread-eagled, on the floor.

"What about chairs?" Toby stands up and peers into the bedroom full of mattresses and the bare little kitchen with its Formica-topped table and four mismatched chairs.

"We have chairs, what do you think you're looking at?" I lean back, with my elbows braced.

"Where's da tittens?"

"I mean chairs, chairs like you sit in, that are soft."

"And a sofa. Right, Toby," prods Madeline.

"We'll get those in time," I say defensively.

"Where's da tittens? Where's da mama tat?" Beth tugs at my shirtsleeve.

"And on Wednesday, we can go pick out a phone. You guys can pick the color."

"Red," says Toby.

"And what about Daddy?" Madeline is keeping her voice casual.

"Your daddy will stay in the farmhouse and you guys can see him whenever you want to."

"Red is a stupid color. Harmony has her own phone in her room." Madeline changes the subject. "It's a banana. Can I have my own banana phone?"

"You don't even have your own room anymore, stupid!" Toby shouts in triumph.

Beth curls up in my lap. "Where's da tittens?" she murmurs as she slips into sleep.

When I go to draw a bath for my children and there is no hot water, I am hit by the weight of what I've done. In nine years of marriage I never once even changed a fuse. Beth is asleep in a huddle on her youth bed; Madeline and Toby prance around the tiny bathroom, clad in underpants and shivering. "Why are we here, and why is this tub so yucky?" asks Madeline. I don't have the words to answer Madeline yet and I'm looking for the hot water heater.

"Here, Mom." Toby has scooted into the kitchen ahead of me

and located the hot water heater in a narrow dusty closet. "I'll bet it's that button," he says, reaching down and turning it on.

"I didn't move here to take your childhood away," I tell my five-year-old son. "I moved us here so you could have one." Toby rolls his eyes at Madeline.

I go into the bedroom to untie Beth's shoes and slip them off and to pull covers over her filthy little self. I hope this will give my two older children the opportunity of talking together about some of this chaos, some of the unknown, out of earshot of their erratic mother. I remember when Eve and I would dissect adult behavior under our covers at night; making our own sense of it, trying to harness a world where we lacked control.

. . . . .

The next evening while preparing dinner, I discover that, among the staples I failed to move from the farmhouse, I can also list salt. I could fake almost anything else. "Kids, I'm going to run very fast to the store. I'll be back in two shakes."

Madeline looks up from her coloring. "You mean you're leaving us here? By ourselves?"

"Honey, the store is only five blocks away. It's not like at the big house. Beth is buck naked, by the time I get her dressed I could be at the store and back."

I am relieved to find the A&P not very crowded. As long as I'm here, I pick up some fresh fruit and the paper towels I keep forgetting and ice cream sandwiches for a special dessert. There is only one cashier and the line backs up while she calls out for a "price check." I begin to panic as the line does not move. Finally, in what seems like ten minutes, but is probably only about three, I get my turn, pay, and dash out to the parking lot. I plop the groceries down on the seat and turn the key and nothing happens. Not even the usual groaning of the ignition failing to catch. I try again. "Shit, no, no!" I can't even call the children, we have no phone. They are alone, it is their second night ever in town. I try the key again and again. I bang the steering wheel and throw open the door of the station wagon.

Now the parking lot is deserted, no one arriving, no one leaving the A&P. I run into the store. A bent old lady is going through the checkout line, all the other shoppers are gliding carts down the aisles in the unconscious dream of grocery browsers. Now I'm almost positive I left the kitchen stove on. I remember Madeline's fear of fire. I want to scream, "Help, somebody help me!" But I fear my own hysteria, that I'll begin to scream and will be unable to stop and will get carried off. Then I'd never get home to my children. I stumble back into the darkening parking lot, just as a pickup truck pulls next to my station wagon. I am at the driver's side opening the door before the man in the baseball hat can even turn off the motor.

"Mister, excuse me, mister, but do you have jumper cables?"

The middle-aged farmer is amused at my high-powered rush. "I might, I just might, little lady. Guess you're in—"

"Please, mister, my kids are home alone. And they're so little." The man's face changes, he is out of his truck and fumbling in the truck bed's tool case in a matter of seconds.

· · · · ·

There are three front windows in our shabby town house, our new home. As I drive up, I see that all the lights are on. Each one of my children is framed in a different window. They are standing on the windowsills, legs together and arms spread out. They are frozen there, a miniature Calvary. Perhaps it is some child's game. My heathen children know nothing of crucifixions. I stop the car in front of the house, they don't move. Then I drive around and park the car in the back of the house, by the kitchen door. I try to catch my breath, calm myself. When I walk in, they are waiting for me. They have turned off the stove and have set the table. They have found a candle and have lit it. They thought I wasn't coming home. They have made up spells to bring me back.

CHAPTER VI

*E*RIC RETURNED TO TOWN AND WAS JUST
not as upset as a father and husband should be coming home to
an empty house. Of course the house wasn't really empty, there
were plenty of things in it. Just no wife and kids. Eric is coming
by our little house to talk this afternoon. Again, Rosa has taken
my children with her to the country club pool. She has been such
a rock these last few days. Eric warned me, when he called, that
he hasn't a great deal of time. I catch myself in front of the
bathroom mirror getting ready to fix my hair. For some reason,
this amuses me. "This isn't a date, this is a summit meeting.
You're not Sandra Dee, you're Golda Meir," I tell my shaky reflection.

"Can I fix you some coffee, or a glass of water, or something?"

"No gin?"

"Nope, nothing alcoholic. Sorry." I pull a clean glass from the dish drainer.

I'm standing by the sink and Eric is sitting at the kitchen table, checking his watch every few minutes. I used to like that about him, that he was so busy, so important. It made me feel safe. Even after the children came and he was too busy to help, or be involved, I liked protecting his time. I look at him now and finally see what so much of that was, or is. A wall between himself and feelings. Like Alice's White Rabbit, he is so busy scurrying from the same appointment to the same appointment that he leaves no time for amazement or passion. This man has just lost his family and he's checking his watch. It leaves me to wonder what I've been avoiding by living so long with the White Rabbit. Maybe I was allowed to remain Alice, got to go through childbirth, homemaking, and a crumbling marriage wearing a starched pinafore. All the womanly stuff was just a pretend game. Inside I was allowed to stay a little girl, bewildered by the White Rabbit.

"What should we do about the house?"

"You keep the house, Eric." I wouldn't want that place of bad memories, that cemetery for love's illusion. I also know Eric considers the house legally his, since his parents paid for it.

"I've been advised it's not a good idea to use the same lawyer. If you don't have any objections, Katherine, I'd like to stick with Tom. I've already called him."

I am filling the glass with ice cubes. "Rosa's next-door neighbor is a lawyer, I guess I could—"

"Sounds as good as anything else you could come up with."

"Fine, Eric."

"Keep the station wagon. My parents are going to let me have their Volvo. By the way," he adds, tongue-in-cheek, "they send you their best."

"Return it, of course." I toast the air above his head with the water glass.

145

"And child support, you'll be wanting child support. I mean, at least until you garner the Pulitzer for journalism."

I am now refilling the ice tray. We are almost out of ice. Madeline always returns the trays empty to the freezer. " 'Sarcasm is the protest of the weak,' Eric. Remember that?"

"Tom tells me I can charge you with desertion, sweetheart. So my position isn't all that weak. I'm holding all the cards." I slam the freezer door.

"Well, I'm holding all the kids, Eric. You just take your Waspy money and run. I don't need you, we don't need you."

"I could fight you for the kids and probably win too."

"You'd lose. In court the judge would ask you their names and you wouldn't be able to get them straight!"

Eric is standing now, his voice controlled. "Don't get so emotional, Katherine. We both know the children should be with you. We'll talk visitation, or whatever it's called, in Tom's office. Or at Rosa's next-door neighbor's, if you'd prefer."

He checks his watch one more time. I am certainly getting the point. "I just think we should have a third party present the next time we talk." Eric is heading for the door.

I turn on the faucet and fill the glass. The sound of running water makes me remember our first night together, the rainy New Orleans night when all things were possible. The screen door slams. I think of those two people, how different they were, and yet how much the same. Now I hear his car back out of the rocky driveway. There are a million accusations I could fling after him, but I can't hold Eric accountable because I never wanted responsibility for myself. This whole marriage, these nine years, some part of me had stayed within that dream, that fantasy, of two lovers kissing in the rain. What a long way we came, without ever noticing the journey. I slowly sip the glass of ice water I'd meant to give to Eric. I sip the cool water and deeply wish it was pure bourbon. "Good-bye, Elfin One." I toast the empty air once more.

. . . . .

The children test me constantly. With the dwindling funds left from my mother's insurance policy, we go out to buy furniture. When I get to the store they don't want to leave the car. I have to bribe them.

"Grand Furniture gives free Cokes. They give away Coke in those cute little bottles."

"I thought you said Cokes were bad for us," Madeline challenges me. "That if you left a nail in a glass of Coke it would dissolve the nail. Is that what you're trying to do to our guts? Dissolve them?"

In the store Toby starts up a game of hide and seek with his sisters. I don't want to pick out any furniture without involving the kids, giving them a real say in our new life. But every time I see something I can afford, that's halfway decent looking, I can't find my children. The clerk wishes he hadn't grabbed us up when we walked in. I can tell he's willing to give his commission, maybe even his job, to the first passerby, if we'll just leave. I hate to shop and have no plans to try another store. It's Grand Furniture, or no furniture. "Toby, Madeline, dammit all. Come here, right now! You too, Beth."

"Mister, do you give seconds on Coke?" Madeline is pulling her Shirley Temple imitation. No one has told her she is much too skinny to swing it.

"No he doesn't. He wants to know, and I want to know, what you think of this couch. It's a hide-away. When Papa comes to visit we can fold it open and he'll have a place to sleep."

"I think it looks like dog shit."

I grab Toby by the back of his neck and slam him down into the sofa's matching chair. "That'll be enough out of you. You just sit in this dog shit chair until we're ready to leave. Understand?"

I smile serenely at the salesclerk, who is not looking at me. He's watching Beth, who has just climbed onto the sofa in question and is squatting to pee. I grab her, but it's too late. We buy the sofa, not the chair, but the sofa. The store has free delivery.

. . . . .

"When I first walked in that office and asked him to put me on full time, my greatest fear was that he'd open an old file and toss all my free-lance articles on his desk. And they'd be smeared with red pencil, bloody with corrections."

"Sounds like you're champing at the bit, raring to go," says Esther.

"I don't really dread work starting, in fact I look forward to it. I just hope there is a reversal process for atrophy of the brain. I also dread what my suddenly taking off for the workplace will do to the kids." Rosa, Esther, and I are sitting under the trees in Rosa's yard. "That will be a lot more radical for them than not having a dad. Eric was like an occasional visitor to their lives, rather than a parent."

Jeff is pushing chicken around on the barbecue grill a few yards away. He and Charlie, Esther's husband, are drinking beer and tending the fire for our Labor Day picnic. In deference to my new sobriety, we women are sipping iced tea. The five children are in the play yard on the other side of the house.

"Your kids will be fine, great, in fact," says Rosa.

"Remember, our mothers didn't work, and look at us," says Esther, crossing her eyes and sticking an unlit cigarette in her ear.

"Our mothers didn't work and they didn't read psychology." Rosa smiles over at Esther, who is now trying to keep the cigarette balanced in her ear, while she reaches for another one to smoke.

Rosa continues. "Some of the weird manipulations they pulled are amazing. But then, imagine having to raise kids without 'Captain Kangaroo.'"

"Or 'Sesame Street,' for Christ's sake. Wonder how we learned to read," Esther says with exaggerated wonderment. She has abandoned fake fingernails for false eyelashes and is now wearing her hair cut very short and bleached an eerie blond. With her eyes opened extra wide, she looks for all the world like a Kewpie doll.

"Eric's mother told me that when she was having kids the current theory was not to hold the babies, that it would spoil them."

"Well, that certainly explains your warm and loving husband, Katherine. Ex-husband," Rosa adds as she gives me a little pat on the head.

"I just have this image of Eric, an infant crying and crying. And his mother deliberately not picking him up." I take a sip of the sticky tea. "It kills me."

"Just so long as the mothers always get the blame. Charlie tosses a ball with Nathan about twice a month, and he's in the clear. Nathan gets in a little trouble at school and it's my fault 'cause I weaned him too soon, or spend too much time away from home. Every time I think of *Portnoy's Complaint,* I want to lodge my own fucking complaint. Where was good old Dad while Portnoy's mom was fucking him up?" Esther is not terribly sympathetic to the writings of Philip Roth.

. . . . .

My first day at the office is one of the longest of my life. Each time I look up at the clock, the minute hand seems to have slipped back one dot. I labor over an introductory sentence while all around me my colleagues, the young and glib, pull and exchange finished sheets of paper from their typewriters. I can't remember how to spell the simplest word and worry over using up the ribbon and not knowing how to change it on an unfamiliar typewriter. When I walk into the lunchroom to eat my peanut butter sandwich, the raucous conversation slows, then stills. My fellow workers stop talking about office intrigue and the latest movies to ask polite questions about my children, my new neighborhood. When I try to smile and politely answer their questions, I think peanut butter has glued my top lip to my teeth. I return to my desk and grab the dictionary to look up how to spell "regional." By the end of the longest day of my life I have one very rough draft of an article about a university research center. I make plans for a future as a waitress at the Greyhound Bus Station coffee shop.

. . . . .

The children and I are gradually falling into a pattern. I've made a deal with the editor that I can work on portions of my columns at home. So I'm free by three o'clock each day. I pick the kids up, stop by the grocery store, and run errands with the children in the car. When we first began our new household, I discovered my children didn't have a clue about sitting to eat, in a humanlike fashion, at the table. Eric and my extended cocktail time hadn't been conducive to family dinners. Gradually the children pick up basic skills, like sitting in their chairs, rather than standing. They learn to chew with their mouths closed.

"Toby, put your napkin on your lap."

"Yeah, Tob, cover up your ugly penis."

"Madeline, this wasn't what I had in mind for dinner banter."

"Dirls don't have a penis, wite, Mom?"

I cut Beth's pork chop into little pieces as she climbs out of her chair. In addition to training my children to break bread in a traditional fashion, I'm working on getting Beth to sleep less. Tonight she is staying alert all through dinner.

"He don't even got his penis on."

"Get out from under the table, Beth."

. . . . .

"Katherine, poetic writing has its place. But its place is not in a story about the university taking over downtown real estate. Your editorials are fine, well, they're all right; but, frankly, your straight reporting sucks."

The editor is being kind. I know I'm keeping my job because he sees me scrambling around with my three kids. The man is not being professional and I'll be damned if I'll punish his kindness with amateur writing. I've given up my lunch hour to sit in on a journalism class at the university. I get up every morning two hours before the kids do and write and rewrite my pieces by dawn's early light.

Michael, a young journalism graduate from West Virginia, has been helping me at work. Whenever time permits he checks my copy before I turn it in.

"There are hardly any marks on this article. Am I getting better, or what?" I sit on the edge of Michael's desk.

"You're getting better."

"You swear?"

"I swear. Now can I talk you into cutting your class and going to lunch with me?" He is a lanky, long-haired redhead. He looks like a basketball player. He looks a lot like that Walton guy who had some connection to Patty Hearst's kidnapping.

"Not a chance, young man. That woman is kind enough to let me audit her class, I'm surely not going to be an ingrate."

He stands up and puts a cover over his typewriter. "Look, Katherine, I'm not all that young. And everybody cuts at least one class."

"Not me, I'm making up for lost time."

"How about dinner then, or a movie, or, or we can take your kids to the circus."

I grab a fistful of my shoulder-length hair and pile it on top of my head, alluringly. "Michael, are you trying to date me? Am I Anne Bancroft? Are you Dustin Hoffman?"

"Come on, Katherine. I'm twenty-three years old!"

I let my hair drop. "And to think I thought you were young. Michael, I'm nearly thirty, I'm too old to date you."

"You won't be thirty for almost two years. I went through your file."

. . . . .

Eric's parents are visiting so the kids are spending all day Saturday and Saturday night out at Eric's. Michael and I have just returned from a long afternoon hike in the mountains. Now I'm sitting in his small garage apartment watching him cut up vegetables.

"How'd you learn to cook?"

"You don't know that I can. The proof of the pudding . . ." He holds the large knife by its handle and the tip of the blade, rapidly chopping a stalk of celery into paper-thin miniature crescents.

"Julia Child wishes for such perfect celery slices." I reach down to rub my calf. "God, I'm sore already. I'll probably need crutches by tomorrow."

"What did you expect, after hiking for three hours in flip-flops." Michael puts down the knife and reaches for a dish towel.

"They were my sturdiest flip-flops. I just hate women in those combat boots."

"Katherine, hiking boots are vastly different from combat boots. Here." Michael kneels in front of me and puts my foot on his thigh. "I took a six-week course and now know how to give one dynamite massage."

He pushes my jean leg up and begins to knead my sore muscle. I know I should object, but it feels so good. He works in silence, first one calf, then the other. I lean back in the chair, close my eyes, and listen to the slow drip of the kitchen faucet, Michael's breathing. All of a sudden Michael takes his hands from my leg, leans back, and slaps his open palms on his thighs.

"We have all night to fix dinner. How 'bout I heat up some oil and give you a real massage? Music, candles, the whole shebang."

"You mean I get naked? Is this a trick?" I sit up.

"Not a trick, a massage. You can leave your clothes on." He stands. "It won't be the same, but you can leave your clothes on. Or we can just forget it. Cook dinner, go to the movies. You name it." He heads back toward the chopping board.

"You mean that, don't you? Whatever I say, we'll do."

He faces me and leans his lanky frame against the sink. "Of course I do. This is your first night off in, what? Three months? Two? Most of my nights are free. Of course we'll do what you pick." He folds his arms and gives me the kind of grin Toby gives when he finishes putting together a puzzle.

"Try ten years. Try it's my first night off in almost ten years." I walk over to him and press my open hand to the side of his face. "I think I'd love a massage. You do all your heebie-jeebie ritual stuff and I'll go take my clothes off."

When I walk out of the bathroom wrapped in a musty towel, Michael has cleared the covers from his bed. He's turned out the lights and lit candles. Wonderful piano music is playing and the drab bedroom seems transformed. Michael steps up to the bed, holding a small jar of, what I assume is, oil.

"Do you like the music? It's Keith Jarrett, his concert at Köln."

"It is perfect," I say, and stretch out on the bed. The flannel sheet feels warm against my stomach.

He slips his fingers into the top of the towel. "O.K. if I take this off?"

I nod into the pillow. Like the sounds are part of the music, I hear Michael rub his hands together. When he presses his hands onto my shoulders they are warm and I smell the faint scent of almonds. His thumbs stroke the tendons in my neck.

"Ow!" I raise up on my elbows.

"Relax, Katherine. I feel like I'm untangling knots, not like I'm touching a beautiful woman."

I do. I gradually, and finally, relax. Michael moves his hands over me, starting at my neck and moving down to my feet, without speaking. The record stops, then starts again. He must have set it to automatically replay. When Madeline was little I used to do that with "Old MacDonald." She'd sit half the afternoon listening to that same song and I'd be able to steal reading time. His hands feel wonderful, slow and sure.

"Now turn over." His voice comes out of the music.

I turn over, keeping my eyes shut. In my life, I've only been naked with Eric. If I keep my eyes closed, it won't be like I'm really naked. His fingertips rub oil into my temples.

"Relax, Katherine. Open your eyes, let go."

"Feel this," I say, and take his hand and press it over my chest.

"Feel this . . ." Michael takes my hand and even through his shirt I can feel his heart beating as hard, as tellingly, as mine.

He leans over for more oil, presses his hands together, then moves them from my collarbone, over my breasts, down to the hollow of my belly. For a long time he touches me, until I begin to move under his hands.

"What a wonderful body. I knew, I just knew it would be beautiful."

"How can you say . . . my belly is scarred, I—"

He bends down and kisses me. Then, his voice muffled as he talks into the road map of scars on my stomach, he says, "I knew these would be here too, and I knew I would want to kiss them." His hands stay on my breasts, his mouth moves over me, the music plays, I'm lifting my hips to him and before I know it, or can think, or speak, I'm climaxing. His hands move over me and I come again. I'm floating and flying, I can hardly breathe and yet I'm breathing the purest oxygen. This has never happened to me and I try to move away from him, twist back over on my stomach, and feel his hand lifting, pulling, opening my thighs.

"No! Stop it, Michael, stop it."

He takes his hands away and lies down beside me. "What— what's wrong, Katherine?"

"It—this feels too good. It's not right. And what about you? Look, you still even have your clothes on."

He pushes my hair back from my damp forehead. "I know, I know that. My time is coming, or . . ." He grins at me. "I'll come in time. Relax, Katherine, it's not bad to feel good. You're paying attention to the ghost of Catholic pasts." He slowly runs his forefinger over my lips. "And I'll come in time, don't you worry. Right now, pleasuring you is pleasuring me."

"That's a new one on me," I say, and pull Michael's sweet young face to me. I kiss him for the first time.

. . . . .

Through some kind of warped legal maneuvering, my children are to spend Christmas with Eric's parents, so my father and Eve are visiting us for Thanksgiving. Eve has become engaged to one of her LSU statistics colleagues, but hasn't brought him with her because we have no room for him. My father is horrified that his grandchildren and his daughter live in a tiny house while Eric holds on to the farmhouse.

"Daddy, you couldn't pay me to live there. It's too isolated and there are too many bad memories."

"Think of your children, Katherine."

"That is who I'm thinking of, or whom. I like it that in the night I can hear all three of them breathing. I like sleeping with Madeline."

"Yeah, me too," Eve adds dryly. She, my oldest daughter, and I have been sharing a bed.

"Well, at least let's get those poor kids a pet."

They return from their shopping trip and, in addition to three bags of toys that will only clutter this little house irrevocably, my father has bought a hamster, cage and all. The kids are jubilant. I haven't the heart to tell my father just how much I don't want to be in charge of one more life. It takes more than I have most days to just keep loving, being loyal, to these children. I think, as an act of compassion for my children, I would pass my motherhood on, if there were really anyone to pass it on to. The hamster's bright little eyes make me want to cry. I don't want to be in charge of one more life, even one so minor. My father is only trying to help.

He is trying to help when he goes outside to trim the rose-bushes away from our clothesline pole. Eve and I watch him through the little window above our sink.

"He has aged so much since I saw him last."

"He misses her, Katherine. He's not getting over it."

The kids are playing around my father's legs and he blinks in the sunlight that seems to blind him as he tries to trim the autumn bare vines. He reminds me of Robert Frost at Kennedy's inauguration, that same white-haired, bewildered presence. My father accidentally cuts the clothesline instead of a strand of rosebush. He looks toward the house to see if anyone has been watching. Eve and I duck.

. . . . .

It is Thanksgiving morning and everybody has gone for a long walk so I can have the small kitchen to myself. It is four months since we moved to this house and I still lack most of the utensils I need to get up even an ordinary dinner. I didn't sleep well in the crowded bed last night, the turkey isn't fully thawed, and the goddamned hamster is running round and round on its squeaky wheel. I take a finger full of Crisco with the intent of oiling the wheel. But when I open the cage, the hamster shoots out.

"Damn!" I wipe the glob of Crisco off on a paper towel and head after the hamster just in time to see it scurry under the bedroom dresser. It burrows back in the corner between the dresser and the wall. I can't quite reach the little sucker. Without thinking, I pull out the dresser. The mirror that has been propped on top of the dresser drops down behind and pins the hamster. The hamster is screaming, I mean really screaming. Its scream sounds human. I start to scream and cry too. As I cry, I pull the dresser out all the way. I lift the mirror, and take hold of the hamster at the same time. Miraculously, the little creature is still alive. But when I put him back in his cage, I see that his hind legs are dragging behind him. Maybe he is only stunned, or bruised. Maybe he'll be fine by the time the kids get home.

"Ohh, that turkey smells great!" Eve is a bustle of holiday enthusiasm. The kids are piling through the door behind her.

"Papa! Look at our hamster. What's wrong, do you think?" Toby kneels by the cage.

Maybe it'll be O.K. by tomorrow, I think. Maybe I can build a little go-cart for its hind legs. My father kneels beside his grandson. I can tell he thinks he's screwed up, thinks he's gotten a bum hamster for his grandchildren. I don't want to tell anyone what happened. I don't want them to know how much the hamster was hurt, how it screamed. How it was all my fault.

Mercifully, the little fellow lives until after my father and Eve return to Louisiana. I tell the kids not to mention the hamster's death when their grandfather calls.

. . . . .

"In the backseat of his car, if you can believe it. Long legs and all."

"Katherine, you're gonna break his heart."

"No, no, you have it all wrong, Rosa. He's going to break mine. Michael leaves for someplace in central California in two weeks. We've both kept that as a deadline."

My kids are asleep in our only bedroom. Rosa, Esther, and I are sitting around my kitchen table.

"How do you feel about that?" asks Rosa. "About Michael leaving?"

"Sometimes I think that if I asked him to stay, he would. But then what would I do?" I light a cigarette and blow out the match with a breath of smoke. "I mean, he's just a boy. A great

157

lover, but a boy. The sex is great, but what does sex have to do with life?"

"He's your first. I mean after Eric. Right? Zombie man doesn't count." Esther is amused. "You Catholics amaze me."

"Esther, go dye your hair, or something. Let Katherine finish. This is the wave of the future, I swear. I read a fairly scholarly article, saying more and more older women will be attracted to younger men as the women's movement gathers momentum."

"Doesn't sound scholarly to me, sounds like *Cosmo*. And I resent you implying my hair is dyed." Esther raises her middle finger in Rosa's direction.

"I didn't 'imply,' I 'inferred,' you did all the rest." Rosa laughs and grabs at Esther's obscene finger. Then she turns back to me. "But really, how is he around the kids?"

"I don't want to confuse the kids with a man who is just 'passing through,' so he's only come over here a couple of times. Totally chaotic dinners. I mean, you can imagine. After they're asleep, we sneak out to his car. Thank God I have a driveway. I just wish Michael weren't quite so tall."

"A whole new world is opening up. When we were getting you out of that house, I didn't even think about you dating, or finding a new man. It's happening so fast." Rosa wears her dark blond hair the same way she did when I met her. Since beginning graduate school she dresses more conservatively, otherwise she looks the way she did seven years ago.

"Come on, Rosa. I told you. It's a fling. You two had yours in college. I'm having mine now."

"Retrogressive fucking," Esther adds.

. . . . .

Michael looks tired, he has shadows under his eyes and even his voice is tired. "I agreed to take this California job before I ever met you. Now it is killing me to go. It feels like a mistake. I'll miss you, Katherine."

"I'll miss you too." It is Michael's last night in town and I've hired a baby-sitter so we can have a little quality time. He and I are stretched out naked on his bare mattress, sharing a cigarette. We're surrounded by boxes and the last minute debris of packing.

He leans up on his elbow, "No, I'll really miss you, Katherine. Not like I'd miss cigarettes if I gave them up, or will miss the good folks of the *Leeston Gazette.*"

"I am one of those 'good folks,' " I say, blowing a stream of smoke in his face.

He bats the smoke away and continues. "Why won't you take me seriously? You avoid any real conversation, any attempt at intimacy. Is it because you're afraid to take yourself seriously?"

"You're not Jimmy Olsen after all. You're Sigmund Freud." I run my fingers down the red fur of his chest. "Sigmund, I don't think anything could be more serious than raising three children all alone."

He grabs my hand, gently, as I open my fingers over his lower belly. "You didn't have to be alone. You could have let me in. I wasn't just interested in humping, you know. I would have been glad to do more things with your kids."

I am wiggling my wrist, trying to get out of Michael's grip.

"Katherine, you seem to need to have your men be bad guys."

"If you let go of my hand, I'll show you a magic trick."

It makes me slightly desperate to think this is our last time to have sex. What a brief interlude this has been. I will miss this, this body grappling, this pure, pure pleasure. This new world that has just opened, and now, is closing again. I don't want to talk, I want to make a great deal of love. As though I could store love-making the way a camel stores water for the desert.

"I don't want to leave you, Katherine. Are you listening to me at all?"

He doesn't know that sex can last longer than love. I lean over Michael, let my hair fall in his face, and quiet him with a kiss.

A n n   G o e t h e

. . . . .

Marie has joined me for Christmas. I thought of going to Louisiana, but the kindly editor has asked that I be part of his skeleton crew. I get to pay Bill back for all the rope he's given me and I get to avoid Christmas in Louisiana without Mother. Not that my little house without the kids is exactly festive.

"On the first date, like public school kids? Really, Katherine?"

"Rosa had the same reaction, Marie. Remember, Michael was a kid. These young guys are used to playing things straight."

Marie pours another cup of eggnog for herself. "Did you like it?"

I smile and nod, emphatically, "It was great. He was my friend and he was my first real lover. These young boys are very into pleasing their women. I recommend it."

"Yuck." Marie has a foamy white mustache but sits across from me as if she is a perfectly normal person.

"Marie, remember Sister Helena telling us that women are made to give and men are made to take? Sweet Michael never heard that lecture."

Marie laughs and raises her eyebrows, which makes me laugh. "I have this theory, Katherine, about us Catholic girls, or at least convent girls. Sex is too big a deal, we wait too long. When it comes along we either hate it or we love it. We're frigid or we're nymphos. I'm the former. Which was a real turn-on to Dr. Jekyll. To quote your well-spoken daughter, gross, gross, gross."

Marie still has her mustache and thinks I'm laughing because she does such a great Madeline.

"Did I tell you that my mother said she saw Susan's grandfather in that fancy old folks' home outside Lafayette? She said his mind is completely gone. As soon as Mrs. Blake died that old man just fell apart."

"And she was so mean to him! I'll never figure the man-woman thing out." I drop back on my pillow.

160

"Mama said most of the money got left to Susan and they're trying to get her to come back to the States to untangle things. I hear she doesn't want to." Marie reaches up to turn off the light. "Just like a Communist."

"I tried calling her old number when I left Eric. No answer."

"Same with me," she mumbles.

We lie quietly in the darkness on Madeline's mattress. Just as I'm about to drift off, I get an idea. "Marie, why don't you move here? We have florist shops in Leeston too, you know."

"I saw that, you have two. No thanks, I'm a city girl."

"Woman, you're a city woman."

"Same difference, Katherine." My friend sounds cranky, "Don't start all that feminist crap. You're paying your own rent and suddenly you're a revolutionary."

I sit up. "You're so New Orleans, Marie. I'd rather clean other people's bathrooms than be a female in New Orleans. All of you are kept women. I mean you were an extreme case, but even the married ones. In fact, especially them."

"That is a really rotten thing to say, Katherine. Just because you're mad at Eric doesn't mean you have to be mad at everybody."

I reach up and turn on the light. Marie grabs her pillow and puts it over her face.

"It's the truth. And I'm not mad at Eric. I would be mad, I'd be crazy, in fact, if I hadn't been able to leave him. Getting out of that marriage was another chance at life and another chance at mothering. So, I'm not mad at Eric. But that's not what I want to talk about. I want to talk about the women of New Orleans—at least our class of women—being stuck in the nineteenth century. That city is one big Good Ole Boys Club and all the women are being held captive by the Junior League. Exposing your mind, if you're a woman, is tantamount to exposing your breast on St. Charles Avenue."

Marie's voice is muffled under the pillow. "Let's just make a few sweeping generalizations here, Katherine." She lifts the pillow. "I certainly wouldn't want to find you being fair. I swear, Susan goes off to Europe and Communism and you take her place, putting everybody down. I don't care about any kind of club or the Junior League. I just want to go to sleep." She flops the pillow back on her face.

"I don't care about them either. I just love you, Marie. Even if you're outta time, like the Stones say. Merry Christmas." I turn out the light and lie for a long time thinking of all the changes that have come in five months. I feel that I slept through the Big Show, but am starting to catch up by reading all the old reviews, hanging out in the lobby. The talk at the newspaper, the new world Michael opened for me, the way of enjoying, meeting, my children all are part of my catching up. Nineteen seventy-four is drawing to a close and, after the long sleep, I lean toward the new year with anticipation.

. . . . .

"Happy New Year, Katherine! Thought I'd call and see if you were longing for your old copy editor. The only letter I've gotten from you was pretty colorless."

"Oh, Michael, I wrote that when the kids were in Delaware at Christmas and I was feeling blah. I'll write a real letter soon." It is good to hear his voice. His timing is bad, though. When the phone rang I was just getting ready to pour the milk and Madeline shot me a look as if I were deliberately sabotaging our holiday gathering. Toby takes the milk carton from my hand.

"How are the kids?"

"They're great. Michael, I have a million things to tell you, but we're just sitting down to New Year's dinner. We're having black-eyed peas for money and cabbage for luck."

"It's the other way around, Katherine."

"Right. It's just so chaotic here. But that's what I meant." Toby is carefully pouring the milk, every glass to the very brim. Beth will immediately soak herself with the first sip.

"Look, I'll let you go, but write, O.K.?"

"I will. I will, I promise. And, Michael? I miss you. We all miss you, everybody at the paper misses you."

. . . . .

Our first winter in the little house in town is almost over. We are learning to live our new life when the phone call comes from Louisiana. It is Eve. "Katherine, there is very little explanation for it, but Daddy has suddenly taken a turn for the worse."

"What does that mean? People say that in bad television shows, Eve. 'A turn for the worse.' What does it mean, what does it really mean!" I am holding the office phone and banging my head softly against the wall.

"Big sister, I think it means our daddy is dying . . . Katherine?" I bang my head a little harder. "Katherine?"

I take a deep breath. "I thought he lost his voice, that was all. I thought he was in the hospital being tested for a form of existential laryngitis. I thought he was whispering, whispering like maybe he wanted to speak to spirits, like maybe it was a way for him to talk to Mama, or the past, that he could sneak into the past. Like maybe if he whispered, like you do in the library. You know how in the library—"

"Katherine! Listen to me, Katherine. He has asked for you. He seems to really need to talk to you. Can you fly down here? Can you get a plane?"

"A plane?" I ask vaguely.

"Stick with me, honey. Yes, a plane, an airplane. Can you fly down here pronto?" Now I have twisted the phone cord around my wrist. One of the reporters is looking at me, anxiously.

"No," I moan. "I can't. I can't fly there. I haven't any money, the children . . ." The cord is pulled so tightly the veins in my hand are bulging.

"Katherine, I'll give you the money, we just need—"

163

"I'm coming, Eve. I'm driving, with the children. I'll be there just after sunrise."

"O.K., fine, Katherine. Drive straight to the hospital. He's in Sacred Heart Hospital, Room 229. Can you remember that? Room 229."

"Tell him to wait. Tell Daddy to wait, tell him we're coming, tell him . . ." I hang up the phone. As I turn to walk away, the receiver jumps from its hook. I have forgotten to unwrap the cord from my wrist.

I dash into each of the kids' classrooms babbling, like an idiot, to their teachers. I have tried so hard at their schools to seem rational and capable. I belong to all the goddamned PTAs. Every single day I brush Madeline's hair until it is shiny and braid it into neat tight braids. No one would ever guess how crazy and chaotic our mornings are. How we can never find the hairbrush and Madeline has always lost her homework and Beth won't get up and Toby absolutely hates whatever we're having for breakfast. I spent a half week of my paycheck to buy Toby a pair of shoes that look like all the other pairs all the public school first-graders wear. I send Beth to her nursery school in little pastel dresses, the sashes tied perfectly. Now I am blowing all my groundwork. These teachers will feel sorry for my children because their mother is a crazy person who crashes into their classrooms demanding her children. Like they are certificates of deposit that have matured on the day of a bank failure.

"Where are we going, Mommy? Why do you have a pencil stuck in your hair?"

We are heading to the house. I figure I can dedicate ten minutes to packing for four people for an undetermined length of time. "Madeline, we're going to Louisiana to see Papa. He's very sick." Madeline starts to cry. "Don't worry, honey, Papa will—"

"But you said I could go over to Harmony's house after school. You said," wails Madeline.

"Is he gonna die?" asks Toby. He is huddled in the backseat

with his arms folded. When my father and Eve last visited us, Daddy spent hours out in the yard with Toby. There were a lot of secrets and a lot of anti-women-bossing-men-around talk.

"Our tat died. Wite, Mommy?" Beth is cheerful and alert.

"Put your seat belt on, Beth."

Toby's voice is even quieter. "Like Granny, huh? He's gonna die like she did."

"What's a Dranny?"

. . . . .

I am on Louisiana I-10 where it stretches over the Spillway swamp as the sun begins to rise. Farther from Bellebend than I want to be, though I have broken speed limits all night. A few hours after midnight I hit a dog on an Alabama highway and didn't even slow the station wagon. Now slender-legged water birds stand as silhouettes backed by the swamp's shadowed palmetto leaves. Louisiana, *la Louisianne.* I roll the window down to smell the water, the mud scent to the air. First light is tinting far-off Lake Pontchartrain a bloody pink. The air is warm, and I think of my father's tenacious defense of Louisiana as "God's Masterpiece." I consider waking the children to show them the swamp, the birds. Then I remember the feeling of falling asleep in the backseat, with my parents driving, the grown-ups in charge. It never occurred to me to doubt that they knew the way. If I wake my children, they will only worry that we might be lost. Besides, we're an hour from breakfast and I need to meet my land alone.

I missed what my father had to say to me my first day at Holy Name Academy and I missed what he had to tell me on my wedding day. I won't miss this message, I won't. "Hold on, Daddy," I whisper to my whispering parent.

. . . . .

If God bothered to look, He'd be really pissed to see what has been done to His Masterpiece. It is almost full light as I drive onto the bridge over the Mississippi into Bellebend. As far as I can see, the sky is dense with gray smoke, lit by flares from burn-off valves in the big oil refineries. The riverbanks, where I played as a child, look like an atomic wasteland. The air is foul and my window is rolled tightly up. I don't want my children inhaling this trash. I think of my father's rantings about the greed of Bellebend citizens and politicians, selling off great expanses of land to oil refineries, fertilizer plants. "Thirty pieces of silver. We've been betrayed for thirty pieces of silver," he always says. I don't wake the children until after I've crossed the river. The last time I was here, I must have been oblivious, I didn't see this horror. The avenue of trees that welcomed people entering Belle-bend is gone.

The hospital is a small two-story building not far from the bridge. I pull into the deserted parking lot and stop the station wagon near the front door. Beth and Madeline have their eyes open, but are still lying down. Toby is sitting with his back to me, looking out the rear window. "Do you guys want to wait in the lobby, or here in the car? They don't let children in hospitals. I won't be long."

"Can we have Terrios?"

"At home, Beth. At Papa's house. I'll be right back, then we can go to Papa's and get breakfast. I just want to let Papa know we're here." Since no one moves, I assume my groggy children have opted to stay in the car.

The wide elevators in hospitals always give me the creeps. I choose to take the stairway. The second-floor hallway opens at the top of the flight of stairs onto a very small waiting area. The room to the right is 201, the room to the left 231, I turn left— 230, 229. I walk into 229, but Eve must have made a mistake. This room is empty.

The cheap beige spread is stretched tightly over the bed. The curtains, pulled back from a window overlooking a barren sugar-cane field, let a hazy light into the empty room. I run my fingers lightly over the ridges of the bedspread. "Two, two, nine; two, two, nine. Eve's numbers, Eve knows her numbers. She's not like me, she knows her numbers." I think I am whispering. My father has whispered in this room. I will whisper with him, it's not too late. "Moon, tars, Daddy."

He got well. That's it. He sat up in the middle of the night and was cured. While I was racing through the night they couldn't reach me to say "false alarm." To say everything is going to be fine. He is a good man with faith in God and miracles happen for those people. There is no message, no important message, nothing that he can't tell me later, later when there is more time. My children are waiting for me. They are hungry and we can go home, home for a big Louisiana breakfast. Eve and Daddy will both be talking at once. And I can rest. They can love these children for a little while and I can rest from the long, long trip.

. . . . .

When we pull into the driveway of my parents' house, the truth is a muffled gong banging against my chest. I don't want to get out of the car. I don't want to go in. My father is alive until I walk into the house where he lived. Out here I can go on lying and he'll go on living. When we get out of this car, my father will be dead.

Though it is only seven in the morning, there are four or five cars parked in the driveway. I can see that all the lights are on, and I see people moving behind the curtains. I turn off the motor and sit very still, with my hands in my lap. The children are rattling the childproof locks.

"Mom, this is it, right?"

"Right, Madeline. This is it." I don't move.

"Well?" Madeline is exasperated.

"Does Papa have tereal at dis house? Does Papa have Terrios?" Beth is leaning over the seat patting my cheeks. Then the car is quiet.

The children are waiting for me to tell them what to do. Beth tumbles into the front seat and climbs on my lap. She squeezes my lips to make "fish lips" and then laughs. "How 'bout a little tiss, Mommy?"

"Papa isn't going to be here, is he, Mom?" Toby's voice is very quiet.

When we walk into the house the people gathered in the living room stop talking. One of Eve's friends, a kindly woman named Jean, stands and walks over to hug me. "Katherine, you must be exhausted." She kneels in front of my children. Madeline hates this and steps back. "My name is Jean. John has been fixing breakfast for you. I'll bet you're hungry."

"Terrios?" asks Beth pleasantly.

Eve walks in. "Katherine!"

She opens her arms, and I wrap mine around her and whisper into her ear. "Help me with this, Eve. I've got to get these kids situated." She lets go of me, hugs the children, and leads them into the kitchen with promises of excess syrup for their pancakes.

I begin to sleepwalk around the room, greeting an old friend of my father's, greeting my parents' next-door neighbor. I meet Eve's fiancé, John, and a couple more of Eve's friends. Eve returns; she has left the children eating pancakes in the kitchen with Jean.

We sit on the picnic table under my father's beloved oak tree. The warm air in late February is as unreal as this entire trip. Eve is speaking slowly, tears are running down her cheeks. "I'd been beside his bed all night. He fell asleep at about two. A real sleep, gentle, you know? And I drove back here to take a quick shower and change my clothes. When I returned, he was gone. At first I didn't know, I thought he was asleep. His arms were crossed on his chest. You know, the way they always showed the dead saints on holy cards? His arms were crossed on his chest and the room was quiet. Too quiet. I put my fingers to his mouth. And he wasn't breathing. The room was very dark. If I'd turned on a light I would have known he was dead. I hate that he was by himself. I told him you'd be here, that you were on your way."

All day people come by, kind people carrying great dishes of spicy Louisiana food, cakes and pies made with too much sugar. The visitors help themselves to drinks from the bottles of bourbon and gin and mixers sitting on the sideboard. They tell stories about my father. Wonderful stories. I keep my children nearby so they can hear the stories. The children watch me, looking for signs of breakage, but I am a rock.

In the late afternoon Jean takes my children off to play with hers. She lures them away from me with the promise of an actual video game in her home den. Shortly after they leave an old boyfriend comes by. Philip and I had a gentle teen romance going the summer I left for Michigan. When I returned from my times with married Jim, I had outgrown poor Philip. I know he still carries a torch. He's always been nervous around me; he wrote a very long letter to me the night before he got married.

We are surveying the remains of my father's winter garden. "No one in my life made a stronger, a more humane impression upon me than your father, Katherine. I know that's true for plenty people around here. He was a good man," says Philip.

"I keep waiting for him to walk out here with a tray of drinks for us," I say, wondering why, with my children gone, I'm still unable to cry.

"Well, if I can do anything, anything at—"

"You can," I say suddenly. "You can make love to me."

Philip looks as though I have slapped him. "What? I don't understand. What are you saying?"

I take a step closer to him. "I'm saying I want you to make love to me. I want you to have sex with me . . . Please."

"You don't know what you're saying. Katherine, sweetheart, you're just upset."

"Philip, you asked what you can do. That's what you can do, you can service me. As they say."

169

He backs away from me, his eyes are watering. "When . . . how?"

I reach out and take his hand and run my fingers lightly down his palm. "Now. And however you usually do it. I don't need anything fancy. The missionary position will be just fine."

"Katherine, your daddy died a few hours ago and—"

"And I need you between my legs. If you don't lay me down and enter me, I'm not going to make it. Please, Philip."

I lead him into the musty closed-up garage. My father's old Buick gleams in the darkness. "Let's take our clothes off outside, it'll be easier," I whisper.

After we've undressed I put my hand on his chest and feel his racing heart. I kneel on the gritty concrete floor and overcome my own small revulsion to touch this frightened man with my lips and my hands, until he is ready for me. We climb onto the backseat, I close my eyes and spread my legs. The leather feels smooth and cool on my bare back.

When I finally climax, I am sweaty and flushed, and I begin to cry. Philip holds me for a little while. Then I ask him to leave. He does as I ask; he quietly dresses outside the car and quietly leaves. At the funeral, this gentle man won't be able to meet my eye, and I can add using him to my list of wrongdoings. I lie in a damp naked heap in the corner of the backseat of my father's abandoned car and cry. I cry for my father and for my mother and for all that is gone.

. . . . .

"You think we may have a Father Thing?" I ask Marie. It is the night before the funeral and Eve is reading to my children while my old school friend and I catch up in the living room.

"You mean the way we gravitate toward men with silver hair?"

"You know, so much of what happened with me and Eric just really wasn't his fault. I screwed up any chances we had to be partners. Sorta the way I always confused 'minotaur' and 'mentor.'"

"That's right, Katherine. Blame that disaster on yourself. I mean, you were almost twenty years old. Of course you should have whipped that old boy into shape!"

"Don't mess with anyone you can't look square in the eye is gonna be my new motto," I say.

Marie is nursing a glass of straight bourbon and is slumped in my father's chair with one leg slung over the worn armrest. "I think the long nightmare with Dr. Jekyll may have cured me," she says. Like me, Marie is still adjusting to single life. Though she walked away from her sicko surgeon lover unfettered and empty-handed. A true fresh start, no children, no division of property.

"Electra notwithstanding, I know I can't imagine life without Daddy," I say. "It's not even that we saw one another that often. It was just that total acceptance, that knowing that no matter how much I screwed up, he'd be there to catch me, to save us. I hate that my children have to grow up not knowing him. I—I . . . Marie, remember Sister Helena sitting by the glow of that little lamp at the end of that long marble hall?" My friend nods. "Don't you wish we could just go and crumple up at her feet and tell her how differently things are turning out? Don't you just wish that we could?"

. . . . .

The day following the funeral, when I am packing the old station wagon for the trip back to North Carolina, my grieving sister comes to get me. She walks me into the backyard with her arm around my waist. Eve shows me a basketball hoop set up in the far corner of our father's lawn.

"You know, after you left Eric, Daddy naturally assumed you and the kids would come here to live. He had that basketball hoop put up for Toby." Eve takes her arm from around my waist and points to the basketball hoop.

I think how Toby is several years away from being tall enough to even dream of throwing a ball through that hoop. It reminds me of the tricycle Daddy bought me long before I could reach the pedals.

"Katherine, I think he would have lived, if you had moved here. It would have given him a reason. He was at such loose ends, so confused and sad when Mama died. When he put that hoop up, he was like his old self." She walks away from me and sits on the picnic table. "Why didn't you, Katherine? Why didn't you come home?"

I stand back, slightly away from my sister. "I—I don't know. It didn't occur to me, I guess. I sorta think of Bellebend as where I'm from, never where I'm going. I—I made my bed in North Carolina, I guess that's where I thought the children and I should lie."

"Even if it killed Daddy?"

I am fighting tears. "Eve, listen to what you're saying! Listen."

I have lost both of my parents. I am an orphan. All that is left of my childhood is the grim, pale woman facing me. Yet—yet, if I had a gun in my hand right now, I think I would kill her. She is calling me a murderer, the killer of our lost father. I would shoot Eve through her suddenly cold heart. Instead, I turn around and go inside to help Madeline find her schoolbooks.

When Eve gets married she will ask me to be her maid of honor, or her witness, since the wedding is to be a small one. I will beg off, or out. I will say I can't take the time off from work. I will tell her that the children are too needy. The truth is that I have no intention of ever returning to Louisiana, God's Masterpiece, the Dream State, the Cancer Corridor. The Land that God Forgot. To me, the river now means death, the mighty trees stripped of Spanish moss mean death; the famous Louisiana good times don't roll, they toll death. The truth also is that I am stepping away from my injured, outspoken sister; second child of our lost parents. For good.

Our farewells are tight-lipped and restrained. Eve, like Wednesday's child, is full of woe. When the children and I leave Louisiana I drive off before first daylight, on purpose; so I don't have to see the ravaged land of my childhood in the light of day. As the station wagon goes over the Mississippi River bridge, the flares from the oil refineries are reflected in speckles over my rearview mirror, a hellish spray of farewell confetti.

· · · · ·

We return to our cold North Carolina house at about midnight. The children are cranky and thirsty and I am as tired and empty as I'll ever be. The only thing in our refrigerator is lemonade. I pour a cup for each of us and empty the pitcher. Tomorrow I'll go to the store and we'll start over. I'll buy milk and good fresh things to eat. The children sip the bittersweet drink silently and seem comforted. This barren house isn't much, but they take it to be their home. They are home. I think, "Take and drink this in remembrance . . ." A midnight communion.

"We're going to be all right, kids. The four of us will do just fine."

CHAPTER VII

"*Y*OU SURE HAVE HAD YOURSELF A BITCH
of a year or two. Do you think you're in danger of cracking?" Rosa
has stopped by the newspaper office to hear about the Louisiana
trip.

"Maybe later, I haven't got the time right now."

"Bad sign, bad sign. Repression creates dangerous neuroses.
Death, divorce, new job, new house, more death, and now famil-
ial estrangement. A combination of any two of those makes you
prime nervous breakdown material."

"Rosa, you are a perfect example of why women shouldn't be
educated. A little bit of knowledge is a dangerous thing. Take
your psychology master's and, and—"

She leans over and pulls the cigarette from my mouth. "And
how do you think it makes your poor kids feel to know their
grandparents died of cancer and now their sole participating parent is smoking her brains out?"

I grab my cigarette back. "It sure beats drowning my sorrows. If the gods can refrain from making my life any more akin to a nineteenth-century melodrama, I'll quit smoking in a year. That's a vow. On the anniversary of my father's death I will lay aside the wicked weed forever."

.   .   .   .   .

And I do. A year passes where the only mishaps are a few bad report cards and a few overdrawn checks. The entire year I tread softly, I am careful not to rock the boat. I put aside, unanswered, the few letters I get from Michael and I put aside all thoughts of him, or any lover. I'm never late to pick the children up, I don't copulate or drink or even leave my children with baby-sitters. It is like a deal with whatever powers have been slapping my little family around. The old ladies in Bellebend used to light novena candles in the church to hold the demons at bay, I'm never late for carpools. As the rest of the bargain, at the end of the year, I quit smoking. Which does nothing for my disposition.

"I hate your guts! You are such a witch that little children run when they see you coming. Why don't we just move out of this house and into a gingerbread house so you can roast us in your oven!"

"That does it, Madeline. I'm cutting off your fairy tale supply. From now on the only thing you'll be allowed to read is the lives of the presidents." My daughter and I are standing in our much too small kitchen yelling at one another.

"Funny, Mom, everything is a big fat joke."

"Look, Mommy is a little irritable right now. I was just trying to take a nap. This house is too small. When you opened the refrigerator, it woke me up."

"Please start smoking again, Mom, please?"

"Nothing doing, a deal's a deal. Now go do your goddamned homework."

. . . . .

Though we talk on the phone occasionally, almost two years have passed since his first and last visit here; now Eric has come to the little house to talk to me again. The kids are in school, I've left work early for this meeting. Eric called me at the office this morning to say he'd accepted a department head position at a small Maryland college. He'll be leaving town at the end of the term. He wants to talk about the sale of our farmhouse, the final division of property. Once again we are at the worn Formica table in the kitchen of the little rented house.

"I know you've been wanting this for a long time. Eric, you deserve it, you really do." What else can I say?

"Thanks, Katherine. With my folks getting older, it'll be good to be closer."

I just nod, I don't mention that his children might need him more than the old folks. I make up a little movie in my mind, where Eric is in the bleachers cheering for his father as the old man hits a home run in the Geriatric Little League. Then his bent, withered, old mother is spinning round and round in a pink tutu as Eric claps from the front row of some auditorium. The three of them bake cookies together and play darling practical jokes on one another. Eric teaches them how to color inside the lines.

Meanwhile, our children glare out at the empty place where their dad is supposed to be.

"Come take whatever furniture you'd like and I figure I'll give you half of whatever I get for the house. That ought to set you up pretty well."

"That ought to buy us a house with more than one bed-room."

"Look, Katherine, I told you that you could have had the farmhouse, that—"

I lean across the table and put my hand over his. "I know, I know, Eric. You did the right thing. You've been fair. You really have."

Eric takes his free hand and places it over mine. I think of the children's game "Paper, Scissors, Rock"; paper covers rock, scissors cut paper, rock breaks scissors.

Eric is talking. ". . . was it? I mean, what happened to us, Katherine? Everything just changed. What happened?" His thick chestnut hair is now almost completely silver.

I place my hand on the side of his face. With my forefinger I trace the lines beside his eye, they go so much deeper than mine. He's still a handsome man, though. This man I made babies with, and grew up beside. And outgrew. When he starts to kiss the inside of my palm, I stand up and lead him into the only bedroom. Early afternoon light has settled on the rumpled covers of the mattress that lies a few inches from Beth's outgrown youth bed. We don't take our clothes off, only tear at them, then tumble on top of one another and into the pool of light. When I climax, this loveless, sad, last act of sex feels like falling off the edge of the world, falling through black space like the corrupt robot in *2001*.

. . . . .

The kids and I worked together to fix Eric's farewell supper. Now the five of us are crowded around the kitchen table, eating as quickly as we politely can. For all our own reasons. I know Eric wants to get home to a drink, my kids are uncomfortable seeing their parents together, and I am just plain old uncomfortable. I want this ill-begotten feast to end. The children have been noncommittal with their feelings about their dad leaving town. Though Eric saw the children infrequently, he had been in town. He'd been around. They could say they had a father. He even showed up occasionally at their school functions. He took them out to eat about once a month and to the rare university functions planned for children. When our fun supper is over, we all walk Eric out to his car. The children and I stand and wave as he backs out of the driveway. His car turns onto the street, rounds a corner, and disappears. " 'From where the sun now stands, we will fight no more forever,' " I murmur.

"Why did you say that, Mom?" Toby asks, "What does it mean?"

It means it's not his fault, or all his fault, that I made him in the image I needed. He could have been a nicer person, it's true he could have been a nicer person. He didn't have to be such a bad guy. But he never could have been my father. Since he couldn't compete, maybe I wanted to keep him out of the running.

"What does it mean?" Toby asks again.

"I don't know," I say, and walk back toward our little house.

. . . . .

I've won an award for one of my features stories, a story about a general store, in the mountains, that hosts a musical jamboree every Saturday night. The North Carolina Journalists Awards Banquet is in Raleigh and I'm driving there with the editor and his wife. The newspaper is putting me up in a hotel, and paying all my expenses. I've been packing and unpacking for over a week. This is the first time I've left my children overnight, ever. Rosa is keeping all three while I'm gone. I'm returning the favor, and will keep Harmony, when she and Jeff go off to Cozumel for a spring vacation. I leave for my humble night away in an hour and still haven't finally decided on what to wear to the banquet. We're in Rosa's bedroom and I'm trying on one of her dresses, a beige silk sheath.

"I think it's too long."

"That's why I thought you should try it on, Katherine. That's the style."

I look in the mirror, turning sideways, checking the effect of my brand-new short haircut and Rosa's dress, which almost touches my ankles. "The new style turns us short folks into Munchkins . . . 'Thank you, ladies and gentlemen, for this wonderful award, I am very honored. In closing, I would like to say . . .'" I make my voice very high. "'Follow the yellow brick road, follow the yellow brick road, follow—'"

"The Tin Man and Glenda are going to leave without you, if you don't shake a leg. I have one more—"

"Mom!" Toby's voice is urgent and interrupted by Madeline's high-pitched scream. Rosa and I fly out of the bedroom. "Mom!"

"Mother, hurry!" Harmony and Toby are running inside to get us and we can hear Madeline screaming in the driveway.

Madeline is lying at the foot of the long, slanted asphalt driveway, tangled in the wheels of Harmony's bike. Beth is crouched beside her sister, patting her foot while Madeline screams and screams. Rosa and I run down, and kneel beside Madeline. My daughter is one solid brush burn. She seems to have skidded down the driveway on the right side of her face and most of her body.

"My arm, my arm, my arm," howls Madeline. Her left arm is under the bike at an unnatural angle.

Rosa is driving. I'm in the front seat with Madeline moaning quietly in my lap. "It's going to be all right, honey. It's O.K., it's O.K." I stroke the unbloody side of her face. The other three kids lean over the seat, watching Madeline with fascinated horror.

"Mad, if you had a mirror and saw yourself, you'd vomit," says her best friend encouragingly.

"I already want to vomit," adds Toby.

"Is she gonna die, Mommy?" asks my youngest. We are halfway to the hospital before I realize I'm still wearing Rosa's expensive silk dress.

After she is cleaned up, Madeline's flesh wounds don't turn out to be very bad. She is brave and holds tightly to my hand, without making a sound, when they set her broken arm. Her pale scraped face, looking at me as though I could possibly have made this not happen, breaks my heart. We walk out into the emergency waiting room and find Rosa had already bought a pack of magic markers for the kids. So Harmony, Toby, and Beth are ready and waiting to autograph the new cast. They argue over who gets to go first.

"How about I treat to Italian?" offers my ever ready friend. "I called Jeff and he'll meet us at Angelo's."

"I'm certainly dressed for dinner out. Especially the tomato sauce part. Sorry, Rosa. So sorry."

About the same time the editor is accepting my award in Raleigh, I'm picking pepperoni off Beth's slice of pizza in Angelo's. I try not to wish that I had left just a little earlier for Raleigh. Or that Madeline had been able to hold back disaster just long enough for me to make my getaway. I suspect I'll never get away.

.   .   .   .   .

After literally months of house hunting, we find a place I can afford and that the kids like. It is a square gray house on a dead end street. The small yard has large trees in the front and even an already-built tree house in the back. Each child has a bedroom upstairs and I have a combination bedroom study downstairs, next to the living room. The living room has a fireplace and the basement is dry. I take it as a good sign that I no longer need to hear my children breathing as they sleep.

"Can we get a cat now that we have our own house?"

"Let's sit on that for a while, O.K., Madeline?"

My daughters are supposed to be helping me unpack books and load them into the bookshelves lining the living room. Toby is upstairs hanging and rehanging a poster of Joe Montana that Eve's husband, John, sent to Toby as a housewarming gift. It speaks volumes about our family that the kitchen stuff will be the last group of boxes we unpack.

"I'm 'lergic to cats," says Beth proudly.

"You are not, we used to have a cat, stupid. In fact, a lotta cats."

Beth stands and dusts off her still dimpled knees. "We did not."

. . . . .

In the rented house years my children had been reluctant to invite other kids to our shabby home. Now Madeline wants a birthday party. She has it all planned. The children are to be dropped at our house for game playing, then we're all going to Angelo's for pizza. Their parents are to pick them up at Angelo's. I make the mistake of not checking the guest list.

"Oh-oh, Toby, I've been counting. That's number twelve getting out of the car.

"Thirteen, Mom, there's two of them getting out of the car."

I line up a few more paper cups on the dining room table. The house and stairway are filled with little girl squeals.

"Mommy, why doesn't Madeline wanna play Pin the Tail? I told her it was fun."

"Would you please go tell Madeline that I want to talk to her, Beth?"

Madeline sails in on the crest of her popularity, her face flushed. "Do you really want to talk to me?"

"Honey, counting you, there are fifteen people at your party. Counting Toby, Beth, and me, that's eighteen. How are we expected to all get to Angelo's in our car?"

"You could leave Toby and Beth here."

"Be serious, Madeline . . ." She has gone spinning off in a swirl of friends.

"Girls make me sick," says Toby.

"Me too," agrees Beth.

We are packed in the old station wagon. Toby, Beth, and two of the less popular eleven-year-olds are in the front seat, the backseat is down, and the rear of the station wagon is jammed with thirteen girls. Arms, legs, heads, elbows protrude from all the open windows. The girls are shrieking and giggling as I try driving, unobtrusively, at a snail's pace through town. We haven't gone eight blocks when a police car circles us, then signals us to pull over. I'm still trying to unpack myself from the front seat when the officer reaches the car.

"Oh, Katherine, I didn't recognize you."

"Officer Graves, anything wrong?" I hope I look in charge.

"It is, like, a violation to have this many people in your car."

"Don't worry, they're not people, they're girls!" The officer tries to reach in and pat Toby, but of course his arm can't get past me.

"Look, I have to radio for a backup here." The policeman heads to the squad car and pandemonium breaks out in our car.

"Are you going to jail?"

"Was he wearing a gun?"

"Are we all arrested?"

"Mom, are we still getting pizza?"

I feebly wave my hands. "Wait, everybody! Calm down. I know the policeman from my job at the newspaper. I don't think he's really mad. He'll probably just give me a ticket and then we'll go to Angelo's."

But instead, another squad car arrives and they divide the kids among the three vehicles. Sirens and red lights flashing, the police drive us to Angelo's.

As I tuck Madeline in on the evening of her eleventh birthday, she takes my hand. "Mom, this was the best birthday I ever had. None of my friends could believe how fun that was with the police. It was like a parade, a parade for my birthday."

"It's the power of the press, baby." I kiss my skinny daughter and turn off the light.

. . . . .

"Toby, what in the hell are you doing?" I walk down the back steps to confront my stoop-shouldered son.

"What does it look like?"

"It looks like you're trying to start the lawn mower and you ought to know better. I already told you that the thing is too damned powerful." I gather him into a protective hug. "I got bad advice when I bought it. The mower runs on its own and practically tears my arms off. Losing your arms could seriously set back your baseball career. Think of it."

He slips from my grip. "I didn't even know you knew I played baseball."

"Of course I do. Besides that, the lawn won't need mowing again until next spring. There are only about twenty blades of living grass out there."

"Nobody ever gets a turn to talk but you." Toby kicks the side of the lawn mower and slams into the house.

·   ·   ·   ·   ·

Marie has called to tell me she is buying a house. She talks on about interest rates, showing off her fiscal savvy. Marie sounds happy. "Best of all, both of my parents are finally speaking to me again. Now Daddy says that my owning a house will scare off prospective husbands. If you can believe it! Between you and me, I think he's just as pleased to think of me as a, quote unquote, 'spinster.' The Dr. Jekyll period was almost harder on Daddy than it was on me. Almost."

"Wait, Marie, let me move into the stairway. The kids are fighting. I can hardly hear you." I settle on the bottom step and stretch my legs in front of me. "We've been in our new house a year and you still haven't been to visit."

Marie laughs. "Look out, Katherine, with that house, and all, you might scare off prospective husbands."

"Yeah, like three unhousebroken kids don't. I never could understand people who ran ads in the Lonely Hearts column.

Now I do. I have wonderful friends, but I need to be beautiful. I think an attentive man could turn me beautiful. And, it goes without saying, I need to get laid."

"I don't want to make you nervous, Katherine, but Sister Helena may have this line tapped."

"Sometimes I'm so lusty that the bed sheets touching my skin set me off. In the Middle Ages they believed in something called an 'incubus,' a naughty little male spirit that crept into the beds of women at night. For me, it's Sears' percale cotton sheets."

"Get out and meet people," says Marie.

"Easy for you to say. Maybe I could run one of those ads. Then, when I hooked a man, I could spike the kids' canned spaghetti so they'd sleep while I had wild abandoned sex." The whole time I'm talking on the phone, my free ear is covered to block an argument over whose turn it is to put away the dishes.

"My mother's Lafayette connection says that Susan is still single too. The three of us must be some kind of record for Holy Name Academy."

Toby and Madeline reach an impasse and abandon the kitchen. The downstairs quiets enough for me to continue without shouting. "It was a subliminal message from the nuns. Think of the simplicity of their lives, no bills, no interest rates, no broken-down cars, and Jesus, the world's best listener, as a bridegroom."

"Seriously, some kind of partner would surely help you," says Marie.

"Well, what about you?"

"Never again, I love my solitude," says Marie. "But you . . . I bet someday your prince will come."

I lean against the second step. "I don't count on it. My mantra these days is 'Help is *not* on the way. Help is not on the way.' "

. . . . .

One autumn Saturday night, I am reading late and feel the weather getting a bit chilly. When I go into Toby's room to add a blanket to his bed, I discover his bed is empty. I look down in the basement, in the yard; look again through the three bedrooms upstairs, one bath. It doesn't take me long to be sure that Toby is not in the house. A hundred things can happen to a little boy out alone in the night. I try to think of none of them, I am so scared I can hardly swallow.

I go in to wake up Madeline. "Honey, Toby is gone. I'm going to look for him."

Madeline doesn't even sit up, "Mom, that's what the police are for. Let them look for him."

"Last resort, Madeline, last resort," I say, and pull the covers under her chin.

My son has been a loner of late. No best friend's house to check. I get in the car and drive around town looking for a nine-year-old boy. The movie theater is showing *Annie Hall*. Not Toby's cup of tea. I pass all the campus hot spots and all the video arcades; somehow it doesn't occur to me to check any of those places. They'd toss his half-pint self right out. I'm murmuring to myself, "Help me find him, help me find him. Let him be O.K. and I swear I'll never yell at him again. I swear."

On a whim I turn onto the road on the town's outskirts that leads to the municipal park. In the middle of the shabby wooden bleachers by the playing field, I see a lone figure, a small one. My son has walked over three miles from home. The wind whips the nightgown trailing under my overcoat, as I walk across the field. Toby doesn't move. I climb up and sit next to him. I want to scream "Where have you been, you little son of a bitch? I've been scared half out of my mind, and you are punished until you're forty. God dammit!" But I don't say anything. I remember my

185

vow. And I want my son to grow up to like women. Right now I wouldn't lay any money on it.

"Mom, remember when I played Little League baseball?"

"Sure I do. Mondays and Wednesdays. Right?" He doesn't answer. "Right," I say again.

"How come you never came to my games?"

"I came to your games," I say defensively.

"One, Mom, you came to one. I was the only kid there who didn't ever have anybody in the bleachers."

I put my hand on his knee, and he moves away from me. "Toby, I didn't know you wanted me to come. Baseball . . . well, I don't understand baseball, and all those parents always made me nervous. But if you'd said it was important, I would have come."

"I hate not having a dad. You know, I lie awake at night thinking about how great it would be to have someone to throw a ball with. Just throw a ball. Forget all that other Dad stuff, camping and that fishing and hunting shit."

"Toby."

"Anyway, I just want you to know I hate not having a dad and I hold you responsible."

I rest my back on the bleacher above us and hunch into my coat. "If you want a dad so much, how come when your father asked you to visit him you said you didn't want to go?"

"He's a jerk," says Toby dismissively.

"He's your father."

"He's still a jerk."

"Listen real carefully." I pull Toby's open jacket closed and zip it up. "Just because you think your dad is a jerk and you go around saying he's a jerk. Just because, don't think that's any guarantee that you won't grow up to be a jerk. Mark my words. Nobody's a jerk on purpose."

"Don't change the subject."

"Changing the subject is all I can do. I certainly can't produce a dad. Now, are you coming home?"

Toby nods and starts to walk down the bleachers. I follow and catch up with him. "If you ever run away again, you leave a note." I take his hand. "Do you hear me, you little shit?"

.   .   .   .   .

"I don't know, Rosa. It's one losing battle after another. I fear the future. I don't see my kids improving. Anybody could do a better job. Even Joan Crawford." I have fled to my friend's house after a devastating conference with Beth's teacher.

"My smart little seven-year-old is in danger of failing first grade. If you can believe it. The teacher says she can get absolutely no work out of Beth. That Beth is agreeable and friendly, the other kids like her, but Beth won't work on her numbers and letters—"

"She gets that from her mother."

"Funny, Rosa."

We're sitting on Rosa's back deck overlooking a spectacular view of valley and several mountain ranges. I've recently returned to having an occasional drink and we're sharing a small pitcher of sangria.

"Go ahead and laugh, Ms. Fat Cat with her unbroken home and model kid. I have it from a very good source that Harmony hoards peanut butter cups in her sock drawer."

"It doesn't mean Beth isn't smart or is a troublemaker." Rosa takes small bites of orange peel as she talks. "My guess is that she needs to be a little kid a little longer. What's the big deal? Let her hang out in first grade driving her teacher nuts until Beth is ready to assume the trappings of maturity. Like reading 'Run Jane, Run' or whatever."

"I can just hear Eric's parents. 'We tried to warn you about Southerners' inbreeding.' They're gonna make it my fault and make my baby sound like that banjo player from *Deliverance*."

"The little pink-faced guy with no eyebrows?"

I nod.

. . . . .

Eric calls from Maryland one evening. He says he has called to speak to the children, but needs to tell me his news first.

"I'm getting married Katherine. I'm getting married in about a month."

"Another whirlwind courtship, Eric?"

"Not really," his voice is cheerful, "I've known her for almost a year. I met her at AA."

"Whew, that's a bigger bomb than your marriage. AA, huh? So, this, this . . ."

"Barbara, her name is Barbara. She was doing a research paper on alcoholism and—"

"Another student, Eric?"

"Yes, but—"

"High school, or college?"

Eric laughs. "Anyway, Katherine, we'd like the kids to come to the wedding."

"Oh, so Barbara will have some little playmates?" It is a very good sign that Eric is still laughing when I go to call the children to the phone.

CHAPTER VIII

TODAY I AM INTERVIEWING A UNIVERSITY guest lecturer, a man who will fly in from Boston once a week for the academic year to give a special lecture course for the College of Architecture. When Ian Richter walks into my office, I immediately like him, instant attraction. He's not terribly handsome, just appealing, that patrician look I'm such a sucker for. He has sandy, rumpled hair, blue eyes, a great profile; he is tall, with the unstudied, slightly soft body of an intellectual. From his vita I know he is about two years younger than I. We are winding up the interview, which I'd actually prolonged for the pleasure of this man's company.

"That's about it, unless you'd like to suggest something else for me to ask."

"Maybe you could go to dinner with me tonight and give me a quick tour of the town."

I'd noticed him looking at my bare left ring finger. I pick up the folder of information I have on him. "It says here you're married."

He smiles. "Very. Does 'dinner' have another meaning in the South? Have I, unknowingly, compromised your virtue? Should I have proposed 'suppah' instead?"

We both laugh; then I say, "I have three young buckaroos at home. If I'm not with them every night for 'suppah,' they will turn to drugs, junk food, and cheating on their homework." Inexplicably I add, "You are very welcome to join us, though. I think we're having stir-fry. Vegetarian. You could see how the natives truly live."

Why am I doing this? I never mix work and family.

I've invited a perfect stranger, a perfectly married perfect stranger to dinner with my family. And I am setting the table with our matched stainless. Ian Richter arrives at six-thirty on the dot. He is carrying a wonderful tub of Brie and a stack of Western comics.

"For the buckaroos," he says, tongue-in-cheek.

The children are at their most obnoxious. "Pass the snot balls," says a gleeful Beth.

"How about some ear wax with those snot balls," Toby asks helpfully.

Madeline says nothing, she is reading Western comics at the table.

"You know, guys, I've read the literature, and this phase isn't supposed to start until around seventh grade," I say. "Only Madeline is allowed to be so disgusting. And she's too busy being rude."

"If I put ear wax on my rice," asks Ian, "will it still be vegetarian?"

Toby and Beth are interested. The bespectacled Madeline doesn't even look up from her comics.

The children have cleared the table and are supposed to be doing their homework. Ian is helping me with the dishes.

"It was really kind of you to invite me to dinner. You're a

good cook. Even though no animals were sacrificed." Ian has figured out my cupboard arrangement and is putting away dishes as he talks. "I really hate eating alone in restaurants. I like to make a ritual of dining, any kind of ritual. Except the ritual of lone man at table unfurling napkin."

"Mom." Madeline walks into the dining room as Ian and I settle at the table with coffee. "Toby has the remote control and keeps changing the channels. Would you go upstairs and break his arms off?"

"You're almost thirteen years old, Madeline. Can't you handle this?"

"You're always on Turd Face's side 'cause he's younger than me." Madeline sits as though she plans to join us for the rest of the evening.

"I've told you not to talk that way in front of me. You're supposed to pretend you never talk that way. Especially in front of company. Besides, it's 'I,' not 'me.' "

"Well, me was just trying to warn you in case you were wondering what's smelling up the house, it's good ole—"

"Madeline, dammit! You're supposed to be doing your homework anyway."

She tips her chair back, dangerously. "Me finished."

"Bring it down here and show me."

"I can't, the only thing me had was my science project, and—and the glue's drying."

I turn to Ian. "Gee, I'm so sorry you don't have kids. How can you stand missing out on all this?" He laughs. "Anyway, if you have to get back to your hotel, feel free to flee. I have to go upstairs and check on Madeline's glue."

"Mom"—Madeline's voice is injured—"I can't believe you don't trust me!"

"If you don't mind *I* browsing through your books, *me* will just stick around." Ian is already heading into the living room.

I return several minutes later and find Ian engrossed in a large book on Van Gogh. He looks up. "It is amazing that all of his color was done in the last two years of his life. Did you know that?" I nod. "Intimidating, right?" I nod again. "And this"—he points to a painting of a portly middle-aged woman, sitting in front of wildly floral wallpaper—"this woman was the postmaster's wife in Arles. She's about the only visitor Van Gogh had the first time he was in the mental hospital."

"I didn't know that," I say, sitting beside him.

"She was apparently very kind and visited him almost every day. She brought him a special kind of baker's roll that he loved. Van Gogh did three paintings of her and, in gratitude for her kindness, let her choose one. She selected this one. She had a good eye, it's the best."

"Poor Vincent," I say, "now they think all his craziness was an ear infection."

"I thought it was migraines." He closes the book. "Revisionists at work." He crosses his hands behind his head and leans back on the sofa. "On to other pursuits of truth. Had Madeline done all her homework?"

"Of course not. It seems so ironic that I went directly from feeling guilty about not doing my homework to feeling guilty about not doing their homework."

He sits forward, looking amused. "So, you were one of those bad children that didn't do homework?"

Conversation, real adult conversation with someone from the outside world. A handsome, educated man is choosing to stay in my messy, noisy house and talk to me. This isn't like the conversations I grab, on the run, with my friends. This conversation has the undertones of flirtation. It sounds like a beginning, a fragile, slightly dangerous, beginning.

"Obviously you did yours. You were always a good boy?" Ian nods. "You didn't ever rebel? You didn't steal hubcaps or get a tattoo?"

He leans back again and puts his feet, gingerly, on my scarred and dusty coffee table. "Nope, I didn't rebel until my sophomore year at Columbia. And even that was short-lived. I . . . ." He pauses, looks at me, then continues. "I would get loaded and go around the city taking leaks on architecturally significant build-ings."

I twist around to face him full on. "You what?"

"Come on, Katherine. You heard me. I splashed on the Em-pire State Building and on the New York Public Library and on the UN Building."

"You mean like some kind of raging King Kong?" I ask.

"No, like some kind of sneaky wino. I found out-of-the-way corners in the wee small hours of the morn and I—I left my mark on them. It was a stage, O.K.? A brief stage."

I am laughing. "Don't tell me your father was an architect!"

"Well—yeah. Matter of fact, he was. Freudian, right? Gropius was my father's mentor, so I made a specialty of the Pan Am Building."

I laugh again.

"Ellen, my wife Ellen, says it's primordial, like wolves staking out territory."

. . . . .

The following Wednesday, Ian joins us for dinner again. This time he appears at the door with a bottle of brandy and a package of bakery cookies. "Cookies for us, brandy for the kiddos. Ought to be a quieter night, huh?" he says as he walks in.

"Look, Katherine, when I called you this afternoon, I felt like a bit of a jerk. But I really enjoyed last week and—and until I can make friends of my own, will you let me hang out with youse guys?"

"Sure, Ian. I never know when I'll be in some strange town giving one of my sought-after lectures on the effect of journalism upon the political structure of Leeston, North Carolina, and I'll need a friend."

He follows me into the kitchen and lifts the pot lid. "If you're ever in Bean Town, absolutely. Hey!" He is glaring into the pot. "It looks like you have dead cow in here."

I'm tossing the salad. "Don't worry, no one suffered. It died in its sleep, surrounded by its loved ones. Its last request was to be served at my family's feast."

"Fine, I'll eat it then."

"You're a funny man, Ian Richter."

"You're a pretty funny woman, too, Katherine, whose last name I can't remember."

"Don't worry, I change it all the time."

"Marry often, do you?" He's slicing the bread, now. He pulled out a bread board and is slicing bread, taking over my kitchen.

"Seldom, actually. The truth is, I've meant to take back my own name, Roberts, but the kids have a fit. 'Don't you love us?' they say, and 'Are you ashamed of us?' So I always do a personality profile before I give my last name. If you looked like PTA material to me, I'd definitely be Pierson. Which reminds me, where is dem little Piersons?"

. . . . .

He comes on Wednesdays. Those mornings I always wash my hair. I begin to buy scented shampoos. I get makeup hints from the women in my office and, for the first time, start to line my eyes, wear mascara. "A good friend," I tell myself. "A good male friend. Some good strong male influence for my children." Unless his plane is late, he meets me for lunch before his class. We are often joined by some of his graduate students, and I enjoy the heavy architectural talk, though much of it sails over my head. It's a nice balance to the Wednesday night dinners at my house. Where my kids outdo themselves. Madeline has stopped bringing a book to table, all the better to join in the erudite conversations.

"Mom has a boyfriend, kissy, kissy, kissy." She pushes at her small wire-rimmed glasses with her forefinger.

For some reason, I haven't told the children Ian is married. He never mentions this in front of them and now it seems too late. Irrelevant.

"Ian, is it true that Boston is full of fags?"

"That's 'homosexual' to you, young man. Your mother has assured me this is a liberal household. Else I'd sup alone at McDonald's."

"That's a good idea," says Beth. "Why don't you sup alone at McDonald's with us?"

One Wednesday night Ian takes us all to Pierre's, an overpriced mockery of a French restaurant. Ian orders for us. The kids are very impressed.

"Ian, Toby says those aren't really snails. He says they're slugs from off dead bodies." Beth insisted on arranging her own hair for her night out on the town. A pinch of it is precariously drawn into a pencil-thin ponytail, but most of her hair frizzes around her face in tight dark blond curls.

"I think, if we ever come here again, we should leave the young children at home," says Madeline facetiously as she butters her French bread.

"Anyone want to talk about the decision to return the Panama Canal to Panama? Wasn't that a nice thing?" Ian asks, with a straight face.

One Wednesday, the children prepare a horrible half-cooked dinner for us. One Wednesday, Ian doesn't show up.

It is the raw time of the year when no one has yet adjusted to the early nightfall. The November days seem cut off at the neck. I haven't heard from Ian for over two weeks, though I know he has met his classes. He has been in town. I checked. He just hasn't called. I have difficulty sleeping, and lie awake running his last visit over and over in my mind. When I finally fall asleep, my dreams are erotic and disturbing. I wake up feeling unattractive and abandoned. The kids don't mention him. He seems like an ominous empty place at our table. The second Wednesday with no word from Ian, I took the kids to McDonald's, a first. Tomorrow will be the third Wednesday and I am thinking of Ian and finishing the dinner dishes when the phone rings.

"Katherine, this is Ian, Ian Richter."

I smile, even though I am shaking so much I'm surprised I haven't dropped the phone. "You're the only Ian I know, first names are fine. Particularly since you don't even know my last name."

"You're still funny."

"I figured that was why we haven't heard from you, Ian Richter. You couldn't find us in the phone book."

His voice changes. "You haven't heard from me because seeing you was becoming—is . . . I guess you haven't heard from me because it was too important. To me, at least."

"And to me." I sigh. "This is long distance. Right, Ian?"

"Right."

"But you can afford it. Right?"

"Katherine, I'd like to take you out to dinner tomorrow night. Alone, if that's all right. At that fancy French place with the bad food. If that's O.K.?"

"That's very O.K., Ian Richter," I say.

When I hang up the phone, I stand for a long time with my hands, one on top of the other, pressed onto the phone's receiver.

. . . . .

"You didn't really think you could 'just be friends'? Men and women can't do that." Esther takes a long, deep drag of her cigarette.

I am meeting Ian in a couple of hours and my friends have come by for an afternoon visit.

"Don't ask me what I'm doing, Esther. I really think, I really thought . . . You know, male company for my kids. That I could—"

"It's O.K. to be horny. I mean, really, when was the last time you were laid?" Esther leans across the coffee table to give my hand a pat. "That Michael boy is almost the only lover you've had. How long ago was that?"

"Almost exactly four years."

"Four years ago, God!" Esther bites her knuckle.

"Sweet young Michael. Lost to the grape fields of California." I sigh and look with envy at Esther's cigarette. "He still phones about twice a year. Still single, a nice catch like that, and talking about grape pickers and unions. He seems so far away."

"Astute, Katherine. California is far away and you can't do it with a phone. Though you can certainly try."

"From what you say, you certainly love sex," says Rosa, ignoring our lewd friend. "You're a juicy little number, someone ought to be plucking you from the tree."

"You mean fucking her from a tree, or in a tree, or by a tree."

"Esther! Don't be gross. And stop with the inanimate objects." I reach over to stub out the cigarette Esther left smoldering in a coffee saucer. "And don't tell me my two married friends are sitting here advising me to have an affair with a married man."

"Well, I've done it," Esther says. "Nothing beats experience."

"You're exaggerating. You can't really count that music teacher, he was more like a puppy." I cock my head, puppylike, toward Esther. "Besides, that was a fling, you've certainly not had anything serious."

Esther drops off the chair and sits, Buddha-like, beside the coffee table. "How come this would have to be serious?"

"Because that's Katherine's way, Esther. That's why."

"I'm scarred by my Catholic past. And I can't afford babysitters, so I can't waste money on something casual."

It's Rosa's day to pick up our daughters from piano lessons, so she stands to go. "I guess I'd like to live through you, a bit, Katherine. I've been with the same man since before they stopped delivering milk in glass bottles. Besides, I love hearing all your little Tracy-Hepburn dialogues. The man sounds quick of tongue."

"Yum," says Esther.

. . . . .

When I walk into Pierre's, Ian is already at a table, and he has already ordered a bottle of wine. He stands up when he sees me, and I freeze. For a second I forget that part where you keep walking. I am so glad to see this man, I forget how to walk. I'd forgotten how unkempt his hair is and that he wears dress shirts, sleeves rolled up and exposing his forearms, no jacket. "You were early. I could have—"

"Katherine, you look wonderful, you—"

We are talking at the same time, we are both still standing. I'm afraid Ian will touch me, I'm afraid he won't. We laugh at ourselves, and he pulls my chair out for me. Now we are both sitting down, and we're both silent.

The waiter comes and pours my wine and backs away. Ian breaks the silence.

"So, Katherine. What are we going to do?"

"Do we have to do something? I mean, can't we just—just—you know, keep on keeping on?"

"You mean, 'be friends,' " he says.

"I have this friend," I say, "who claims it is impossible for a man and a woman to be friends. But we could give it a try."

"Since you called this person a friend, I must assume she is a woman," Ian says, stroking his chin wisely.

I taste the wine. "Delicious." I put the glass down again. "And you're smart too. Now I know why the university is paying you a trillion dollars to teach one course."

"Do you really want to change the subject," he asks.

"Yes. No."

The waiter approaches our table, then sees we haven't even opened our menus. Ian reaches across the table and runs his forefinger over my wrist in a wavy pattern. I actually feel a chill run up my back.

"Forgive me for asking," I say, "but has this happened to you before? Please tell me the truth."

"The truth, Katherine, is not even once. I swear. In nine years, not even once have I done more than look at another woman."

"I hate that it makes me feel better. But it makes me feel better. I still don't want to have an affair with you. I mean, I'm trying to think that I don't want to." I run my forefinger round and round the glass rim. "Affairs are tacky. I ought to know. In my former life, I had a couple done to me."

"O.K., Katherine the Rule Maker. What do you suggest we do? Become blood brothers? You do need to know I am nursing some fantasies about you. And they aren't very brotherly. And there's one other thing I need to talk—"

"I want us to be like our seven Wednesday nights were," I interrupt. "I mean, there were seven of them. But who's counting? Maybe a little different, sometimes without the kids. But then, sometimes with them." I lean on the table to move closer. "I missed you, Ian Richter. I horrified myself with how much I missed you. And they missed you too, they missed you too much to even mention your name. Toby really missed you, which touched my heart." I pick up the menu. "My son has so needed to be around a good man."

I open the menu, then put it down because I can't think about food with Ian looking at me so intently. Ian reaches across the table and lightly touches my hand. I think he is going to say something about how terrific my children are. But he doesn't.

"I can't play surrogate dad to your kids, or even uncle." I feel the blood rushing to my face, and turn away from him.

"That wasn't what I was asking, saying, I was just—"

"Katherine"—he takes my wrist—"Katherine, let me finish. Please look at me."

"What?" I turn back. "What?"

"You know that Ellen and I don't have children. There is a little more to that than I've told you." He pours more wine into his glass.

"A few weeks ago I was in one of those electronics stores, and I saw a game I thought Toby would get a kick out of. I picked it up and had even taken it to the counter. Another little bribe. Then I thought about what I was doing. I left the game there before a clerk could wait on me. I turned around, walked out of the store, and decided not to mingle in your life anymore. See, Katherine, putting it frankly, I'm generally not too crazy about kids. I can do the—"

"But you're so natural around them. I—"

"This is difficult, Katherine, let me talk this through." He rests his hand over mine. "I can do the short-term razzmatazz with kids. It's the long doses that stump me. I'm not a 'children's adult.' I'd been trying to maneuver a way to see you without the children, to ask you for some 'nights off.' And I know your life is all about children. But I can't seem, right now, to not be in your life. So—so please listen to me."

Now Ian is the one who has turned his face away from me. He speaks slowly. "When we talked about kids, Ellen and I decided there was no place for children in our lives; she's devoted to the museum, I'm a workaholic. Shortly after we married Ellen had some female trouble and, while she needed surgery anyway, I convinced her to have her tubes tied. Then, about two years ago, Ellen started talking about children. She said she wanted babies. She wanted to carry a child inside herself. I made light of it and that has been between us, ever since. Like a grudge."

He rolls the wineglass between his hands, then looks up at me. "I should have been regretful, but I wasn't. I didn't want children. Now I find myself getting in good with your children, sometimes even enjoying your children . . . Do you see what I'm saying?"

"God, yes." I try to keep my voice steady.

"I am very interested in Katherine. Though I'd like Katherine all to myself, I even like her kids and I'd certainly like her kids to like me. For self-serving reasons, it would make it all easier. Beyond that . . . pursuing you, looking forward to being with you, doesn't seem nearly the betrayal forming a relationship with your kids is." He takes a sip of his wine. "Somewhat of a double betrayal, of Ellen and of the kids. If that makes any sense."

"Of course it makes sense." I push away my barely touched wine. "The convent is many years behind me. There's been a lot of blood under the bridge. I certainly had a good idea of what was going on with you and me. I guess I felt like it was fair. You know, sorta even. Ellen had just about all of you and the nice house and the great education, the dream job at the museum, and, and probably a real nice car. Right?" Ian nods, and smiles. "And a very nice car. And I got three to six hours on Wednesdays for part of a year. I got to be pretty and funny and sometimes my kids got to be around a man who wasn't a total jerk. All of a sudden, we're outta kilter here."

"Katherine." He reaches for my arm, but I pull away.

"Ian, I don't know enough about gambling to figure what to do here, so . . . So, I'm just going to go home, to my house, to my 'likable' kids. Instead of—" When I push my chair back, I knock it over and freeze in indecision.

"I'll get the chair, Katherine. You go on. I'm sorry." It is the last thing I hear.

I am sobbing by the time I get into the car. "The hard part is over. I don't need anybody's help. I don't need anybody's husband. She has you, and I have them. And I am all they have!" I yell to the empty car.

. . . . .

"Katherine, at least he was being honest. He didn't have to tell you the truth."

"Rosa, honesty isn't the point. Just because you're honest,

you shouldn't use it like a credit card. Honesty doesn't entitle you to a free ride."

"I guess you're right. I guess your dream suitor was maybe a wolf wearing sheep's clothing. Tasteful, but a costume." Rosa shakes her head regretfully.

"Or Scrooge disguised as Santa," I add.

"I didn't really think you could get that good repartee and good romance. It wouldn't have been fair."

For almost twelve years, now, Rosa has been my sounding board. If she's ever come to me seeking solace, in all these years, I have missed it. We're back in my living room dissecting last night's time with Ian.

"I'm trying to figure out why it makes a difference. Why I have to turn down what he was about to offer. I just know I do."

Rosa sounds wistful when she speaks up again. "It doesn't sound like too much to ask. I wanted to encourage you, I wanted to, to maybe ride in the backseat while you had this discreet, witty, naughty romance. But your instinct is right, you have to protect your kids. They could have gotten really hurt."

"I mean, it's not like I wanted to marry him. And I don't know what upsets me the most, that I let my kids get hooked on someone who was, somewhat . . . no, not somewhat, he was really using them. Really. He admitted as much. That I let my kids get hooked on him, or that his poor wife . . . and I hate that I'm saying 'poor wife,' in that I was a 'poor wife' myself . . . gave up babies for him." I begin to pound my heel on the coffee table. "Now he's chasing a woman with babies. Yuck!"

Rosa leans back on the sofa. "They're not really babies, Katherine."

"You know what I mean, Rosa. You know that the thing that took our virginity was not having sex with a man." I stand up to make my point. "We lost our virginity when we had our first child. You and I will never—I'll never again truly sleep at night. Madeline will be sixty years old and my phone will ring at three in the morning and the first thing I'll think is 'My baby, which of my babies is hurt?' There are days I pull up to my house and dread walking in, dread the arguments, the chaos, the raw need of those children. But they are mine, my babies." I drop down next to Rosa. "I never understood violence until I became a mother. Now I know I could surely rip the throat from any monster threatening them, threatening my *babies*. I'm five feet tall and I could kill a three-hundred-pound man with one fist if he meant any harm to one of my children. They are my babies, they—"

"Calm down, Katherine. Easy, friend, easy."

. . . . .

Eve and John stop by to visit us on their way back from meetings in Washington. In the past year or two Eve has been making it a point to stay in touch. She obviously comes to visit the children, so I am surprised she has stayed behind with me tonight. We are sitting by the fire on a sleety late December evening. John has taken the kids bowling and I tell Eve the whole Ian story. The courtship that's not a courtship, the sad barren wife, Ian's easy cheating way with my kids. I tell Eve how much I loved Ian's wit and his looks and how opposite our lifestyles were. How being with him seemed to make up for all that I had missed in all these adult years. I tell her how he looked when I left him at Pierre's.

"Go for it, sister."

"What do you mean, 'go for it'?" I ask.

"You know, Katherine. Life really is a beer commercial. We really do only go around once." Eve and I are sitting in front of the fire nursing cups of hot cider.

"If this is it, really it, then we have to do it right. Do what we think is right," I say.

"Katherine, you have as much right to happiness as that priggish museum marm. And why does the man have to like your kids? Go for the ride. Maybe he's a great lay. Eat, drink, be merry, and fuck your brains out. And he told you the truth, he could have kept on pretending he was Mr. Rogers. It's all fair . . . You ought to know that, being a blonde, and all," she adds facetiously.

The fire is dying, and I jiggle the coals with a poker. "See, Eve, I have to disagree. I don't think I could have sex with someone who doesn't like my kids. Better he hated my body."

Eve shakes her head. "I thought you had become a feminist, Katherine. Your kids aren't your body. They're separate from you. You have as much right to a sex life, a love life, as Eric does."

"And, Eve, if you're going to talk feminism—what about the 'sisterhood'? What about Ellen Richter?"

"What she doesn't know won't hurt her. Ian isn't her property, any more than she's his. It's not like he's calling home lying about working late. It's not like she's sitting up waiting for him." Eve empties her cup of cider. "When we were kids, I resented that you got to go to Holy Name Academy and I didn't. Now, I am so glad I missed it. That big dose of Catholicism fucked up your mind. Forever. You make everything too heavy, Katherine."

"It's not necessarily Catholic, Eve. The Hopi Indians say, 'Never hurt another living thing.' That's their whole religion."

We sit quietly and watch the glowing ashes. Then Eve speaks up. "I have something to talk to you about. I mean, it may seem a little out of place. . . . Anyway, John and I are going to have a baby."

"Eve!" I put my hand on her arm. "What wonderful news, Eve. I didn't even know you and John had sex. I thought you were too intellectual."

"Well, actually it was all done with computers."

"Aha, that's more like it. When is the little Einstein due?"

"Near the end of July and that's what I wanted to talk to you about." She stands and adds a few small pieces of wood to the fire.

"Almost the same time we found out about the baby, John heard he was getting the Fulbright he'd applied for to go to Pakistan."

"Oh no, Eve, not at the same time the baby's coming?"

"You got it, big sister. Anyway, he's been working on this book about their elections which are, of course, in late July. This is a once in a lifetime, blah, blah, blah. The point is, John is going— I'm insisting he go—and I'm sure as hell not planning to have a baby in Pakistan. I want to do natural childbirth and, Katherine . . . Katherine, we're wondering if you would take John's place at the delivery?" She dusts her hands off and leans back, not looking directly at me. "Don't answer now."

There is a long silence. I jiggle the kindling, but it doesn't seem to be catching. I realize Eve has come to mend fences. She must regret what she said to me after Daddy's funeral. I also realize that I am still angry. "I can't, Eve. I'll tell you right now. I wouldn't want to set you up. I just can't."

I'm afraid to look at my sister's face. I'm already getting that clammy feeling; I see the flare of the refinery burn-offs in my rearview mirror, I can almost smell the foul air. I know as well as I know anything that I can't go back to Louisiana. And I can't let bygones be bygones with my sister. "I just can't, Eve, I—"

"It's O.K., no big deal."

"I kind of assumed you weren't ever going to have babies. You seemed to think all my child rearing was a big cop-out, so I—"

"I mean, my friend Jean can do it with her eyes closed. It's really no big deal, I just thought, you know . . ." We sit without speaking and watch the fire die down to nothing.

. . . . .

I stop listening for the phone, and I stop my extra mascara on Wednesdays. I manage to stop everything but my thoughts of Ian. I am a woman in her thirties and one day, when the local oldies station plays "Unchained Melody," I have to pull my car to the side of the road, like a melodramatic teenager. That part of the song about hungering for a lover's touch and asking the lover to wait just kills me.

A n n G o e t h e

I dream I am sitting across a small table from Ian, telling him that I am listening for a message from my father, an urgent, lost message. Ian is smiling at me. He reaches over and slowly unbuttons my blouse while I talk. I am wearing a silk camisole; his thumb brushes my nipple, lightly, again and again. Just that, that one gesture. I pull awake and my bed seems on fire.

. . . . .

The phone rings one evening and I'm relieved at the interruption. Bill wants me to do an article on tax evaders and sham tax shelters. I've brought home a stack of pamphlets, trying to grasp an understanding of straight tax shelters. This has to be an all-time low in boring assignments. If I pull this one off Bill will make me features editor. I'll deserve it.

I'm still making notes as I pick up the phone in the kitchen.

"Katherine, it's Marie."

It doesn't sound like Marie, it sounds like a disembodied voice, a messenger, coming from the floor of the ocean. I suddenly know I don't want to hear this message. There is a long pause. I am still holding my pencil and begin to scribble a small dark circle on the kitchen counter. It is my turn to say something, but I don't.

"Susan is dead, Katherine. She's dead."

I make the circle smaller and smaller. It is pencil lead, I'll be able to wipe the markings off with a sponge, before the children see what I have done. But, for now, I want to see how small, how dark, I can make this circle.

"Are you still there, Katherine? Did you hear what I said?"

"She's not dead, she's in Europe. She's . . . What are you saying, Marie, what—"

"She's not in Europe. She's in Arkansas. Or she was in Arkansas. She's been there for two years. She took her grandmother's money and set up a commune in Arkansas, and . . ." Marie is gasping for breath.

I circle the pencil over and over, building a tiny heap of carbon dust.

Marie begins again. "She set up a commune in Arkansas and she and her lover were walking in the woods and stopped to kiss and a redneck shot them. Killed Susan dead and the lover is still in the hospital and my mother thinks the redneck is going to get off scot-free 'cause Susan's lover is a woman. She and Susan were lesbians and Susan's commune was just for lesbians. No men were allowed, not even male children. And now she's dead."

"Arkansas? Marie, this doesn't make any sense."

I cross my index finger over my middle finger, smudge up the dark pencil dust, and streak it across my cheeks as though I could smear this horror, this outrage into some ancient ritual, turn the real to symbol. I keep holding on to the phone with my other hand.

When Marie begins to really sob, I join her. We cry together for a very long time; then, wordlessly, hang up.

· · · · ·

Rosa and I are having lunch at a pizza joint near my office. We meet every Tuesday for lunch. I'm telling her about Marie's phone call. Though, of course, Rosa has never met Susan, over the years we've shared fantasies on the fortunes and travels of my brilliant girlhood friend.

"How do you mourn someone you haven't seen in sixteen years? Is it like clearing space on the shelf of your life? Giving away outgrown clothes that are still in perfect condition?" I'm huddled in the corner of our booth, my arms wrapped around my knees. "I thought, as time went by, our cupboards became more and more full. Mine seem to be emptying. Rosa, I'm thirty-three years old. I'm too young to know so many dead people!"

"You are, Katherine. I've never lost anyone close to me, and I'm older than you." Rosa pushes her crust over the greasy pizza pan.

I look up at her, "I'm thirty-three and Susan is still eighteen! The most brilliant person I ever knew. Why did this happen? Why didn't she come back? I always thought I'd see her again. Susan could have put everything in context. All these years she's been my touchstone and she never gave us a chance. She just walked away from me and Marie. Hell, she even walked away from you. She never gave any of us a chance."

"It's not fair." Rosa comes to my side of the booth and pulls her arms tightly around me.

"We spent four years together, we planned our futures together. We had no secrets."

Rosa is patting my back while I rage. "It is goddamned not fair."

"Rosa, I've been crying on your shoulder for as long as I can remember."

"It's just because they wouldn't let you take your mammy when you left the ole plantation, Scarlett. I'm the best replacement available."

"Tell you one thing, though." I move from her hug and take one of her hands between mine. "Someday all this one-sided stuff is going to slow down and then I'll be able to help you out."

"Heaven forbid," says Rosa, slinging her free arm around my shoulder.

. . . . .

It is an afternoon in late February, a month after Marie's call about Susan. I am at the typewriter in my office, struggling with an editorial on Kissinger and the Shah. In the piece I am portraying Jimmy Carter as a befuddled host whose guests have taken over his party. I look up and Ian is standing in my doorway.

"How was your Christmas?" I ask inanely.

"We went to Switzerland, skiing. How was yours?"

"We went to K mart, shopping."

"You're an incorrigible smartass, Katherine Whatever-your-name-is. Can I close this door?" His face contradicts his casual tone.

There is some reason I shouldn't let him in, but I can't recall it. "Are you going to touch me?" He nods. "Then close the door."

I meet him halfway across the room.

. . . . .

Most Wednesday nights we go out to dinner, just the two of us. I gradually let the children know Ian is married, and both Ian and my children circle one another with considerably more distance. He is clever and sensitive to little nuances and, though Toby stays aloof and resentful, Ian manages to build a new and fairly loose friendship with the girls.

I look at Ian with less illusion, still every Wednesday feels like a holiday, a feast. The walls come down stone by stone and we reach for one another with words and with our hands. We talk about our cold months apart as though they were some trial, some test we endured. Our few hours together, our triumph, our reward. I think about Eve's advice and take off my mama hat and put on my woman one whenever Ian is in town. I try to feel I'm entitled to whatever he offers. That I'm entitled to something beyond the unbroken chain of children, work, housework, bills, children, and work again.

Ian has been back in my life for over a month and, incredibly, we still haven't made love. The children spent a week with Eric during the December holidays and aren't due back there until their traditional week of the Fourth of July visit. I am too well known in Leeston, so Ian and I have no place to go. We have ruled out groping sex parked by the duck pond with the rest of the horny campus lovers. Though, after our dinners out, we often drive down to the river to kiss and touch in the shelter of the winter trees and rocks. I can't interest him in car backseats. It may be a class difference. We laughingly suspect we might even be getting a perverse pleasure from the torture of the long, creative foreplay.

"Katherine, we have to do something. I'm growing hair on my palms. Put your kids in an orphanage and move me into your house. Let me be your native boy. I'll fan you with palm leaves."

"You'd like that." I pull back from him.

"Hey, a joke, all right?" The window is rolled down so that we can hear the river tumbling over the rocks. Our clothes are partially unbuttoned under our open overcoats.

One Wednesday night Rosa has my kids over to her house for a long dinner. Ian and I make our first love in my bedroom study. It is wonderful, but rushed.

"Are you sure you can't call your friend and ask her to keep them overnight," Ian asks as I start to get dressed.

"I have a thing about getting my kids to bed on school nights. You don't know how tenuously balanced we are. I feel that if I break one bit of our routine, my family will be like Humpty Dumpty and all the king's horses and all . . ."

"Katherine, this can't go on. I want to make real love with you."

I lean over to stroke the side of Ian's face. "One thing I've been thinking of . . . Rosa and Jeff own a little cabin off in the mountains. Very isolated, no phone, wonderful views. I'll see if we can use it."

"Next week? I'll stay an extra day."

Now I run my fingers through his thinning blond hair. "It may not be for a while, because of the paper. Bill is taking on a new reporter at the end of April. I know that's a long time, but it's impossible for me to leave on weekdays right now. If we go off, I want to fall asleep with you, and take a long, slow time waking up."

"Ahh," says Ian.

. . . . .

When Ian is in Boston, he calls me a couple of nights a week from his office. My children are amazingly disruptive and seldom leave me alone while I talk. Though they pretend not to know who I'm talking to. I won't let myself think of the lessons they are learning in deceit. Or the lessons in bribery. Tonight I've parked them in front of a trashy TV show with popcorn and sodas. For a change I hear Ian's every word.

"Katherine, Ellen told me yesterday she is going to Italy for two months. She leaves in early July. It's the same time I have that big design job in California. Meet me out there. I've talked to my attorney friend. Remember I told you about his beach house I designed near Big Sur? He'll turn the place over to us. You'll love it. I've looked at my calendar and, except for two days, I can clear two full weeks. Afterward, we can drive along the coast, down to L.A. and I'll show you the town. Then, the next day, I'll put you on a plane back to North Carolina. You already told me you have accumulated at least a month's leave time from the *Gazette*. It's perfect!"

Our worlds are so different. This man just doesn't know. I have let him into my world and he still doesn't see it. I press the phone against my ear and don't say anything.

Ian continues, "You've never been West. We can have time and solitude, you and I, alone, beside the Pacific. You can explore far and wide the two days I'm gone, I'll leave a map. You can take long, hot soaks in the sunken tub to rest up from and for our perpetual lovemaking. I'll leave food and wine and great books. Please, please say you'll stay out there with me."

"The kids too, Ian?"

"Come on, Katherine. I'm very serious."

"I am too, Ian. I'm not leaving my children for two weeks."

"Doesn't Eric usually keep them about then anyway? I mean, that's why it is so perfect."

"Well, not for two weeks. I mean he does have that new wife. They do need time to themselves."

It is out of the question. I can't even fantasize California. I refuse to see my children as obstacles, although they certainly seem to be at this particular time. Ian is inviting me to dance as the children hold me by my ankles. Walking is a miracle, dancing almost unimaginable.

"Anyway, first things first," I say. "Let's work on Rosa's cabin. We haven't even spent a night together. If you snore, I'm definitely not interested in a string of overnights."

. . . . .

Finally, with untold maneuvering, I get the loan of Rosa's cabin in the country for a Wednesday night and arrange to take Thursday morning off from work. I'd planned to have the kids stay with Rosa, but she has a conference in Atlanta. One of Ian's students gladly agrees to take care of the kids. I tell my children I have an overnight meeting, for the paper, in Raleigh.

I drive to the campus lodge to pick Ian up and he staggers out to the car laden with two brimming-full grocery bags. Enough supplies for a week in the country. As he awkwardly drops his packages in the backseat and climbs in beside me, I suddenly wonder what I am doing driving off to spend a night with another woman's husband; driving off and leaving behind a trail of lies. Something seems to be urging me to turn around, to cancel. I don't know what Ian is thinking, but we are very careful not to touch on the drive. We are both nervous, our conversation is strained and artificial. We talk in brief spurts about his class and my afternoon interview. The president of the university had openly challenged the governor's new budget, I got the scoop.

When I turn onto the long gravel road to Rosa's cabin, the sun is low in the sky. The spring fields dip toward woods iridescent with new leaves, and the woods climb into mountains that balance the coloring sky. I make a weak joke about the bags of groceries.

"Candles," he says, "I bought candles. How do you feel about candles?"

I keep my eyes on the road. "What do you have in mind? I mean is this for some kind of perversion, or are these the tiny kind you put in cakes, or . . ."

"I guess, well, Katherine, what I had in mind was illumination."

"Sounds good to me. Of course, Rosa has got electricity in her place. So candles aren't a necessity."

How do men and women talk when they have a long time together? Especially when they are from different worlds? This evening stretches ahead like a down escalator we need to ascend. This is very awkward. I've made a mistake.

When we walk into my friend's cabin, it seems too dark, dusty, abandoned. Though I know Rosa thoughtfully tried to straighten up for us her last time out here.

"I—I guess the bedroom is up those stairs," he says. "Think I'll take the candles up there, now. Meet you in the kitchen, O.K.?"

I've unpacked the shrimp, two small steaks, artichoke hearts, the hearts of palm, the whole pineapple, the cheeses and bread. I've put the bottle of white wine into the fridge to chill and have uncorked the red. I am at the sink, washing lettuce, when Ian returns.

He stands behind me and takes my hands, he holds them under the cold water. He presses his body tightly across my back and moves his hips against me. Turning my wrists under the cold water, he strokes the insides of my arms with water, washing them with icy water, moving his hands down to the water and up my arms again and again. Without letting go of me, while kissing my neck and shoulders, he reaches and turns on the hot faucet too. When the water is warm, he cups handfuls of it to my breasts, soaking my blouse, then unbuttoning my blouse and cupping warm water to my bare breasts, to my belly. I take my wet hands and touch him, touch him where he is pressed behind me. I am bent with my head almost in the sink, licking water from his forearm. Ian abruptly turns off the faucets, takes hold of the open bottle of wine, and leads me upstairs.

The small loft bedroom shimmers. He must have lit twenty candles; the bed is turned down, and the room is warm with light. We undress one another slowly. We make love most of the night, pausing in our lovemaking only long enough to share thirsty gulps from the bottle of wine. When we finally rest, we cannot sleep.

A few hours before dawn we wrap one another in blankets and go out to look at the sky. Ian points to distant constellations and tells me stories of their namings. Cassiopeia in her chair and the bow of Sagittarius. When we come back inside, we cook together and make an opulent, obscene breakfast of steak and shrimp, cheeses and bread washed down with cold white wine. We eat everything and drink most of the wine.

At sunrise we go back to bed and sleep for a few hours, co-cooned tightly together in a blanket. In the mid-morning we wake up and make love again. We shower together and get back to town just in time for Ian to meet the airport limo. I drop him off and head for the newspaper office.

. . . . .

Something is wrong. When I walk through the door, all activity stops.

"Bill." The secretary keeps her eye on me and bangs on Bill's closed door. "She's here."

My boss walks out of his office with doomsday on his face. "Katherine, everybody has been looking—" He stops, looks around at the still office. "Come inside." He closes his office door behind us.

"About an hour after you left here yesterday. We got this call. Look, Katherine, no one knew where you were. I mean, I have my suspicions, but we tried—"

"What, Bill! What's wrong? My kids, my children, my—"

He puts his hand on my shoulder. "It's Beth. Now listen, Eric just called from the hospital, and—and—"

"Eric? I don't—I don't understand. I mean, Beth is O.K., right? There's nothing . . ."

Bill is getting his keys from his desk. "Come on, I'll drive you up there. We can talk in the car." I follow him out the door. I want to grab the corner of his jacket. I want to hold on tight. I don't want my feet to touch the floor.

In the car he tells me that yesterday the kids had just gotten home from school and the baby-sitter was watching TV with Madeline. Toby was mowing the lawn, Beth was sitting on the back steps watching him. It seems the mower hit a stone, a small stone was flung by the blades and hit Beth in the temple. When the sitter went out to check on them, Toby was, obliviously, still struggling with the oversized mower and Beth was lying on the ground, at the foot of the stairs. Lying there, still breathing, but not moving. Phone calls, neighbors, an ambulance; Toby and Madeline with Esther, more phone calls.

"They called the office first to find out how to reach you in Raleigh. As you can guess, I had no idea of what anyone was talking about. Somebody got ahold of Eric, maybe Esther, I don't know. He caught a plane and managed to get to the hospital about ten o'clock last night. Some big deal surgeon flew in from Atlanta."

A vein in Beth's temple was severed, something about pressure on the brain. They operated at four this morning. While I watched Cassiopeia reclining in her sky chair, my baby was lying on an operating table, her mother standing naked to the stars.

"She . . . Katherine, she's in a coma. No calls yet on if she's going to make it."

"No calls, no calls," I mutter over and over. Bill is pretending to drive, but the car really isn't moving.

"Bill, right after Beth was born . . . It was an early summer evening and all three of the children were asleep, so I left the farmhouse for a little walk. I was just going to be gone for a few

215

minutes. Anyway, I walked over a rise in the field and came face-to-face with a baby rabbit . . ." Maybe I could get out and run beside the car.

I continue. "A tiny little thing, immobilized with terror at the sight of me. I took one look at that helpless creature and milk cascaded from my breasts. I turned around and ran back to the house with milk flowing down my front, like blood from a knife stab at my heart."

Bill just nods, pretending to drive, but the car isn't moving. It's a sunny spring afternoon. So why am I asleep? Why am I having this wrong dream?

"No calls, no calls . . ."

At the hospital a grim-faced Eric is waiting for me in the lobby. I follow him up to Intensive Care. My baby lies immobile and dwarfed on an outsized bed. Her head is wrapped in white and machines surround her everywhere. Tiny TV screens are running the story of her life in zigzag patterns. Beth is pale and so small. The fingers of her hands are loosely curled, but I can see her fingernails are dirty. Maybe one of the nurses has a nail file and I can sit here and clean my daughter's fingernails. Beth is sleeping. I am holding her hand in mine.

"Remember, remember, Eric, when she was really little and she slept all the time?" I whisper. "Remember that? And for a while I was glad that she slept so much, I really wanted her to. And then I didn't want her to. She would fall asleep and I'd wake her up. When she got sleepy, I would distract her. I would say, I would say, 'Beth, look at that Momma bird trying to find worms for her baby.' I would say, 'Beth, guess what hand the penny is in.' I would say . . ."

We are back in the lobby. No one is allowed in Intensive Care for very long. Not even mothers.

Eric lights a cigarette. "Barbara got in this morning. She's rented a car and has gone to pick up Toby and Madeline. Esther sent them to school today, she said that was her best idea for what to do with them. Anyway, Barbara is bringing them here.

I've gotten rooms for everybody at that motel across the high-way."

This is a new Eric. After all these years, he sounds like a parent. Sobriety has done wonders for him.

"Katherine Roberts!" I have a phone call at the reception desk. It's Ian.

"I called your office and heard. How are you? How is Beth? I'm—"

I hang up the phone and go back to watch Eric smoke his cigarette. A few minutes later a very lovely young woman enters the lobby holding hands with Madeline. Toby is following, slowly, behind them. The woman has to hold the door for Toby for a long time, waiting for him to come through the door. His head is down, but when he looks up and sees me, he runs toward me. I bend on one knee and open my arms.

This isn't what Toby has in mind.

"Where were you? You weren't where you said you were going to be. You weren't there. You're a liar! A liar, a liar—"

"What about you, little buckaroo?" I stand and jam my hands in my pockets. "I only told you a hundred times to leave that mower alone. Now see what's happened."

Toby's face drains of color, from an angry red to white. Without another word, he turns and walks away down the corridor. I watch him, his narrow shoulders slumped. He looks so tired, and so old as he walks away.

He's a little boy whose world keeps breaking on him. What's wrong with me? What's wrong with me? I am a mother bitch devouring her pups, tearing them up and swallowing them, one by one. Please, God, let Beth be all right.

"You handled that real well." My daughter shoots me a rotten look and heads off after her brother.

"Katherine," Eric says in an out-of-context way, "Katherine, this is Barbara."

I turn to the lovely dark-haired woman who is now holding on to Eric's arm. "I bet you just couldn't wait to meet me," I say, grimacing.

It is the third day. I haven't been to the motel room Eric has so thoughtfully provided. I haven't left the waiting room outside Intensive Care. I've slept sitting up and now my feet are so swollen I can't wear shoes, and sit barefooted in the hall. Rosa is sitting beside me. She's just handed me a little bag of toiletries.

"Thanks, friend. Rosa to the rescue, as usual. My wonderful friends. Marie has called, I don't know how she heard . . . maybe you? She sent flowers for Beth, balloons for Toby and Madeline. Esther has been in and out . . ."

I rest my head on Rosa's shoulder. "She's only sleeping, Rosa. I know she's only sleeping. You know how tired these little ones get? I hope her dreams are O.K. Toby used to have such horrible nightmares. I'd tell him to turn his pillow, you know?"

"I know," says Rosa. She takes out a brush and begins to brush my hair.

"I turned the pillow of bad dreams over and over. Those times my children drifted away or were in trouble? I always felt I was pulling on boxing gloves, ready to fight. But I was never able to find the opponent. I whirl around looking for the enemy and find only my own shadow. There is no one else to blame. So I am the enemy, the shadow boxer."

"Katherine, you just need some sleep. And, if you don't mind my mentioning it, a bath. She's going to make it. She will. Beth is a tough little fighter and she just does things her way." Rosa fumbles in her purse. "Room 321. Take a shower, I'll sit here and not move till you come back. I'll send someone, in person, to pull you out of the shower if there's any change." She hands me the key.

. . . . .

It is Sunday afternoon. Eric and Barbara have gone to lunch with Toby and Madeline. Madeline has happily told me that Barbara is

218

teaching her to do embroidery. Toby continues to steer clear of me and has taken to following Eric, like a puppy. I watched the four of them leave the hospital talking to one another in a relaxed way. Life seems to be going on, though I can see no reason for it. The nurse says I can have my five minutes with Beth.

I stand and watch her shallow breathing. I would breathe for her, become her breath. I would lay down my life for her, surely I could be her breath? Now I am trying to remember how she breathed when she wasn't lying in this bed, wasn't a small lost sleeper flung among these machines. I try to remember Beth, just Beth, her life, her healthy life. I can picture her when she was learning to ride Toby's two-wheeler. But what was she *thinking* while she learned? How did she *feel*? I've always just assumed my children are part of me. I realize now I've only known how I felt about taking care of, watching over them. Even when I thought I was, I wasn't really watching *them*. Who has she been, this child, this daughter? And Toby and Madeline? Who have they been, separate from me, separate from reflections of my self?

I run our lives by like a silent, out-of-focus, movie. I have marked the passage of time by their births, yet I don't remember them being there. I only remember *my* experience of their births. What do they wish for when they close their eyes and blow out birthday candles? What are their wishes and who hears them? I love my children enough to die for them, but not enough to spend time listening to them. I can't remember any conversations with my children. Who are they really? What are their good dreams? I don't know. After all this time, I just don't know. These children deserve better than this. They pulled a bad ticket in the mama lottery.

When I walk out into the hallway Eric and Barbara are returning. They come down the hall, holding hands. "Those two can't get enough of McDonald's," Eric tells me. "You should have seen Toby—"

"Do you want them, Eric? Do you want these children, Eric and Barbara? Whatever of these children manage to survive.

Would you like to take over now?" A terrible weight is beginning to lift. Soon I will be able to float away.

"Come on, Katherine. You're just tired, tired and distraught."

I flop down in a chair. "Eric, nobody says 'distraught' anymore. It has fallen out of fashion, as they say. I know I'm tired and 'distraught,' but my wits are about me. We can talk later." I press my fingertips, pulling my eyelids over my too dry eyes. "You know, I'll keep on keeping them if you don't want them. If you don't want these children I've had all to myself all their years. But, otherwise, I'm ready to give up. How about you take over? How about you have your turn?"

A few minutes later a nurse runs out, followed by half the staff. "She just woke up! She woke up and looked around and now she's crying like a seven-year-old with a bad headache!"

The nurse is also crying. I take this awakening as a sign. For once, I have done the right thing. The children will be better away from me, they'll find salvation elsewhere. They will have a good life with Eric and his new wife. My decision to let go of my children was like the prince's kiss and my daughter is Sleeping Beauty. We all rush into Intensive Care to welcome Beth home from her long sleep.

. . . . .

We are back home. Beth has been moved to the Leeston hospital, they will release her in a couple of days. She's just fine. It's near the end of the school year and Beth's teacher has been kindly going to the hospital to catch Beth up. As soon as summer vacation begins, the three children are moving to Maryland. Eric has agreed to take his children on. He thinks it is a trial run. He doesn't know I have washed my hands of mothering. I think he's agreed to have the children through Barbara's prodding. Sweet, young, innocent Barbara. It will be like an instant family for them. Everybody potty-broken and verbal.

I overhear Madeline talking to Harmony on the phone. "Barbara says I can have a canopy bed. We're going to pick it out when I get there. And ballet lessons."

Toby is still not speaking to me. Our meals are silent and careless. I order out for pizza or fried chicken and let the children pour their own Cokes. We've begun to eat on paper plates.

"Mom, you're the one always talking about the environment. Trees died for these plates." Madeline, a moralist to the end.

. . . . .

Rosa has come to my office to talk to me. She is furious. "You can't mean it, Katherine. You can't. You don't know the damage it's going to do to them."

"Why?" I push back from my desk. "They're going with their father. Where does it say only the mother is a true parent? Where does it say that? Don't tell me you're jumping on the bandwagon for 'biological destiny'? I have a uterus, so I don't have a choice."

"That's not the point, it's just so radical, so sudden. You are the only parent they know. You've been it for them, even before the divorce, and now—"

"There's the point, Rosa. Now it's their father's turn. They'll have two parents and grandparents and all this middle-class shit they always wanted and I couldn't give them. I'm doing the right thing."

Rosa leans over the desk, she is pleading. "It will be like a death to them. Children who lose the caretaking parent, in child-hood, those children are bereft forever."

"I don't want to hear this, Rosa. I've loved them too hard and too long. I'm the, the . . . I'm the bull in the china shop of love. The harder I love them the more I hurt them. I can't do it anymore. I'm no good at it and I can't do it anymore! I know they'll be better off. Hearing otherwise only causes me to be afraid and I'm goddamned tired of being afraid! O.K.?"

Rosa turns and leaves the office, without another word.

. . . . .

Ian stopped trying to reach me at the hospital. The Wednesday after we get home I call him at the Campus Lodge. "Oh, Katherine, your voice. I'm so glad to hear your voice. I'd talked to a surgeon friend at Mass General about Beth—" He interrupts himself. "I called the paper, Bill told me she's going to be O.K. I was so worried about her. And I knew, I knew if Beth died I'd never see you again. I'd never—"

"I tell you what, Ian. I want to talk and to make love and drink wonderful wine and spend time with you. But you and I are never to talk about my children. All right?"

"Katherine, I want to be in your life, I want—"

"All right, Ian?"

"All right, Katherine. As soon as I know what the rules are, I'm ready to abide." The relief I hear in his voice makes me angry.

. . . . .

"But you'll still be our mom, right?"

"Right, Beth. I'll be your mom and Barbara will be your mom too. You'll have two moms." It is hard to breathe while I say this. Am I a liar, or a dreamer?

"Two moms?" Beth's brow is furrowed under its little crew cut.

"And two houses. Well, sorta two houses. Mostly you'll be in Maryland, in a beautiful house. That will be your new home."

Her fingers play with the fringe of hair circling her bandage. "But this house is beautiful, I don't want a beautifuller house than this."

I lift Beth onto my lap. "You'll change your mind. Just wait."

I think to myself, "Please change your mind, Beth. Go with the winner."

· · · · ·

"You keep avoiding any discussion of the future. Katherine, you remind me of a little kid closing her eyes because she thinks it will make the bad monster go away."

"That's a good name for the future, Bad Monster." Ian and I are sitting on the rocks at the river. It is his last day in Leeston. The surrounding mountains hold their full green and bird songs are rivaling the sounds of rushing water.

"Today I taught my last class. It's the end of my course, but it's not the end of us. I'm certainly not leaving you behind for good."

"Leave me behind, Ian. I'm a fling. I'm an affair, your little piece on the side."

"We're in love, deeply, intensely, in love. Dammit!"

"Affairs are supposed to be passionate and intense," I say wearily. "Everybody feels this way. All the sneaking around is like an aphrodisiac."

Ian grabs a fistful of my hair. "O.K., that does it, I'm drowning you. If you are going to besmirch this passion that tears me from sound sleep, if you insist on making it common and temporary, I'm going to drown your ass!"

I take his hair and pull him into me and kiss him on his face and his neck.

"That won't work, Katherine." He closes his fingers over my lips. "I'm asking for a very small commitment, two weeks. I'm not asking you to marry me, I'm just asking you to shack up in Big Sur with me. It's only two weeks. I'm in love with you. Sure, I want to make a lot of plans with you, but right now I'm only asking for this one."

I let go of him. "Think about how you felt for Ellen when you first knew her. I know my love for Eric pulled me from sound sleep too."

Ian stands and flings a rock into the water. "For God's sake,

223

Katherine. You were nineteen fucking years old. You had nothing in common with that man."

"We read the same books. You don't even read literature, Ian."

He throws another rock. "I'm gonna get a library card. I'm gonna read a book every night. I'm gonna write book reports. You'll see."

Neither one of us mentions that there'd been no future plans until I surrendered my children.

. . . . .

"Toby, a truce. Let's just have a truce." The children leave tomorrow. Eric will arrive in a van and he'll drive the children and their possessions off to Maryland. He has refused to sign any papers. Eric wants to make sure the kids are adjusted and that Barbara can handle this sudden new role before we do anything legal. I am signing full custody over to him, whenever he is ready. But now Toby has got to be set free. We need to mend our rickety fence before he leaves.

"You know Beth is so much better that they say she's going to be smarter in school than she was before the accident. Really."

Toby just leans on the edge of the sofa and stares into space. "I mean, not that Beth was ever what you could call straight A material. But they think her remedial reading classes are over forever. She's that much smarter. In fact, they're thinking of taking all the dumbest kids at Leeston Elementary and lining them up and throwing rocks at their heads. Really."

Toby plops down on the sofa. "That's the weirdest thing you've ever said. And you have said weird stuff."

. . . . .

The van is packed. Harmony and Rosa have just left, after tearfully telling the kids good-bye. Madeline is slumped on the front steps, holding her little eyeglasses and sobbing. Toby is sitting on the front seat of the van, where he has been for the last half-hour, ready to go. Eric walks out of the house. "I can't find Beth anywhere."

I circle to the back of the house, climb the rope ladder, and find my young bald daughter hunched in the corner of the tree house.

"I'm gonna stay, O.K., Mom? I'll just live out here. I won't be any trouble."

I take her chin in my fingers and kiss her. "Sweetheart, you're going to have to go because Madeline and Toby are going. They need you. Well, especially Toby needs you. He needs someone to be on his side against Madeline, because she's so bossy." I start down the rope ladder and Beth follows. "You know how good you are at being on Toby's side."

We get to the front of the house and Beth sits beside her sister and starts patting Madeline's back.

I lean into the van and kiss Toby. "I love you, fella. I love you very much and I hope you get on a good baseball team up there."

"I will." He's looking straight ahead, tapping on the dash-board like a steel drummer, biting his lower lip and looking straight ahead.

I kiss my daughters and take each one by the hand and lead them out to the driveway. "I'll write to you and I'll want to hear about your new rooms and your new friends. It's going to be fun."

Eric lifts Beth up and she, silently, grabs my arm. He is trying to pry her fingers loose. Madeline wraps her arms frantically around my waist.

"I don't want new friends, or new anything. I want to stay!"

I'm not listening. The girls are incoherently screaming and crying. Eric and I work together to get our daughters into the van, to close the door.

I remember trying to jam fuzzy kittens into a picnic basket. I was alone then. And it was a long time ago.

225

Now the doors are closed. Eric kisses me quickly on the cheek. "They'll be fine." He walks around to the driver's side, starts the van, and drives off. I stand at the foot of the driveway waving in the late May sunlight, though there is no one to wave to.

I go back inside, put very loud music on the stereo, and ferociously begin to clean the upstairs, to clear out all the evidence. I jam abandoned toys, old drawings, baseball cards, school pictures, plastic jewelry into large garbage bags. I don't pause to look at anything. I hold my breath, fighting nausea. My hands are shaking and I have to open the windows for air. Yet I keep working, cleaning. It is dark when I'm finally satisfied.

I go downstairs to the kitchen, without turning on any lights. I grab a fork, open the refrigerator, and pull out a bowl of pasta. I prop my foot on the bottom shelf, put the bowl on my knee, and begin to eat by the light of the open door.

"Free at last. Good God Almighty, I'm free at last." My voice is a cracked whisper scuttling, spiderlike, through the abandoned house.

. . . . .

The last time I was my own agent I was a fresh-cheeked girl, with no car and little income, in the Old South where unescorted females waited by the phone. And if it didn't ring, they stayed home. Now I have a house, a car, a career, and a great deal of life experience.

The singles gang at the newspaper opens up for me, these young, unattached people let me into the world of late night dancing and movies and bar-hopping. I take to it like to a ladle of cool spring water after a long walk in the desert.

At first it is hard to believe that I can just pick up and go to a movie. No major plans have to be made, no supper hurried through, or prepared early and left on the back burner, no babysitter. If you want to go to a movie, you walk out of the house, get in your car, drive to the theater, buy a ticket, walk in, and sit down. I keep waiting for someone to stop me. Nobody does. I see more movies in the first two weeks the kids are gone than I've seen in five years. I avoid movies I would have shared with the children. If I see any kids at the "adult" movies I choose, I resent them. I am sick and tired of children. My dues are more than paid and now my time is my own. It will take a while, I know it will take a while, but I'll learn to own my time.

The children have been gone for almost a month and still Rosa and I haven't patched up our quarrel. "Rosa, would you be interested in dinner out? My treat."

Her telephone voice sounds crisp and artificial. "I don't think so, Katherine. Jeff's out of town and Harmony and I have planned a big night together." Neither of us bothers to say "good-bye" when I hang up. "It's time for new friends, anyway," I mutter to myself.

· · · · ·

"This stuff is fantastic. No wonder all those hippies gave up the revolution for it."

One of the reporters has brought marijuana over to my house and we're sharing a joint and a bottle of very inferior red wine. Mark has been hanging out with me fairly steadily since I began my single life. He's a student and works half-time at the paper. We are just lighting up, this is my second time to smoke the "devil weed." The first time was several nights ago at a party. I got very stoned and was very funny. I regaled a room full of people with the story of my sex education classes at the convent. I remember acting out the poor little sperm searching for the gone-forever egg. The little sperm was beside himself, but the elusive egg had zipped through the chute. Pot must make it very easy to laugh. The next morning my sides were, literally, sore. I had laughed so hard.

"It sure must have made the revolution more fun," Mark

says, as he refills my wineglass. I inhale the smoke deeply, recall-
ing my happy days as a cigarette smoker.

The living room begins to look misty and soft, as if the walls
might be made of clouds. "Whoa, I'm getting a little lost, here,"
I say. Then I don't know if I've said this out loud, or to myself. I
look at Mark to see if he has heard me.

He is smiling at me and reaches over to pull a lock of hair
away from my face. No, that's not what he's doing, he's unbuttoning my blouse. It takes a long time. When I go to help him,
he moves my hand and puts my fingers in his mouth. I can't
believe how good this feels, this boy sucking my fingers and smiling at me. Good ole Mark.

"Are we going to do it, Mark, are we?" Have I said this out
loud? I must have, because now I'm unzipping Mark's pants.
Everything feels so good, so very, very good.

The next morning I don't even remember what happened
until I walk out into the living room and see my clothes on the
floor. I dread going into work, but when I get there and see Mark,
he is his same young affable self.

. . . . .

"I don't know, Esther. It's still a big deal to me. As much as I
enjoy it, I can't see being casual about sex. I wanted to put on a
mustache and a fake nose to walk into the office."

Esther and I have gone to the river and are sunbathing on a
flat smooth rock in a curve of the river, just below the rapids.
There are college students on the other rocks but the noise of the
water protects our conversation.

"Get over it. Fucking is fun and you surely deserve a good
time. If Ian hadn't shown up, your hymen would have grown
back." Esther is slathering suntan oil over her short brown legs.
"Of course, Ian might not be thrilled to hear of your indiscre-
tion."

"You mean, no fair cheating on a cheater?"

"You sure have been hard on your boyfriend since Beth's accident."

"I swear, some days I don't know how I feel about Ian. Most times I think I love him, I certainly know I always lust for him. Still, there's something about that lust that always recalls Beth's accident."

"Are all Catholics so masochistic about sex?"

"I don't think it's just Catholicism. Maybe it is also because I was molested as a child. Nothing really big deal. A dirty old man grabbed me. I ran away." I put out my hand for a hit of suntan oil. "Nothing happened. But it made sex so, so threateningly mysterious. I thought that old man could see something in me I couldn't see. I stayed afraid of whatever I thought he knew and I didn't. That's always been just around the corner from my pleasure. That part of me I can't see, but maybe the man can."

Esther caps the suntan oil. "I didn't know you were molested. All this time and I never heard that. How old were you?"

"Oh, about seven." The oil feels good on my slightly sunburned legs.

"Poor baby. If anyone had touched my Nathan when he was little, I would have tied 'em to the back of my car and driven eighty miles an hour down a hundred-mile-long gravel road. The fucker!"

"Atta girl, Esther. Actually, I think I blocked it for a time. I know I didn't tell my parents. I remember my mother saying, 'Katherine, you used to be such a sunny child.' It must have changed me for a while. Anyway, if I remember, I buried myself in books and dealt with it. Rosa claims I haven't dealt with it. I think Rosa is on the lookout for another Sybil. I think it would cheer her up if I had a multiple personality." I lean over to wash the tanning oil from my hands.

"She is worried about you, you know, Katherine. Not because of your childhood, because of your children. She thinks you aren't dealing with letting them go."

I dangle my hand in the water, still incredulous over the

clarity. I remember the first time I ever came to this river, how much I loved it then, how it bonded me to this place.

"I'm dealing with it. She's wrong. I write to the kids every week. They're doing fine and I'm doing fine." I rub my hands together under the water and watch a thin film of oil rise to the surface. "Eric is bucking it a bit. He claims it's more difficult than they thought it would be, that the child bride is having a hard time. No joke! I'm not worried, though, my guess is that this instant family will, in the long run, help Eric and Barbara's marriage. Rosa's wrong, this whole thing is for the best. Also, I wish she'd try to restrain herself from discussing my business behind my back."

Esther drops the capped bottle into her beach bag. "You aren't exactly being fair, Katherine. You know fucking well she's tried to talk with you. Think of all—"

"Think of all she's done for me. You think I don't know? She's got it too together, what could I ever do back? Wish her hard times so I can be the one coming to the rescue?"

Esther doesn't answer. She seems to be concentrating on the sun lightener she is working into her hair.

"She's just pissed because I don't think the way she does. I guess I'm backward. Not having a college degree and all." I splash the water and watch the droplets catch the light.

"Un-huh." Esther has pulled out a comb and is lifting sticky strands of her hair toward the sun.

"I tell you one thing, Esther. I have figured out how come men are so far ahead of us in the world. You wouldn't believe what I'm getting done at the newspaper. In addition to the features section, almost a third of the articles in last week's issue were mine. Nine, I wrote nine pieces!" I stand, lock my fingers together, and stretch. "And they were damned good too. When you're not driving carpools and rushing home to fix dinner, the ole career takes off!"

I walk to the edge of the rock, toward the deep side of the

river, and dive. The late June sunlight slashes through the deep clear water and washes golden bars across my arms.

When I get home the empty house seems stale to me, stale and sterile. I walk upstairs and the three bedrooms accuse me with their bright starkness, the stripped-down mattresses, the bare dresser tops. I decide to put sheets on the beds. I carry a set of Felix the Cat sheets into Toby's room. As I lift the mattress to tuck the sheet under, I feel the edge of a book, a slender cloth-bound book. I pull it out and it's a journal. It couldn't be Toby's, Toby is definitely not the journal-keeping type.

I open the front cover and it is inscribed by Rosa, in neat broad printing. It says:

Toby, I am giving you and Madeline each a journal. This will be the first Christmas you have spent away from the farmhouse where you've lived all your life. You probably can't even read this yet. But I will read this to you and Madeline can read it.

When your heart hurts and you feel like you can't tell your secrets to anyone, write them down in this book.

Your friend, Rosa.
December 1974.

How exactly like Rosa.

There are only three entries in the journal. And none of them are dated:

My popa Deid He is My bes Fren
Garnny deid
the Hamter Deid
I don no why

I saw my DaD today. He wave at me. I lik his car.

231

This is my birthday. I am 7. My Dad fourgot to call me.
My Dad is besy. My mom bake my cake and it was gret.
My mom is smart. She is prety. David is my best frend.

I hold my forefinger on the last entry, close the book, and press it to my chest.

"Jesus, Jesus, Jesus, Toby. I don't know why either, I don't know why they died. I don't know anything. Your smart mama doesn't know a thing. And I don't even remember your seventh birthday. And I miss you, Toby, I miss you, I miss you!" I'm crying and burying my face in the mattress, searching for the scent of my lost son. I rub my face over his mattress like a hound following a forgotten trail. I think to myself that something happened on the way to a happy ending and we all got lost.

"You go on ahead, kids. I'll wait here," I sob.

None of this turned out the way I planned, or thought it would. I can't find a pretty way, or a funny way, to tell this story. Once upon a time there was a little girl. Her daddy loved her very much. He was her best friend. He told her she could do anything in the whole wide world. Then he gave her away to a prince. The prince was not her best friend. The prince gave her children as playthings. They were little dolls that were supposed to keep her from noticing that the prince had left her alone. She ran away from the prince and while she was running she kept dropping the dolls, dropping her children. She'd go back and pick them up. But after a while, she'd gotten them so dirty and broken she couldn't play with them anymore.

I cry myself to sleep in the tangle of red and black sheets.

CHAPTER IX

*W*HEN THE PLANE LANDS AT THE SMALL Monterey Peninsula Airport, I want to leap out and race away from its slow taxi in. It has been almost six weeks since Ian and I have seen one another. We're both more brown, his hair is longer. I go to kiss him as he reaches for my luggage. Then, when I catch on and go to hand him my luggage, he leans to kiss me. Finally we laugh and drop the luggage and hold one another in the midday light of the strange, strange land of California.

"I'm not going to let you go," says Ian. "I'm sorry you'll never get to see the beach house, or the ocean, or even the parking lot. I'm going to hold you until I am kudzu and you are a Georgia tree."

We stop at a florist shop, just outside the airport. "Pick anything you want, Katherine. Let's have a big bowl of flowers by our bed and flowers on our table. I want to see you in the light and surrounded with flowers."

A young Chinese man pulls out the flowers I select from behind the glass. "More," says Ian, smiling. "There is much light where we're going." I select deep blue irises and white roses, several stems of white and purple flowers that the young man says are a form of trailing orchids. He gives our flowers to an elderly woman to wrap. She walks to the case of flowers and takes out a perfect bright red rose. She speaks in Chinese to the young man, then adds the flower to our giant bouquet.

"My mother says, since you are lovers, she wants you to have the loveliest rose. A red one. Red is for luck."

We drive out of town and the car begins to climb. "Oh, Ian," I sigh, "how beautiful!" We are driving along a cliff above the ocean, the unbelievably blue Pacific Ocean. On the curves ahead of us and behind us rounded cliffs push into the sea like massive prehistoric whales, nosing out into the water. I think how I would have loved to show all of this to the children.

Our car, filled with the scent of flowers, is climbing higher. Now I've crawled halfway into the backseat to look behind us. Ian is chuckling at my amazement. "Jesus, I didn't know anyplace in the United States was so high above the ocean. Are you sure this isn't Monaco? I keep expecting Princess Grace to come careening by."

Eventually, we turn off the highway onto a sandy road that twists through a fantasy forest. Small streams wind through beds of fern, and thick, almost furry, vines are strung through the branches of the most enormous trees I have ever seen. "Ian, are those redwood trees, the famous redwood trees?"

"Uh-huh," he says, as if he'd planted them himself.

"It's so dark in these woods. What happened to the ocean? You know I don't think I recognize a single plant. California really is another planet, isn't it?" Ian stops the car. The road has ended. We are still in the woods, I am confused.

He gets out and opens the door to the backseat. Ian hands me the flowers and hoists my bag over his shoulder. He gives me his hand, and we follow a narrow path through the woods. "Do

234

these woods smell like heaven, or is it all the flowers? It seemed so quiet, and now I hear—"

"Look." Ian is almost whispering. "Look." The forest has abruptly stopped, and the path opens onto a small white beach. The whitest beach I've ever seen. The turquoise ocean slips around a large black round boulder on the rim of the perfectly white beach. Behind the beach, and enclosing it, there are high gold hills arching and climbing higher and higher toward a cloudless sky of blue so bright I have to close my eyes for a second. Ian looks at my amazed face and starts to laugh.

"Do you see the house?" he asks, smiling. I look all around and then shake my head. He proudly points over my shoulder. To our direct right, halfway up the hill, is a bluff, and on the bluff, nestled into the hillside, is the beach house. It is built of pale wood that is almost the same sandy color as the hills. Most of the small building is curved glass facing out to the sea.

"It looks like a secret," I tell him. He takes my hand again.

Just as the way up the hill becomes steep, steps begin. Ian leads the way up steps of weathered railway ties that have been embedded in the hillside. There is a small grassy front place before the house. I see that what I thought were windows is actually a series of French doors. They are all latched open. "What about bugs?" I turn to Ian.

"There is a Big Sur ordinance against bugs. They send all their bugs to Third World countries."

"Rich people think of everything," I mutter.

We walk into one large room, filled with light. Most of the low ceiling is made of thick glass, tinted pale green. The back wall has a small stone fireplace and a series of cupboards and drawers and bookshelves, made from the same wood as the house. There is a thick sheepskin rug in front of the fireplace. The room is dominated by a king-sized bed made of handhewn oak. A vibrant green Mexican embroidery is thrown across the bed and almost buried beneath a tumble of large pillows of many colors, a deeper green blanket is folded at the foot of the bed.

The far left alcove is a small kitchen, built around a butcher's block. In front of the kitchen, also facing the sea, is a table of the same oak as the bedstead. I have never seen anything so lovely. I will never forget it.

"You are good, you are very good. Ian, this place is beautiful. It's almost creepy beautiful."

"You can't tell, but we're stocked up so we wouldn't have to leave for weeks. I flew in yesterday and spent the whole afternoon shopping," he boasts. Ian wraps his arms around me, and we stand facing the Pacific. "The owner built it as a love nest," he says, kissing the back of my neck. "But his woman left him before they ever used this place. He almost never comes up here."

I take his hands from around my waist. "Give me a little time. All right, Ian? I feel a bit jumpy."

He steps back easily. "How about a swim? We have two weeks, Katherine. There will be time for everything."

Ian gives me a pair of straw sandals and we walk down the steps and across the white beach to the sea. "I warn you, Katherine, this isn't the Atlantic. This water is cold." We hold hands and run into the sea, which is so cold it knocks the wind from my chest. But it still feels wonderful. We ride the great waves and play in the frigid water until it seems as though our limbs are almost locking from the cold. We run, screaming with cold, up the steps again.

On the far side of the studio is a tiny stone patio with a shower that seems to be coming from the rocky hillside. We stand together and let the hot water pound over us. Ian is careful not to touch me. Then we step through a set of French doors into a small skylit bathroom.

"For you." Ian helps me into a deep green terry cloth robe. He kneels to tie the belt. "Do you like it?"

I run my hands along the soft cloth and nod. He grabs a brown robe, like mine, from the other wooden peg and we step into the big room. Ian crosses to the kitchen and takes a bottle of red wine from a cupboard that seems filled with bottles of wine lying side by side.

"Would you mind getting that blanket from the foot of the bed?" He is uncorking the wine.

When we walk outside, Ian is carrying the wine, two glasses, and a small plate of sushi. I spread the blanket, and we sit, facing the sea.

"What's that wonderful smell?" I ask as Ian hands me a glass of wine.

"Wild sage," he says. "All of this growth is wild sage." We sit, looking out to sea and sipping very wonderful red wine, nibbling the small bites of sushi.

"Ian, is that what I think?" I point to the ocean.

"Dolphins," he says.

Five dolphins are playing just offshore; their sleek dark bodies form curved stitches in the glimmering ocean. How my children would love this sight. Off to the right, the sun is a bright ball, almost ready to sink into the water. The sea is turning gold, and the dolphins are getting darker, shinier. This must be paradise. And I am an amputee in paradise.

"Katherine, watch those cliffs there." It seems that at the same time the sun is dropping into the water a thousand birds burst from the faraway pale cliffs over the ocean. As they come closer, I see that the birds seem to be all kinds, pelicans and sea gulls, pipers and birds that look like inky egrets. They pepper the multicolored sky and swirl past us, above the golden water and glistening dancing dolphins.

"The Garden of Eden must have been like this," I say. "Before Adam and Eve had a conscience." I rest my head on Ian's shoulder, and he pulls me closely into him. I slip my hand over the grasses and pull a bunch of the coarse wild sage, crush it in my fist and lower my face to it.

"Katherine, almost since that first night at your house, my dream has been to bring you here, to this love nest that has never before held lovers." He strokes my hair with his fingers.

237

If I don't love him, who do I love? I rub the crushed sage over my chest, open my robe, and bring Ian's face to me.

. . . . .

Each perfect day blends blue and gold into another. Most mornings we wake up early when the studio is enclosed in fog and we can only hear the ocean. We drink fresh-squeezed orange juice and coffee in thick mugs and make a large decadent breakfast.

Some days I feel as though I am convalescing from a severe and nameless illness, on others I feel like an impostor. I've sneaked onto the pages of somebody's absurd romance novel. In the late mornings Ian and I go down to the beach and ride waves and race one another along the smooth white sand. I keep seeing things that I wish I could show to the children, the tunnel the ocean has carved through the rocks, the golden grass of the hillsides beside the sea. At the same time, I glory in not having to care for anyone. Instead, I'm the one being cared for.

Ian shows me that the ocean side of the round black rock has a ledge for sunbathing and for diving during high tide. We turn almost the same shade of copper. Sometimes, when I see Ian's shining dark body coming from the water, I have to catch my breath. He seems so beautiful to me.

We don't eat lunch but usually take a small cloth bag of fruit and wine with us into the woods. The forest seems prehistoric and is so dense it muffles, then extinguishes, the roaring of the surf. We find a mossy place by a trickling waterfall where we share a bottle of wine and sometimes we make love.

I lean over to chew Ian's neck. "You still taste like the sea."

"That's because we are all made of the ocean. Didn't you know that?" I shake my head. "We are. Ninety-seven percent of our bodies are salt water. Like the ocean."

"Maybe it's not the ocean," I say. "Maybe it's tears."

Ian jams the empty wine bottle into the cloth bag. "Katherine, this is the best I can offer. I only want to make you happy."

"I am happy, Ian. Really. It's just that I was thinking this morning about how I used a large portion of my inheritance from my mother to buy a sofa, one sofa. A sofa your friend wouldn't want to let into his tasteful hideaway. I'm trying to adjust here. Trying to put things in perspective."

Each evening we take wine to the bluff and watch the sun set and the birds take to the sky. After the sun goes down, Ian always lights a fire, and we eat our supper on the sheepskin rug, our plates on our laps, and the serving dishes spread out in the fire's glow.

I always thought that if I got away from my children I would want to have sex morning, noon, and night. But sometimes, when Ian reaches for me, I think I hear Beth crying. And I freeze. I tell myself it is my morbid imagination, but then when Ian enters me it is so painful that I bite my lips until they almost bleed. And he doesn't seem to notice. Other times I'm ravenous.

I wish I could slip into an unquestioning love of this man, I'm trying hard. I've found that drinking helps. I don't want to spoil my only shot at paradise, so I drink a great deal. The drinking makes me wanton and, I think, pleasing to Ian. Tonight I dance naked for him in front of the fire, conscious of how the glow of the flames looks on my copper skin. I dance holding a bottle of brandy and sipping from it as I dance. The room is warm and I am warm. I am hot and very dizzy. I will dance until I believe in love again. I fling my head from side to side so that my damp hair slaps my face and fans out in a whirl before me. This makes me even dizzier. The room goes round and round, the beautiful room, and the fire glows on my lover, the man who would not give his wife children, as I go round and round. The man I think I can have now because I don't have children either.

My father is leaning over me. There are flames behind him. I am naked. I try to cover myself, cover my nakedness from my good father. The flames make shadows over his face. He looks so worried about me. The fire bothers me. I don't know where it comes from.

"Daddy? Daddy, are we in hell?"

He laughs and it's not my father, it's Ian. "You've had way too much to drink, Katherine. I'm going to carry you to bed."

Sometime during the night he enters me. "It's no good, no good, no good!" At first I am horrified, and pound at him with my fists, then I remember he's not my father. He's Ian. I remember and start to cry and lift my hips and close my legs over him and pull him tightly into my body. As if I could fill all my empty places with him.

In the morning Ian treats my hangover as the truly awful thing it is. He nurses me, bringing me juice and vitamins. He talks in a low voice and plays soothing music. A swim in the freezing ocean and a long massage in the sun restore me. By the evening I am starving, ready for a big dinner and more wine and lovemaking.

Tomorrow he leaves for his two days in the city. We have just finished our supper of poached fish, and I am wiping the last of the avocado salad up with a crusty piece of French bread when Ian starts to speak. "Are you happy?"

I lean over and slip the last mushroom into his mouth.

"Because," he says as he moves the dinner clutter from the rug and I stretch out with my head in his lap, "I've never been this happy, Katherine. In my life, never."

I take a deep breath and turn my face away from him. "It's so beautiful here, Ian, that it's make believe. That night in Rosa's cabin? That was the best night of my life. I loved you. I think I loved you purely. After everything you'd told me, I still had to have you in my life. I just knew I loved you, married, or single. I loved you and I felt I knew who you were." I take his hand and rub it, as though I am comforting him. "That was the new part, for me. I made up poor Eric, created him in some image I needed, or expected. Who knows, I may even have made up my wonderful father. But, that night I thought I knew you. My

Waspy, funny, gentle, generous lover." I drop his hand. "And I can't talk myself out of believing the price for that knowledge was too high. Now I hardly know anything."

He is hurt, but I can tell he is trying not to frighten me away. He speaks gently, as he would to a wild kitten. "Give it time, Katherine. Give yourself time. Your life has changed very radically and we can just take it easy."

A hungry—but ready to run away—lost, wild kitten.

"I have a better idea of what it feels like to be Ellen than of what it feels like to be you, to be Ian Richter. Isn't that funny?" I get up and begin to pace.

"I think one reason lovers gaze into one another's eyes is to find their own reflections. To learn love of self. But, when I see you loving me, I can't love myself because I'm worried about who you are, and why you love me. In all that has happened, I forgot who you are. Except . . ." I pause. "Except I know you are a man capable of deceiving his wife. And you are a man who does not want children. You love me more, now that I don't have children. And I love you less."

"No, Katherine. That's not fair and it's not—"

I lean down and place my hand over his mouth. "If I don't know you, Ian, I'm not sure what the point is. I look at your world and realize you've never lost anything. The last five years of my life have been about nothing but loss. We don't match. We don't reflect one another."

The ocean is pounding in the darkness behind my speech. Ian is sitting by the fire, head tilted. He is trying to understand, trying to listen. I kneel beside him. I take his face between my hands. "I know you can't even imagine what I know. Don't you see? And it makes me lonely."

"Katherine, you're not giving me a chance. It's true, I can't manufacture hard times. I surely can't say I have had any that could compare to yours. But why can't I use that to make your times, or at least your times-to-come, easier?"

"As simple as that, huh, Ian?"

"Katherine, you are determined to set up barriers for yourself. You would even set up roadblocks on lovers' lane, if you could. That is something I do know about you. And even something I love." He leans to the cupboard beside the fireplace and pulls out a bottle of Grand Marnier. "I'm not a bastard, or not a total bastard. I have spent time thinking all of this out. And don't worry about Ellen. No matter what happens with you and me, Ellen will be fine. I promise." He stands to get two liqueur glasses.

"You just don't get it, do you, Ian? I'm speaking another language."

"Just tell me what you want, Katherine!"

"I want to know another person. I want a faith in love's permanence. I want permission to be happy." I can feel him kneel beside me. "Love dies, one way or another, it always dies!"

"Look at me. Look at me, Katherine. Love is not a dead thing or a bad thing. Love is good. Our love will make us good. We will get this behind us, and we'll either have a long, rich affair and part friends, or we'll get married." He takes a sip from his glass, as he hands me mine.

"But," I say, taking the glass, "don't you see, I just—"

He kisses me and fills my mouth with the liqueur he has warmed in his own. Some of the Grand Marnier flows out of my mouth, down my jaw to my neck, where he licks it away. He dips his forefinger into the glass and begins to paint letters on my body with liqueur. I dip into my glass and reach for him. We are kneeling in the light of the fire, while the ocean of the other side of the world roars outside.

. . . . .

The next evening he calls me from Los Angeles. It is the first time the phone has rung in the eight days I've been here. And at the first ring, I turn icy cold. Even though Ian told me he'd call, when the phone rings I become terrified, afraid to answer, more afraid not to. It is a relief, a strange relief, to hear his voice.

"I wanted to check on you, Katherine. I wanted to see how you're doing. See if you're pining away for me. And I have news, real—"

"I've had quite a lazy day, Ian. Though I feel like I sneaked into someone else's house and I have to be careful not to move anything." My day hasn't really been lazy. I ran and swam, tried to pound all thoughts from my head with violent exercise. It wasn't a lazy day, but it was mindless. I look at my arm and see that it is dusty with a coating of salt.

"You can push the whole damned beach house into the sea, if you want to. Listen, I have something to tell you, something amazing. I called Ellen, caught her in Florence, and told her . . . well, I didn't tell her about you, only told her I thought I wanted out of the marriage. She didn't sound surprised, or angry. We talked for quite a while, and quite calmly. I swear to God, Katherine, she even said she'd been thinking along the same lines."

"See, Ian," I want to say. "See, love always dies."

He is still talking. ". . . called Boston after I talked with Ellen and checked with one of my contacts at the *Globe*. I went on and on about your work. You can have a job in their features department in a minute."

"*I am trapped,*" I think, "*trapped.*"

The day still holds the light, and there is movement on the water that could be dolphins. "Wait, Ian, I think I see the—"

"Just be ready when I come back. It's going to be like at Rosa's cabin again. It will."

It isn't dolphins, it is the shadows waves make, at their crest, in the last light of day.

"Katherine, I take this as a sign. Everything is going to be fine. The Chinese woman's rose really worked."

When I go outside to shower I find a tick buried in my pubic hair. I take a long time to pry it away from me. Then I don't know what to do with it. So I just lean over and put it on the ground.

That night when I finally get to sleep I dream I walk up to a gardenia bush beside the sea and the bush is filled with blue-birds, all different kinds of bluebirds. The strange large vibrant bluebirds with the black wings I have seen flashing through the Pacific forest and the small American bluebirds that flit near the riverbank in North Carolina; there are miniature blue humming-birds and indigo buntings. In the dream I reach out my arms for the birds, and they fly to me, they cover me. They aren't afraid and land all over me. The smallest birds on my fingers, the largest on my shoulders. I turn to go and show the birds to the children. But when I get to the studio, the birds are gone. I had thought they were nestled between my shoulder and my neck, but they have disappeared. When I wake up, it is midnight, and my hand is clutched into a fist on my shoulder.

. . . . .

"Why did I know, with the goddamned phone ringing at three in the morning, why did I know it would be you, Katherine?"

"ESP, Eric. But enough about you. How are the buckaroos doing?" The phone is cold in my hand, as cold as the stone floor on my bare feet.

He seems to be collecting his thoughts, there is a pause be-fore he speaks. "I don't know, Katherine. Some days they seem fine, some days not. Beth is despondent. I was afraid it was the head injury, but the doctor says no. Madeline has been—

I can't hear this. "They're just adjusting, Eric. I mean you didn't think they'd bounce right in? They'll be fine."

"Barbara isn't doing so great either. It's more than she thought it would be. And—and—Katherine, we just found out Barbara is pregnant."

"Congratulations, Eric. What do the children say about it?

I'll be they're thrilled. You're going to end up with your own little Brady Bunch, yet."

Eric is obviously speaking carefully. "They don't know, we haven't told them. I want to talk to you, Katherine. Barbara and I have been thinking—"

"I have to go now, Eric."

When I bang the receiver down, the bang resonates over the sound of the fog-bound ocean. I don't need another guilt trip. If I don't know anything else, I know I need a life of my own. The children are not hot potatoes. They are wonderful little people, little Piersons, and that's Eric's last name, Pierson, not mine. I did the best I could and now it's over.

Dear Ian,

Something has frozen my heart. I believe that. I also believe in sin and that we must pay for our sins. And that, sometimes, sin comes disguised as freedom, sometimes as love. Beth paid, and I paid, for one perfect night.

You believe in love. You brought me to this ocean hideaway and, to you, this was a new Eden. We were entitled to forbidden fruit because we cherished its taste so well. While it is true, I ate the fruit and even savored it, I think paradise can easily become the mundane and wine made from forbidden fruit will surely sour. I believe love always dies.

I have learned from your gift of the sea. I have walked this beach and have watched the changing of the tides and the play of light that, in the late day, turns the sea to molten gold. Each morning the same sea is obscured by mist and beneath the mist the sea is gray. I have searched for the faith that what we have discovered together is so precious, it might hold the light. Instead, I find that,

245

right now, today, I haven't the courage to chance more inconstancy. On your part or mine. I hold us both accountable. Perhaps it's only that I don't love you enough. Or that a frozen heart cannot love.

I have to go away. At least for a while.

Please don't look for me.

In the late morning of the second day Ian is gone, the day that he promises to be back in time to watch with me while the sun falls into the ocean, I pull my suitcase from the cupboard where Ian stored it. It is still packed since I have had little need for the trappings of the real world in this paradise. I leave the rumpled, disjointed letter for him on the table under the vase of faded roses.

On the long walk through the woods I am plagued by butter-flies. I don't have a plan, but I do have a friend, one friend in California. The sandy road is a steep one, and, when I reach the highway, I am winded. The first vehicle to pass stops for me. It is a battered turquoise pickup truck, driven by a woman who is perhaps thirty years older than I am. Her coarse gray hair is in one long braid down her back. Two hawk feathers hang from her rearview mirror.

"Where to?" She has thrown open the passenger door.

"Where are you going?" I ask.

"To Paso Robles." She seems amused.

"Is that anywhere near Templeton?"

"Very near."

"Could you drop me off where you're going, then?" I say, standing firm by my luggage, not wishing to presume.

"One of the many good things about seeing time pass is that you come to understand how very much of it there is. Get in, little one. I'll drive you to Templeton."

"Do you know where Hummingbird Lane is?"

"No I don't, but we're a long way away. The address can wait."

"This is the first time I've ever hitchhiked."

"I guessed that."

When we drive along the high road, I turn away from the sea and look at the round brown and gold hills, the tired sparse grass. The sea is too beautiful and would remind me of all I have just given up.

"Not from around here, are you?" I shake my head. "You don't look like you belong."

"I don't."

She smiles and we hardly talk again for about fifty miles.

"Do you have children?"

I shake my head. "No."

We have left the sea road and are driving inland. The landscape is very different. It reminds me of the old Roy Rogers movies. Come to think of it, those movies might have been filmed here. I can see Roy leading his loyal horse Trigger to drink from that wide smear of creek before it disappears into a grove of dusty trees. Trigger would dip down to drink, then Roy would jump on his back, and they'd gallop another twenty miles to fetch the doctor back to the young widow burning with fever in the distant hills.

"No children at all?"

"None. I had a cat, but it died," I say, and think "Ask me one more time, old woman. Let me be Peter, let me deny them thrice."

"No man neither?"

"None. I had a dog," I say, "but I ran over it."

Deep canyons are topped by rings of enormous oak trees, the sky is more blue than any sky I could imagine. I always thought California was crowded, but we drive miles without sight of any houses. There is an occasional sign for a vineyard, all the signs seem to be on the highway end of twisting dirt roads. I think I am already starting not to hurt so much. I will get over it and Ian

247

will get over it. It will be hard when he gets there and I'm gone. But it's easier this way. Not so drawn out. All of that beauty was making me mad. And his "good news" trapped me. I thought I wouldn't be able to get away. But it looks like I have.

"If men are dogs, maybe you are a lover of women?"

I turn, incredulous, from the window. "Excuse me?"

She is still smiling her easy smile. "I say, have you ever been with a woman?"

What does she have in mind? Maybe, out here, everybody wants something. What will I do if she grabs my breast?

"Oh. Oh, *been* with a woman. Sure, lots. I mean I had a sister and I went to a girls boarding school and a girls college. Come to think of it, I've been with many more—"

She touches my hair, like a mother, or a nun. "Does it make things not so immense when you joke about them? Is that your way?"

"It is my way," I say simply. "It has always been my way. It's just lately that it hasn't been working real well. If you mean sexually, have I been with a woman sexually, I'd have to say no. I mean, I mean thinking about it, I don't think I could pull the mouth part off. I already love women. I mean, I think I do. But I just don't think I could nose around down there with my mouth."

The Great Squaw starts to laugh. "Me neither," she says.

"One of my friends was, or became, a lover of women. Then she died of it."

In another ten miles the woman speaks again. "In the old ways, you know what they called us? They called us 'She Who Bleeds but Does Not Die.' They thought we were very great magic. Women, they thought women had powerful medicine. Because of our monthlies."

We have left the main road and entered yet another land-scape. There is no grass and the canyons are gone. I would say the land is desert, except that massive oak trees are everywhere and we drive over many bridges, small bridges stretched across wide stony riverbeds with small streams running down their middles. The bare fields hold beautiful horses, mostly Arabians. They are so pretty, but I don't see how they can thrive in this grassless land. We pass a sign that says Templeton.

"Is this it?" I ask.

She doesn't bother to answer, instead she pulls into a gas station and goes inside for directions while I pump gas. We get back into the truck at the same time.

"I'm pretty sure it's 809 . . . 809 Hummingbird Lane," I say. "There! There, I see his car. The same old car."

Michael's baby blue 1967 Oldsmobile convertible is parked in front of a small, slightly shabby, Spanish-style house.

When she drops me off in front of Michael's house, this woman, the Great Squaw of Big Sur, untwists one of the hawk feathers from her rearview mirror and hands it to me. "There's many worse things than being alone." She smiles again.

"I know," I say, and close the door.

"Jesus Christ, Katherine. You're the last person I ever expected to see at my front door!"

"Well, I did owe you a letter."

"You've owed me a letter for about three years. I wasn't exactly on my way to check the mailbox."

He's wearing his red hair shorter than he was four years ago and he may be thinner, but otherwise, Michael looks pretty much the same.

"Boy, Mrs. Robinson, you look great. That's a leisure time tan-of-the-idle-class, if ever I saw one." He's holding the screen door open for me.

"You got that right, Dustin. And don't knock it till you've tried it."

I drop my bag in the middle of a large room containing an old TV set balanced on a wine crate and, on the far end, one leaning couch that is covered with a bright turquoise Indian spread. The kind of spread you buy in a store where sitars are playing in the background and the air smells like patchouli. Another corner holds a work table containing a typewriter and several shaky stacks of books.

"And you obviously haven't tried it."

"Oh, this. I haven't entered the interior decorating stage of my life yet. Besides"— he motions for me to follow him—, "I spend most of my home time out here."

We walk through a kitchen made colorful by walls covered with an erratic collection of Mexican tiles and down two steps into the backyard, which is really an arbor surrounding a stone table and benches.

"This is so nice, Michael."

He grins. "The wooden trellises, the table, the benches, and, of course, the grapevines were all here when I got the place. But I put in the stone flooring with rocks from the riverbed. And the view, if you can call it a view, also came gratis."

The rest of the yard slopes gradually down to what I guess is a riverbed and, beyond that, there is a rounded hillside, which is so carpeted with bright yellow flowers that it looks like a sunlight reservoir.

"I've been saying this for more than a week now. But California is not the world. Nothing that I've seen here is like anything I've ever seen. And nothing is what I expected." I sit on one of the benches and gaze out.

Michael settles himself on a bottom step and says, "I know you're going to mention how you came to be here. I mean, I know you didn't just show up, because this is the first day I've taken off in more than a month. Or who knows? It may be a great psychic connection."

"Well, mostly I'm here seeking shelter from the storm," I say, pointing to the flawlessly blue sky. "I have part of a plane ticket departing from L.A. in four days and can't afford another way home. So, can I hang out for a few days?"

Michael leans back on his elbows. "*Mi casa es su casa.*"

"I'll earn my keep. I'll dust your TV. I'll carry river stones. I'll gather grapes in my apron and smush them in your bathtub.

Assuming you have a bathtub. I'll even clean the bathtub if you offer me a beer, an ice cold beer. I've such a thirst."

Michael jumps up and drawls, with an exaggerated West Virginia accent, "Well, bust my buttons, if I didn't recall nary a morsel of hospitality!" He opens the screen door, then turns back to me. "I thought you didn't drink. I remember that distinctly."

"It was a deal I made with the powers that be. Seems we all had our fingers crossed."

The afternoon has grown long and the sun no longer touches the hillside. I can see the flowers in their natural color, not liquid gold, but a calm yellow, like butter, or the inside of lemons. Michael has been telling me about his work. Not his work at the newspaper but the work that consumes, it seems, every free moment he has.

"The first time I met Chavez he was holed up in this convent, on a hunger strike. The man hadn't eaten for days but he was so friendly, so open. I tell you, Katherine, after being out in the fields with the farm workers, an Anglo face is cause for, for want of a better word, cause for *disgrace*. But Chavez couldn't have been more friendly to me or more hopeful for his people. I don't know where he gets all that damned hope."

Michael stands up, goes into the kitchen, and comes out carrying two more cold beers. He barely pauses in his conversation. Meanwhile, I'm trying to ease into another round of culture shock. Yesterday at this time I was sipping from a bottle of wine that probably cost more than Michael pays in rent a month. Now he's talking to me about the people who may have picked the grapes for that wine.

"You say California is a different world. You want to talk different worlds, Katherine, see how the farm workers live. They are not fighting to join the middle class, you understand? They are just asking for someplace to take a piss when they are out in the fields in all the hours of daylight. They're asking for running water for their families in the little overcrowded shacks they are loaned while they labor in the Anglo fields. The women give birth in steaming hot shacks with dirt floors and there isn't even any fresh water for them. Many of their babies die." He leans his head back to finish the last sip of beer. "And this is America."

"This is California, land of the lotus eaters," I add encouragingly.

Michael talks while the shadows become long. When it is dark, he lights a scented candle and goes into the kitchen and returns carrying two plates of steaming black beans. We eat in silence. I am thinking of the stories he has told me and I think he is resting from his anger. He has told me he got involved with the migrant workers when his newspaper sent him to report on a bombing. Irate Anglo field managers had bombed a migrant settlement. I look at his earnest face in the flickering light and am amazed that I had missed the change in it.

"You know, Michael. This struggle now is like the civil rights struggle was ten years ago. Cesar Chavez is like Martin Luther King and the migrant workers are like the black people were." I run my fingers over my empty plate and lick away the last bit of sauce.

"I remember, when I was a girl, I'd wake up in the middle of the night on a Saturday night and I could hear the field workers, the black field workers, singing on their way back to the plantations. Most of them didn't have running water either. My family, especially my mother, was getting involved in civil rights and I'd wake up and hear that beautiful singing and think how it was a way of life that was passing away. All of that, the thick scented summer nights, the feel and taste of the Mississippi River air, the black people singing and living together as a community. All of that is gone, the good and the bad. Such a big change in such a brief time."

Michael stands. "I doubt if any of the workers would say it was a brief time. I don't know about you, Katherine. When you tell your pretty stories it sounds like you care more for the story, your version, than for any truth."

He stacks the plates, balancing them on his arm as he scoops up half of the beer cans. "And I have to get up in a few hours. I really need my sleep. O.K. if I put you on the couch?"

I nod and Michael walks into the house.

. . . . .

When I wake up the next morning it is evident that Michael has been long gone. I pull the turquoise cover over my head and try to block out the light and block out thought. I want to sleep but, of course, I can't. So I'll earn my keep.

I walk into the kitchen and see that Michael has left a note leaned against the coffeepot:

> *If you heat this up in a pan, along with some of the canned milk from the fridge, you'll have one fine cup of coffee. There are rolls in the cupboard and some honey. Didn't mean to be such a shit last night. I'm glad to see you. I'll be home a little after dark.*
> *Mi casa . . .*
>
> *Love, Michael.*

When I walk into the bathroom, in the light of day, I am horrified. The bathtub is the filthiest I've ever seen. The rest of the room is pristine by comparison. The peeling linoleum floor, the leaning toilet, and the rust-stained sink seem worn, but relatively clean.

Michael's bedroom is the only portion of the small house that shows any care. A patchwork quilt—maybe the handiwork of a mountain grandmother—lies crumpled over the brass bed. There is an oak armoire and a massive, hand-tooled trunk at the foot of the unmade bed. The entire room is coated with dust. I decide to tackle the bathroom first.

I have emptied the can of cleanser without making a dent in the deep stain ringing the porcelain tub. Under the sink in the kitchen I discover a bottle of bleach and that finally improves the appearance of the tub. I also like what the bleach does to my hands, they look raw and useful. I sweep and scrub and dust all day. Michael doesn't seem to have a stereo anymore, so I turn up the kitchen radio full blast and clean and try to sing along to country western songs. All of this is mindless and feels as though it is keeping me from losing my mind. "Don't think, scrub the sink," I chant during the challenging songs, the ones with lyrics I can't guess. I am trying to sing and chant the last week, the last few months, from my mind.

In the late afternoon I stick a ten-dollar bill into my shorts pocket and head down the road in search of a store. I find a small grocery store where I feel like I'm the first outsider to ever enter.

The three or four people visiting together in the store abruptly stop talking when I walk through the door. A dark round-eyed little boy peers at me from around his mama's skirt. The child stares as if Toby has sent word ahead that the short little woman with the good tan is really a female dog who devours her pups. When I buy the chicken and a six-pack of beer, I also buy a Tootsie Roll pop. I smile at the little boy's mother and squat down to offer the sucker to the little boy. Who immediately begins to howl and scream. Maybe Ian has cause to not like kids. I'm squatting in the middle of a grocery store, holding a lollipop, while a group of strangers glare at me as if I am Son of Sam.

. . . . .

"Don't know the last time this house smelled so good." Michael walks in maybe an hour after I've expected him.

I take one look and understand his bathtub. It's hard to believe there is white skin under the coating of deep gray dust; he's gray from head to toe, except for his fingers, which are stained purple. When he goes to open the just-cleaned refrigerator, without even washing his hands, I block it with my body.

"Oh, right," he says, and crosses to the sink. "I just do this one day a week. I figure if I'm going to write a book about these people, if I'm going to use their lives, I'd damn well better walk a mile in their moccasins." Michael is cheerfully splashing stained water over the edges of the kitchen sink as he talks.

"Tomorrow I'm back at the paper. If you want to drop me off, you can take the Olds and drive around to see the sights. Sorry I can't give you the Grand Tour in person."

. . . . .

I had driven all the way to the coast, but the sight of the Pacific made me miss Ian so much I could hardly breathe. I drove off as if those turquoise waters could swell up and drown me in a great tidal wave of regret. I stopped for lunch at a little inland Mexican restaurant and had one enchilada, one margarita, and two beers. I don't miss anybody, I like being a drinker again. Now I'm speeding down an interstate, or freeway, whatever the lotus eaters call their highways. I'm wearing a sundress and the convertible top is down. Another flawless day.

As I pass one of those giant trucks, I casually look up and see the driver is staring down into my car. The wind has blown the skirt of my dress up and the truck driver is getting an eyeful of my newly tanned thighs. I start to pull my skirt down, then I think what harm is it doing?

I turn the radio louder and drive side-by-side with the truck, pretending to be concentrating on the road. I don't look at the driver again, but I know he's still watching. My skirt flutters and I pretend to smooth it, but I'm really pressing my fingers between my thighs, touching myself. I leave my hand there for a few seconds, then accelerate and pass the truck driver. My heart is pounding and I can hardly believe what I've just done. The truck speeds up and pulls just behind me. I speed up and slow down and he stays with me. It becomes its own rhythm, our speed does —slow, then fast.

We are driving through the land of canyons and there is little traffic. I pull out into the left lane and the truck driver pulls alongside me. I let the wind blow my skirt up again and then I put two fingers to my lips and lick them. I'm slowly and seductively licking my fingers and driving over sixty miles an hour down the highway. My skirt is above my waist and I'm caressing the tops of my breasts with my wet fingertips. I don't look at the truck driver. I'm smiling and looking at the road.

I've become two people, one is excited and feeling powerful and free; she is touching herself and giving a strange man reason to touch himself. Another me is watching this with horror, and that second "me" is watching the highway too. It is a good thing the other "me" is watching, because up ahead, in the eighteen wheeler's lane, there is a rickety farm truck bumping down the road. The wooden truck bed is filled with tattered, dark-skinned men and the old truck can't be going more than forty miles an hour.

I grab the steering wheel with both hands and scream. The truck driver must suddenly see the puttering truck too, because his brakes make a horrible sound. I floor the car and pass the old truck. It is filled with Michael's people, weary workers on their way to another field.

In the rearview mirror I see the eighteen wheeler swerve, almost jackknifing, over the highway. Finally the driver seems to get control again. He pulls to the side of the road and stops while the rickety old truck continues on its oblivious way.

I turn onto a side road and drive down it until I find a place to pull over. I open the car door, lean out, and vomit. When I raise my head the two-colored landscape spins in front of me. Then I rest my sweaty forehead against the dashboard and try to remember all the words to the Act of Contrition. "Oh my God, I am heartily sorry . . ."

That night I can't get to sleep. After Michael goes to his room, I lie on his lumpy sofa and try to sleep. Finally I pad into his bedroom.

"Michael?" I whisper.

No answer.

"Michael, I can't sleep. Can I sleep with you?"

He throws back the covers to make room for me. "Maybe this bed will be good luck. I surely wasn't having any trouble sleeping."

He doesn't say anything else and I lie, stiffly, on my side of the bed. I don't think that Michael has gone back to sleep. I hear him sigh, I can feel his wakefulness.

"Michael, don't you want to make love?"

"Nope."

I stretch out my arm and put my hand on him over the covers. "Yes you do. You do want to make love!"

He takes my hand and holds it tightly. "Back in West Virginia we had people called 'Sin Eaters.' After someone died, his folks would go call for the Sin Eater. The relatives would lay the deceased out in the parlor and set up a great feast all around the body." Michael's voice is quiet and slow in the darkness. "The Sin Eater would come and eat and eat. The mountain folks believed that the food represented the sins of the dead person and that the Sin Eater could eat the sins away."

He puts my hand to his lips and kisses it softly. "Sin Eaters weren't exactly what you would call socially acceptable. They served a purpose and they were paid for it. And they certainly ate well."

Michael abruptly throws back the covers and kneels, straddling me. I reach up and pull his face down to kiss him, then he helps lift off my T-shirt.

"Katherine, I think I might be your 'Sin Fucker.' Or really sorrow, not sin, your 'Sorrow Fucker.' I feel a terrible sorrow in you. I thought if you wanted to tell me where your kids are, or what you've been doing in California all this time, I thought if you wanted to tell me, you would." He is touching me, caressing me.

"It's like when we were lovers in North Carolina. You were

troubled, but you never talked to me, Katherine, you just fucked me."

He enters me slowly, with kindness. We move for a long time in silence, I am slippery with sweat and Michael is holding back, waiting for my climax. When I come, I think I will never stop coming and moan and cry until I am only crying. Sobbing and holding on to Michael as if he could keep me to the earth, anchor me in the wind that is sweeping away every single thing I have ever loved. What isn't taken, I discard.

Michael wipes at my streaming eyes and runny nose with the corner of the sheet. "Poor Katherine, poor little Katherine, she's grieving with her cunt. It's O.K., baby, it's—"

I sit up and push his hand away. "I don't want to be comforted, or understood. That's not what I need from you." He puts a pillow against the backboard of the bed for me and one for himself.

"Maybe you just need to talk."

And so I talk. It doesn't make me feel better, but it makes me feel less selfish. I tell Michael how scared I was all those years of loving my children alone, how unprepared. How I'm too old to feel like an orphan, but I am an orphan. And I tell him about falling in love with a married man and being punished for it. How I was punished and my children were punished. I tell him about the perfect, perfectly awful perfection of Ian's world on Big Sur; paradise after original sin. I tell him the only good thing I've ever done is give my children away, but that it hasn't made me good. I tell him about the afternoon, the truck driver.

And he just listens. He listens and he doesn't judge. I don't know how he can do that. Halfway into just about any story, I've judged it. Michael only listens and when it starts to be daylight we go into the kitchen and he fixes scrambled eggs and coffee with hot canned milk.

"Why couldn't I have fallen in love with someone like you, instead of someone like Ian?" I ask, with my mouth full of eggs and toast.

"I don't know, Katherine. That's a damned good question. And you're not the first pretty woman I've ever wanted to ask it of."

. . . . .

Michael has left work early so he can drive me to the airport. The top is down and we speed through the bright, strange landscape holding hands. I feel rested. For the first time, since Beth was hurt, I feel rested. Last night we sat in the arbor and just talked. We talked about newspaper work and what deadlines do to style, how the California mountains don't seem to be even cousins to the ancient Appalachians. We talked about the best book in the world, the best movie, the best way to eat French toast. Good easy talk and, while we talked, I realized I'd never had a male friend before. At age thirty-three, I'm making my first male friend.

Esther would be amazed. She would probably say Michael can be a friend because we've already been lovers. Maybe she is right. Though I think it is that I've finally stopped playing Scarlett O'Hara at the Twelve Oaks barbecue. I seem to be ridding myself of that particular curse of my generation of Southern women.

We pull up into the Piedmont loading zone and Michael takes my hand in both of his. "Katherine, back home, when you want to transplant a rhododendron, you get an ax, or even a shovel, and you chop off the outspread roots. Then, a couple seasons later you go and dig up the whole plant. The roots that were left have curled tightly up under the tree, almost in a self-protective ball. It makes it real easy to lift up the plant."

Michael is rubbing my hand now, as though it was cold. I'm trying to pay attention to him, to not be distracted by the loud-speaker announcing flights, by the airport bustle of comings and goings.

"Honey, you seem to me to have chopped off so many of your

roots, you've lost track of the live ones. And—and well, just find out where the good ones are. And when you transplant? Well, make sure it is in good soil. Not all the transplanted rhododendrons make it."

When Michael takes my face in his hands and kisses me on the forehead, I start to cry. I cry and grab my travel bag and get out of the car without saying good-bye. I hardly ever say good-bye.

In the airport I stumble into people, apologize, and then stumble again. After I get my ticket checked, I lose my way to the departure gate in the crowded airport. The wait is not long. I file with the other passengers through the twisting tunnel to board a plane bound for the East. The stewardess must tell me twice to buckle my seat belt. I can't remember how and need help. The plane lifts into the air. It seems so slow. I watch the waters of the Pacific from the plane window until they become part of the sky and disappear. When I talk of my time here, I will probably say, as always, that everything was beautiful. Perfect.

. . . . .

I have left the windows open and the rented car darkens and seems cooler as I enter the avenue of oaks leading to the entrance of Holy Name Academy. I park the car in the shade of one of the giant ancient trees and gaze over at the graceful old dormitory standing deserted in the summer sun. It is unnaturally quiet and the white-columned building shimmers, like a mirage, in the heat.

Time has made the building smaller, but more beautiful. I remember the first time I walked through the doorway. The doorway that I know opens onto a long, glossy gray marble floor. I followed my father through that time. I remember I was angry, but I don't remember why. I walked down that marble hallway, that first time, only concerned with the right to wear lipstick, the vague hope for a boyfriend, a fear that my Bellebend friends would forget me, a desperation to be genteel and wild. I loved James Dean and Pat Boone. When I left, when I walked out of that doorway the last time, I believed in the Holy Catholic Church. I wanted to write great poetry, I wanted to save the world and stay a virgin and be sophisticated and never grow up. I loved Jack Kennedy and William Shakespeare.

When I step onto the covered brick walkway to the main building and smell the sweet olive trees, it is as though the sixteen years have not passed away. The dappled shade, made by jasmine vines, soothes me and I almost hear girlish voices singing "Coeur de Dieu sauve le monde. . . ." The scent of the air, the cloak of moist heat, the feel of patterned bricks under my feet return all faith to me. There is an all-seeing God, and everyone who loves, loves forever. Susan walks a few steps behind and innocence returns to me like a thing of seasons. I am dizzy with the rush of remembrance.

Then I step again into the sun and it all leaves as quickly as it has come. The heat slaps my face, I stumble on a step down I hadn't remembered and I am thirty-three years old, feeling lost and, once again, tired beyond my years.

In the main hall ceiling fans stir the dusky air, the building smells vaguely of incense and furniture polish, and seems empty. Have they all gone away? Have the holy and perfect nuns all left for the disco? Is Father Shea in India with the Beatles' guru? Did I make up Holy Name like so many of the other fantasies that dressed my past? I step back into the sunlight of the columned gallery and gaze over at the alley of ancient pines. I smile to think of the conversations, the mysteries Susan, Marie, and I struggled over in that scented sun-streaked darkness. Sir Lancelot was as real as Ian. Goodness and evil only came in two colors. We would never have sex, but we would have many children and we would be perfect mothers. Our daughters would all attend Holy Name. The nun who finds me sitting on the railing of the gallery tells me that Sister Helena is, indeed, still at Holy Name. Father Shea

261

is now in Alabama, but Sister Helena might be in the garden cutting flowers for the chapel.

The nuns no longer wear habits, they go into modern life disguised as ordinary women. Sister Helena's civvies look as close to nun garb as possible. She is such a small woman, kneeling among the roses, in a long, plain dark dress. Without her cowl and veil she seems so exposed, her pink scalp showing through the wisps of silver hair. I have to take several deep breaths before I gather the courage to go to her. I pick my way through the flower beds and kneel beside her. Sister Helena goes on clipping the long roses, placing them in a basket at her side.

"Sister?"

"Yes, my child?" She addresses me as she did in those years, but looks at me without recognition.

"You taught me, Sister Helena. I was a student here."

"English. I taught English, Emily Dickinson was my favorite. And Gerard Manley Hopkins, a Catholic, you know. A Jesuit," she says serenely.

"I remember, Sister. He wrote 'As kingfishers catch fire.' "

She carefully clips another rose. "Many of my children had trouble with sprung rhythm. He invented it, Hopkins invented it, you know. He was a Catholic, a priest."

"Yes, I know." I push the basket closer to her as she moves among the roses. Her skin is translucent, it is like fine linen writing paper, crumpled, then smoothed open again. I think of how she looked, reading by the small lamp, in the nights of my girlhood. I think how much I wanted to rest my head on her lap, back then, how strong she seemed. A mockingbird calls out from the branches of an oleander, the air is soft with the scent of pine and sweet olive.

"I'm Katherine, Katherine Roberts. I wrote poetry. Do you remember me, Sister?"

"There were so many . . . They are all my children and I love them dearly."

I run my fingertips over the rippled apricot edge of a petal.

"Sister Helena, I wanted to tell you that my—my mother and my father have died. My parents are dead, Sister. Even though I know it's not really my fault, I feel like it might be. Susan is dead too. And I—I also wanted to tell you that I have given away my children." I slip my finger deep within the smooth petals of the rose.

"These things happen, sometimes," she says as she gently moves my hand away from the flowers. She reaches to cut another rose. I place the basket closer to her and stand up, dust my knees, and walk away.

I had come for absolution and now I discover there is no one left to hand it out, that even absolution is a solitary thing. I drive away from Holy Name without what I have come for; yet strangely eased to see the school is as beautiful as I remember. That the gardens are large and laced with paths, and that sunlight truly does streak through the ancient pine trees leading to the chapel. *These things happen sometimes.* My mother said that too. There must be something to it. For the life of me, I can't figure what. It will give me something to think about on the long drive from Louisiana's Arcadia to the Delta.

. . . . .

I am not too late. Eve answers the door, wearing a purple maternity dress. "You look like an eggplant," I say.

"Well, I feel like a pumpkin straddling a watermelon."

"You could call yourself a one-woman roadside stand."

Eve steps out on the green-floored porch. "I wasn't expecting you." She opens her arms to me. We are both crying.

"Just because I can't reach all around you doesn't mean I'm not hugging you, you know."

"I know, I know," she sobs.

We walk into the living room. The midafternoon light filters through sheer white curtains and shimmers over the dustless floors. Most of the old furniture is gone. The room has been

redone with plants, my sister's watercolors, and beautifully refin-
ished antiques.

"God, this room never looked so great."

"Thank you for coming, Katherine, thank you, thank you."

I turn to face my sister, "Thank you for not slamming the
door in my face. And for holding on to that baby," I add.

"Please don't give me credit for not having the baby yet.
Honey, if I could bounce down the River Road on a pogo stick, I
would have."

"Have you been to see the Voodoo Queen, do you know what
the little digger is going to be?"

"Most of the bets are that it's a boy. The trade, with John
going to Pakistan, is that the baby is a Roberts. It keeps our
name. I'm going to call him Jason, Jason Roberts."

"Why not Robert Roberts?" I ask. "That would be resound-
ing."

"You know why!" She takes my face between her hands and
kisses me square on the mouth.

"RR, I like that," I say. "Like good ole Roy Rogers."

Eve has shown me all around the house, the changes she and
John have made on the house. Now we are sitting in the old
kitchen. Which is very much the same as when I last saw it,
almost four years ago. The tiles on the floor are new, but still
black and white.

"Revisionist tiles, huh?" The same large oak table. "We have
six or seven months to catch up on, Eve. Or maybe four years."

"Well, let's just start on what got you here."

As I finish the story of leaving Big Sur, I place my hawk
feather on the table.

"Just like that, Katherine. You just walked away from Ian, just
walked away from that California dream?"

"I guess so. Today I think I love him still and yesterday I was
positive I didn't. I also suspect Ian of necrophilia."

Eve reaches over to test my forehead, as though I have fever.
"Katherine, I—"

"One night he entered me while I was sleeping. And that was like a metaphor. It seems like the less feelings I had, the more he loved me."

"Warpo human nature, not necrophilia," my sister says comfortingly. "I don't want to sound like a bigot, but, generally speaking, men aren't great at expressing, or even feeling, their feelings. It sounds like Ian was really trying, trying to feel and to be open with his feelings. At the same time you were closing yours down."

"Then there was the perfection of that place, of our borrowed life. It didn't fit me. I think I need some disorganization and need to think there are people living better than I am, so I don't have to feel bad about living good."

"Was it really that beautiful? You do have a tendency to romanticize a bit, to make Dachau look like Disneyland."

"Who knows? I think it was. California sunlight through that thick glass made it seem we were dancing underwater, in the house, in the broad daylight. I mean, you can't really improve on Big Sur." I'm thirsty, I've been talking too much and I'm thirsty.

"It sounds like he is offering you a new life, a fresh start. Some creature comfort and a chance to be yourself."

"I mean, matching robes, for Christ's sake! That's not me."

"Tell him how you feel about that kind of life. Those days of doing everything the man's way are over. If you really want a new life, and you say you do, if you really want a new life, grab some control of it." She squeezes my hand, hard. "Don't just give up on it, Katherine!"

"After you give up your kids, giving up anything else is easy."

"You know, it crossed my mind that one reason you let your kids go was so that you could have a new life with this new lover." Eve leans back and rests her hands on her vast belly.

"Not at first, not when Beth was in the hospital. But later. Later, when I realized I was really going to let them go. It was the first time I ever thought of having a life to myself. It started sounding real good. And real deserved."

"Do you miss them?"

"No . . . Yes, of course I miss them. My little phantom limbs. The place where they were still hurts. Everything I saw at Big Sur I tried to see for them. Beth wakes me up coughing at night; Madeline and Toby shook my empty house with their arguments. I stumbled over their toys and books. But their toys and books had all been sent away. The house was intolerable. I missed them terribly. But now, now you know, I can write. Maybe get a job with a real newspaper, maybe write a book." It feels so good to be talking to my sister again. I reach past her and pick up the feather.

"I can stop postponing my own life, and get on with it. And God knows those three are better off, much better. The child bride has the kind of energy for them that I don't have anymore. Eric gets another chance at being a dad. AA has made a new man of him and everybody deserves another chance."

"Everybody, but you, huh, big sister?"

I run the hawk feather over my open palm, and continue. "They have a great house, great schools, grandparents a half-hour drive away."

"You might walk away from Ian's offer of the good life, because you suspect it couldn't make you happy. Yet you think a nice organized life is better for your kids than life with you."

I lean over and pat Eve's stomach. "It's different with kids. You'll see. I feel good because now they have everything they need."

"But they don't have you," my sister points out redundantly.

"That's probably the best thing about their new situation," I say, and push the feather out of reach.

"You are a good mother, Katherine. Maybe a little eccentric, but a good mother. What happened to Beth could have happened if you'd been home, or if they'd been at Eric's."

"You know what? It's not just that, almost losing Beth. I was awful to Toby too." God, I have too much to say. And I am so thirsty. "It's the—the—I don't know, this is probably the wrong thing to say to a woman about to have a baby. But it's the horror of loving them. It's been too long, it's been too hard. I feel like I have heart damage, irreparable heart damage. What you have there, inside of you, may be the very best part. That baby is so protected, you can be so in charge. It's when they come out that the trouble starts . . . Look, I should shut up."

Eve leans across the table and strokes my face. "I can take it, Katherine. I have the firm faith of the converted. You were a child, sweetheart, when you had Madeline. I am a fully growed woman. You just go on and talk. It's good for what ails you. Actually, it's good for what ails us both. You talk."

I walk around the kitchen opening cupboards. "These modern pregnancies. No beer in the fridge, no bourbon in the cupboards."

"A tall glass of skim milk ought to do you just fine. Now, go on, Katherine."

"So then the bundle of dependency comes out, out of the water-walled womb, and the trouble starts. I remember once, when Toby was a newborn, I remember I'd hung his receiving blanket out in the sunlight to dry. I bathed Toby, and carried in his blanket to wrap my little baby in the soft sun-warm cloth. And I did, I bundled him up so nicely. Toby suddenly began to scream, a terrifying scream. Turns out there was a wasp in the blanket." I open and close the cupboard door.

"Toby's mother had wrapped him up with this horror. My tiny little baby had a wasp fastened to his infant chest. I'd done my best, and there it was."

I close the cupboard one last time. "And then—then—when Madeline started school, maybe the second week of school. I waited with her, holding her hand at the end of the driveway, waiting for the school bus. She's all fixed up for kindergarten, you know. Remember she had those little braids? Anyway—anyway— the bus comes and she's going up the steps of the school bus and trying to wave good-bye to me at the same time and she slips. I mean she didn't hurt herself, or anything, she just stumbled. All the kids on the bus started laughing. The little shits."

I am crying and pacing the black and white tiles. "I mean, what's Madeline going to do? She just trudges up the rest of the steps and the kids are laughing and the school bus door closes and off it goes. My daughter's pale humiliated face pressed to the window as the school bus drives off. And I saw that."

I wipe my eyes on the short sleeve of my blouse. "Can you imagine the hurts, the tiny humiliations and exclusions that go on, that have gone on, that I don't even know about? Can't stand to think about. Want out of heart and mind forever. One second your kid is sitting on a step watching her brother mow the lawn, the next second she's clinging to life by a cobweb strand. No, no I don't miss them. I'm relieved. I'll just be an aunt. Maybe that won't be so damaging."

I slosh skimmed milk into a glass and slam the carton back into the fridge. "And look, I'm very aware that this is all nothing next to those mothers Michael told me about and those mothers in Central America, or mothers in those famine countries, holding their babies, those swollen-bellied babes, holding them while they die. Imagine those war-zone mamas, imagine the heroin babies, imagine some mama looking at her raped and battered nine-year-old daughter. What's a wasp sting to those mothers? Motherhood ought to be outlawed. We should all be aunts! Now, God dammit, I'm going to pick up a six-pack. Then I'm going to fix you an absolutely great dinner."

. . . . .

"The ancestral bed. You and John sleep here, in Mama and Daddy's bed?"

"Sure do. But don't worry, big sister, we don't fuck here. When we want to fuck, we go to the Holiday Inn, or if we can't wait, we just rut around in the backyard."

"So, little Robert Roberts, my nephew, was conceived right

here." I pat the high mattress of the four-poster bed. "You know, Eve, I can remember them, well one of them, probably Daddy, reaching over this high old bed to haul me up when I'd had a bad dream. We were so safe, growing up in this house, with those parents."

Eve is using a little step stool to climb into bed. "Yeah, except for the poorhouse wagon always being on its way to pick us up. Or Mama crying herself to sleep 'cause Daddy had spent the house payment on a piano for you, a piano you would never play. We were safe except for worrying about the Klan bombing our house, or Mama leaving Daddy, or the devil dancing off the end of Daddy's sword and roasting our little Catholic souls."

Eve smooths her gown over her great belly and continues. "We had a great father, but I don't think you let him be real, Katherine. He screwed up like everybody screws up. You know, you really were sorta a normal adolescent, but he freaked when you became a teenager. He overreacted and, for all practical purposes, abandoned you. Madeline brought you back into his good graces."

I sit up. "I don't remember that!"

"Of course you don't. It doesn't make a good story. Remember how embarrassed he was to look at you when you were pregnant?"

"Yeah." We both laugh.

"Night, RR." I fall asleep with my arm flung over my sister, my palm pressed open on the great swell of her belly. We are together, my sister and I, we sole survivors of our fierce recaptured past.

. . . . .

Two nights later Eve is shaking me by my shoulder. "Katherine, wake up! I think, I think I've wet the bed."

"Well, one of us has wet the bed," I say groggily, moving my hand over the sheet. Then I jolt awake. "It's your water, your water has broken!"

"I know that. We have to go, we have to go now." Eve has grabbed on to the bedpost and is slowly pulling herself up. I slip down from my side and rush around to steady the footstool. "You need to call Jean. Her number is, her number is, I can't—" Something has finally shaken my sister.

"I'll find her number. You just get your little Lamaze bag, or whatever."

"Jean has that. When I hire myself a coach, I get the best."

After I call Jean, I find Eve in the bathroom trying to clean herself off. "You haven't seen your feet for two months, what makes you think you can handle this?"

I run a large towel under warm water, kneel on the bathroom tiles, and wash between my sister's legs.

I pull a cotton smock from the closet and help slip it over Eve's head. She lowers her arms to clutch her middle. "Oww. An all-time champion stomachache. Maybe this isn't such a good idea. I'm thinking of calling everything off."

"Come on, let's get you in the car." I head for the door.

"Katherine, come back. You're naked, honey."

. . . . .

Jean is waiting in the hideously lit reception area. Forms have already been filled out, Eve signs a few dotted lines. "What about the small print. They're not going to pull any fast ones, hey?"

"Shut up, Eve," says Jean.

They flop my sister into a wheelchair. As they wheel her away, she looks over her shoulder with apprehensive good humor. Then she is gone. I feel like there is something I wanted to say. But now she's gone.

"Where's the fathers' waiting room?" The woman behind the desk is slightly bewildered. "You know, where I smoke cigarettes and pace until my nephew is born." She points me in the right direction.

There is a phone in the waiting area and I feel like, since I don't smoke anymore, I should call someone.

New Orleans information gives me Marie's number. I listen to the phone ringing in the small New Orleans house set up for one. My childless friend has never learned to fall asleep with one ear cocked for disaster. On the ninth ring she answers, sounding vague and still asleep.

"Yes?"

"Marie, it's Katherine."

"Katherine, what's wrong?" Her voice seems almost to echo, as though there is some emptiness, a hollow place on her end of the line.

"Nothing's wrong. Eve is having her baby. I wanted to tell someone." A cigarette would be magnificent right now.

"Well, that's wonderful, honey. What is it?" Marie is trying to wake, to rise to the occasion.

"She's having it, it's not here. I understand that can take a while." I see Jean, dressed in a gown and shower cap, heading down the corridor toward me.

"Where are you, Katherine?" asks Marie.

"At the hospital, of course."

"The hos—"

"Look, Marie, we'll call you when it's over. I just wanted someone I love to know a little Roberts is on his way. Hope four wasn't too early to call. Bye, Marie."

Hanging up is almost as fun as calling.

"Your sister is making big trouble. Good thing Bellebend doctors are easily intimidated by LSU professors. That dumb guy probably thinks she can get him good tickets to the Tigers' football games. She wants you in with us."

"Jean, I know zip about this stuff. I mean it's all done with breathing, right?"

Jean whips off her shower cap and fluffs her hair. "Eve said,

271

through the miracle of drugs and the lateness of the women's movement, you missed the births of your children. She's damned if you're going to miss the birth of hers."

I sit down and take a deep breath. "You know, Jean, I've never even looked between my own legs. It seems, I don't know. . . ." I stand again. "I guess we should find a shower cap for me, huh?"

Eve's pains have been regular and sharp, her jokes have been regular and not so sharp. She has started the special breathing, the panting, and Jean is doing her coaching job, encouraging, saying how great she is, how smart.

Eve stops, mid-pant, to say, "I guess that makes me a smarty pants, huh, Jean?"

"Now do you see why they drug women?" I say. I'm trying to stay out of the way, but within Eve's line of vision. The male doctor is in and out, but mostly it is a room of women. And everyone but me seems to know what to do.

In the last half-hour everything has gotten more intense. And I'd like to leave, I hate watching my sister's pain. But she asked, so I'm staying. Now I have a job, I get to feed Eve little chips of ice. The bright room is very cold, but she is sweating and flushed and thirsty. I slip tiny slivers of ice between her lips.

"Cool," she says. Eve is struggling to talk to me. "When Daddy, that last time when Daddy was sick, he would ask for water—"

She arches and pants, Jean says the time is closer. Then Eve continues. "He would ask for water and when, when I brought it to him he'd say—" another contraction, more activity—"he'd say for me to give it to Mama. He'd say, 'Give this water to your mother, she favors . . . Give this water to your mother, she favors her water so cool.'"

A hard contraction, more panting, a nurse leans over my sister, puts a small machine to her great belly, then steps away. Eve is crying, though I doubt she knows this.

"Katherine, Katherine, I favor water so cool."

"You'll have it, my sister. You'll have it."

Jean is on one side and I'm on the other. My sister keeps her eyes fastened on me. She is squeezing the circulation out of my hand.

"Swat," she says.

" 'Swat'? What does that mean, Eve? I don't—"

"No, squat, I want to squat. Help me off, I need to squat!"

Jean strokes Eve's forehead. "The time is much closer—"

Eve arches and screams, she pants some more.

"You want to squat because that's the natural way. Turns out it isn't convenient for medical personnel." Jean explains.

"The fuckers," Eve snarls. I slip more ice between my sister's lips, she pushes my hand away. "Together!" She yells, then starts to laugh, she's laughing and crying.

"Remember that time, Katherine, when we had the flat tire at night on—" More panting, she arches, then goes on speaking. "—flat tire in the rain on the Airline Highway and of course Daddy didn't know how to change a tire and you and he went to try to flag down a car, and—and a car trying to stop, to help, skidded and hit our car and shot it forward? You and Daddy thought Mama and I had been killed and we thought you two had, and—and—nobody had. We all survived. That night in our bed you grabbed me—"

I don't know how Eve is managing to keep the thread of her story.

"—you grabbed me in your sleep and woke us both up yelling 'together, together, together.' Remember—"

This is the hardest. Jean begins to shout, "Hold it, hold it, don't push yet."

The doctor is back, the nurses are zipping around like seasoned shoppers through revolving doors. Eve is screaming, "Down, Katherine, down!"

It's all crazy and Jean looks up and says, "The baby's coming, she wants you to watch!"

I trip down to the other end of the bed and stand just behind the doctor. The baby's head is squashing itself to come from the center of my sister. The doctor is pulling—and must be hurting —the baby by its incredibly malleable head. The baby comes out like a bewildered, beached, wet, wrinkled swimmer. A creature from the sea turning to the air and becoming a creature of air and light. His little fists are clenched and he shouts, like he can't believe this is all happening, like he is his own coach.

"A girl!" announces the tallest nurse.

They lay the baby on its mother's, my sister's, chest. The little wet slippery creature streaks Eve with blood and mucus from her mother's insides and begins to squall. Eve makes a tent of her fingers to crown the baby and with her forearms pulls the child into herself. Something very intimate is happening with those two and I feel that we should all leave the room. Though no one does. I think of old Robert Louis. 'Hush, hush whisper who dares . . .'

"Katherine," says my sister, finally breaking the silence, while she looks at her baby. "Katherine."

"What," I say. "What, honey?"

"That's her name. I'm going to name her Katherine, Emily Katherine." She kisses her daughter's sticky little head. "Hand this little girl to my sister, to her namesake," she says, looking up at the nurse.

"That's pretty heavy, Eve," I say.

"She's not heavy," says Eve, weakly trying to lift her baby. "She's my daughter."

"Spare me," mutters Jean.

"She gets that refusal to be sentimental from our mother," I explain. And lean over to kiss my sister's crusty, chapped lips and stroke her tired sweaty face, where tiny blood vessels have burst in this race to make life.

My niece is being swabbed by a cleanup team. They could drop her, they could hold her too hard. She's too new and they are all strangers. Emily Katherine is screaming for her family. I am amazed at how much I want to hold her. I turn to step closer to the work crew.

"Do what you must do," Eve is saying, behind me, to the doctor. "I need to drink a gallon of something cool and wet and I need to call my man before I fall asleep for a month."

Then I am holding my niece, the youngest human I have ever touched with my hands. She's barely the length of my forearm. When we fell asleep last night she wasn't a person. Now she is and she has worked so hard to be here. "Coming, ready or not" she has burst into the world. And I watched her come. In my wildest dreams I never thought to see such a sight. Once I watched a man walk on the moon for the very first time, and it was nothing to this. Does she know, will Emily Katherine ever know how damned hard it is all going to be? Did she have any say? Minutes old, my niece has figured out breathing; her lungs, even her tiny limbs, reach for air. In my arms I hold the wish for life made flesh.

She turns toward my voice as I whisper to her, "You want this, don't you? This life thing? However it all turns out. Ready or not, you want it."

Her lips mime very small kisses and little Emily Katherine covers her eyes with her fists. Like someone waiting for the world to shout "Surprise!"

. . . . .

I walk along the levee on the afternoon of Emily Katherine's birth and look at the distant industries throwing their filth into the air. The air that I believe killed my parents, or hastened their deaths. The air my niece will grow up breathing. Someone has been careless here, very careless. I am also coming to realize that I've been a different kind of careless. I grew up in Louisiana when it was green and gold. When the land lost its lush colors, when it stopped being a pretty story, I left it forever. I have never truly dug in for a fight. I turn my back, give up. All this time I haven't been able to forgive my own wrongdoings. I have been saying there can be no salvation in this world, only retribution. I had forgotten about the state of grace.

I gaze out at the river. In so many ways it is not the river I loved when I was growing up, but it is still a mighty river. It keeps going. I look at the full-grown river trees and the saplings; little trees, just starting. Things are living in this air so unlike air was meant to be.

If it's done right, rhododendron can be transplanted. And the plant will live. It may miss where it came from, but it will live.

I walk along the levee running my fingers through the tall grasses, remembering conversations with my father, our mutual, separate, stumbling search for goodness. *Forgive us our trespasses, as we forgive those who trespass against us.* "Forgive, forgive, forgive," I murmur, and walk down the hill that holds back the mighty Mississippi.

. . . . .

Beth answers the phone.

"Hi, baby," I say, taking a deep breath.

"Mommy? My real mom? You know this number?"

"This is your mama and I miss you way too much . . ." I don't think she hears me, she is calling loudly for her brother and sister.

Now she is back. "Toby says you don't love us. Toby says—"

"Don't say that! Don't tell—"

I hear Toby struggling for the phone. Then I hear Beth crying in the background, and shallow breathing on the phone.

"Toby?"

There is a silence, then . . . "What?"

"Guess where I am. I'm in Louisiana, and you have a new cousin. Your aunt Eve just now had a little girl."

"Great. Another stupid girl." He clears his throat.

"I'm coming to get you, Toby. I'm coming to fetch my children home."

"It doesn't matter to me," he says in a shaky voice. "I mean, you can. It'll be all right."

"Well, good, because I'm coming. I'll get your aunt situated. Then I'll come for you, in about a week, in seven days from today. Find a calendar and mark out each day till I get there. Now can I talk to your big sister?"

.   .   .   .   .

It is almost night and the house of my parents holds the dusk. Soon the fireflies will be out. And then the moon and stars.

We are back on that same Alabama road, racing through the night. I know that I'm a good driver, my children are safe, and we're heading home. "Home," I whisper to myself in the dusky car of sleeping children. Again, the dog stands frozen on the highway. He looks to me for help. Again, I'm going too fast, I can't slow the car in time. I know this. I also know my kind intentions. Again, I hit the dog and he sails past the windshield, over the roof of the station wagon. But this time, this time I slow and stop and park on the side of the road. When I get out of the car, the air is clean and a warm Southern breeze blows wisteria blossoms past my face. I go to wake the children. I carry Beth, her sleepy face nestled against my neck. Madeline and Toby walk just ahead, holding hands. Together we all go back to tend to whatever harm we find.